THE IVY TRIBE

A SIREN LOVE NOVEL

CHELSII KLEIN

CONTENTS

**To the best PA's, friends and awesome women around--
Karen, Zoe-Amelia, and Deanna…**

This book would NOT have happened without you guys. I cannot even begin to express my gratitude to each and every one of you. Ever since you guys took me under your wing, whether it involved edits, advertising, or promoting you have given 110%. I honestly don't know how I got so lucky. Through this book, I believe our friendship has grown and I can honestly say you guys are my go-to each and every day—even if we are just talking about silly things. You're always there. So thank you from the bottom of my heart. (I also can't wait for us to buy our own island (with the hubby's of course), and all the book boyfriends…lay around and drink on the beach 😄.) You guys have truly become my best friends. Thank you so much for all you do.

To the hubby--- Thank you for being my sexy book boyfriend inspiration for the characters.
To A & A Formatting--- Thank you for the wonderful job on my books, and always being there when I have a question.

NOTE TO READER

This book is a little bit of everything. Slow burn; Romance; Dark fantasy; Reverse harem; Paranormal; Erotica; Horror; and the list goes on. I tell my story and add in writing aspects from each that I like but not enough for it to be fully one genre. This book is literally a mix of all.! That being said you are in for one (Hell) of a ride. I hope you enjoy this series as much as I do. Happy reading!

COMING SOON

The Beloved Heart: Book 2
The Beloved Ice: Book 3
The Beloved One: Book 4
The Watchers, A Siren Love Novel: Book 2

GLOSSARY

Realm 1: The King's Realm
    Ruled by: Satan

Realm 2: The Lava Realm
    Ruled by: Queen Mandra
    Watchers: Remy & Lanthrian

Realm 3: The Mentally Ill Realm
    Ruled by: Queen Asgret
    Watchers: Emil & Manic

Realm 4: The Revenge Realm
    Ruled by: ~~Queen Eiseth~~ (RIP)
       Queen Balli
    Watchers: Caligula & Rasputin

Realm 5: The Sexual Realm
    Ruled by: Queen Lilith
    Watchers: Cander & ~~Abel~~ (RIP)
    Jax

Realm 6: The Realm of Emotions
    Ruled by: ~~Queen Fellen~~ (RIP)
        TBC
    Watchers: Envy & Strife

Realm 7: Purgatory
    Ruled by: Prince Anock
    Watchers: Cain & Elijah

Realm 8: The Greed Realm
    Ruled by: Queen Irrithal
    Watchers: Ancitif & Amon

Realm 9: The Sorrow Realm
    Ruled by: Queen Sitri
    Watchers: Chort & Focalor

Chelsii Klein

The Ivy Tribe

A Siren Love Novel

THE DAY OF AGE

*G*etting an envelope from my dead mother should have given me some type of clue on how the day was going to go. It was a Saturday. Just a regular Saturday, except for the fact that this Saturday marked eighteen years of life for me, Akira Black. Woo hoo.

Except, not really.

I stared ahead at the light blue envelope, my name signed across the front, and my heart beating out of my chest. I looked around the familiar kitchen for a clue as to who'd left the strategically placed envelope for me but came up with nothing. I inched forward, feeling nervous. Was this a joke?

Even though she'd died before I even knew her, I recognized her handwriting. I'd kept the love letters between her and my dad sealed away in a box under my bed. If it wasn't for the writing scrawled across it, and her favorite color (robin egg blue) I would have doubted it. When I pick it up, it will probably have her perfume scent floating around it as well.

I was only a couple of steps away from the envelope when the doubt crept back in. This *had* to be a joke. Liz, our housekeeper and my caretaker, was gone on weekends. Maybe dad came home? But I hadn't heard him. Sitting in the kitchen for my midnight cereal craving proved that the envelope wasn't there before I locked up the house last night. Was someone in the house right now?

I'm just creeping myself out. The hairs on the back of my neck rising proved as much. *Breathe. Just breathe Akira.* Rubbing my arms to calm the chills, something still didn't feel right, but I shut my eyes and took a deep breath anyways.

I opened them after a second and looked around the lavish kitchen. Nothing had changed. I was alone again, like always, and the envelope still sat propped up against the center decorations on our island. I let a crazed chuckle out as I moved to retrieve it. It was just an envelope, what was the big deal?

Just as my hand hovered above the envelope, a shadow fell across the kitchen floor through the morning light. I whirled, letting out a shriek as soon as a human form came into sight. It wasn't a second later that I realized the person's reaction mirrored mine. I blinked the sleep away and got a better look.

A girl not much older than me, maybe in college, stood in the kitchen's entryway. She held two black high heels on one looped finger, while her other hand held her purse.

"Umm. Hi. Sorry. I didn't mean to scare you. I just...wait, who are you?" Her statement turned into a possessive question.

I rolled my eyes. "I'm Akira..."

Ring a bell?

She squinted as if thinking. It made the black pile of makeup under her eyes look worse.

"Akira?"

Wow, real groupie here folks. Take in her ratted blonde hair sticking up in the back, and her red party dress hitched up on one thigh, she may not know who I am, but I knew exactly who this girl is.

Just another notch on Axel Black's belt.

I cleared my throat to try and push down the annoyance and disgust. It didn't help.

"His daughter..." *I don't even know why I'm helping this girl out.*

Her face relaxed, and she let out an embarrassed laugh. "Ooooh. Right." She laughed a little more before she composed herself. "I knew he had a daughter, well you, but the magazines always made it seem like you two lived separately. And not only that, but you look way older than the pictures they have of you." She paused, looking uncomfortable for the first time in her explanation, which I didn't care to hear. "Anyways, I just assumed he lived alone. I mean, I wasn't expecting to run into anyone this morning."

Good lord, lightning strike this girl *please*!

The girl stood there a beat longer, taking in the kitchen before facing me again. "I'm Ashley by the way." She started to take a step into the kitchen until I cut it short.

"Door is that way, take a left then right." I turned my back on her and headed to the coffee pot.

After a murmured thanks, I soon heard the front door slam shut. I let the grunt of frustration go I'd been holding in as I filled up the pitcher with water. Why the hell did he have to bring those nasty things home? Wasn't he even concerned with me seeing?

This had to be a joke, the whole day was turning into a nightmare. First the envelope, I glanced over at it like it wouldn't still be there, and now the groupie. I continued to silently fume as I went for the vanilla creamer.

"I see you haven't opened her letter. Or didn't you see it?"

I slammed the fridge door closed to see my dad standing there. I jumped at the sight. "Ugh! Dad! Clothes!" He was just in shorts. Gross. The third thing to ruin my day.

"Sorry, Bear." He said, ruffling my hair as he passed, heading for the coffee cups. "Happy Birthday, by the way."

"*Thanks.*" I wasn't sure why, but I always felt awkward when people wished me a happy birthday.

"And I saw it." Not knowing what else to say.

After sitting down with both our coffees at the kitchen table, it was apparent we didn't spend a lot of time together. It was awkward having him home, and we both sat in silence, taking unnecessary glances around the room.

Dad, or Axel, is the lead singer in the chart-topping rock band from Australia that made it big in the States. Singing is his life…his passion. His passion took a break when he met my mother, movie sweetheart Jade Sonya, who later became Mrs. Black. After three short years of marriage, I came along, and Jade passed away exactly two minutes after giving birth to me. Dad was never the same since, or so I've heard. Now he spends his time mainly on the road. Every once in a while, I'll get a surprise visit from him, and it will be awkward. Like now.

"Listen, about the letter…" He paused long enough in his explanation that I almost thought that was all. I broke my concentration from a random spot on our wooden table, a ding in the wood, to look up.

He was concentrating way too hard on his coffee. "She had made me promise while she was pregnant that if something was ever to happen to her, I would make sure, no matter what, that you received this letter on your eighteenth birthday." At some point in his explanation, the sound of his voice cracking made me look away.

I could ask a million questions. Did she think something was going to happen to her before then? Why my eighteenth birthday? What does it say? Would it say something along the lines of how I'd grown into such a wonderful person? Because that wouldn't make any sense. How could she have known that she's dead? I didn't want to think so spiteful; I loved my mother. Still do. She is kept alive through her movies and the awards she's still winning. But I tried not to be upset about her vacant spot in my life.

So many things brought up to the surface from that letter appearing today. Questions, thoughts, emotions. All things related to her that both dad and I try to avoid at all costs. After another long silence, I cleared my throat and picked a safer topic. "So how was the concert last night?"

He gave a half-smile before answering like he always did. "It keeps it." I never really knew what that meant, but that was his answer anytime I asked about his career. Maybe it was a rocker thing?

Finishing his coffee in record time, he stood, leaving his cup. "Any big plans today? Tonight?"

A groan I meant to stay hidden crept out. "Lunch with Kay and Alex, then..." I paused; did I really want to tell him the plan for the night?

"And then?" I'd caught his interest now. Great, just great.

I cleared my throat nervously. "Dinner with Ian. Maybe. Well, he asked, but I don't know. I mean, he asked me a while ago, but now he's gone on the set, and I'm not even sure if he remembers or...anyways." I finished in a rush hoping he wouldn't press. I didn't have curfews or rules on the weekends growing up, and when dad was home, he didn't care. Only now in the last few weekends had he started making random phone call check-ins. It was almost like as soon as I graduated he decided to care.

"Ian? Ian..." He was thinking way too hard about this. Although if he'd kept up with my so-called love life, or what the magazines called my love life, he'd know I was talking about Ian Wesley. The hunky, twenty-six-year-old actor that had taken over the action movies the past three years. I watched him cautiously while sipping my coffee.

I started to get a glimmer of hope that he wouldn't figure it out. It vanished when I looked up to see his eyebrows touching his hairline, and his green eyes bulging out like a cartoon character. I knew he'd figured it out. I wasn't so worried about him saying no, as I was of him making fun of me. He was the type that pointed and laughed at the pretty boys.

"Ian Wesley!" And here it comes. "*The* Ian Wesley! Oh, no, no, no, no. Not the, *I'll kill everyone to find your evil heart*, Ian Wesley!" Dad laughed, repeating the line that got Ian his big break. It was hard not to laugh with him at his bad impression of Ian because of his accent.

I smacked my hands on my forehead, dragging them down my face in embarrassment. My cheeks felt hot, and I wasn't even sure why. Maybe it was because Ian was the new fangirl sensation, hotter than hell itself. Dark chocolate brown hair, sky blue eyes, tan skin, with a defined muscular jawline and cheekbones. He was a mix between Johnny Depp and Channing Tatum. Any girl would be lucky to have his attention, but I just wasn't sure I wanted my dad to know about my love interest.

It wasn't like love at first sight, music playing, and fireworks exploding in the background. It still isn't that, at least, *that's what I tell myself*. Not only had he randomly showed up at my door one day asking for my number along with a date, but he was a stage five clinger. I was attracted to him, he was fun sure, but I was sure he was just dating me for my status. The moment in our five-month relationship that I started to feel us getting close to the L-word, I pushed away. Every guy has used me for my status. But hey, I'm used to it by now. When you have a rock star dad and a dead movie star mother, what'd yah expect?

After having the rest of the band show up and poke fun at my date while feeding me more bad impressions of Ian, the morning passed and dad was back on the road. Leaving me alone again.

As I made my way up the stairs, the sound of my phone had me sprinting up the remaining steps. I reached the top just as my foot landed on something soft. A millisecond later, the immediate screech of my cat (Aldous Snow) defending his tail, had me screaming myself. Almost falling back down the way I'd come while trying to calm my heart.

"Damn it, Aldous!" I yelled as I righted myself and pressed down the hall. I slowed down at my door when I realized I'd missed the call. The delayed reaction to my scolding had Aldous Snow grunting and hissing from behind me somewhere. He is a miserably prissy cat.

I unlocked my phone to see three missed calls from Ian, I rolled my eyes. Forty-two Happy Birthday texts from friends and family. Three call me texts from Ian, and one from Kaydence that read,

Just making sure we're still on for lunch at 12. –Kay

Time read 11:06 a.m. Holy Shit. I called Kaydence as I rushed to the bathroom.

"Happy birthday, bestie!"

"Hey, thanks!"

"Did you get my text? We're still on for lunch, right?"

"Umm, yeah." I paused, setting the phone down on speaker to work on my appearance. "I'm running a bit late. It might be closer to twelve-thirty. I had a surprise visit from Axel and the band this morning."

"Really?" I'd piqued her interest. She had a mad crush on the drummer.

"Yeah." I looked closer at my reflection, not a pimple, blemish, or red mark in sight. I leaned closer in the mirror. "Holy Shit. Umm, my face is super clear today."

Kay snorted out a laugh. "Good for you?" The sound of a blinker hinted that she was probably already on her way to lunch. I just hoped Alex would be on time to keep her company.

"It's just weird. I mean, my skin looks amazing; I just look...weird today." I continued poking my face and staring at it in utter disbelief with my mouth open instead of getting ready.

"Hmm. Anyways, you never finished texting me last night

about what Ian said." She was more invested in my relationship than I was.

I threw up my greasy blonde hair, thinking of how much the paparazzi was going to have a field day with my shitty appearance, but not so shitty face apparently. "Oh, I don't know. Something about our six-month anniversary..."

"I don't know why you're not all over this guy, Alex and I are still fighting for dibs when you get done." I started to defend myself for the hundredth time about not wanting to get hurt, but she continued on. "I mean, all you two have done is make out. Those dreamy eyes, muscles, and back to those light blue eyes..." She continued on, but I tuned out at blue.

My mom's envelope was still downstairs, did I really want to open it? Why wouldn't I? Maybe it was something I was better off reading after the day was done. I finished throwing some color on my face, which I apparently didn't need anymore, and went for the sundress Kaydence and I had gone shopping for.

Kaydence was still going on about Ian, I rolled my eyes and laughed. "Hey, I'm heading out in ten, I'll see yah in a little bit." I ended the call and headed for a pair of wedges. I usually wasn't the dress-up type, but after my freakishly awesome face, I felt it was necessary. I was even feeling a little giddy as I put the pair of wedges on that we'd bought with the dress. Despite my bad news and awful morning, I was feeling light and excited for the day. Getting one last look in the mirror, I almost did a double-take. I'd grown. I was taller and not from the wedges. I'd seen myself enough times in the full-length mirror in my room to know where my head usually fell. I scoffed, shaking my head to clear the confusion. Maybe I was getting an early onset of dementia since I'd turned eighteen?

Well, best to put this on the crap to address later list.

I grabbed my purse and was on my way out of my room when I felt two warm hands clamp over my shoulders and spin me around. "Boo!"

I screamed as I tried to jump back from whoever scared me.

Ian kept his grip on my upper shoulders and pulled me into a bone-crushing hug. "Ugh, IAN!" I stepped back, grabbing at my racing heart.

"How did you get in here? And...how *long* have you been in here?"

He just laughed and pulled me back into him.

"I can't tell you all my secrets." He said, leaning down and giving me the lightest of kisses.

Despite wanting to keep my emotions in check, my knees buckled. Stupid hormones, at the sight of him, I was in a puddle. What was going on with me today? He looked amazing, he smelled terrific, and his lips tasted...amazing.

"Happy Birthday Akira." He whispered, pulling me in tighter and kissing me again, only this time with more emotion. Our kiss turned into something X rated quickly, and I had to pull myself away, gasping for air.

"Easy, Ian!" He was just as shaken as I was from our kiss, only he still held a look of seduction in his eyes. I looked away.

"You look...wow. I mean, you look amazing. You always do, but today you almost look different. I guess being away from someone you love for a month will do that to a person." I couldn't stop looking at his lips. I stared at his outfit instead.

"You look amazing too." He did. He was in dark designer jeans and a faded vintage T-shirt from my dad's band.

Wait. What did he just say? I met his eyes.

"What did you just say?"

"You heard me Kir, I love you. You're all I think about, dream about. I got physically sick a couple of days ago at the thought of kissing Summer on the set. You're doing something to me, Akira. I've never felt this serious about anyone before. After seeing you today, I can't imagine ever being with anyone else." His brown hair had fallen in his face, I moved it aside to keep it out of his eyes out of habit. He closed his eyes at my touch, and after realizing what I did, I quickly moved my hand back to my side.

I could tell his confession of love was real, but the timing for something so deep seemed off. I couldn't wrap my head around it all, it was like he had to hurry up and get his confession out as soon as he saw me. I shook my head and took a deep breath in, super unsure of how to handle what he'd said.

Thankfully, the sound of my phone ringing brought us both out of our trance. I looked down to see Kaydence calling and the time, 12:40 p.m. Shit! I ignored the call. I'd call her after I got in the car and on the road. "Shit! I'm late meeting Kay and Alex for lunch." I started to pull away, but he wrapped his hand around mine, holding me in place.

"I know, that's why I'm here. I came home early so I can spend a couple of days with you, I'll drive." An eyebrow raised before I could stop it. Was he just allowed to leave a movie set in the middle of making a movie?

He looked around the back of me before smiling. "By the way, I love the new tattoo, why didn't you tell me?"

Huh? I looked back at my full-length mirror as he continued to pull me out of my room. Only then did I notice an ingratiate design of black lines on the back of my neck. "I..." I rubbed my free hand on the back of my neck and then looked for ink. Nothing. I rubbed harder as we made our way down the stairs. When the hell did those lines get there? I tried to explain that I didn't even know they were there, but Ian just continued to mumble agreements like I was playing some joke. Keep the tattoo hidden from the boyfriend joke.

First the letter, then my new height, complexion and now a tattoo. Oh, I almost forgot the half-naked groupie and father situation and having a surprise visit from my movie star boyfriend. Was everyone's eighteenth birthday this crazy?

2

A BIRTHDAY SURPRISE

I thought Kay and Alex would be shocked at the sight of Ian attached to my hand but instead, Kaydence just shrugged, and Alex wiggled his eyebrows at me. *Geez.*

We had decided to meet up at my favorite little Italian restaurant, tucked and hidden away, known only to the locals. I already knew Alex and Kay would be at our table in the back corner.

"HAPPY BIRTHDAY!" They said in unison as we got closer. I felt a smile creep up. No matter what drama was unfolding in my life I could always count on my two best friends. Ian pulled out my chair while Alex cleared the table of the embarrassing display of presents and balloons. I felt like I was turning ten all over again.

Ian leaned over and started to talk when a voice interrupted him. "What can I get everyone to drink?" The voice was rugged, not one of a waiter. I saw Ian's guard go up as he scooted his chair closer to mine. Unlike Ian's reaction, Kaydence and Alex were trying to contain their hormones.

Now I *had* to look up and when I did...I was not disappointed.

I looked into the eyes of the single most attractive being I'd ever seen. My heart stopped. My veins thrummed. It wasn't until Alex brought me out of my stupor that I realized my mouth was hanging open.

"Birthday girl first." He said, peering uneasily between Ian, me, and the hot waiter.

"Oh." I shook my head to clear the cobwebs that had formed. I fumbled with my menu trying to think of what I wanted, but was all too aware of the waiter's burning gaze to my left. "Umm." Where the hell did they keep the drinks on this menu? Why the hell would someone so hot be a waiter? I glanced nervously up for help when Ian turned over the menu.

"Right here." He pointed before taking the menu from me. "Actually, how about I order for you." He said, changing his mind. "We'll get a pitcher of sangrias for the table." I looked at my friends and then nervously at the waiter. Everyone knew who I was and knew my age. I'd been trying to keep my eyes from the waiter on purpose but his delay in response made me glance up.

He stood there staring at me in anger. What the hell did I do? I glanced at my table and then back at him. Ian had a God-like appearance, but this guy put him to shame. Compared to Ian, the waiter had light blonde hair. He was tall, not as tan as Ian, but held the same muscular tone. He also had an edge to him, unpredictability and excitement came to mind when I looked at him. You've heard of bad boys, well this was one of them. It made the guys Ian played in the movies look like wimps.

"Right away." He said, narrowing his eyes at Ian. I glanced back at him to see if he'd noticed the waiter's rude behavior. He did.

"Babe, how do you know that guy?" Ian asked, settling his arm around my shoulders. I was unsettled by the waiter's appearance and for some reason Ian's arm felt out of place. Almost like I was cheating on the waiter.

"I don't," I replied quickly, maybe a little too quickly. It made me sound nervous, which made me sound even more suspicious. Almost like I was hiding something. I wasn't hiding anything. Other than the fact my nerves were on edge. *Geez, I needed to get a grip*.

Alex picked up on the weirdness and saved me from any further embarrassment, only to bring me to the next. "Time for presents!" He sang.

Oh lord.

I suppressed an eye roll and gave my best fake smile. "Yay." They caught the sarcasm.

Kay spoke first. "Listen here, miss! We have never once missed this date with you, and we aren't about to stop now. Plus, this is the best one!" She said pushing forward a black box with a red bow tied around it.

I already knew what it was and was genuinely excited, this really was something I looked forward to every year. I opened the box and gasped at the picture they had placed in the front; tears sprang to my eyes and my throat clogged. Okay, I wasn't usually the sappy type but seeing my mother never ceased to amaze me and this picture was one I'd never seen before.

"Oh my gosh, you guys." I gushed as I started to take the scrapbook out with shaky hands. Every year Alex and Kay make me a scrapbook with all our photos from one birthday to the next. This one held a blended picture of my mom on the day of her graduation accepting her diploma and me in an identical stance and pose getting mine on the same stage. I sniffled and looked up at my blurry friends.

"I don't even know where to begin, I'm just..." I couldn't talk anymore, or I'd break into awful loud sobs with snot and everything.

Kaydence and Alex had tears in their eyes as they held each

other and smiled. "Don't just thank us. Your man is the one who pulled strings to get the photo on the front." I stilled as I felt my defensive wall crumble in a matter of seconds. I set down the book and looked slowly over to my right where Ian sat with a half-smile and smoldering eyes. Guys who are just using you don't do stuff like that. This was something someone did when they really cared. Even loved.

"*You*?" It came out as a whisper.

Ian smiled and scooted closer wiping a tear away from my eye. "Me." He said brushing the stray hairs away from my eyes leaning in and kissing me on the forehead.

This was too sweet, caring, and considerate for me. The kind of guy who did this sort of thing for his girlfriend was not someone who wasn't invested. I lunged into his arms and breathed every inch of him in. He always smelled like rain and safety. I don't know why he did, but his smell always took my mind to those two things.

"Thank you," I whispered into his ear while he held me tight. At that moment there wasn't anyone else but us. It wasn't like we were having sex, but a different kind of emotion, one I'd tried not to play on. If I had been waiting on a moment to know for sure there was something between us other than lust, this was it.

The clearing of a throat broke our hug and I settled back into my chair as the waiter placed the pitcher of sangrias on our table...a little too hard. What was this guy's deal?

It was the middle of the day, but you wouldn't have been able to tell it in the darkened restaurant. Even in the eerie orange glow, I could tell the guy's eyes were abnormally dark, unsettling. They made me feel lustful to even look at. His eyes never left mine as he set down the cups. When he leaned in a little closer to place mine, I was assaulted by the smell of danger, fire, and ice. It took my breath away, eliciting a shiver that I tried to suppress that somehow, I think he noticed, as his eyes narrowed on the out of control pulse in my neck. I couldn't tell if I was scared or excited by him and it spiked my nerves.

I kept my gaze on the table after that, even as I ordered my lunch, I don't know why this guy affected me so much, but I had someone, and that someone was next to me. Kay, Alex, and Ian bantered on about the process it took to get the picture. I was thankful and I loved it, but I was unable to concentrate because of the waiter's stares. Was he staring at me because of who I was? If so, why was he mad? Did he hate my dad's band that much?

A voice flitted through my mind before the waiter backed away to get our orders started. *I made those alcohol free. Alcohol won't work on you now anyways.* I swiveled around in my chair, but he was gone.

How did he do that?

Holy shit, was I just imagining things now?

I shook my head and took a sip of my drink as I turned back to the conversation. I had to be losing it.

"Wow, they didn't make these very strong," Alex commented with a perplexed look at his glass, before shrugging and taking another drink. He looked cute today in his designer clothes and reading glasses. Alex was the stereotypical gay friend that every girl dreamed of having, and I was lucky to call him mine. He came from money which helped with his clothes obsession and perfectly highlighted hair. I would be worried about how much debt he would acquire if it wasn't for his parent's money. But he wasn't all looks. Alex was genius-level smart, and if it wasn't for him, I honestly don't know how I would have passed my end of the year testing.

"I think they are strong enough," Kay said. "What do you think Akira?"

I hadn't detected a single drop of alcohol in my drink. How do you do that when the drink was made from wine, fruit, and Sprite? I had no idea. Not only that but if there wasn't alcohol in the drinks, then I'd actually heard the waiter's voice in my head.

I made those alcohol free. Alcohol won't work on you now.

What the hell did that mean, alcohol wouldn't work on me now?

I dropped it and concentrated on my friends. "So when I woke up this morning not only was Axel and one of his groupies there but an envelope from my mom..."

I went ahead and put it out there. There wasn't a single thing I didn't run by my friends and I knew they would know what to do about the situation.

They both had a look of shock and Alex even set down his drink, but it was Kay who spoke up. "Oh my gosh, like from when? I mean, did your dad give it to you?" I took another drink and shook my head, as Ian he ran his hand up and down my back for support.

"Yeah. I haven't opened it yet. I just. I'm not sure what to expect from it...you know?"

"Well if you need us there when you do open it, let us know." Alex reached forward and rubbed the top of my hand. I teared up at the support as I looked around to my friends and handsome boyfriend. I wasn't sure where I would be without them or how I got so lucky.

Kaydence brushed her long auburn hair back from her shoulder, showing the back of her neck. She was beautiful. She modeled part-time and I wished for the gazillionth time I would have been blessed with her classic beauty. Her green eyes always looked like sparkling emeralds, and unlike all the other fake, hateful people in the modeling world, she was so compassionate it amazed me.

"Hey." We all turned to Ian, who picked up his glass and downed it in one gulp. "Kay do you have the same tattoo as Kira?"

Ah hell, I completely forgot about that thing.

Alex choked on his drink, "TATTOO?!" At the same time, Kaydence shook her head like Ian was the craziest man alive, "HELL NO!"

I put my head in my hands as I suppressed a grunt. Leave it to Ian to bring up the one question I had no answers to, and yeah, I told my friends everything and I was sure I would get around to the mystical tattoo appearance, but I still wanted to try to get it off first.

"Yeah, Kira got this awesome tattoo on the back of her neck!" He turned me around and I heard their gasps.

"Okay, okay," I said turning around and shooing Ian off as our food was set in front of us. "Listen, first off," I paused to say thank you to the waiters bringing our food, super glad not to see the waiter with the dangerous eyes, then continued. "I honestly don't know how that got there." I threw up a hand when Alex looked like he was about to die from not talking. "Second off, no I wasn't drinking or doing drugs. You guys know I don't do that shit unless it's with you and last...I was really hoping Ian was joking. I just found out about it right before we left to meet you guys."

That left everyone looking as confused as I felt.

"So you weren't joking?" Ian asked.

"No, I wasn't." I shook my head.

"Kir tattoos don't just appear. Do you think it's a prank from one of the band members? You said they came home last night, and you know they have those long-lasting tattoos actors and singers use all the time. Maybe they put it on you when you were sleeping?" Alex asked.

I shivered at the thought of someone touching me while I slept, even if it was the guys I grew up around, the thought still creeped me out. "I honestly don't know, but why would they prank me and not say anything about it before they left today?"

Kay frowned, concern taking over her face. "Yeah, that does

seem weird. Let's just deal with it later, okay?" She must have taken in my freaked-out features.

"Oookay, well let's just figure that out later. Like after having a gallon's worth of alcohol and pray it's not some weirdo cancer. Although it is really pretty." Alex said twirling some pasta around his fork.

I laughed. "Agreed."

After eating and fussing over who got the bill, which Ian did, the angry sex God waiter returned and set down another pitcher of drinks with the bill. "Anything else?" I swore he only looked at me.

I shook my head to tongue-tied to say no, while I tried to catch a glimpse at his name tag to look up on Facebook later. Unfortunately, it was too dark to see. Thankfully the waiter left us alone after that and the rest of the lunch went by in a blur.

"Let's go dancing tonight!"

They looked at me like I'd just grown two heads. "Did you just say dancing?" Kaydence asked, taken aback.

I laughed as I nodded. "Yeah what's the big deal? We never go out!" Okay, actually that's all we did most weekends but still.

Alex smiled and glanced between me and Ian. Ian's hand had made its way slowly up my thigh and I had to keep nudging it down. Not that I didn't like it, but we were in public.

"Hmm, I think that alcohol got to the birthday girl." Alex giggled. "I'd go home and take advantage of him." He cleared his throat realizing his mistake, making us all laugh. "I mean her. Yeah, Ian, you should take advantage of that."

Ian just chuckled and shook his head. He was well aware of what team Alex batted for.

Kaydence turned to him with a perplexed look.

I was only half paying attention as Ian inched closer to me. His breath tickled my neck making my head spin.

"Why do you care if they get some?" I heard their conversation continue like Ian wasn't trying to seduce me.

"Hey! Gay or not, sex is sex. Plus ...me being one of the best friends, I will get to hear all about it, and sex with Ian Wesley." He whistled and we all laughed as Alex looked at Ian and turned bright red.

"OhmyGod I did it again. I'm so sorry Kira! I talked out loud again didn't I?"

We all laughed harder. I wiped the tears from my eyes as I looked over at Ian, it didn't take long for my smile to drop. He was staring at me with such an intense look I'm surprised my panties didn't rip themselves off. If I hadn't been lost in his eyes, I would have tried to diffuse the sexual tension rolling off him.

"You're so beautiful when you laugh." He whispered, slowly leaning forward.

The already dimmed lights made it easier for me to tune out the noise around us. I thought I heard Alex say something about heading out, but it got blurred with everything else unimportant. My gaze was locked on Ian's luscious lips even though his deadly stare never looked away from my eyes. My blood hummed and every nerve in my body felt him. His lips lowered on mine and whatever little world still hung around us was shattered at that moment. He wrapped his arms around me as he deepened the kiss and I breathed out a breath I didn't know I was holding, letting his scent engulf me.

It was a kiss so hunger filled and sexual, I was surprised I didn't go up in flames from it. I couldn't contain myself. His warmth, smell, and taste enveloped me, and I was halfway on his lap when the feel of a cold hand broke me out of my daze. I jerked away, breathless, my heart beating out of my chest as if someone had stabbed me with a knife.

I turned to see the waiter from earlier standing above me with red eyes.

Woah!

Lust turned to fear and I leaned back into Ian for protection. His arms moved around me protectively.

"We need to clear the table. I'm going to have to ask you to leave."

I looked over at Alex and Kaydence only to be faced with two empty chairs. What the hell? "Your friends left twenty minutes ago; we cannot hold the table much longer. Not even for the rich and famous." His words were ice down my back and matched his glare. Fear, he was the very definition. Something else seemed to go with his intimidating, bad boy demeanor that I couldn't place.

Also, did I have a major brain fart or how did Ian and I make out for twenty minutes without realizing it? I looked around to see what I was sure would be shocked faces from the other patrons, but nope, at least we were in the clear on that. The place was empty. The creepy waiter had to be exaggerating on the time, I mean, Ian was sexy as hell...but not, Godly stop time from turning sexy.

"Let's go find that club you were talking about," Ian whispered in my ear, breaking my stare from the angry blonde in front of me. He helped me stand on wobbling legs as he grabbed my gifts off the table. Okay, maybe Ian was a little Godly if he could make my legs wobble after making out.

He looked back over to the waiter as we turned to leave. "What's your name man, I never saw a name tag."

"Why do you want to know?" He asked, narrowing his eyes.

Ian mirrored his expression and I told myself never to make him mad. "Because even the rich and famous have their limits. You ever look or talk to my girl like you did earlier and I'll have you fired in a heartbeat. You got that no name?" Ian growled. It sounded almost animalistic and my hand loosened from his grip involuntarily. He tightened it back up around mine as the waiter sauntered over-looking unfazed.

"My name is Cander...and I don't work here." He said in an icy tone. His lips curled up into a deadly smile as he threw down his red "waiter" towel and walked out of the restaurant.

Ian was just as taken aback as me, and I was more than confused at what had just happened. I felt threatened somehow, vulnerable, was this guy stalking me? Had that waiter really talked into my mind? His eyes, scary tone, and even his behavior didn't seem human, but what the hell else would he be? Why did he serve us if he didn't work here?

Ian rushed me out of the restaurant fast after that, the sun shining down on us blinded me like I'd been in a cave for twenty years. If it hadn't been for Ian guiding me down the sidewalk, I probably would have tripped or ran into something at first as it took a minute for my eyes to adjust. My phone vibrated in my purse as I got in the passenger seat.

Please tell me you had sex on the table. –A

Please tell me you did NOT have sex in public, or on the table... - Kay

A rush of embarrassment and guilt riled up in me about my behavior in the restaurant, how in the world could we have made out in public for twenty minutes! It had only seemed like a couple of seconds. My head was spinning by the time Ian was heading back to my house. Envelope, mystery tattoo, and stalking hot waiters.

"Hey, I know you wanna go hit up a club, but it's only three in the afternoon. Do you want to go back to my place? I just got the theatre done downstairs..." My heart raced and I looked over at him swallowing the nervousness.

"Umm." I played with my hands in my lap trying to think of anything other than his smoldering eyes and kissable lips, or the way his shirt pulled across his defined chest.

"Hey." Ian put a hand under my chin and slowly lifted it. "We don't have to do anything you're not ready for. We don't even have to watch a movie, it's your birthday. I just thought you might want to come and check out my place."

I breathed a sigh of relief, yeah sex with Ian was every girl's dream, but I wasn't sure if I was ready yet. I had only just committed to letting him in. "Okay. A movie sounds great and then dancing."

Ian smiled. "Movie and dancing. Your wish is my command." He lifted my hand to his lips, kissing the back of it slowly before wrapping my hand in his and placing it back on my lap. One tiny gesture had made me weak and sweaty. His eyes flickered over at me as a devilish smile curled on his lips. Oh yeah, I had no doubt watching a movie was the last thing on his mind. Damn him.

The hanging out at Ian's didn't turn into a porn session like I was afraid it would. True to his word when we first showed up, he kept his hands to himself. We watched his new movie that had just come out in theaters. It was funny to see him in his serious act, the one that had the girls wet in seconds, when the clingy, vulnerable guy sat next to me. It made it so much better that we both got to make light jokes at his expense throughout the movie.

Talking and laughing with Ian after the gift at lunch was like a three-sixty to what it had been. It felt as natural as breathing and I found myself fighting the urge to reach over and be physical with him. So much for keeping my emotions in check. Going from unsure to really liking someone should have been a big step, but my body was in overdrive and seemed to want to keep going further.

After coming back from the bathroom taking my time noticing my strange tattoo for the first time. It was an intricate design of swirls and loops that covered the back of my neck. If someone had placed it there when I slept, it would have taken them a long time.

I came back to an empty living room. "Ian?" No answer.

"Ian?" I called out as I meandered to another room, the

kitchen. It sat empty as well, his stainless-steel appliances and black cabinets were rustic; it went along with the rest of his sharp bachelor's pad.

Just as I made my way down the hallway, he stepped out from a room. "Hey sorry. I had a call." I stopped the urge to ask who, I hadn't been that clingy, and until today I didn't or wouldn't have even cared, so I didn't need to start now. Ian stopped just short of reaching me and scratched the back of his head, he looked nervous.

"Summer called. She...well, she wanted to know what we were up to tonight and wanted to know if she could join. I kind of told her sure. I hope you don't mind." An animalistic feeling that halted my breath and pushed anger through me came fast, giving me yet another emotion I didn't want to have this quickly...jealousy. Summer was more than beautiful, she was gorgeous, flawless, and also his co-star. Why was she calling him? I shook my head feigning indifference.

"Sure. I mean I don't care, I guess. Isn't she supposed to be in New York on the set?" I asked, then immediately wanted to take it back. I didn't want to act like I cared.

He gave a small smile before wrapping his arms around me. "Everything is on hold until I get back. I'm not sure why she's here, but if you want it to be just us, I can text her. Babe." I looked up biting my lip, hoping the emotions I felt weren't visible to him. "You are my girl. I don't think I've ever told a girl I love her, well, in fact, I'm sure I haven't. Listen, I'm under your spell, no one else's. Summer and I are just friends, okay?" I ignored the questions and thoughts of him having to have "sex" with her in the movie he was shooting and how he felt about that, or him kissing her.

"Okay," I said smiling and stepping back. He kept the distance by stepping forward, I didn't move away as he took yet another step closing the gap between us.

"I know I said I would keep my hands to myself, but I was

wondering if I could give you my present now." His fingertips slowly brushed down my arms giving me goosebumps. I tried to hold back a smile.

"What's your present?" I asked like I didn't know it was a kiss.

He gave me the stare that had won his way with the ladies along with the smile that told me he was up to no good as he leaned forward. I was now backed against the wall; I couldn't keep my gaze from shifting between his lips and eyes. When his hands came up and lightly brushed my neck, my nerves felt alive. I closed my eyes and tilted my head back as he gently kissed my neck. His warm soft lips and tongue were like molten lava in my veins. A warmth in my body started and stopped at my clenched thighs.

"This." He whispered as something cold laid just above my breasts. He pulled back giving me room to look down at a beautiful diamond necklace, it was in the shape of a square with a silver chain. My breath caught as I lifted the chain to take a look at it before looking back to Ian's smiling face. I didn't even notice he had a necklace let alone notice him putting it on me.

"It's beautiful. Oh my gosh, Ian, I love it." I beamed a smile at him. My heart was fluttering in my chest so much I thought I'd pass out.

"Well, I didn't-"

I didn't let him finish. I pulled him to me by his shoulders and lost myself in his lips. His skilled tongue delved deep in my mouth and I gasped at the pleasure. He didn't waste any time after that as he lifted me off the wall and I wrapped my legs around his waist. We were in a bedroom in two seconds flat and I took a second to look around his room after he laid me down on the bed. A balcony overlooking the beach, I'm sure, was covered by sheer black curtains. His room was super clean, not a thing out of place. I stopped looking when the sight of his bare chest took over. My mouth dropped, and Ian quickly picked it back up with his.

I had to fight myself to not give in as our actions grew hungry and impatient. Making out was okay, but both of us were past that. I wanted him so bad I gripped the blankets on his bed to keep from ripping his pants off. He had already gotten me down to my bra and my dress laid bunched around my waist. It wasn't much of a barrier as he pressed up against me, neither was my lace underwear.

"Fuck, I want you so bad right now." Ian whispered, in between kissing my neck and gripping hard at my upper thighs. Like me, he was trying hard not to cross the line. My emotions were in a back and forth battle in my head.

I want him. I want him. I want him.

No, be smart Akira, but I need him. Oh my gosh, I want him so bad.

I was eighteen, I was the only virgin I knew, maybe it was time to correct that.

His thumb sliding under my panties sent my back arching as he unhooked my bra with his other hand.

"I want you too." I moaned making the decision. He stopped his torment and looked down into my eyes.

"I want you, but I don't want to force you." I stared into his eyes and saw something in them I was sure was love. It shut off all doubts that this was wrong.

"I want this. I want you." I said in an even voice gripping his hair. He closed his eyes and moaned as I sat up and kissed his neck.

It was like a tornado after that.

We were ripping at each other's clothes like we were the last two people alive. Just one piece of fabric laid between me, Ian, and my virginity.

He slowly pulled down my panties and I bit my lip to hold back my impatience, I trembled, I wanted him so bad. Just as he flung them off and made his way down my stomach with his skilled lips, his phone blasted in our ears from the nightstand at the same time his bedroom door flew open.

I screamed, my heart leaping out of my chest. Ian covered me with his body as the ringing stopped.

"Shit." He mumbled looking down at the bed with his back to the intruder. I looked over his shoulders, my heart dropping.

I'm guessing it was her calling because as soon as she took in the scene before her, the cell phone dropped out of her hands ending whatever call she was making. She put her hands up to her mouth as tears sprang up in her eyes.

Then, Summer ran from his room.

*H*yper-ventilating, freaking out, or emotional breakdown was an understatement. I would hold it together long enough to get my clothes on and rush out the door. It didn't take an idiot to see that girl was way more than a friend. I couldn't believe I fell for it; I fell for his tricks. He urged me to believe that she was just a friend. Yeah, a friend knew their way to your bedroom and a friend looked shocked and hurt when they saw you in said bedroom with another girl. I was the other girl. Shit that hurt.

"Please! Please! Kira! You have to believe me! Okay, she has a thing for me! I knew she liked me, but I never returned the feeling! Damn it!" Ian pulled on his pants and tried to follow me out. I ran. I don't know where Summer went and I didn't care.

"UNLOCK THE GATE!" I screamed back at him, not bothering to wait for his answer. He would need to open it for Alex to pull up. As soon as I'd called him and he heard my voice he told me he was on the way, and with him literally living down the street from Ian, he would be here in a second.

As I rushed out I passed a black sedan in the drive, most likely Summer's ride. Just as I passed it the gate opened and an onslaught of flashes and questions were thrown my way as paparazzi rushed in and up Ian's drive. Probably thinking the gate was opened for them, although if I would have known they were out there I wouldn't have run out like a moron. Well, actually to get away from the asshole chasing me...hell yes, I would. I still would go through the piranhas of paparazzi to get out of here. Why were they here anyway?

"AKIRA! AKIRA! Is it true what they are saying...!?" A million more Akira's and questions were yelled at me, and I threw up my hand to hide my appearance as tears streamed down my face. They crowded and pushed me trying to get answers to whatever no doubt ridiculous thing they were on now.

Ian was suddenly there screaming for them to get off his property and pushing them back. The sound of honking broke my retreat back into the house and Alex's white Land Rover rushed through the crowd stopping with a squeal of his tires. I pushed forward making my way when a hand jutted out catching my wrist.

"Akira please," Ian begged with his eyes, and we both knew he couldn't say more in front of these sharks and I shook my head and rushed into the SUV.

We fled out of the driveway taking off for my house, me not saying a word until I finally let it all out. It felt like my lungs were caving in and I would never breathe again, I felt the hurt all the way down to my toes. I can't believe how out of control the day had gone and how ridiculous I felt thinking he loved me enough for me to sleep with him. God, I was such an idiot. We had to stop for me to throw up but eventually, we were pulling into my drive.

"Do you want me to stay with you, honey?" Alex asked, rubbing my back. Normally I would appreciate his comfort, but right now I just wanted to get away from everything and everyone.

I shook my head in response, still sobbing as I rushed out of the car and into the house, slamming the door behind me. I didn't even look back as I ran through the house to the back patio, and only then I slowed enough to throw off my shoes and close the sliding door behind me.

It was 6:30 and the sun was still high in the sky, damn summertime. I ran barefoot through the grass until I hit the wooded area at the back of our property. I had found a small pond when I was little, from then on, if I needed to escape, it was the spot I went to. My spot. Almost as if the water had magical healing powers, it didn't matter how bad things got, my spot on the rock by the pond always made me feel better.

A small clearing of wildflowers surrounded the tiny pond on a slight slope. The water was always calm but clear and a perfect blue. Everything in this spot was perfect, full of color, full of fresh air. Today even as I settled onto my rock surrounded by water, I was having trouble appreciating it. I wasn't in love with him. I don't love him. It didn't matter. I didn't have sex with him, I just got really close, and besides, it's not like I walked in on him with another girl. No, I thought, I was the other girl. I let out a shaky breath feeling on the verge of tears again.

Summer was perfect in every way, she was his age, she had a unique beauty about her from her Arabic heritage. Long black hair and beautiful dark brown eyes, perfect statue, breast and legs, skin color.

"Ugh!"

I threw a pebble into the calm water, watching as the ripples danced away from the spot where it sank in. If only I had my mom here, what would she say? Would I feel this betrayed? Would I feel this alone? Tears broke free now and I tried to sniff them back up. I wiped at my face, my hand coming back smeared with black. Damn makeup. I don't know what propelled me to lay down on my rock, it was as big as a door and hung out over the water, but I did, and eventually cried myself to sleep.

A cool breeze flowed over my arm and I shifted on the hard bed to release my other arm that was trapped beneath me. Why was I so cold? I took a deep breath in, feeling an ache in my heart that wasn't there before, and opened my eyes as I remembered the day's events.

I sat on the rock feeling stupid for my reaction, not only that but I could have fallen in the water and drowned in my own pathetic misery. Night had fallen and the sound of frogs and crickets rang out. Fireflies danced and reflected off the water's shine in front of me, it was something that was pure beauty, too bad this moment would be forever stained by my bleeding heart.

Another painful memory of Ian placing the necklace he gave me crept up, the one that I was still wearing, I just didn't understand how something so genuine could have been fake the whole time. The stupid voice of reason I liked to call my annoying angel and devil came now making matters worse.

Maybe Ian was telling the truth about Summer? Why would he go through all the trouble to come back home for my birthday if he was seeing her? He wouldn't bother, they could have been together on the set.

Then the other voice crept in as I listened and sniffled at my running nose.

But she knew the way to his bedroom. Her reaction was not one of a friend but of someone whose heart was breaking. Not only that but how could someone so beautiful just be friends with Ian. They were perfect for each other.

"NO!" I shouted, slapping the water to get the images out of my head of them together. My reflection in the water seemed to be laughing at me as the moon wavered behind me in it. I dipped my hand in the water and pushed the water back and forth to get rid of my pathetic image.

That's when two things happened.

One, the skin that had touched the water felt tingly and comforted at the same time.

Two, after touching the water, all I wanted to do was put more of myself in there.

I couldn't understand how that simple gesture could erase my aching mind, but it did. I shredded my dress leaving my bra and underwear on and under the light of the moon, jumped into my favorite pound. My body responded like I thought it would and I felt immensely comforted by the water. It was almost like it had healing powers.

Normally I was afraid of everything. Especially of the possibility of something fluttering under the water, like a snake or biting fish or maybe something worse that could get me. Hell, I was afraid of my own shadow half the time. But for some reason as I broke the surface and breathed in the night air, I wasn't afraid. I wasn't worried about my sanity even though I was swimming in a private pond in the middle of the woods...in the middle of the night, by myself. Instead, I felt free. I felt like for the first time in eighteen years, even after the Ian incident, I could breathe.

I swam around and enjoyed my time, not once thinking of Ian. I was sure I'd stayed in there at least a couple hours and not once did my skin wrinkle as it used to when I was a kid.

"Hmm." I looked at my hands staring at the perfect, wrinkleless skin. "Weird." I mused, climbing out of the pond.

It was only after all my skin was free of the water that Ian flooded my mind again. It was like the block of all my worries and heartache that the water had helped me to stay clear of was broken and came back as soon as the wicked air of the world engulfed me.

That night I was tortured with nightmares of hellish boyfriends and sea creatures. It was a restless sleep...but when I woke up with a sting in my heart, I had the determination to stay away from Ian, and even more determination to stay around my pond.

3

TRUE LOVE'S KISS

"*N*o time for broken hearts, up now!"

I groaned before rolling over, covering my head with my warm blankets to block her out. "It's a Sunday, you don't even work on Sundays!"

Liz had come storming in, waking me up with the idea that I shouldn't sleep past noon. I didn't want to breathe, let alone be awake. I wanted Ian back in New York, while at the same time here in my room on his hands and knees, begging for forgiveness. Geez I was a mess.

Cold air rushed around me as Liz threw off my covers then promptly started in on her ranting of Spanish cursing and yelling, arms flailing, and everything. I knew there was no arguing once she began speaking Spanish. There was no winning with her after that.

"I don't want to do anything today, Abuela," I whined, sitting up and waiting for her rant to be done. Liz had raised me but I still couldn't understand a lick of Spanish, and sometimes I believe that's a good thing. Other than me calling her my Abuela, which is Spanish for grandma.

"You're too young to know a broken heart, come." She left

me alone after that. And at the term broken heart I was all but a mess, with my heart squeezing in my chest at the same time my stupid bottom lip trembled. I sucked in a *get your shit together* breath while slowly getting out of bed.

"Quit it, Kira," I said, pulling in just enough inner strength not to start crying again.

After dressing in the most basic thing I could find, a pair of yoga pants and a T-shirt that stated *Fries before Guys*...I plopped down at the kitchen island in front of my regular bowl of cereal and freshly made vanilla creamed coffee. In passing the entryway I noticed my phone on the table by the front door, but judging by the black screen, I took it that it was dead. That was fine with me. I didn't want to see anyone today. In fact, today was a good day to soak in my pathetic misery.

"Alex will be here today," Liz stated as she made her way around the kitchen sweeping.

"I don't want to see anyone today," I stated around a mouth full of Charmed Mateys.

Liz scoffed, "No, you sign up for college, and then we shop."

Shopping was Abuela's cure for everything. Growing up, she was the only adult around with dad gone all the time. She was hired to be my nanny and caregiver, along with all the house responsibilities...she also lived in the pool house. She was the sweetest little old Spanish lady, a bit heavyset, with black poofy hair that she teased and hair-sprayed into the cutest old lady hairstyle every day. She also always wore the same blue maid looking outfit with a white apron over the front. All growing up, the memory of her looks stayed the same as if she'd never aged a day. From the time she showed up to the current day.

All my friends loved her too. She was everyone's dream grandma. Caring, supportive, she made the most amazing food that could make you cry, and never forgot to give you money on your birthday. But when she was mad, watch out! She turned into a latino Queen that could kill you with her wicked tongue. On more than one occasion, I got the good ole tongue lashing from my Abuela. Either way, she was my everything, and I don't know where I'd be without her. Although days like today, I know I'd still have my ass in the same stinky clothes as yesterday, Stinky and wallowing in self-pity in my bed with a gallon of ice cream and orders for our guards to shoot Ian on sight.

I scoffed into my coffee, thinking about shopping. Although shopping any other day would be good. There was only one problem with shopping with Liz...we went shopping for her, when I had a bad day.

I took a sip of coffee, letting the warm sweet liquid trickle down my throat and thought about how late I was applying to colleges. My dad had a friend...or my mother did, who'd said he'd get me in the right programs for screenwriting, but I wasn't sure if that was really what I wanted to do now. Alex wanted to do whatever I did, he said that we needed to stick together for the rest of our lives because we were besties for life. So he's waiting for me, until now apparently. It made me feel bad since he could get into any college he wanted with his grades, yet he just wanted to stick by. I loved him for it. Kay had her career in modeling established from when she was young, so she avoided college like it was the plague, even when Alex and I begged her.

"I didn't have plans with Alex."

"I know, he called, and I told him to come over so you two could get college papers done." She paused in her sweeping, her grandmotherly face frowning in concentration. "You really don't have broken heart, little bug. That guy is...douche?"

Coffee came out my nose and mouth, decorating Liz's clean counter as I all but choked on my coffee. "Abuela!" I halfheartedly scolded her. To hear a sweet little old Spanish lady call Ian a douche was more than I could handle this early, especially since she was unsure if that was the right word. I was dying of laughter when Alex strolled into the kitchen.

"Someone's feeling better." Alex said, coming over and hugging me before placing a kiss on my temple. Before I could even say I wasn't, he headed over to make himself a coffee. He didn't get far before Liz waved him away from the coffee cups and told him to sit down. There was no helping yourself in front of this woman. I smiled lightly as Alex took a seat next to me.

"Liz just called Ian a douche." I stated, and he had the same reaction, except without the coffee.

Alex had tears rolling down his face before he calmed himself. "Liz is right Kir. He's a jerk. But on a different note, we are not going to think about that man."

"We aren't?"

"Nope. We are going to have a normal, fun-filled day and then we're going dancing. All but the awesome presents from us, we are going to have a redo of yesterday. Today is your birthday."

I wasn't sure how I felt about that, but so many things had happened yesterday that were screwed up, so maybe that was for the best. I went over the day start to finish in my mind before I decided that's what I needed, but not before I noticed something missing.

"Liz? Where's my mom's letter?" I asked, looking around for the robin blue envelope. I hadn't read it yet, and I didn't want her throwing it away.

Liz looked up at me, her face as white as a ghost and fear in her narrowed eyes. "What letter?"

Umm. "Dad said that mom made him promise to give it to me on my eighteenth birthday. With everything that happened yesterday I haven't had a chance to read it." I gulped around the weird emotion crawling up my chest.

Alex looked perplexed as well. "How is your dad doing? I

heard they weren't going to release him for a couple of days, what really happened? Did he actually break his back?"

"What?!" I stood from the stool, retrieving my phone from the entryway and coming back to the kitchen to plug it in. "What are you talking about? Dad and the band were just here yesterday morning before they left for a show in Chicago. We had coffee yesterday morning, whatever you heard was wrong."

Alex shook his head in confusion, and Liz rushed to put the broom back in the kitchen utility closet beside the pantry. "We just watched him live two nights ago in London, it was live when he fell off the stage."

"But." My head started spinning on its own accord, my heart and nerves thrumming as I looked into his concerned face. "Don't you remember me saying yesterday that the band showed up? Remember? You even said maybe it was one of them that did the prank and..." I took another pause sitting back down on a stool at the kitchen island, running a sweaty hand down my face. "Whatever you heard was wrong, he's obviously fine if he was here yesterday morning."

Liz entered the kitchen from putting her cleaning supplies away with a frantic look as my blood pounded with the unknown. Like what day was it, what year, was I having a mental breakdown, did I just visualize seeing my dad and this letter from my mom, and what about...

"Akira Black! You got a tattoo!"

My heart dropped out of my ass. Yup. Right there on Liz's clean kitchen floor.

Shit. Shit. Shit. How could I have forgotten about that? If it hadn't been for my current dad drama, I would be turning tail and running from the angry Spanish woman at my back. But right now, I needed to find out what was going on.

I ignored her reaction while I dialed dad's number with shaky hands. Liz pulled my hair up and the back of my shirt down to look at my 'tattoo', fussing about it as the phone rang.

Dillon, my dad's drummer, answered on the fifth ring. "Kir, we've been trying to get ahold of you!" His voice was full of concern.

"What happened?" I asked, my voice cracking. I didn't even realize I was crying until Alex brought me over a tissue.

"He, well, ah shit, baby girl. He still hasn't woken up. What do you know?"

Hadn't woke up. What? My head spun with the unknown, and Alex pulled me into his chest, holding me tight to keep me from falling.

"I...I didn't even know I thought..."

Dillon cursed again under his breath, "He's in a coma, Kir. They said he hit his head pretty hard. It looks like we will be in London until he wakes up. You get your stuff and come stay with us baby girl."

I sniffled an mmm-hmm, and then Alex took the phone and finished the conversation while I held onto the front of his shirt and cried. I needed to get to my dad. He needed to wake up. He was all I had left. What was I going to do?

And if my dad had been in London this whole time. Who was at the house with me yesterday morning?

---

*L*iz ran around the house with incense and spoke in another language I'd never heard before as Alex brought me up to my room. I had no idea what she was doing or saying. Weird and unexplainable things such as this were common growing up in this house. It kind of reminded me of something supernatural, like Liz was a secret undercover ghost or demon hunter, or she was some witch warding the house for evil. And although it used to make us all laugh to no end resulting in getting slapped up-side the head, we were used to it by now, which was the least of my worries.

After Kaydence came over, the three of us sat on my bed, and I recapped the past couple of days.

"Okay, you're right Kay, something weird *is* going on but I just don't know how Kira could have just imagined actual people and an object here." He switched his attention to me. "You said they talked to you for like two hours, and that's why you were late for our lunch." Alex shared a concerned look with Kaydence before continuing. "Did you hit your head?"

I sighed in frustration while itching at my irritated arms. "I wish, it would explain a lot more than *not* hitting my head."

Kay concentrated on picking fuzzies off my blanket. "And you're sure it wasn't just a bad dream?"

"Yes." I shook my head; I knew it wasn't. "Yes, I'm sure. I mean, I still have this tattoo," I leaned forward, moving my hair out of the way to show them, "And I have Ian's necklace. Well, I mean, you guys met me at lunch."

"Yeah, but the envelope and tattoo you got when you were alone. Maybe you just had, I don't know, some weird day-dreaming thing about the envelope and your dad giving it to you?" Alex countered.

"Then how do you explain the tattoo? I mean, I couldn't have given myself this." I couldn't help the rise in my voice. Alex shook his head just as confused as the rest of us.

"Oh, wait! You did say that Dillon was over when we were on the phone."

I straightened up with relief that maybe I wasn't going crazy at Kay's observation. "Yes! I don't know guys. I don't know what to think. My dad was here, we talked, he even called me bear and ruffled my hair. I know he was here." I grunted in frustration as my phone went off playing Ian's ringtone.

We all stilled and looked at the phone. I reached over to shut it off or maybe answer it, I wasn't sure, but Kaydence tackled me back at the same time Alex darted for my phone charging on my nightstand. "Oh no you don't! Do not give that prick a moment of your time."

I shoved Kaydence off as Alex silenced the call. "I wasn't going to answer it guys, I was just going to shut it off." I muttered a geez but in reality, I really did want to hear his voice.

"Wait!" I shouted. "Guys, Ian saw my tattoo before I left the house! He was the one who pointed it out, I hadn't even noticed it! And! And he had snuck into my room and scared the shit out of me while I was getting ready! What if he was the one to put it there?"

Alex shrieked back and Kay's eyes turned into saucers. "Oh my God, that's creepy!" Kay said.

"Ugh yeah." Alex shivered. "What if he's like some crazy serial killer, and he marked you in your sleep and was just watching you?"

We all stilled carefully looking around, and I noticed the now too quiet room giving me chills. I shook out my nerves and laughed. "That's too crazy to be true." I cleared my throat. "I hope. Anyways, let me call him and do some investigating." I reached my hand out for my phone, giving Alex a don't mess with me look. "I'm not going to beg for the potentially crazy asshole who broke my heart and could be a stalker to come back to me."

They both looked unconvinced, silently agreeing with each other. "Mmm. Hmm." They both murmured.

I rolled my eyes. "Listen, the last thing I want to do is make up with him after finding out I was the other girl, I just need to prove my sanity here. Please."

Alex sighed in defeat. "Fine, but I'm holding the phone, and it stays on speakerphone."

I rolled my eyes but agreed. "Fine."

Ian picked up on the first ring. "Akira, listen, don't hang up."

I rolled my eyes for the third time while ignoring the stupid flutter in my heart at his masculine voice. "Ian, I didn't call to talk about last night. I just need to ask you about my tattoo."

Alex gave me a stern head nod, and Kay gave me a thumbs up. I'm glad my friends approve but at the moment all I really wanted to blurt out was, *come over and tell me you love me and only me.* Instead, I kept quiet.

"Babe, please, I love you. I kicked her out as soon as you left, you have to believe me. Please!"

But why was the wench even in there in the first place, and how? I wanted to ask.

I interrupted his pleading voice; I didn't need to think any more of that whore. "Ian, the tattoo!"

He sighed. "Yeah, what about it?"

I sat up straighter, I was on a mission. "You didn't happen to...I don't know...maybe put it on me?"

"WHAT?" He yelled.

His reaction had Alex turning down his lips, raising his eyebrows and nodding his head, which told me he believed Ian's response. Kay just gave me a shoulder shrug and shook her head; she wasn't sure.

"Why the hell would I put a tattoo on you? And how?" He asked.

Good question, Ian.

"Okay thanks, I gotta go."

Right as Alex pushed the end-call, Ian pleaded for me to hear him out. I wanted to, but I knew better than to call him back. What he did to me was unforgivable. Even as I kept reminding myself this, the angel voice in my head was saying, *but what if he is telling the truth.*

Yeah, but how did she get in when he locked the front door. My devil said.

Geez, me, and my messed-up conscience.

The day proceeded with college apps, Liz dragging us up

and down the west coast to all her favorite stores and then dancing at my favorite teen nightclub. I had a day full of fun, but still couldn't forget about Ian and now worse, my dad. Not only were we all convinced I was losing my mind, but I also thought I saw the waiter guy twice. Once shopping and then at the nightclub. And every time I thought I saw a glimpse of him, I told Kay and Alex right away, and it only cemented in their minds more that I needed a psych ward. I was starting to think maybe they were right.

By the end of the day, my head was about to explode. I knew what I needed to do to erase the pain. At this point, I was like a crackhead needing a fix.

I headed for my pond around eleven-thirty when I knew no one would see me.

Just like I thought it would, the water eased my pain, and I swam enjoying the pain-free thinking space and the feel of the water against my skin. I still got a weird tingle in the water, but in a good way. It just sucked that as soon as I was laying on my rock, all the emotions came flooding back to the surface. Even more so than the night before. I was a mess with emotions.

What was I going to do about dad? What if he never woke up? And Ian, I thought I loved him at one point in our relationship, so I distanced myself to keep those feelings at bay, but now they were all too clear. I cried. I cried and thought about my newly made plans to fly to London tomorrow night to stay by my dad's side. I cried, wishing I was in Ian's strong arms. I cried to the point of hyperventilating, that produced a sea of black material creeping over my eyes. I stood fast, needing to walk and clear my mind, but I must have stood too fast because black took over my vision.

Right before I passed out, heading straight for the water, the feeling of two strong arms caught me around my waist.

"*C*ome on, Kira, come on baby, wake up." The voice was like water in the desert, but something was too familiar with this voice. It was...

I opened my eyes to a pair of ice-blue eyes staring down at me.

"Ian?" I bolted upright only to be struck again with some more dizziness as I tried to look around. We were on my rock, the moon now high in the night sky.

"Wooh. Easy." Ian helped me steady myself as I sat back down but scooted away, trying to get my confused thoughts in order. How did he know where I was? No one knew about this spot. Why did he think he could be around me after what he did? Anger boiled inside of me, the voice not of reason but doubt reminding me of Summer and her reaction.

I turned to face him shooting daggers at him. "What are you doing here!?" I tried to yell, but I only sounded like a wounded dog as tears blocked up my throat.

He looked pained by my words but also looked understand-ing. Sympathetic bastard. I hardened my stare, letting my emotions turn to stone. I didn't want his pity. "Kira. I got dressed and kicked her out of my house. Liz told me where to find you. I kept my distance and gave you space waiting for the time to try to explain myself. Baby, I love you. It's clear you feel the same way. I'm so sorry you thought there was something between Summer and me."

He tried to continue, but I couldn't let him. Lying asshole.

I stood fast, unable to keep still as I squeezed my hands tight at my sides to keep from hitting him. "THEN HOW DID SHE KNOW WHERE YOUR BEDROOM IS? WHY DID SHE THINK SHE COULD JUST BARGE IN YOUR HOUSE? WHY DID SHE LOOK SO HURT WHEN SHE SAW US? AND HOW DID SHE GET IN THROUGH A LOCKED DOOR? SHE OBVIOUSLY HAS A KEY!" The outburst scared the normal summer croaking frogs and chirping crickets, but only for a second.

He looked away, clenching his jaw, before standing up and stepping closer to me so that I couldn't get away without falling into the water. I looked towards my house, determining how far I could make it before he caught up.

He lifted a hand, but I shifted my face away. "I don't know why she thought she could just walk in my house. I don't know how she knew where my bedroom was. She looked hurt because she told me last week, she thinks she's in love with me. I told her I didn't feel the same, but we could just be friends. When she called earlier that day, she said she wanted to get to know you, and maybe that would help get over her feelings for me...baby, please look at me." I breathed in, finally letting my tears spill over and down my face.

"Where is she now?" I spit the words out with as much venom as I could muster, which wasn't a lot. My throat was raw, and it came out a little above a croak.

Ian looked down at the water, frowning in frustration, tightening the hand he held to an almost painful grasp. "I don't know. I. Don't. Care. I don't love her. I don't feel anything for her! I gave her back her phone and sent her packing while she was still crying. She could be on the other side of the world for all I care. I came after you as soon as she was out the door, I looked all over your house but couldn't find you. Finally, when I showed up tonight, Liz told me to come here. Why the hell aren't you answering my calls? Why do you think I don't deserve a moment of your precious time to explain, Kira?"

My head snapped up at his rough condescending voice. Right before I could snap back at him, he pulled me flush to his hard body, making me yelp.

"Come. Here." He growled. I sucked in my shock when I looked up into his cold stare. The feeling of safety I usually had around him was sullied by the anger in the air.

"That's not how this works, Ian" I started pushing against his chest, trying to break his hold, instead of releasing me, he held tighter.

"Quit struggling Kir, I'm not letting you go until you answer me. You're mine. It's too late to push me away, so whatever little attitude problem you have, you need to squash it. I didn't do anything with her. Drop it and move on."

I sighed. "I...want to believe you. I just need some trust first. I need to know you're not just dating me for my status."

"Trust." He let out a dark chuckle before stepping back, shaking his head in disbelief.

My hand flew to my hip. "Yes, Ian. Trust. I need to be able to trust you if you want me to believe this will work. If you want me to be yours." I made air quotes around yours. It was either that little form of the attitude he asked me to squash or push his ass into the water.

He reached back behind him grabbing the back of his shirt before pulling it up over his head, and off his amazingly delicious abs before tossing it into the grass. My body responded with liquid heat, and I gulped trying to suppress it.

"Ian, what are you doing?" I whispered. Even though his intense stare stayed locked on my eyes, I couldn't return the favor. I was too busy watching his steady hands unbutton the top of his jeans.

"Swimming, Kir." I gulped watching as he unzipped and stripped his jeans down in one swift move.

Why the hell wasn't he an underwear model?

It was hard to close my mouth or break my stare from his perfectly muscled, six-pack ab, tanned body with the sexiest white boxer briefs over his...package, that I'd ever seen, but his amused chuckle had me pulling it together. Barely.

I cleared my throat, pulling my legs together as I bit my lower lip to keep my jaw from dropping again.

"Kir, you keep looking at me like that, and I'm going to fuck you instead of swimming with you." He said, tilting a sexy half-smile before turning and diving into the water with perfect form.

I scoffed at my dilemma. How could someone be both turned on and angry at someone?

He popped back up in the middle of the pond, treading water as he wiped his face and pushed back his hair.

"You coming in?"

"I'm mad at you," I said, knowing I was getting in either way, not that he needed to know that. I may be mad at the bastard, but that didn't mean I would miss the opportunity to swim in the magical water.

He laughed. "And we also decided for you to squash the attitude."

My skin itched in anticipation. I needed that water. Now add in one sexy actor boyfriend. Shit, I was so screwed. I blew out a breath. "Fine. But I still need trust."

The trickling sound of the water floated through the quiet night as he laid back floating on his back. "Yeah, yeah. And you need the time or whatever other stuff you said."

"Ian," I warned, and he popped back up, treading water.

"Yes, babe. I got it. Sorry. I didn't know we weren't messing around. Come on now. I want to swim with my sexy girlfriend."

I watched him for a second longer knowing there was no way I could keep up the angry façade. Honestly, I wasn't sure if what he said was true or not, and if going back to him so quickly made me pathetic, fine. But I didn't want to feel the heartache anymore. Sure we would need to talk more about this, but for now, it was time to kiss his sexy ass and makeup. He must have known by getting half-naked and making me drool would equal forgiveness.

Damn, I was a shallow biotch. Alex and Kay would be so ashamed.

A plan formed in my head, and I liked the idea so much I

couldn't help the crazed laugh that broke free, followed by an ear-splitting grin that spread across my face. I launched off the rock and curled into the most epic cannonball ever. I only felt my hair lift off my head for a second, hearing him shout something that sounded like *oh shit* before the cold silky water bubbled over my body as I sank deep before pushing off the muddy bottom to head up to the surface.

I popped up, clearing the water from my eyes.

"You're a little shit," Ian said laughing.

Smiling cutely before flutter kicking away from him, I pulled out my best flirty voice saying, "I know." I winked before moving further away. I soaked in the feel of the magic water as I closed my eyes and let my body float.

The sound of rippling water caught my attention, and I peeked out watching Ian float up next to me on his back as well, I glanced at the full moon and star-filled sky before closing my eyes again feeling content and calm. At least for a minute.

Ian's ringtone blared out, making both of us jump to attention. "Shit." He said, swimming to the shore. "That's my producer, I need to take this."

I relinquished a sigh coming back to reality. These stolen moments were rare, and it sucks we spent it fighting.

"Yeah." He said into his phone.

Dipping under the water to wet my hair, I came back up to see him walking away. He most likely didn't want me to hear what he was talking about. Psh. Whatever.

Going back to my position floating on my back, I stared up at the stars, my ears under the water, letting a slight hum take over my hearing, further blocking out the noise. My body sang with comfort.

I shut my eyes, letting the atmosphere give my voice the strength to sing. The one thing I loved to do more than anything but was always too shy to pursue. Even if dad was a Rockstar, somehow, I missed the courage gene.

Singing a song of a woman lost at sea with her love, and how they made a grave decision together, I let my voice flow out over the water and through the air.

Follow me always and give me your heart

As the sea washes over my love

Give me breath from your lungs

As I give you the blood from my heart

Be one always with me and we'll drown in the water my love

Death, life all in the same as we give up our love to the shore

I finished the song feeling a tingle throughout my skin. I felt empowered, full of energy, and something else I couldn't place as I finished my song. Taking a relaxing breath in, I decided to see if he was done with his call. But when I opened my eyes and lifted my head up, I was met with empty surroundings. My heart rate picked up automatically.

He was gone.

Looking back at the house, I couldn't see him. I glanced at the rock to see his clothes still in a pile. *What the?*

"Ian?" I called into the silent night air. Was he playing a prank? I would kill him if he jumped out and scared me. I turned in a circle, carefully examining my surroundings but came up short.

Right as I started making my way to the shore, a gurgling sound in the water caught my attention. My gaze flew to the spot in the water where it seemed to be coming from. Now closer to the rock over by the shore, I paused my attempt to get out.

What the hell was in the water?

The gurgling continued as my heart neared cardiac arrest, and my hands shook so hard there was no calming them. Thoughts of monster fish, snakes, alligators, and sharks ran through my mind.

Yeah, it was a closed water pond, but sue me. I was swimming alone in the middle of the damn night and there was a bubbling coming from a spot in the water.

After treading water slowly and trying to make very little movement, I noticed the bubbling water didn't move. Okay...if something was coming to eat me, it would have moved right?

The sudden break of the water as a hand broke the surface from the middle of the bubbling stopped my heart, the black ring though damn near put me in my grave.

Oh my God.

Ian.

I quickly swam over to the spot, seeing the floating of dark brown hair at the top of the surface. "IAN!" His quick jerking movements told me he was trapped, or drowning, or both. My heart slammed in my chest as I reached down, wrapping my arms around his chest to pull him up, but he wouldn't budge. I stifled my cry.

Oh my God. Fuck. Fuck. Fuck.

It felt like something had a hold of him. No matter how hard I pulled, he stayed in the water and only bobbed up an inch or so.

"HELP!" I screamed as I looked around, my face parallel with the water. Frantically looking around the pond and open meadow, there was no one around. Of course, there wouldn't be, but maybe my security would find us?

Dropping below the water, I opened my eyes, not expecting to be able to see at night underwater, but I definitely could...and the sight shot ice through my veins.

Ian's mouth was shut, it almost looked glued. His head thrashed side to side while his eyes pleaded for help. I looked down to see seaweed or some type of plants wrapped around his ankles and wrists. Nervous panic struck my body, and without a second thought, I darted down, grabbing hard at the plants that held him down, pulling with all my strength. They deteriorated under my touch and melted away from his ankles. I floated back from the sudden give of the plants breaking, completely shocked.

What the hell? Why couldn't he break those?

I swam up quickly, bringing him with me. Breaking the surface, I took a deep breath of air, filling my lungs before guiding us back to the shore. Since we weren't far, it only took a couple of strokes.

"HELP!" I shouted again. They had to hear me. I looked around for his phone, not spotting it anywhere.

"Be right back." My voice trembled as I staggered towards his pants on the rock. Slamming my hand down around the clothes. Nothing. Shit. Had it fallen into the water? Fuck.

"HELP!" I screamed again, a cry breaking from my lips as I rushed back over to him.

No, no, no!

Ian lay lifeless, cold and drained of color. His eyes, almost looking grey from their original blue, stared up to the star-filled sky.

Reaching out, I felt his cold, stiff shoulder before my hands flew back to cover my mouth.

"Oh my God. Oh my God. Ian." I mumbled between sobs that wrecked my terrified soul.

How long had he been down there for?

Shaking my fear aside enough to move, I started CPR even though his body was half in the water.

"IAN!" I pleaded while I pumped on his chest before opening his mouth, giving him my air. I listened to his chest, pleading to hear something. Nothing. I tried again, pumping harder this time with shaky hands and a weak stomach. "Ian, Ian. Don't do this. Don't..." I cried out between quivering lips, the roar of my head threatening my consciousness while the pain crept back into my chest.

I ignored it all as I hyper-focused on the cold corpse in my hands.

I breathed another lungful of air between his blue lips. Water dripped down onto his face from his wet curls.

I tried another lungful of air.

Nothing.

I tried it again.

Why wasn't it working? I rubbed my hands up and down his cold arms, trying to warm him awake. Nothing.

The burning of my eyes and throat I could ignore, the panic and sharp pain in my chest I couldn't.

Ian was dead.

He'd drowned.

I let him.

I couldn't save him.

How did it happen so fast?

My world spun as my blood iced.

"NOOOOOO!" I screamed between sobs.

"Help, help me! Someone." We were too far out on the property for someone to hear, even the guards. I knew it was no use in the back of my head, but everything shut down inside me. He couldn't leave me. I laid down halfway on top of him, nestling my head under his chin as I sobbed. "Iaann." I whimpered. I cursed. I cried. Nothing. I needed to get help, but he needed me. I couldn't leave him. I didn't care that we were still half in the water or that we were soaked. He needed my body, I couldn't separate myself from him.

"I love you," I whispered the words I never got to say. Why had I been so stupid? Why hadn't I let our love grow and given us a chance?

I sat up studying his face, a calm falling over me. It felt like my emotions were dripping off me like the water on my skin was doing. The numbness would help me, so I welcomed it.

I wiped the water away that had dripped on his lips from his nose before placing a gentle kiss down on them. I closed my eyes like I always would when we kissed and pulled back only a breath away to plead with him one last time. I didn't dare open my eyes and see his relaxed face.

"Baby, come back to me. I need you." I whispered. I needed it to go out as a prayer. I needed to be heard and felt and answered. It was the only sound in our world. I laid my head down on his hard chest, despite my panic, and sent out prayer after prayer.

Please don't take him from me.

---

*T*he pinkish glow turned orange over the horizon, the first sign of the morning coming alive with its light. Had I laid here all night? My eyes remained unmoving on the meadow that led to my house, but still, I held onto his body my once wet head that I realized was now dry still on his chest. I needed to get help. I needed to help him.

Slowly I lifted my head from his chest, more tears falling and splashing on his skin, as I found the strength to sit up. I sniffled, trying to gain control. I needed to get help.

"I will always love you. I'm so sorry." I whispered, before placing one last kiss on his lips.

My eyes sprang open with panic as his cold lips twitched against mine.

Ian kissed me back.

I pulled back, and he took a huge breath of air as I cried out. I moved away, helping him sit as he turned away and coughed up the water.

How?

We scooted out of the water, and I helped him to his feet. His eyes were distant at first, but only for a minute.

"Kira?" He croaked. I shook my head up and down, plowing into his chest.

"Ian! I thought I lost you, you were...you had. Ian, you-"

He cut me off, running a hand over my hair as we held each other. "I know."

We held each other for a long time, my emotions feeling euphoric, like after riding a roller coaster. I pulled back to study his face. His lips were back to being pink again, and a blush filled his cheeks.

"How?"

He shook his head in confusion. "I don't know. I was listening to you sing, and the next thing I knew, I was walking into the water. It felt like I was in some kind of trance. Then I was trapped under the water. I saw your face in the water, and then everything went black." He shivered. "It felt as if the life just drained out of me, nothing like what I thought drowning would feel like. It was almost peaceful. And, and then I heard you. I heard you say you needed me, and I followed the light until the feeling came back into my body. Your lips were the first thing I felt." I let out a relieved laugh and hugged him tightly.

He lifted my chin and studied my face. "Baby, you saved me...but there's something I need to tell you." I smiled weakly, feeling exhausted all of a sudden.

"What?"

"Never mind." He mumbled before leaning down and kissing me softly.

The tingling started first, and I was only half-aware of the energy I felt.

Ian leaned back, separating our lips as he sucked in a breath like he'd just ran a marathon, he staggered back putting his hands on his knees as he tried to catch his breath. "Ian?"

He looked up weakly and smiled, "We need to do that again."

Was he kidding, he was about to die...again, just from a loss of breath?

"No. Come on, you can stay with me tonight. I want to make sure you're okay, then you need to go to the doctor." I walked toward him and took his hand, which he hungrily grabbed to pull me flush against him.

"Ian." I warned, trying to pull out of his arms.

He just died and now was out of air, he needed to rest, or do breathing exercises or something. Not make out and diminish what little air he had left in his lungs.

He shoved his tongue halfway down my throat in a matter of seconds as he grabbed my ass. I tried to pull away and refuse to kiss him, but it just egged him on more. And to be honest, I didn't want to pull away from how he was making me feel. I knew in the back of my mind it was messed up and wrong, but I couldn't stop. His kiss was filling me with an energy so powerful I felt like my blood was alive. I gave in as he kicked my feet out from underneath me and caught me in one quick motion.

I yelped as he lowered me down to the ground. He was on top of me before I could even think about what was happening. The tingling I had started to feel the last time we kissed covered every inch of my body. We were kissing so fast, so heavily; we were both out of breath but didn't care to stop. He tore off my bikini bottoms, and I let him. Breathing in deeply, I watched as he pulled down his pants. Only then did I notice how dizzy and weak he looked.

"Ian, stop." I said, grabbing his hand and getting a better look at his face. His eyes were different. The blue in them was so light I could barely see them, and his skin looked more than pale, almost translucent.

"No!" He growled as he brought his lips back to mine. This time it was more than a tingle, it was a burst of energy that I felt, along with Ian dropping lifeless on top of me.

"Ian?" I rolled him off me and onto his back.

His lips slowly turned white before my eyes. What? No.

Looking up, his eyes were wide open and just like his lips, completely white. His skin looked translucent like all the blood had been drained from him.

I shook his shoulders. "IAN?"

He laid there lifeless, and somehow, I knew this time in my heart...he really was dead.

I stood on shaking legs, then...I turned and ran.

Somewhere in the back of my head, I knew I needed to get help, but I also knew I killed him.

I didn't know how, but I killed him.

This time I didn't feel sadness at his life being gone, but power. Nothing more. No other emotions. It felt good. I'd just cleared the trees running at full speed when I slammed into a chest full of muscles.

I fell back, hitting my head, hard. Black dots spotted my vision.

"It's done." I heard a familiar voice say.

I looked up but couldn't see from my swaying vision.

"Took you long enough." I closed my eyes and grabbed my head. The pain was still there, but the dizziness had stopped.

"I already took care of the body, but now you need to complete your transformation." I heard him talking, but I didn't know who it was or what he was talking about.

"Complete huh?" I asked, hoping that made sense.

I opened my eyes to see the figure bend down, his knees popped as he rested his arms on them and continued to study me. "Yes, what do you feel like doing?"

I thought about it, I didn't know. I ran through what just happened in my head. I just killed Ian. I waited to feel something, but nothing came. I ran through the previous moments when lust filled my body. I felt tingly and powerful and...turned on.

Thinking about the feelings brought them an instant later.

I didn't want to feel those though. So I didn't answer the person and stood.

"Akira, what do you think I'm here for? Only an Incubus can complete your transformation."

What?

I found my voice. "Move." It felt and sounded powerful.

Bringing up my hand to block the bright morning sun, I was able to get a good look at the person who'd knocked me down.

I gasped. "You're the waiter?"

"Cander."

Cander grabbed my wrist and pulled me against him, I tried to struggle free, but my struggles stopped when I saw his gold eyes start to glow.

"Again. Took you long enough." He said before slamming his lips onto mine.

Black swarmed my vision, dizziness striking me as I lost control of my muscles...I felt my body fall. Somehow, I was the one that was drowning now.

4
THE START OF 72

 I woke up naked in a stranger's bed. I looked around the unfamiliar room as I wrapped the silk sheets tighter around myself. *Where am I?* Keeping the sheets around myself, I crawled to the corner of the bed, trying to find any shred of clothes that could be mine. Nothing. No clothes.

I leaned back on the bed, feeling the pounding of my head and the churning in my stomach. It felt like I had the biggest hangover in history.

"Clothes are in the dryer. They'll be out soon." Cander said, coming into view from around the corner. I let out a scream before grabbing at my pounding heart. He was like a ninja, I hadn't even heard him. He narrowed his eyes at my reaction and licked his lips before turning to face me with a look of annoyance. "You don't always have to be so jumpy. It isn't even in your nature."

I don't know if it was his last words that brought on the flood of memories or the tone in his voice, but visions of the night before slammed into me at full blast. My heart sank. The last thing I remembered was kissing...Cander? *Shit!* Taking in our kiss, and the situation with me naked and him standing by

the bed in nothing but boxers, it was hard not to assume something had happened. I felt myself slowly freaking out and
muffled it as best I could. I needed to figure out what was going
on. Cander just stood still, watching me with the same annoyed
look on his face that he seemed to save especially for me.

I opened my dry mouth before I chickened out. "Did
we...you know?" I asked, looking down at myself and then him.

He let out a sigh before bringing his hand up and rubbing at
his forehead. "You'd remember it. Now get your clothes, and
let's get going."

Go where? Did he think I was just going to go places with
him? I needed to go home. *No.* I couldn't go home anymore. I
was a wanted criminal. I somehow murdered my movie star
boyfriend. The pain hit me like it should have hit when it
happened, and I couldn't fight the tears this time. They poured
down my face silently, I looked away from Cander. I didn't need
him scrutinizing me for my actions.

"I know you're new to this, but this crying shit has to stop.
It doesn't solve anything." I glared over at him just in time to see
him leaving the room with the door slamming.

Asshole.

I got up, pulling the sheet from the bed and wrapping it
around myself. Yeah, I usually didn't cry as much as I had been
lately, but it hadn't been the best week. I peered around the first
corner I came to, it was a closet and bathroom. I decided the
door Cander walked through would lead me to wherever the
washer and dryer might be. It seemed a little shocking that he
took the time to wash and dry my clothes. This guy looked like
the selfish uncaring bad boy type. The type that shot first and
asked questions later. Not the kind that did laundry.

I left the room quietly, walking down a lavish hallway,
undoubtedly in some type of mansion. There were chandeliers
in the hall for shit's sake. The only problem with finding the
laundry room was that the hallway looked to have about a

million doors and almost seemed endless. I turned back to the room I was in before I got lost. This place was intimidating. *And I thought I was rich.* If Cander wanted me gone so fast, he'd just have to go retrieve my clothes. Another question that had me on edge was, if we didn't have sex, what did we do?

It felt like I sat on the edge of the bed forever before Cander finally made another appearance. "What *are* you doing?" He almost sounded amused. I must have heard wrong.

His expression wasn't any different than the hard glare he usually sported with angry gold eyes. "Get my clothes so I can leave," I demanded.

Cander was dressed in a black leather jacket, black jeans, and black riding boots. It looked good with his bad boy demeanor. "And where do you plan on going? You're a wanted killer, *Akira*, surely you don't think you could just walk around in plain sight."

I stood wrapping the sheet tighter around me. "You don't think I don't know what I did! Who are you? Why am I here? And why am I naked?"

He walked over to me with an icy stare. "It's not my fault you don't remember what happened last night. I told you who I was. I told you who you are. Next time try to keep up. We have less than seventy-two hours for you to complete your transition, so hurry up. And. Get. Dressed." He spat in my face as he stepped back and motioned to a set of clothes on the dresser I hadn't noticed before. My heart hammered in my chest, but I refused to move from the anger boiling in my veins. He wanted to intimidate me that much I was sure of, and if he thought because he had big muscles and a sexy face I would bend to his will, he had another thing coming.

Cander stepped even closer, looking my body up and down. I refused for my body to react. "Oh, and Kira?"

I glared as a response.

He smiled and leaned even closer, his lips brushing against

my ear. I held my breath to keep still. *I can hear your thoughts*. He whispered into my mind without even moving the lips that were still up against me.

My heart stopped, as heat flooded my cheeks. So I hadn't just imagined hearing his voice in my head in the restaurant.

"Nope. That was me, babe."

"Ugh!" I screamed in rage, pushing at his chest. "How?"

"How about getting dressed." He said, laughing as he sauntered back out of the room. I just stood there, unsure of what to say.

I dropped the sheet from my body and stomped over to the dresser naked. *He was such an asshole*. I snatched up the clothes on the dresser and headed for the bathroom. Once inside, I put on the black lace push-up bra. *Seriously*? It had underwear to match. I put them on with shaky hands. The jeans someone laid out for me, or most likely Cander laid out for me, were skintight. I had a tight black shirt and leather jacket that looked too close to his on the pile. I threw them aside and looked in the mirror. I had imagined myself looking like a complete wreck. The past twenty-four hours had been an emotional roller coaster.

What I saw instead had me laughing. I couldn't stop. I'd finally cracked. My hair was not only curled and longer. It was a completely different color. Brunette. It looked like I'd just stepped out of a hair commercial. Flawless would be how I'd describe it. Not only that, but I hadn't put on makeup. I leaned closer in the mirror, rubbing at my eyelids, cheeks, and lips. It looked like I had eye shadow, mascara, lipstick, blush, and powder on my face. Even though none of it would rub off. I laughed until I cried. I picked up my hair at different angles hoping somehow a wig would fall off and reveal my once blonde hair. Nope.

Not only was it not a wig. My damn tattoo had grown. It was now circling around to the front of my neck. It was beautiful but way too much. How the hell could I forget getting a tattoo? I needed some therapy and a white padded room.

What the hell was going on? After the laughter came the hyperventilating, then the dizziness. I couldn't remember anything after Cander had kissed me last night. Still, apparently, I'd had the biggest makeover of my life after killing my boyfriend. I climbed into a stalkers bed, naked. I probably got a boob job as well. They were at least a C cup, via what my bra read.

A loud banging on the bathroom door had me jumping out of my skin. Unfortunately, it didn't help my nervous breakdown. "Akira, we don't have time for you to freak out. We have to leave. Now!" Cander roared before kicking open the door so hard it slammed into the wall behind it, making plaster float down onto the floor. He stepped through, looking like an avenging angel. While I just stood there in the middle of the bathroom with a tear-streaked face looking like a mental patient.

"What is happening to me?" I crumbled to the floor, the cold tile was welcoming on my hot cheek.

Cander's hand wrapped around my upper arm, pulling me hard off the floor, forcing me to my feet. He forced me to look at him. His hand was digging hard into my arm, I held back a cry of pain. "Get your shit together, Akira! Look!" He growled, shoving me towards the mirror while his other hand flipped back the hair from my shoulder, and pointed to my tattoo.

"If you don't complete the transition within seventy-two hours, you will-"He stopped and let out a growl. "Damn it, Akira! I made a promise to get you through this!" He let go of my arm, and I stumbled forward, catching myself before my head slammed into the bathroom mirror.

I turned and faced him, anger rolling off me. "Don't ever lay a hand on me again!" I screamed.

Cander walked forward, backing me up against the bathroom sink, he didn't stop until he was flush against me and his face inches away from mine. His eyes drilled into me, making me shiver in fear. He had a look that would have people begging for mercy.

Whatever. I wasn't going to cower because he could narrow his eyes. Anger riled up in me.

"I will touch you whenever and however I like." My heart stopped, and fear started to trickle in at the realization that he could. He looked me up and down the best he could for being so close before stepping back with disgust on his face. "Fortunately for you. I would rather do anything other than *touch* you." He stepped back, grabbing my jacket off the floor and dragging me out behind him.

He stopped just before we stepped out of the bedroom. "Can you follow me, or am I going to have to drag you along like a good little dog?"

Dick.

"Yes, I am." He said a self-satisfied smile on his face. I nodded once, and he finally let my arm go.

I followed him down the fancy hallway. "What transition are you talking about?"

We came to what I assumed to be a front door, and he opened it and motioned me through. "The transition to becoming a Siren." He said it so matter of fact. I laughed as I stepped through the door and looked back. Just for him to poke me in the back and growl to keep moving.

"You're kidding, right? A Siren? Like a mermaid or nymph thing from mythology?" I had no idea where I was walking. It was a cloudy day and looked like we were in the middle of a desert. Not a soul, plant, or object in sight other than hard, dry dirt.

Cander walked up beside me but ignored my question. Whatever, he was probably just lost shuffling and nosing around in my head where he didn't belong. *Hmm. Cander is a dick. Cander is stupid. Cander is ugly...Cander is-*

"You're so mature."

"Stay out of my head and answer my questions!" I looked around and noticed a white-barked tree with green leaves that looked massively out of place. A Harley sat underneath it. *Oh.* So that's what these clothes are about.

"I'm babysitting. We're looking for a person named Jax before you're trapped here." Here, in the desert?

Cander sat on the Harley and looked back to where I stood. I shook my head. Hell no. Those things were dangerous and just no. Cander noticed my defiance and rolled his eyes. "Do you want me to tie you up and leave you here? That's your other option."

"Why are you such an asshole? I'm going through a lot right now!"

"No actually, you aren't going through anything until we find Jax." He said, revving the engine to life.

"I'm not getting on until you tell me who Jax is. And what a Siren is and who you are." I yelled over the noise.

Cander growled in frustration. The look he gave me did more than just shoot fear through me, it made my heart race, but in a good way. I shook my head to dispel those emotions. "Jax will extend your deadline; he's the gatekeeper of the Fourth Realm. A Siren is a demon. I'm a demon. You're in Hell. Now can we get on with it?"

I didn't believe it but shuffled for the bike anyways. Demon? Hell? Did he really expect me to believe any of that? As soon as my leg wrapped around the other side of the seat, he took off. I flew back, and if it wasn't for him reaching back and grabbing my leg, I would have been left in the dust we were now making across the dry ground.

I instantly wrapped my hands around his stomach and leaned forward against his back. I had never been on a motor-cycle before, I couldn't tell if it was normal not to be able to breathe. Was it from the wind in my face, or was it just the hot, dry air suffocating me? Either way, I dipped my head down and used him as a shield. Cander didn't move or seem to mind my closeness as we roared on. We rode through the blank abyss for what seemed like an eternity until his voice broke through my thoughts, and we finally slowed down.

Try not to show anyone the marks on your neck. Don't talk if you can help it. If asked a direct question, tell them what I tell you to say.

I rolled my eyes and leaned back from him. "As you wish."

"That's what I like to hear." He said out loud as he dropped the kickstand and got off the bike. He was a smug asshole most of the time, but he was still sexy.

We were parked amongst ten or so other motorcycles in front of a broken-down bar. In the middle of nowhere. How original.

Cander grabbed my upper arm and pulled me close to his side as we walked in. The lights were barely existent, along with the stench of stale beer and cigarette smoke. The whole place was a joke. Something you'd see in a biker movie. The place even had rock-n-roll music playing from the corner jukebox. Cliché and non-threatening.

"Coming from the girl who is in Hell." Cander's voice broke through my thoughts, once again invading my mind. I hated it. I hated him in there.

Can't you just shut it off? I thought back to him, giving him a side glare.

Believe it or not, I'm using this ability to protect you. Now. Keep. Quiet.

"I- "I started to tell him off when he squeezed my arm impossibly tight to the point I almost screamed when pain shot up my arm.

Be. Quiet. He threatened into my mind. I complied this time, cradling my arm when he dropped it.

"Cander. Has Lilith sent you to collect?" The bartender asked, startling me. I hadn't even seen him let alone anyone in the bar besides us a second ago. Was that normal for people and things to just appear and disappear here?

Cander's eyes shifted from right to left, scanning the bar in what looked like suspicion. "Do you have anything to collect?"

The bartender looked nervous. He looked over Cander's back shoulder quickly before swallowing his visible nerves and shaking his head. "No." The guy's eyes shifted towards me.

Cander stepped in front of me, blocking the guy's view of me. I rubbed at my arm, holding back a whimper. Yeah, I was a baby when it came to pain, but it was definitely broken. I could hardly move it. Great.

"A Siren?" The bartender asked. "I wasn't aware you had moved on from Ariel's death." Cander's body stiffened at the name. I was instantly curious, but it didn't take a genius to guess she was someone special to him.

"Leave that alone, Crow." Cander threatened.

Crow, the bartender, ignored him and put down the glass he was cleaning as he glanced around Cander to me. "Hey, baby. You wanna take a break from the man whore and sing me a nice little melody?"

I started to back up in fear when Cander's voice entered my mind. *Don't show fear. Act disgusted and above him. Look down your nose at him and push out your chest. Don't be intimidated by him.*

I did as he said and then more. I stepped around Cander to stand beside him as I held my head high and wrapped my arms around Cander's tight bicep. "I'm not interested in..." I paused, looking at the disgusting man with black slicked-down hair up and down before finishing. "Your kind." Then I glanced at Cander from the corner of my eye to see he was about to burst with laughter but quickly contained himself and picked back up the rough act.

The bartender narrowed his eyes at me in anger but moved his glare to Cander. I'm guessing the bartender no matter what, or who he was, wasn't going to mess with Cander.

"Where's Jax?" He asked, shaking his arm free of me. I didn't mind. My left arm was throbbing from moving it in the first place.

"Asgret summoned him the night before last. I hear she wasn't very pleased with his last stunt." He scoffed. "I can't believe he actually went. He's as good as tarred."

Time to go. Cander spoke to my mind. I stood there expecting him to finish his conversation with Crow, but instead, he turned on his heel and grabbed my upper arm hard and dragged me out with him. I looked back one last time to see a group of men step out from a back room. All of them dressed in black biker clothes, rough and dangerous looking. Fear shot through me. It was clear they were coming for us, but why?

We ran to the bike and took off so fast the back tire skidded in the dirt, but we flew forward in seconds.

What was that? I asked him via mind speak.

"Hold on." He said, trying to pull my left arm around him that was hanging by my side. I screamed in pain as black dotted my vision.

Cander, noticing my pain, looked back to see my dilemma as he turned sharply to the right. We were out in the middle of nowhere. There were no plants, no trees, rocks, or landmarks to tell me where we were. So the sharp right turn seemed a little ridiculous to me.

"We're going back to Earth." He answered my thoughts.

A second later, the once grey sky opened up, forming a huge black hole. The bottom of the hole touched the dirt floor. I tried to tell Cander to stop, but the fear gripping me had my heart in my throat. The only response my body would give was to squeeze tighter to Cander and hope that we died fast. Right as the front tire touched the black opening I was sure was a wall, we drove right through it. For a mere second, all the air in my lungs collapsed, and it felt like I was being squeezed to death. It passed, and before I knew it, Cander was revving the engine as we passed a semi on a two-lane highway.

"What the hell just happened? Why were those guys chasing us? Are they still chasing us?" I looked back but couldn't see any other motorcycles racing towards us.

We passed a sign that read- "Now Entering Las Vegas City Limits."

"Why are we in Vegas?"

"Because that's where the portal comes out at. We'll crash here for the night, while I make a few phone calls and figure out my next plan."

It didn't take long for us to find a hotel and before long we pulled into the MGM Hotel and Casino. I had doubts they would let us in. Well, me anyway. Not only did I not have an ID, but I wasn't even twenty-one. If that wasn't enough, I was now also wanted for murder. I sat on the bike as Cander walked towards the entrance and then stopped.

"Are you coming?" He asked, clearly annoyed.

I got off the bike like the good little captive I was and followed cradling my broken arm. Whatever, if he wanted to try and get us a room, he could. I just wanted to go home. I needed to turn myself in. If the whole hotel thing didn't work out, "transformation" to this Siren bullshit or not, I was going home, and that was final.

To my surprise, not only did he get us a penthouse, but no one asked questions or wanted ID's as he handed them a black credit card. We remained silent, both lost in our own thoughts, well I was anyway until we got to the room.

"Let me see your arm." He said, turning to me.

"No. You'll probably just break it more." I turned and headed for the kitchenette for some water.

Cander stepped in my way, coming out of no where.

"Akira, I can heal you." He said, backing me up against the

wall. The whole scene taking place reminded me of Ian, and my heart squeezed in my chest.

Before I could protest or maneuver around him, he pushed his lips against mine. The instant his lips were on mine, all feelings of anger, confusion, heartache, and anything else I was feeling no longer existed. They were instantly replaced with a dazed feeling and a desire to do only one thing. That thing was in front of me. The tingling I felt the night before returned all over my body, but I ignored it and deepened the kiss. I didn't mean to let a moan escape me, but I couldn't help it as I pushed myself up against him. Cander returned my kisses, but I had a feeling he was holding back. I didn't care. The only thing I could think of was that I wanted, no, needed more. *More*.

I grabbed his jacket with both hands and urged him to come to me. He didn't budge. Instead, he broke away from me and cleared his throat. I was still in a daze, a beautiful lust filled trance while I tried to catch my breath. "Feeling better?" He asked, studying my face. He didn't sound out of breath or anything.

I couldn't talk, my throat and body pounded with need. I lifted an eyebrow, trying to calm my breathing. Hopefully, he knew that meant I had no idea what he was talking about.

Cander looked down at his jacket and then back to me, raising his eyebrows. I was confused until I realized I was gripping his jacket with both of my hands.

My arm was completely healed. As much as I could for being backed against the wall, I stepped back and examined my newly healed arm. "How...I." I didn't know what I was trying to say. How did he do that? Thanks? I don't know. It didn't matter. When I looked up, he was already at his bedroom door, slamming it shut behind him. He'd left without waiting to hear a single word come out of my mouth.

5

THE RIGHT ANSWERS

"*O*kay, so let me get this straight."

We were in the living room. I had begged to go out and blow off some steam and go dancing, he said that was a horrible idea, and that a better plan was to take this time to get all my questions off my chest. Had I known what I was getting into I would have pushed to go dancing. Why did I want to go dancing? Well, I felt like I had so much built-up energy I was going to explode, and dancing has always been my back up.

I sat up straighter trying to calm myself. "You and Jax, are part of a group in Hell or Purgatory or somewhere down there," I pointed to the floor as he gazed at me with a bored expression. "Called the Watchers. You represent the demons that can cross realms, possession, and sexual, and Sirens. All I need to know right now is that yes, Sirens can look like mermaids and that I'm in the transition stage to becoming a Siren, and if I don't complete it, I'll die. Oh, and Sirens are demons who kill humans to survive." I said the last part all in one breath, then took a deep breath to replenish my burning lungs.

We'd been at this Q and A for almost an hour. Yeah, I'm a little slow. But when he'd first explained the little bit that he did,

I was stuck on a Siren's definition for so long that he finally told me that it was like a mermaid and that I didn't need anymore. Okay, so. Hi, my name is Akira, and I'm a mermaid. *Holy shit.* I *cannot* wait to wake up from this dream.

"Finally," Cander said, standing up and looking out the window at the lights from the strip. He'd taken off his leather jacket and stood in a tight black beater.

"Can I call and check on my dad?" The question had no sooner left my lips, and he'd turned, his eyes glowing and growled. "No!"

Okay? I tried to think about how long I'd been gone, twenty-four hours...maybe? Okay, okay. No big deal, other than the fact that dad was in a coma, and the band was probably wondering why I missed my flight. But if the news got out about Ian, what would they think? What if my dad woke up to that news in London? I needed to get to my phone fast.

"Wow, I cannot believe you're actually thinking about your phone right now. Typical teenage girl."

That's it. "Are you freaking serious?! Can you seriously stay the hell out of my head! Yeah, so I was wondering about where my phone was, so what? What else do you want me to think of?" I yelled standing up from the couch. I dug my heels into the carpet to keep from storming over to him and either ripping off his shirt or slapping his face. I wanted to do both, and it only fueled my rage more.

When he didn't turn around or say anything, it really made me lose it. If I could use my demon powers to blow someone up, it would be Cander. He laughed at my last thought. "Do you seriously have to be so mean, and an asshole and so...stupid!" Okay, there were a lot of things Cander was, but stupid wasn't one of them. Unfortunately, my anger had shut off my thought process, and it was the best I could do on such short notice in the middle of a good lashing.

Cander turned around and grabbed the beer he'd been

drinking from the side table. He took a slow drink and set it down, leveling me with a neutral face before turning back around. UUUGGGGHHHH! My brain shut off, and with it, all reasoning. I stormed around the glass table in front of me and took off towards him. Attempting to sprint in such a small space, I headed to tackle the asshole into or preferably right out of the glass window.

I was only a breath away when he turned lightning fast and brought me to a halt as he caught both my wrists. I struggled to move forward while I grunted and screamed profanities. I tried to move forward and beat the hell out of him but he was too strong. If I could just land one punch, I would feel better. Cander didn't even flinch as I struggled against his hold.

"Akira, stop. This is pathetic." It only fueled me on. Why was he such a bastard? Why wasn't he more understanding, caring?

I stopped struggling and when he eased his grip on my wrists I jerked them away from him. I paced in front of him, trying to calm myself.

"Okay. You will answer the rest of my questions, and you will stay out of my head." I demanded, feeling that was more reasonable since I couldn't beat it out of him. I had no doubt he could lay me out in a matter of seconds, but it still hadn't stopped me from trying.

Cander looked defeated. "What other questions do you have?"

I thought about all of them and tried to sort through the pile that formed in my head. I needed to start with the most important ones first. "Okay. How do I stop the transition and just be a human?"

Cander smirked before shaking his head. "You can't. Next question."

"WHY NOT?" I yelled in his face.

"You want to keep asking questions or not? Next. Question."

Fine, what the hell ever. I walked back to the couch and looked around at the black and white designed penthouse, trying to keep my stare on anything other than him.

"Okay...What *do* I have to do to complete the transformation?" Not that I planned on it. Yeah, the little mermaid was cool, but I wasn't cool with the title of a demon. If I had to pick being a demon, I'd rather die.

Cander took another drink of beer before answering, taking his time to just piss me off more. "I thought you said alcohol didn't affect me anymore! Why are you drinking it?" He paused mid swallow and glanced at me before putting down the bottle. I concentrated on his soft, pink lips and wanted to lose myself in them again.

And then there's that awkward moment when you want to be a beer bottle...

Damn it, Akira, stop thinking like that! I shook my head, trying to clear my thoughts. *Holy shit, I needed to calm down.*

Cander tried to cover his laugh by clearing his throat, but it broke through anyway. I hated him. He grabbed his beer and sat down next to me on the couch, it was antagonizing, and I knew he'd done it on purpose. I scooted away but he ended up following.

"Okay! That's it! Why in the hell am I so horny!" Now he did laugh. I buried my head in my hands, hating that I actually said that out loud.

"Because you get your power through kissing, fucking, and killing."

Umm, that's not what a mermaid did. They sang under the sea with Flounder and talked to seagulls. He continued like I wasn't freaking out in my head.

"And you're in your transition stage, and you're probably the only virgin Siren I know. In order to complete the transition, you have to be of age eighteen, take your first sacrifice through a sexual act and *make sure* you complete the act during or immediately after your kill. You killed him during foreplay. This not only makes you extremely powerful but extremely horny since you never released your pent-up energy. Not only that, but you must also get powers from a Succubus or Incubus through a sexual act. Meaning you will still need to have sex with me anyways, even if you had finished with Ian." He sat so casually, with his hands clasped together and his elbows on his knees, you'd think this was an everyday conversation. I was still too shocked to talk yet. It was a lot to take in.

"I was there to make sure you completed the transition. I lied and told them you had. I figured I would get you to have sex with me after we got back to the realm. Instead, I got you naked, and all you were interested in was asking questions and crying about Ian. We've gone through all this before. I'm not sure why you don't remember it. I'm guessing from a power hangover. You have to release some of it, or it will get too strong and kill you. Anyways, I gave up and left you alone that night. We'll be on the run until you complete it. I bring in the newbies, you, to the realm. Since you and I are missing, well...technically we're on the run."

I found it hard to believe that I'd denied him sex but shoved the thought away. "Okay, so you're saying...if I don't have sex, I'll die, not only because I won't complete the change but because I'll have too much built up energy?" Geez, this was turning into a messed-up version of a vampire movie. I grabbed at my aching head that had been continuously pounding ever since waking up.

"Yeah, those headaches will keep getting worse too."

Okay, the solution was simple. I would just have sex or die. I knew what I needed to do. "Okay. Well, I'm going to bed." I said, not feeling a bit tired. I tried to think of him as a cover thought while I walked to my room. I needed to think of a way to end it fast. I could overdose on something if I had any pain pills. No. I shook my head and then quieted my thoughts. Cander is so hot. Blah, blah, blah. I had my thoughts hammer on about him for another couple of minutes as I stepped into my bedroom, shut and locked the door, and made my way to my bathroom. Maybe a hot shower would help things? And get this color out of my hair. And get the tattoo off as well. Good plan.

I started the shower and shut the door, locking it as the steam built up around me. I began to strip, I looked in the full-length mirror on the back of the door at my body now only in the black lace underwear and bra. I continued to examine my body when I got another thought. Drowning. I could drown myself. I twirled around fast, getting ready to switch the shower to bath water when Cander appeared in the blink of an eye in front of me. I yelped as I flew back.

"HOLY SHIT, CANDER!"

He ran a frustrated hand through the hair that had fallen in his face, and his eyes looked back up into mine, slightly glowing. "Kira, my job is to make sure you complete the transition, do you really think I'm going to let you kill yourself. Not only that, but I just told you, you're a Siren, and you were going to try and drown yourself. Really?" He looked at me like I should have known that. Well, shit. It's not my fault; I'm new to trying to kill myself *and* being a Siren.

The steam was filling up the bathroom now, I had only turned on a soft glow of lights, and with me in my bra and underwear, the whole situation was dangerous. Dead sexy man, the mood was set, I was horny as hell. I backed up against the bathroom door, flattening my hands against it to keep myself in place.

"Cander, leave," I said with a shaky voice. I concentrated on the floating, fancy sink that looked like it was made of glass, then to the floor, then to the handles on the medicine cabinet. Anywhere but on him. He noticed.

Cander stepped forward, and I only glanced at him long enough to snatch the towel from the bar on the wall and try my best to cover up my front. "Akira. You know what kind of demon I am. Not only can I read your thoughts, but I wouldn't even have to do that. Sex is what I live for. I can pick up on the hormones you're throwing off, and it's enough to drown a city full of people. Not only that, but I'm not going to be able to contain myself much longer around you if you don't calm down."

Like it was my fault I was feeling like this! I tried to think of bad things to change my emotions. "You have sex to survive. Why would you think I would want to have sex with you when you have had sex with a million girls?" The accusation didn't calm me. I tried it again. "You probably have all sorts of STD's."

He walked up to me, so close, all I'd have to do is inch forward. "Is that all you got Kira? Because right now, I'm still reading that you want me...badly." I swallowed my frantic heartbeat and looked at the ceiling, but the soft golden glow of his eyes cut through my vision.

He never tore his eyes away from me as he shrugged off his jacket and it thumped to the floor. My lower stomach and every organ down there thrummed and ached in need. I needed him so bad, but I also couldn't let myself become something so evil. Your first time should be with someone you love. My thoughts didn't help, and he'd taken off his shirt. I could feel myself get wet. I couldn't even stop my body's response to his heated stare and ripped abs.

"Won't there be repercussions to intermixing, or...I don't know. I'm a Siren, and you're an Incubus." I was grasping at straws.

He reached forward, tugging the towel from my grasp before closing the gap, making my chest melt against his. He reached down and intertwined our hands as he slowly lifted them up. "Keep trying." He whispered.

THE RIGHT ANSWERS | 75

Keep trying? I couldn't even breathe! My breasts pressed up against his chest made me whimper from the feel of him against me.

He leaned forward slightly, kissing my neck. I closed my eyes as goosebumps took over my body and I leaned my head back, bliss muddling my brain. His hands now had mine trapped above me. "Umm..." I didn't mean for it to sound like a moan. I tried to think of another reason to stop this madness. Is this really how I wanted to go out? By the hands of a demon? If I'd rather die than be a demon, I had every right, even if it felt like my fantasy had come true.

His kisses were now at my jawline. "Come on Akira." He breathed.

Suddenly the damn voices were back. *What's the big deal, give in just a little? Let off a little pressure. What could a little making out hurt?*

Cander's lips hovered over mine, my eyes were still shut, but I could taste his hot, spicy breath.

The other voice arrived just as I almost met his lips. *Don't lean forward. Don't give in. You don't want to be a demon. You don't want to kill people for power.*

I shook my head, opening my eyes. I'd never seen Cander's eyes glow so bright. Not only the determination, but the glow told me he was done waiting. He dropped my hands and brought his own to my breasts as his lips met mine. I lost control. I couldn't help it.

I wrapped my arms around his neck as the second voice kept shouting at me how wrong this was. I didn't care, it *felt* right.

It kept trying anyway, as Cander kissed every inch of my body. My bra falling to the floor. *Just think of how many others he's touched. Think about the eternity in Hell you're condemning yourself to. Think about how you don't even love him.*

"Kira, come on, you know you want it," Cander whispered from his knelt position as he ran his lips under my belly button.

He was right. I trembled I wanted it so bad. Cander was making his way back up my body taking his time with my breasts. Sucking, licking, kissing, doing everything to keep me soaking wet as one of my hands pulled his hair, and the other held his hard bicep. He unzipped his pants and kicked out of his jeans. My heart tripped in my chest.

What if I wanted him but didn't want to be a demon?

He pulled me to him as he sat down and positioned me on his lap, facing him. I straddled him feeling how hard he was and had to fight the urge to rub against him. Why would he give me the power to get away?

Because you don't want to get away.

He whispered into my mind while alternating between grabbing my ass and running his hands up and down my back, then gripping my hair while kissing my neck. He was right. I didn't want to. "Akira, you have me. Take me." He growled, shoving his fingers inside me before I could think.

I gasped and arched my back, falling into his trap. He laid me down and climbed on top of me before tearing off, and I mean *literally* tearing off my underwear. "You're ready Kira." He pulled down his boxer briefs, and my breath stalled. I wanted him so bad. I needed him in me.

Okay. It was all I could think when he continued to touch and tease me with unfulfilled desire. I was entirely under his spell. Not a bit scared about the idea anymore, I was ready, and God did I want it.

Cander brought himself level with me, slowly running his hand down my face, and I knew what was going to happen next as his lower half came towards me. Just as his tip entered between my folds, all thoughts burst from my head, as a voice whispered into my mind.

You truly are a daughter of Satan if you can kill the love of your life and fuck a man immediately after.

All emotions shut off.

Cander stopped kissing me and shifted back, looking in my eyes as the glow in his shut off completely. If I was wet before, I was completely dry now. I felt sick to my stomach, not turned on. I felt ashamed and weak. I sat up and away from Cander, hugging my knees to my chest. Since that stupid thought, the only thing I could do now was think of Ian.

Cander sat back and looked confused as he stood up, grabbing his clothes, and taking a step back from me. "Congrats Kir, you can officially say you beat the lust of an Incubus." His voice was thick and out of breath. He turned around and in an instant was gone. My heart pounded painfully fast. I wasn't sure why that happened or where that voice came from, but craziness didn't even sum up what just happened.

The bathroom was so hot and thick with steam that I had to shut off the shower and step out into the bedroom in order to breathe.

How in the hell did I get in this situation? Why was I a Siren? If I was one, did that mean my mother had been one? *No, because dad would be dead.* Did I want Cander just because I was turning into a Siren? Is that the only reason he wanted to have sex with me, or did he want to have sex with me because he liked me?

"UUGGGHHH!" I screamed, throwing the glass vase off the table beside me. It shattered against the wall, and I had no doubt Cander heard. I wasn't sure if he cared though, since he was probably back to being his asshole self.

I needed to get away from him. I needed to get out of this situation. If I could stay away from everyone and hide, maybe I could wait this out and just die. I didn't want to wait to die, but with Cander here, it wasn't much of an option. I needed to sneak out. I rushed back in the bathroom and took a quick shower trying not to think any more about it. I would act like I was sleeping and then sneak out. Couldn't be too hard, right?

"*R*EALLY?" He roared in my face, right after he slammed me against the back of the elevator. It hurt.

I remained silent and kept my gaze down. "You have the mortal world *and* all of Hell looking for you, and you decided to *sneak* out! Stop being so stupid Akira! I knew this was going to be a challenge given your age, but this immature bullshit is becoming too much!"

Okay here's the thing, I'd done a lot of thinking in my twenty minutes of free-thinking space away from Cander. It was time to ask him the questions I'd come up with. "Okay, why don't you just force me to have sex with you? Better yet, why do you even want to have sex with me when you're helping me run from what I'm supposed to be turning into?"

The elevator dinged on our floor, and he hauled me out of the elevator by the back of my neck like some delinquent. He ignored me, so I moved on to some more. "Who's Ariel?" No answer, but a growl. He flung me down on the couch in the living room, pacing angrily in front of me.

He remained silent, so I continued. "What if I want to complete the change, but I don't want to have sex with you?"

He paused. I almost thought he was going to continue pacing when he turned to me, and I immediately regretted my taunting. His eyes were bright red, and his blond hair was crazy and hanging in his eyes. He looked scary beyond reason as he marched towards me. I stifled a cry.

I leaned as far back into the couch as I could. He slammed his hands on the back of the sofa on either side of my head and roared in my face. It was one of pain and frustration. For the first time since I'd met him, I was scared to death of him, and he finally looked like what he'd been saying he was. A demon.

He stood up, his eyes going back to gold, his breathing shallow and hard. "Akira. I will give you two choices right now. I'll agree to stay out of your head while you make this decision. So choose wisely. You can either get into bed and have sex with me or leave and never look back. But. Just know that you are wanted everywhere you go. You don't have money. You don't have a phone. And walking around the way you look, your chances of getting raped is very high, and then you'd still become what you're trying so hard not to be. Have sex with me, and this can be all over. You can take your oath back in the realm, and you'll never have to see me again."

Cander turned and walked out of the room after that. Leaving me to the most difficult decision of my life. Have sex with a demon and become a Siren who will kill people. Or take my chances on the streets without resources, everyone knew my face, and those who don't, want to rape me. Isn't that what I wanted? To take my chances out on the streets and escape from everyone and everything? How bad could it really be? But then how bad could being a Siren really be? I had to have gotten the demon gene from someone in my family, and they made it work without sucking the life out of people. Or maybe they just picked random people to become demons, like in some mega demon lotto picks? Wait, none of that mattered.

"I'm giving you five more minutes before I make a choice for you!" Cander yelled from his bedroom. His choice would be sex; I had no doubt. Would I have sex with him if it wasn't these circumstances on the line? What if it was just sex? Would I do it then? Okay, that doesn't even matter right now.

What do I want? What do I want? I had no idea. Ten minutes ago, during my futile escape, I wanted to leave. Now, after Cander pointed out the obvious, did I want to go? I'd been sheltered, rich and spoiled all my life. Could I really make it out on the streets with nothing? I guess it wouldn't really matter anyway since I would be leaving only to crawl in a hole and die.

"Time!" Cander yelled as he entered the room. Had it really been five minutes? Okay, that didn't matter. *Think. Think. Think.* What did I want? Ian. The name came automatically, and I didn't understand why. Why one minute was I so eaten up over a boyfriend I'd been so unsure of, and the next wanting him and crying like he was the love of my life. It wasn't helping, a whole new crop of emotions rushed to the surface of my brain, and I couldn't stop seeing his face.

Cander now stood in front of me. His eyes were wild with emotion, but at least they weren't red anymore. His jaw clenched, and his nostrils flared. He hadn't calmed down. "I can see what decision you're going to make before you even make it." He shook his head, his eyes flashing back to red.

"How am I a demon?" I wasn't sure if he knew, but I had to know.

He ignored my question and sat down facing me on the table in front of the couch. "Leave."

"You want me to leave?"

He stood and motioned for me to move toward the door. "I do. Now leave. I'm done." Was I in shock, or was the pain in my chest more than feeling hurt? But did I really expect him to beg me to stay?

"Fine!" That was easy, he made the decision for me. I didn't want to stay anyways!

I stopped my march to the door, turning to see he was following me out. "No. Answer my question first. I need to know how I became like this. Was it my mom?"

I could have sworn I saw a flash of sorrow, but I couldn't be sure. "Another one."

"What does that mean?"

He ran a frustrated hand through his hair to keep the stubborn hair out of his eyes. It just fell right back down. I moved before I even knew what I was doing and pushed the stubborn pieces out of his eyes. Almost like he had been shocked, he shied away from my touch.

I was more offended than hurt. What the hell could cause him to react like that to me when I was only trying to be nice? It was a gesture out of habit, and he acted like I had the plague.

"Fine!" I roared as I watched him scowl at me. It was clear now what he really thought of me.

I walked to the door and opened it. I turned back, asking the one thing that I knew I would always wonder as long as his name or face came up. "Who's Ariel?" I guess I was wondering if I really ever stood a chance. Did I want to have sex with him, well duh? But did I also feel like my "like" for him could be more like a relationship? Well, I kind of hoped it could. So I needed to know. I hated the jealous feeling I got when he said someone else's name.

He didn't give anything away in his stance or eyes. "She was my wife." He spit out the words with as much venom as a snake. His glare icy cold, he didn't need the red in them for me to feel like a victim in a dark alley.

There was one more thing I wanted to know before I left his care. "How did she die?" Yeah, I know I was being a bitch, and pushing for his personal information, but just like how I didn't feel remorse for Ian after I killed him. I didn't feel it now.

He looked pained, and the torment I could tell he held finally broke through. His eyes swam with unshed tears. "I killed her."

That was all I needed to know. I turned around and true to our deal, didn't look back as I shut the door and headed for the elevator. So it was true. I wouldn't be able to have a normal life. That also answered the question of my heritage. No one in my family was a Siren. Just me.

Like usual, I was alone again.

6

A LIGHT IN THE DARK

*O*kay. After the anger died, I realized walking around the packed sidewalks of Vegas was only making me tired. I didn't know where I was going. I didn't know what I was going to do. I only had a couple of days to live, if what Cander was spouting was the truth. What have I always wanted to do? Find the love of my life, see the world, become the next big screenwriter, maybe produce movies? I wasn't sure. I had found the love of my life, or I thought I had, but clearly that didn't pan out.

Why wouldn't Cander tell me if my mom was a Siren? I shook my head in frustration. His face and our conversations kept replaying in my head.

I stopped walking and thinking long enough to realize I had no idea where I was. How did I get so lost? I could still see the glow of the strip, bright lights over the now rundown up buildings I was standing amongst, but it was clear I had gotten away from the usual traveled areas. A low whistle had me looking left, down the street to where a guy stood and leaned against what I assumed to be a bar.

"Hey baby, you lost?" He called, swirling his beer bottle around.

I looked around, even though I knew he was talking to me. This part of Vegas was obviously not well known.

"I won't bite. In fact." He paused, flicking away his cigarette before pushing off the wall and heading for me. "I'll buy you a drink."

His tone, which at first sounded taunting, turned considerate. I should be scared. Instead, I was intrigued. I turned his way. Black shoulder-length hair shadowed his rough-looking face. His green eyes were piercing and sexy. I took in his profile some more as he got closer and I headed his way. Yeah, he looked dangerous, but it was a turn on. Was that the demon in me?

A couple of feet away, the guy paused, glancing over my shoulder before backtracking, completely turning around, and running back to the bar. *What the hell?*

"Are you trying to get yourself killed?" A low, dangerous voice said from behind me.

I turned around to see Cander standing a couple of feet away, red eyes shining with anger. I wasn't sure what to say. Part of me wanted to accuse him of being a stalker and tell him to leave me to die, but the other part was flooded with relief at a familiar face. My feet hurt from walking, and I had nowhere to go.

Cander's eyes died down to his familiar soft gold. He opened his mouth to speak and then shut it. It was clear that he was still mad, but he didn't know what to say, or maybe he did know what to say, just not how to say it.

"Cander, why are you following me? You told me to leave, so I did."

He stood there, an internal debate still clearly going on inside him. "Come on. Let's go back to the hotel."

Really? "No."

I knew what I wanted to do. Find a phone, call Alex or Kaydence and tell them everything and ask for help. They had always been there for me and would come to spend my last days with me. It was something I had planned on doing but got too lost in thought to act on.

Cander walked over, grabbing my arm. I sighed with annoyance and rolled my eyes as he dragged me along. "Holy shit! Really? You kick me out, and now you're back to wanting a prisoner. What was the point in all of this? Why did you let me go in the first place?"

A hint of a smile played at his lips. "I guess to see how far you'd get."

"Wait!" I practically shouted. Cander paused, narrowing his eyes before leaning towards me as if he was getting ready to get a speck of dirt out of my eye.

"I need to go to the bathroom," I mumbled innocently, putting on my best pleading face.

"UGH! Damn it woman! I'm just trying to help you, why do you have to play games?" He yelled, letting go of my arm.

I glanced down at my arm and then back to him in confusion. "Sorry, I have to go to the bathroom!" It was a lie; I didn't have to go. I just wanted to find someone that would lend me their phone in a last attempt to call for help. I could have sworn I'd kept my mind clear of that plan, especially since it came to me last minute.

"No, Akira, you don't! Why couldn't you just be an easy assignment and crawl into bed with me?" He took a step forward with determination in his eyes. "Am I that ugly? Is there something wrong with my chiseled body? Is a hair out of place?" He said, getting in my personal space. Not that I minded, my body flushed from his nearness.

I swallowed, taking a step back. "If this was just another job to you, why didn't you just make me have sex with you, or better yet just leave and go on to the next girl? I guess I just don't get it, Cander!" In the little time I had known him, I knew better than to taunt him. But *I just couldn't help myself.* "Why am I so special? Wasn't killing your wife enough for you? Why do you want the same fate for me, and if you don't and you are on the run with me, then why are you running at all? Why have anything to do with me?" I yelled while holding my ground.

His eyes weren't red, but they had started to glow sometime during my rant. I didn't know everything yet but knew enough to know that he was turned on when that happened. How did anything I say turn him on?

Cander walked up to me and lightly trailed his hand down my cheek. I hated that it made me shiver. "I'm a demon, Akira. I'm a demon of lust, pleasure, and raw, passionate...sex." I gulped as his hand trailed my collar bone. "I do bad things. I'm bad. I'm always going to want to fuck you before I miss a deadline, even with that aside, I made someone a promise. I promised I would make sure you made it through the transformation."

"But I thought-"

He put a finger to my lips to stop me before I could finish. "I've been summoned. Meaning you have to make your decision for good. Akira, being a Siren is who you are. You can't run from it any more than you can tear out your DNA."

He was still tracing his finger lightly over any exposed skin he could find. I'll have to admit, it was calming me down, along with his calming voice. "So it was passed down to me from someone in my family. Can you tell me who?"

He shook his head, a distant look crossed in his eyes before he dropped his hand and abruptly looked across the street. I followed his gaze but saw nothing but a brick building. "Cander?" I asked, feeling the hairs on my arms rise. It had grown too quiet, and the air felt...too cold.

Cander ignored me and slowly turned in a full circle until he was back to looking across the street at the empty sidewalk and building.

"They won't touch you but take this just in case." I looked down to see Cander holding out a knife and underneath it was his black wallet. "Run to the hotel, don't stop until you're back in the penthouse. There's money." He paused, glancing around us again. His voice picking up pace. "Directions on what to do next. Take this too." He shoved the knife and wallet at me and went back into his pocket, retrieving his phone.

I still didn't see anyone or anything around us. What was he freaking out about? "Cander, what's going on?"

"I already told you." A wicked grin spread across his face. "I've been summoned." Then he leaned forward as if to kiss my cheek, paused, and then turned around and disappeared into thin air.

Holy hell. Holy hell. Did he really just leave me on my own? I fumbled with the long red-handled knife for a little while trying to figure out what to do with it while at the same time glancing around to make sure people didn't see me holding such a weapon. I decided to put it in my boot, after all, that's what people did in the movies, right? After three failed attempts to make it fit comfortably so I could walk at the same time, I said screw it and decided to hold it in my jacket. Hopefully, no one would scare the shit out of me and make me end up using the damn thing on myself.

After figuring I'd just hold the knife, I stuffed the phone in my pocket after wrestling with the idea of calling my friends. But really, when I got to thinking about it, would that really go over so well?

"Hi Alex, hi Kaydence. I killed my boyfriend by sucking the life out of him, and now I'm turning into a Siren...No, no Alex, they aren't like the little mermaid, although we can look like that sometimes. We're mean mermaids, not nice.... Ha, ha, that's funny, Kaydence I was just thinking of how funny it was that I was going to die a virgin."

I flipped open the wallet, and a piece of paper fluttered to the ground.

"Directions"... It read on the outside, I picked it up after tucking the knife down the front of my pants. The cold blade pressed against my thigh. When I unfolded the note, I just about screamed, I didn't see anything. Upon looking closer and moving under a streetlight, I saw what Cander had written towards the bottom. *Keep walking Kira, another note awaits at our place. Incubus Love —C*

I blushed when I read *our place* and I quickly corrected it. As I walked on, I folded the note back up and shoved it into my back pocket. I had no idea where I was or how to get back to the hotel, but that could be fixed. I pulled out Cander's phone, which is the biggest smartphone known to man, and went to work on the GPS. Walking distance to the MGM was thirty minutes! I sighed.

I walked. And walked. The closer to the strip I got, the more I saw people and the crazy nightlife of the place around me. For some reason I felt at home in the city of sin, maybe that was a good thing considering I'll probably die here. After a very exhausting walk in the boots I was given to wear, I was finally able to tug them off when I got to "our place."

I went to the kitchen to grab some water, I'd been dying of thirst. I figured the thirst was due to the killer headaches I'd been having. Even though they were really my pent-up energy from not having sex. Wow. The die-hard expression of, *I need to get laid*, took on a whole new meaning to me now.

After drinking five tall glasses of water, I almost felt better, until the tingling started. I carefully set down the empty glass, reluctantly looking down to my chest, which was tingling. No magical glow. Nothing that looked unusual. I shrugged off my jacket and pulled down the front of my shirt and gasped. What the hell? My tattoo was growing. Twirling and moving over my skin, down my neck, over my collar bones to my breasts. The tingling sensation grew as the intricate lines and twirls continued to move between my breasts. They slowly wrapped underneath them, splitting off in separate directions before sliding down my ribs on both sides. I tore my shirt over the top of my head and rushed to the bathroom. Was I just seeing things?

Nothing could prepare me for what I saw in the full-length mirror on the back of the bathroom door. My tattoo expanded from the back of my neck, down my body to my hips, the natural makeup was enhanced and my face had gotten prettier as well. If that was possible. My hair had also once again changed color. Raven black, but with an almost indigo shine and thick loose curls. I wasn't sure what I expected out of this whole process, but this was not it.

More numb than possible, I walked shirtless into the living room, listening to the city sounds below me. The lights from all around were shining brightly into the quiet penthouse, and I'd never felt more alone in my whole life. Sitting on the glass table in front of the couch was a piece of paper folded in half. Like one of those ones that hotels use to leave little notes on your pillow. It read,

Look back at your directions. —C

Ookay? I pulled out the knife, phone, and directions, setting them down and looking at the "directions".

My dearest Siren to be,

I'm so glad you've decided to come back to the hotel. Now, since I will no longer be with you to complete your transition. Or what I like to consider, sex with Akira. You will have to find another Incubus. Don't worry. I covered that part. Find Jax listed under my contacts. Text him the date, time, and your name. He will find you. Stay at the hotel. Oh...and before I forget. Just in case you're sitting there thinking, but I don't want to be a Siren, blah, blah, blah. You really have no choice now.

I'm depending on you to save me. Yes, Kira. The egotistical asshole needs your help. Good luck, from your Incubus love. —C

Okay, let's just put aside for a second that none of this was written on the "directions" when I first read them. Oh, and the fact that unlike Cander in real life, the letter-writing Cander was pleasant. Now concentrate on the last part of the letter. Cander needed me...to save him?

...What????

BOOM! That would be the explosion in my head right now. Save him from what? He had been summoned. The word summoned formed in my head in a Transylvanian accent that made me think of Dracula. *You have been summoned; I am going to suck your blood.* I stifled a laugh. Okay Kira, enough playing around. Time to put your game face on. He thinks I need to save him, and it's clear he thinks I need to complete the transition to do that. What now?

I'd paced the length of our penthouse at least a hundred times. Sleep wasn't going to happen even in my exhausted state. Okay, would it be worth completing the transformation to save Cander, when it would potentially risk hundreds of other lives? Eventually, I conceded to the "directions" and texted Jax. I wasn't sure whether to laugh or cuss when I saw that Cander listed him as YOURNEWLOVER. Smart-ass. Seriously, how long was it going to take this guy? Did the "directions" work both ways?

I sat down with a pen and the "directions", that was now blank and attempted to write back to him. Would it disappear and work like some *Harry Potter* paper and pen? Here's to hoping.

Okay Cander,
I'm not sure how this stupid magic paper works, but there's a lot of

variables that need to be factored in before I give in to your demands and I want answers.

I'm not sure if you'll get this or how you're writing back to me.

What do you need saving from? Or who? Where are you? Who summoned you?

Answer my question about my mom.

I don't want to be a demon. I'd like to think I'm a good person Cander...

You're not. -C

Shut up!!! And answer my questions!

You're running out of paper. —C

Fine. I'm not going to save you. I'm not going to be a demon Siren who sucks the life out of innocent people just so that I can live!

You're sexy when you're mad. Much love —C

That was the end of the paper. "AAAAGGGGHHHHH!" And my temper. I stood up, chucking the stupid hotel pen at the window, crumpling up the "directions", and holding the stupid ball of paper in my fist as I paced the carpet. "UGH! I HATE HIM!" The urge to rip up the stupid ball of "directions" was extreme. The heat in my face and the shaking was just a portion of the anger I felt. How the hell was I supposed to cope when my appearance was changing every five seconds and I only had a couple days to live? No answers. No friends. No boyfriend. No help. Nothing. Stupid, all this was stupid.

I un-crumpled the paper as I stomped toward the pen, I needed to try again. The paper sat just like it had when I'd crumpled it up. Our conversation still in the same place. Jeez. I blew out a frustrated sigh as I brought it to the coffee table and tried to flatten out the wrinkles. I felt parched, my mouth was dry, and my headache was going strong. No. No way was I drinking any more water, the tattoo would just grow more along with my hair again. I turned on the T.V. as I plopped down on the couch, ready for a distraction. The magical box, what my dad referred to it as, didn't end up helping.

Candles, memorials, and shrines popped up, followed by cries of grieving people in front of a blown-up picture of me wrapped in Ian's arms. Both of us were smiling. Both of us in love. Both of us alive. I stood, walking to the T.V. in a daze as the reporter's words broke through my stunned hearing.

"...Akira Black is still missing. Although cops have removed her from the list of suspects, the question still remains. Is she dead, or could she be on the run for killing her lover? Back to you..."

I shut off the T.V. and dropped to the floor along with the remote. The reporter's words circling my mind as the picture of us flashed in my head. Alex had taken that picture with his phone not long after we first started dating. The day I had to admit to myself that I really liked Ian. The same day I also started to push myself away so I wouldn't get hurt. Guess it should have been the other way around.

I felt a bubble of emotions rising up in me as my eyes burned from the tears. The room felt too small and everything swayed even though I was kneeling down on the floor. How could everything get so messed up so fast? I eventually shut my eyes to ward off the dizziness and laid on the floor, letting my raging emotions take over. I curled into a ball on the floor and cried my eyes out, snot and everything.

"Crying never got anyone anywhere." I shot up from the floor and turned towards the amused voice, stifling my next sob.

The guy that stood beside the arm of the chair was a demon. The eyes gave him away. They shined bright gold, along with their unnatural brightness, the shape of his pupils was another indication of his status. They were vertical, like a cat.

"I'm Jax." He shrugged as if that's all he could tell me. He was Asian. Along with his beautifully colored skin, he had sharp features. I continued to take in his unnatural hotness as I got to my feet, wiping the tears from my face. Even without him saying a word, I knew he was everything Cander wasn't. If Cander was the bad boy type, Jax was the hot best friend that you eventually fell in love with. Boy next door type, maybe?

"What now?" It was the only thing I could come up with, although as soon as that question broke through, I realized there were more important questions I could have asked. Like...how did you get in here? How do I know you're really Jax? How did you know where I was? Those just to start with, of course.

Jax stepped forward, thrusting a light blue envelope at my stomach, breaking my reel of internal question. "Read this, and then we'll get to work." He stepped back, flipping his head in an overly confident yet sexy attempt to get his jet-black hair from his eyes.

I fumbled with the letter with shaky hands for a little too long before processing what I had. "How did you get my mom's letter?" Connections were lining up, and I wasn't sure if I was ready for the possibility. If Jax had this letter from my mother, it must have been her that passed on the demon gene, or whatever it was that made me a Siren. My mother was a Siren.

I stumbled to the couch, ripping at the envelope as I went. The paper was thick and coarse, odd, not standard stationary but something else entirely. I saw the words written out for me to read, but I shut my eyes, mentally preparing myself for something I was sure was going to be hard to take in.

"I came all this way to help you, and it wasn't just to watch you sleep in front of a letter instead of reading the letter." Jax said. I'd almost forgotten he was there. His voice was like silk. I could see how he could draw women in. I sighed. Time to face the music.

To my precious daughter,

Happy birthday my beautiful girl. Let me just start by telling you that nothing could prepare me for the day your father and I found out we were expecting you. It was the happiest day of my life, second to this one.

The day you turn eighteen. Yes, my sweet girl, even though I won't be there with you, today is already one of my happiest days.

You have always had me with you through the years growing up, my blood runs through your veins along with your Siren heritage. I always knew I wouldn't be able to be with you after you were born, but that's how the world works with these things. I'm so sorry if you believe me to be selfish. Daughter, trust me when I say my dearest Axel will take care of you and love you no matter what- never forget that.

To be a Siren is something no history book, myth, or even some movie can tell you about. Baby girl, this transitional phase will be the most difficult. I've been told this by someone I hold dear, and I will let you in on it as well. Just because a demon is what you are, it doesn't make it who you are. Understand the real meaning behind it. You can choose to lead a good life and embrace your heritage at the same time. It is scary at first, but it is who you are meant to be.

You were a special case and were only able to be born because of how deeply your father and I loved each other. Sirens are not born everyday, baby girl. Remember this when you make your decision. Find the Ivy Tribe. If you choose not to be a Siren for some reason because you do not wish to kill, seek them. They will help. You will have plenty of questions and not a lot of answers, and for that I'm sorry. I'm sorry I won't be able to help you through this transition.

My last advice to you, my sweet girl, is to make sure you are in the water when your tattoo is complete, this above all else is important. Remember this information. I love you with every ounce of my being, please know that baby girl. I love you always and forever.

Siren Love- Jade.

I hadn't even realized that I was crying until Jax stepped forward with a tissue.

"Directions."

Huh? I blinked away the tears as I folded up mother's letter with carefulness and used the tissue to rid my eyes of the moisture. I handed Jax the letter. "What?"

This time another paper was thrust at me, this one being Canders "directions." I unfolded the wrinkled paper.

Ivy Cove.

2239088 W. 34 Way.

Indian Ocean/Atlantic/Pacific/Oceans Point.

Good luck, little Siren.

Incubus love –C

"Where to Miss. Black?" Jax asked, holding my mother's letter in one hand and a Will in the other. The choice was simple now that I had read my mother's letter. I stood folding the directions and put it inside the pocket of my jacket, before retrieving Cander's knife and phone. I knew what he was asking, life or death. I just hoped I was making the right choice.

7

TO CHOOSE LIFE

"So, you can read minds like Cander then?" I guess I shouldn't be shocked, but the thoughts I'd been having about Jax had been nothing short of pornographic. To say I was embarrassed would be an understatement.

The corners of his mouth twitched up as he shook his head. "If you're as good as your imagination makes you out to be, me and you will have a good time." I just shook my head and laughed. He'd been at me about having sex the whole two hours we'd been in the car. I just couldn't believe I finally decided to have sex.

"So, you have any questions for me?"

I sat up straighter in my seat. "Umm, yeah!" I bit my lip in anticipation. I needed to tread carefully with my questions. If Jax was anything like Cander, he would shut down after one or two questions, before I got any real explanations.

"Well..." He looked away from driving to give me an exasperated look.

"Okay. So, a Siren..." I wanted to go through everything to get my facts straight. He nodded, prodding me along, and I wished he would keep his eyes on the road. He looked forward at my thought, biting his lip as he smiled. "Is a mermaid...*No*...Is a *demon* that can shift into a mermaid and who has sex to survive? Where does the water and the whole mermaid thing play in?"

He chuckled. "Cander really didn't tell you anything, did he?" He sighed before continuing. "Think of a demon, no, scratch that. Think of all the demons and think about it in a way that we are all different kinds of things. Kind of like animals, but there are all different types of animals. Okay. Now think of demons in that way."

I interrupted. "Yeah, I know Cander said there were Incubi, Sirens and other types, but I still don't- "

Jax gripped the steering wheel so tight that I heard a crack. "No! Just listen." I nodded and sat back in my seat, fighting the urge to rush through the explanation and get answers. I took a mental note that Jax did not like to be interrupted, and it was apparent demons had short tempers. Noted. I felt a little more than antsy, but I didn't want to get on his bad side.

"There are a lot more than just two or three types of demons, Akira. There are millions." I gulped when I heard millions. "Hell is separated into realms. There are nine realms in total consisting of seven Queens, one ruling Prince, and one King. They each run a different realm. Each realm contains different demons. Are you following?"

"Yeah..." The thoughts of animals and zoos popped into my head. Maybe he shouldn't have compared them to animals.

"We are in the Second Realm, and Lilith is our Queen. We are the demons that are allowed to cross realms. We are possession and sexual demons. Sirens, Incubi, Succubi, Spirits. We survive off of killing people, wreaking havoc, and bringing power to our Queen, she then powers the realms. The nine realms power the King, or Satan. Each demon has a certain job and the ability to complete that job. An Incubus and Succubus can weaken or kill their prey through the act of sex. We suck out a person's soul. We can also read hormones to gauge our prey. Our beauty plays a part in our ability. Spirits or possession demons can possess a human's body. Through that ability they draw power, or a person's soul, by wreaking havoc with the person they possess and their life. All the while, keeping the fear and evil in the world about the King. They can take the form of a ghost to complete this goal."

We were heading to Florida. He said the Ivy Tribe could only be reached by water and the road sign read, "Florida Two Hundred Miles". "I'm catching on and not to change the subject, but how did we get this close so fast?"

I swore his eyes twinkled, even though their shape made them appear intimidating, somehow it made him more charming. Jax was exactly like I thought he would be. Charming, sweet, playful, talkative, sexy. Not that Cander wasn't sexy, but Jax was the complete opposite, and I loved spending time with him.

"Demon." Was his only answer.

I rolled my eyes, making sure to make a show of it before turning to stare out the window. He continued his lengthy explanation. "Sirens." I turned my full attention to him now. "They also get their power from sexual acts, but it isn't their main way or the *best way* for a Siren it get its power. Drowning is where they get their power."

"What?"

"Yes." He laughed loudly, and I could tell it was taking all his ability to control himself.

"Then why am I so...you know. Why do I want to have sex all the time? And why do I have to have sex for the transition? I'm lost."

"You need to be transitioned by an Incubus to transfer some of our power or sexual charm to you. Drowning for a human, is fear. Sirens get power from fear, but Sirens are the weakest of the demons, so they need to kill their victims without the human killing them first. Have you not heard of a fatal mermaid's kiss or song? Or the old sailor stories where the mermaids are the bad guys? They would lure the sailors or fishermen into the water with their beauty and sexual charm. If the human wasn't in sight of the Siren, the beauty of their voice could trance a human into the water. Then from there, is the drowning part. When the human realized the mermaid's intention, they would try to overpower them. Do you remember how Ian was dying but couldn't think or act because he wanted to kiss you? You have that power, but you need even more to keep the men from overpowering you in the water. We sexual demons have the power of a Siren times one hundred. Akira, you're immune to our sexual charms because of what you are, but not all the way. Cander could have used his powers and made you turn. Anyways we're getting off subject."

At some point, the sun had risen, and I was on to my last twenty-four hours. Jax continued, "Okay, so you can turn into a mermaid to drown people, to survive off their fear. You also have your beauty, voice, sexual charm, and deadly kiss to kill people."

My head had gone from headache to full-blown migraine. I was in so much pain. Would this really be my life? I would have to live in the ocean, or I guess near water and kill innocent people to survive. But in that case, I could pick my victims. I could live with my friends and family.

"So, my mom..." Where did I want to start?

I felt the end of his cold fingers slide along my jawbone. I glanced over as he lowered his hand and took mine in his. The gesture was friendly and straightforward, but it made me ache to be touched more. "Hey, why don't we just take a break from Q and A for a while? Lay back and take a nap, we'll be there in about thirty minutes."

I was tired, and even though I hadn't slept in the past twenty-four hours, I didn't want to sleep my last day away. "I'm okay." I squeezed his hand to reassure him. It was odd. I should feel weird or offended that he would hold my hand so easily and without permission, but the way he held it was friendly. Even though I felt an attraction to him like I did with Cander, Cander was still on my mind most the time. I needed to know what had happened to him.

"Is Cander being held where you were when we went looking for you?" Jax narrowed his eyes. This was news to him.

"When did you go looking for me?" He returned his hand to the steering wheel as the SUV bumped and shifted over the now rough terrain. The road sign had said two hundred miles, but Jax said thirty minutes, and at some point, we had turned off the highway and were on a less traveled road. What was going on?

"He took me to this bar. I don't know. Right after Ian died. He said we needed to find you, and the bartender said you were being summoned or something."

My stomach was way past uneasy, and for some reason, Jax took the bumps and potholes with a hard pedal, almost like someone was chasing us. I wanted to slow down but gripped the oh shit handle instead.

Jax picked up my thoughts at some point. "We are still going to Florida, but we will use a demon portal to get there. It's something we use to get to different realms. Your tattoo is down to your waist, you need to be in the water before it reaches your ankles." Jax explained. How did he know that my tattoo had grown that much?

"Okay? So, where is Cander? He said I needed to save him. Where is he? Oh, and how does this magic paper thing work, I have a few choice words for him."

Jax smiled and shook his head. "I bet you do. It's a charm, from a rogue Magical. A magical must have charmed or put a spell on that paper for it to work like that. Whatever it is, it acts as a beacon spell. It traces your movements or your thoughts and relays them back to the owner of the paper. In doing that, Cander can communicate back to you. You can communicate to him only when he is willing to hear from you. I'm guessing your writing comes in the form of thoughts that he can hear, and he just thinks what he needs to write back to you. I don't know how it works for sure, that's just a guess. As far as where he's at..." Jax paused. He looked conflicted. Almost like he knew where and what Cander had gotten into, he just didn't want to tell me.

Before I could get any information out of him, a black hole ripped open the morning sky, and we were driving the Land Rover through it. I held my breath and closed my eyes, clutching the seat to the point of ripping the leather with my fingernails.

Jax's laughter had me taking in some much-needed air and looking around to see a "Now Entering Miami" road sign. Oh holy hell, I would never get used to that way of travel. "I hate that," I said after catching my breath.

"I can tell. Now, as far as Cander goes. Who did you talk to at the bar? Do you know the bar's name? Anything specific about what was in the bar?" This time he didn't sound like he was messing around. This time, it seemed like he really had no idea where Cander was or what he'd been up to.

I thought back to the bar and the bartender's nasty grease-covered hair and how he hit on me. I thought about how Cander broke my arm, being his normal pain in the ass self. Jax started laughing. "Okay. I'm not all too happy about where you were and that you guys were chased off by Crow's men, but the way you talked to Crow." He paused to sputtered out another laugh. I couldn't help but smile, and I was going to ask how he knew what I said, but I remembered once again about his mind-reading abilities and remembered how I had replayed the scene in my head. No wonder he was laughing, Jax seemed to think that whatever I said to Crow was pretty funny as well.

"What was so funny about what I said?" I asked, feeling lame. All I'd said to the guy was that I wasn't interested in his kind?

Jax started laughing even harder, and I was afraid he would wreck the car. "Akira. Stop. Please." He was wiping tears from his eyes; it was apparently so funny. I was glad he was getting a laugh at my expense, but really? "What?!"

Jax pursed his lips to keep in another round of laughs and took a deep breath before explaining the situation. "Akira, Crow is a Siren."

My mouth formed an "oh" as I sat there feeling like a fool, my cheeks were on fire. Wow, I am such an idiot.

"Hey. No big. A lot of demons, for some reason, don't like to date within their group. It isn't anything uncommon. I just think that Cander - and myself - found it so funny because you had no idea what you were doing or who that guy was at the time. No big. No foul. Just funny. Lighten up chick." Jax teased as he parked the Land Rover.

I swallowed down my fear, trying to put on a brave face. We were parked somewhere along the shoreline, but somewhere obviously not well known. We were the only ones parked on the secluded beach. Jax unbuckled his seatbelt and turned his body to face me.

"So, what now?" I asked, feeling more nervous than ever. I'd been thinking about sex since the moment I'd started this stupid transition, and now that the moment has come, I'm ready to run and hide.

"Akira. You don't have to have sex. At least not right now. Not if you don't want to. I can tell you're scared. Would you rather find the members of the tribe first and get through your change?" He asked, looking genuinely concerned. Not at all what I thought a demon would act like.

I thought over his offer. The whole thing seemed pretty scary. Transition to me seemed like something the little mermaid went through to be a human, but in reverse. Not only that, but with the thought of having sex, only two people came to mind. First, Ian. Then Cander. I was more than attracted to Jax, but we'd only known each other for a day. Jeez, was I putting too much thought into this?

As if reading my mind, my tattoo answered for me. I felt the tingle as it grew, wrapping down and around my legs. I couldn't really see what was going on because of my skintight jeans and the boots I had on over them, but I could tell that it had stopped at my knees. I took in a breath. "Okay, take me to the tribe."

---

he tribe was nothing like I'd imagined. After going through a rock - that happened to be a secret door - and down a flight of stairs, we walked forever under the ocean in a transparent walkway with Ocean life teeming all around us. When it got too dark to see little lights appeared along the walkway. I figured it would be hard to breathe being this far down in the ocean, because of the depth pressure or something, but everything seemed normal with my breathing. When we came across a huge black looking vault with two guards holding spears, I knew we'd arrived. The whole scene was something out of a movie. Obviously, my dreams of creating movies would skyrocket to success if I ever made it out of here.

The two guards worked together to open the door upon seeing us, never asking for identity or questioning the reason for our arrival. The only explanations I could figure was that they were expecting me, or that their security system needed to be updated pretty badly. Once the doors opened I couldn't help but gasp out loud. From the tunnel to the arched doorway, this place turned into a whole other world.

People, which I assumed were Sirens and other demons, went about here and there. Walking around and popping in and out of stores. I would never have known we were underwater at the bottom of the ocean had I not traveled down here myself. Above me was glass, or the same transparent material that made the tunnels, formed in the shape of the town square.

The Sirens, both male and female...were beautiful. They all had a pearl-colored fabric woven around their perfect bodies. No tattoo like mine, but gills covered both sides of their necks. Even though they all had different colored hair, the females wore almost the same style: long, wavy, and hanging down their backs. The males were much different, all the same dark brown color, but very different styles. Some in braids, some long, some short, and some in the middle. Either way, they all had a common feature; they were dead sexy.

I was just thinking about wiping the drool from my chin when Jax broke my attention. "The Bessel. It's the main place for the Ivy to do their shopping or anything else mortal they have to do. We're headed to the Dome; it's where the council for the tribe presides. They will hear your case and decide if they are willing to accept you or not."

I was more than a little taken aback by this, I came all this way, what if they didn't accept me? "So if this wasn't a sure thing, and I have to be in the water...probably within the next thirty minutes, why did we risk it?" Okay, so I didn't want to be a Siren at first, but after reading my mother's letter, it was like my mind had done a three-sixty, and now I wanted to be one. Was this a sick joke? What happens if they say no?

Jax pulled me against his side as we walked, rubbing his thumb against my waist. He lowered his mouth to my ear. "Then I guess we need to find a room." Heat rushed up through me, and my nerves were on edge. That and feeling him against my side, his thumb rubbing circles on my hip...I was totally at a loss for words. I was honestly afraid that if I opened my mouth, it would be to tell him to take me right then and there.

I scoffed at the thought, knowing that Jax was listening. I

had a dead boyfriend who I was still in love with. Cander, who was a huge asshole, but I couldn't get off my mind and now Jax, who was pretty much the perfect man. Take that into consideration, along with the current information that I could choose to be a good Siren and not have sex or be a bad Siren and have sex. When all the while, I didn't want to kill, but I did want to have sex. What the hell had I gotten myself into?

8

THE TRANSITION

$\mathcal{T}$he Dome, or what I thought of in my mind as the throne room, was decorated like an underwater fantasy. It was the size of a stadium, designed with blue and silver colors with crystals that adorned the glass thrones where the council sat. Basically, on everything the decorator could put them on. The Dome wasn't made of the usual transparent walls like the rest of the Ivy but instead decorated in a dull silver stamped tile, same as the walls, ceilings and floors. Everything was beyond sparkly, making the room emanate a soft blue glow. Maybe that's what they're going for?

The council was composed of one female Siren, who sat on the middle glass throne upon the highest perch. On either side of her were two smaller glass thrones which two male Sirens occupied. These males looked just as young as me but even more terrifying. Not the kind, loving, hippy type mermaids I had envisioned. They also looked like siblings. The males were identical, and the female had all the same features other than the obvious male and female differences. She had golden eyes, flaming red hair, and sharp, perfect features.

The council was located on the opposite side of where we

walked in, and my side already hurt just from looking at how far we had to walk along the light blue carpet. Jax, either reading my mind or seeing my discomfort, took my hand. "Don't speak unless spoken to." I would have normally rolled my eyes. It was like I was stuck in a bad movie, you know, the ones with the predictable lines and characters.

I looked over to Jax to indulge my screaming sarcasm. "And don't go past the red line, and always answer with Your Excellency or My Queen." Smart-ass 101, Cander would be proud. Unfortunately, Jax didn't find it as funny.

After a mile-long walk, we stopped by a pool that I hadn't noticed before in front of the council's thrones.

"How interesting." The female council purred. Her voice was young, but the way she spoke, even those two little words, she spoke with wisdom and age.

The two males looked to her as she continued to look me over with a raised chin. Jax stepped away from me, I guess, to give her more looking room. Upon looking closer, her eyes were not only gold, but they were in the shape of a star. It was trippy. "I'd always wondered when they would make another Siren." She said, rising from her chair. The males on either side of her raised as well.

My whole body itched to step closer to Jax. I felt vulnerable, threatened, and small under her stance. She started to make her way down the blue colored glass stairs towards me. Her long pearl-colored dress trailed behind her. The other council members each took one of her arms as they made their way. Their faces were expressionless, I couldn't tell if that was a good thing or a bad thing. I looked to Jax, and he jerked his head for me to look forward before lowering his gaze to the floor. So much for any sort of comforting words.

"Do you think you're an exception to the rules, young Black?"

Umm, what rules? Shit, there were rules?! And shit, she

knows who I am? "Umm..." My tongue froze after I realized it was a rhetorical question by the look of her raised eyebrows.

"How far is your transformation?"

"To- "

She cut me off with an outstretched hand. The council members were now a couple of feet away from me. "Show me!" She yelled impatiently.

I jumped as her loud voice echoed across the space, but then immediately went to work unzipping my boots and tugging up my jeans. It was a good thing the tattoo was already at my knees, or I would've had to take off my - entirely too tight - jeans altogether.

"Hmm." She shrugged off the men's arms and walked closer before circling me, stopping in front of me so she could raise my chin. I gulped at her hard stare.

"Normally, I would ask the Siren in favor a series of questions. Why? How. When...but I already know those. I hadn't expected to see you here. Yet here you are. Why would I go against your ancestors?" She dropped my chin and stepped back, waiting for an answer. It was hard to stare at her eyes for too long, uncomfortable barely summed up the fear I felt when I saw them. I concentrated on her bright red hair instead.

Jax, who until that moment acted no more than a regular coat rack, stepped forward. Why he chose now, I don't know, but it was about damn time. "There is a lot of her mother's influence and knowledge in the information she has," He paused, bowing his head to give the appropriate respect. "That brought Akira to know the ways of the Ivy."

Other than looking at him like he was a bug on the bottom of her shoe, his explanation seemed to appease her. "Okay."

The two male council members flanking each side of her shrugged and nodded in agreement. "Seems harmless to let her try." And the other followed with, "Yeah, try." he scoffed. As they walked to the female member, they each took one of her arms before making their way back to their thrones.

Jax stepped back to my side, breaking my concentration on the trio. "Okay. Now's the hard part. Get naked and jump in the pool. If you can last through the test of the Ivy, you're in."

I scoffed but started to feel the unwanted tingle over the skin at my knees. The tattoo was spreading, and I didn't have time to find out what this test entailed. I shrugged off my jacket and tugged off my boots as I hobbled over to the pool. Did I have to be naked?

Yes. Jax answered into my mind. I glanced back to see a satisfied smile on his lips that I rolled my eyes at.

My heart was pounding, and I felt the eyes of the council and Jax staring at me. My tattoo was almost to my ankles. I threw off my shirt and bra in one swift movement, feeling the rush of cold air hit my chest, making goosebumps cover my skin. I tugged off my jeans and underwear and let my toes curl around the edge of the pool as I watched my body start to glow. Did I really want to do this? Would it hurt to die? At the thought my body acted on survival and screamed for me to jump.

I covered my breasts with my arms and took in a deep breath of air as I bent my knees. Well, here goes nothing. For a second I could feel my hair lift off my shoulders, and right before I closed my eyes and tucked my knees up, I saw all three council members smile a knowing smile. Before I could worry about what the smile meant, the tingle of my tattoo hit my ankles right when I landed cannonball style in the water. The rush of water and bubbles took over my hearing. I let myself sink further down as I continued to hold my breath, and I straightened my legs to see my ankles.

Nothing but tan feet, with red nail polish and tattooed ankles, were in front of me. I looked around the pool as my dark red hair floated at the sides of my vision, other than that nothing or no one was in the pool with me. Great. This was a joke. The whole damn thing. I must be crazy, probably in some mental institution trying to drown myself right now. I let the thought go as I made my way to the surface. I had somehow sunk towards the bottom of the pool. Which, now at a better look, was still further down, or the pool was bottomless. The thought brought unease swirling through me. I need to get out of here.

There was the wavy outline of four figures the closer I got to the surface. It felt like I'd only been down there mere seconds, but the burn in my lungs told me it must have been longer or being a mermaid didn't mean what I thought it did. Panic was setting in. Why was it taking so long to break the surface? I lunged up and kicked as hard as I could. I was moving, but not as fast as I wanted to. If I didn't get to the surface, would I drown? Was that the test? This had to be the test. My lungs felt like they were caving in, and I didn't know what to do. Cander said I couldn't drown, but now that seemed like a very real possibility. Jax could read my thoughts; why wasn't he helping.

Jax, help me! Jax!

Silence. I pulled harder at the silk-like feeling of the water around me, but it felt like the closer I got to the top, the slower I was going. My heart was slowing down. Was that a good thing or a bad thing? It wasn't a good time to be an idiot about this type of thing, but I was grasping at straws. If I just passed out and never sucked any water up, would I just float to the top and they would fish me out? What do I do? I stilled as my skin started to tingle. The tingling made my body feel numb, was this what it felt like to drown? I needed to do something!

I let out what little breath of air I had, to try to relieve my pain. Big. Mistake. When you're panicking, and void of breath, rational thinking apparently stops working because even I couldn't stop what my body did next.

I took the biggest breath of water imaginable through my mouth and nose.

The water burned as it filled my nasal cavity and sucked down my throat. I tried to cough it up at the same time I strived to hold the non-existent breath. Pain, like never before filled my body. I knew I had failed. My body was filled with water and I started to convulse. I couldn't feel anything. Just as my eyes began to roll to the back of my head my throat was sliced open. Literally.

My eyes ripped open at the feeling and my body stopped convulsing as it tried to expel the water. My legs pulled together as a black glow surrounded them. I breathed in another attempt for air, and to calm my reaction. Heat, so hot it felt almost cold, filled my legs, and I watched as my skin melted off them.

"HELP!" I screamed for Jax. This wasn't the pretty version of getting a tail I'd imagined. It was blood, boiling skin, and pain.

I reached up to feel where my throat had been sliced, both sides had been ripped into three lines... Gills? I didn't have time to think because the glow disappeared. I realized not only did I have a black scaled mermaid tail in place of my legs, but I also no longer had trouble breathing.

In my stunned realization of what was happening, I stopped panicking and started observing my transformation. The tattoo on my neck, chest, and stomach started to crawl over my skin as it shined white and started to rise. It was freaky. What began as a moving tattoo, finished with white scales moving over the surface of my skin and formed what looked like an ivy colored bra over my breasts. I reached out and touched my new tattooed bra as the bright light died down.

I almost didn't notice my hair floating around me which had turned back to its original blonde color.

You can come up now, little Siren.

My head shot up when Jax's voice broke through my thoughts. Up. Holy crap, how long had I been underwater?

I flipped my tail and was surprised when I shot up towards the surface. I had never had a tail or fin, or whatever this thing was called, obviously, but for some reason knew precisely how to work it.

I broke the surface, with not only the council and Jax's faces, but with the room surrounding the pool full of new faces. Some were happy, some surprised, but none of them matched the anger on the councils' faces. Or the desire on Jax's.

I wasn't sure what to do, so instead, I just waded in the water with my tail.

The place remained quiet as the observers looked at the council and me. I knew what Jax had said, but the silence was killing me.

"Can I get out now?"

I should've kept my mouth shut. Not only did my question fill the Dome with a roar of laughter from the onlookers, who I assumed were part of the tribe, but the council looked even angrier - if that was possible. Jax laughed along with the crowd. I couldn't do anything but let my face turn red and look towards the council.

It was one of the males who spoke first as he lowered his face to his hands. Apparently, my question had given him a headache because he rubbed his temples before moving to rub between his eyes. "You could try, but you won't be able to walk on a tail, and you can only transform back in the water."

I let out a small, "Oh," More to myself than anything. This made Jax laugh harder. Traitor.

"Do you know why this is called the Tribe of the Ivy?" The female finally spoke; she answered herself before I could. I'm guessing she did that a lot. "Because of the red gills, ivy colored bra, and tail of its members. Others possess black colorings and blue gills. Unfortunately, you possess both."

The laughter had long died, and now the place was bone-chillingly quiet. I was guessing the coloring of the black tail and ivy bra was a bad thing. Try as I might, I couldn't see what color my gills had ended up as.

"You will change and stay in our care until we come to a conclusion." At that, the guests turned and started to leave, and Jax knelt to my level at the edge of the pool.

"Looking good little Siren." I scoffed, as he grinned. "Are you going to stay in there all night?"

The question was a good one because I was probably going to have to if someone didn't tell me how to change back. I looked down at my lazy swinging tail, keeping me afloat. Was there a magic button?

The female council member's demand broke my attention from my tail. "Oh and will someone please feed her!" I watched her stomp up the stairs to her throne. She was clearly annoyed with me.

"Why is she such a bitch?" I managed a whisper, but Jax acted like I was going to explode for even thinking such a thing.

"Pearl can be a bitch, just ignore her."

I couldn't keep in my laugh. "Pearl? That's really her name?" I laughed some more before Jax silenced me by bringing his finger to my lips. His eyes still held the same smoldering look as earlier, and the feel of his skin against my lips, even a small gesture, flamed my hormones. I moved my head away from him, and he dropped his hand.

"Don't do that," I warned. I didn't know how this whole Ivy, or non-Ivy thing worked, but I assume that if I were to turn my virgin ways now, I'd end up in Hell for sure.

Jax's face was a mixture of amusement and confusion. "Then don't laugh like an angel."

We had somehow gotten closer, either he was leaning towards me, or I was to him. Either way, we were too close. "I thought I was a demon." *Did I want to kiss him?* I couldn't break my stare from his lips. They were a darker shade of pink. I could feel the heat from his body, I needed to back away, but it was comforting.

"Akira, you're playing with fire." *Was I?* I could tell he wanted to kiss me too. I wasn't sure what brought this on, but the clearing of a throat brought me back to reality and had both of us rushing back like a repellent.

"You know a Siren and an Incubus is a dangerous mix Prince Jax."

Jax looked as though he'd been slapped. "You know that is not my title!" He yelled as he stood up. A rush of about ten guards entered from the sides of the Dome at his raised voice. I'd never seen Jax mad, but there was a first for everything. His gold eyes were red like Cander's got when he was mad.

Pearl looked unaffected. "Ah, that's right. You traded your title from Prince to gatekeeper."

Jax ignored the guards that were slowly walking with what looked like harpoons around the pool. "And you traded the title of your fellow brothers and council members to incest man servants!"

The guards stopped their approach with stunned looks on their faces and glanced back at Pearl, who looked madder than Hell itself. "How dare you insult me!" Red flags were blaring in my mind, and my heart rate had picked up. I needed to be by Jax's side! I needed my legs!

The guards snapped out of their stupor and charged forward at the insult of the head council member, who acted more like a Queen than a council member. The water around me started to bubble, and a tingle flitted from within my tail. Jax stood at a stance ready for the attack as my legs formed, and I was once again no more than a naked girl decorated head to toe with a tattoo. I hoisted myself out of the water on shaky arms and pushed back the pain in my bright red legs as I stepped up beside Jax, ready to help. I was sure I would be no match against ten guards with harpoons, but I had to try.

"ENOUGH!" The guards stopped at the joined voices of the council males.

Jax was breathing like an enraged bull. He only gave me a wavering glance before pulling me behind his back while keeping one hand protectively over my right side. "We will stay in my realm until you come to a decision."

He didn't leave them much of a choice because a second later, within a bright white light, we were standing in a black and silver decorated bedroom the size of four of my bedrooms combined. I was fully clothed.

"How did you do that?"

Jax was no more than a step in front of me when we appeared, he closed the gap pretty quickly at my question and circled his arms around me. "Job perk." I wanted to ask if it was a perk of a Prince or gatekeeper but kept my mouth shut.

His thought must have been way different than mine because his lips landed on mine before I could stop him. I pulled back despite my raging hormones, and he looked more than hurt at my reaction. "Jax." We needed to talk about everything that just happened. We needed to save Cander. We needed to do a lot of things.

"This is something we need to do. You need to feed." I stepped out of his arms as if I'd been shot. I couldn't kill him.

"No!" I shook my head to reiterate my seriousness, but he ignored me and stepped forward.

"Akira," He paused to let out a small chuckle. "You need to feed off of someone immortal. The Ivy feeds enough to energize them, but not enough to kill humans. You will kill your first time. You need to feed off an immortal. You need to feed off an Incubus. If this gets out of hand, it won't be the end of the world to lose your virginity, and you will gain power from me. The power that you need."

His reasoning made sense, but at the thought of sex, Cander popped into my mind, not the once love of my life Ian, but the arrogant, angry demon who left me to die. I let out a frustrated sigh. Jax was right. I was exhausted and felt drained of life. I needed to feed, especially after transforming.

Jax stepped back into his position and kissed me before I could protest again, but it didn't matter, I could no longer think when he was kissing me like he was. It was breathtaking. I tried to keep Cander out of my thoughts, but Jax kissing me only provoked the memory of Cander and our last kiss. I shook Cander away at Jax's frustrated grunt. His hands stayed put, his fingers spread against my back, but the pressure of our bodies increased the more we kissed. I couldn't help but move into his hard body. The tingle, heat, and power coming into me was beyond help. I didn't even know he was pushing us back until I was up against the wall. I knew when I had taken in enough power; it was like a splash of water against my face along with the image of Cander. I broke our lips apart. "Jax, I'm better now." I didn't mean for it to sound so sexual, but that's how it came out, and it didn't help convince Jax. He tried to go in for another kiss. I shifted the best I could out of his hold and glowing gold eyes.

"I know you're thinking of Cander, Akira, but he is never going to want you like that. Not how you were with Ian. That's just not how we are." I couldn't deny I had been thinking of Cander, but was that what was happening? Did I want Cander to take my virginity because I thought we could be something more? I liked him, but it was just my hormones. Or was it?

I took another healthy step away along the wall. "I was thinking of Ian. You must have been confused about who you saw."

Jax shook his head and turned from the wall to face me. "I only saw you."

Was I hearing right? "I thought you said that Incubi didn't think like that. I thought it was all business to you?"

"It is." He ran his hands through his hair and walked over to the bed, throwing down Cander's *"Directions"*, before turning and walking out of the room with a slam of the door.

All I could do was stand and stare. Did Jax like me, like really like me? "Don't I have enough guy problems" I muttered as I headed for the paper. I felt energized after "feeding" or whatever that was from Jax. I didn't want to stay in a bedroom and await the council and that awful woman Pearl to make her decision. I would explore after checking on Cander.

Dear Siren,

Congrats by the way on the title. There will be lots to do once you are accepted amongst your new tribe, and you will be. For now, I need you to come and get my ass out of the Fifth Realm. There will be a great reward for you when you achieve this goal. Right now, you are alone in Jax's room, awaiting his sexually frustrated self. If I didn't want you to sneak off without him, I would have you pat him on the back for me and tell him that I know the struggle. Your one tough virgin to crack.

Anyway, I need you to return to that bar and get help from your good friend Crow. Oh, and make sure to let him know you're claimed, and he won't touch you. Take a pen and everything I gave you before I left and get out as soon as possible. My bike is parked out front. Good luck.

-Incubus Love -C

9

THE TRUTH

*A*s soon as I read the "directions" from Cander, I glanced guiltily around the room like Jax was going to pop up somewhere and try to stop me. But even if he did, it wouldn't matter. How did Cander expect me to sneak out and ditch Jax, learn to drive a motorcycle on-demand, and then find Crow in some biker bar? Even though I didn't know where any of that was. Then on top of all of that impossible pile...save him.

I folded the note and unfolded it again, reaching for a pen on the nightstand by the bed. Which was placed next to all the other stuff Cander had left me. I found it odd that he left all this stuff here and wasn't worried about me taking off. Well, I guess technically we were just making out, and well, I really did want to think he was helping me. So I guess I'm not really a captive.

Lucky for me, the note was blank. I was guessing that meant Cander expected a reply, and that's just what he was going to get.

Hello delusional prisoner,
I'll start by reiterating...delusional. Cander, how in the HELL (lit-

erally) am I supposed to do any of that. All of that is impossible without Jax's help.

Before I could finish my thought, the slow bleed of ink from Cander appeared, and I knew he was going to write back before I got what I wanted to say out. Grr, damn him!

I was taken prisoner because of Jax.

Okay, explain...

There's no time. Sneak out. Hop on the bike. It will literally drive itself to Crow. Hold on, and Crow will help you from there. He knows everything.

I stared, wasting time like an idiot as my heart picked up from the rush of adrenaline. Did I really think I could do this? Did I want to do this? The thought alone was beyond scary.

You're my only hope, little Siren. I know I've been a jerk. Tribe, no tribe. I guess what's done is done, but there are some things that I left unexplained to you, and I want to make that right. Don't be scared, just do it. You're almost out of time.

Forever in your debt. —Incubus love, C.

S hit. End of paper. Okay, okay. You can do this Akira. You are a badass, sexy, Siren mermaid thing who needs to pull up her big girl panties and save one sexy, infuriating Cander from somewhere in the fifth quarter of Hell. Wherever that was.

I laughed at my last thought while I gathered my stuff and turned towards the French doors on the opposite side of the bed. They lead to an outdoor patio from what I could tell, and I had no idea what laid outside those doors. I had a pretty good feeling that I needed to believe this was actually Hell, and if that was the case, shouldn't I be worried about the monsters and demons of Hell?

With my racing heart, I made my way over to the doors. Every footstep sounded louder than the last, and I was sure I was taking entirely too long, trying to be quiet. Isn't that how it usually goes though? You are always more painfully aware of just how much sound a footstep can make when you're trying to be quiet.

By the time I made my way outside and eased the door shut, I remembered just how hot and cliché Hell's atmosphere was. If people only really knew how close their thoughts were to the real place. I would laugh out loud if it weren't so sad. Everything looked and felt the way it did the last time I was here. In fact, taking a second to look around as I wandered in the dark for this supposed motorcycle, I realized two things. One, either Jax and Cander had identical mansions or two; they lived together…awkward. There is nothing like two super-hot babes living together in an over-the-top lavish mansion and both wanting to have sex with you.

I found the bike under the same tree as last time, yup they lived together, and yes, it usually took me this long to catch onto things. I hopped on the demon powered bike and sent up a quick prayer that Jax wouldn't hear it roar to life.

And that it did…roar, anyways.

I gripped the handlebars so hard my hands were void of blood and practically numb. I wanted to squeeze my eyes shut out of fear, but the unknown kept them open. Plus, I was watching behind me, waiting for Jax to appear. He never did, though. What was tying him up so much that he didn't know I had left? Would he even care if I left? I shook my head clear of the thought as the bike led me forever through the dry, empty world.

---

*T*he biker bar was packed, with who I could only assume were demons, and I was literally the only female. *Ah, shit.*

Crow was behind the bar just like last time. This time, he seemed locked in an amusing conversation with his customers because he didn't even notice me. Unfortunately, everyone else did, which made me think he was deliberately ignoring me. Catcalls, and hey babies only contributed to my shaky hands. I know Cander had told me the last time we were here to stand tall and act like everyone else was beneath me, but without him by my side, it was a lot harder. I kept my pace even, and my stare on the preoccupied bartender.

Look up, look up, look up. I wanted him to help me so I could get the hell out of here.

I reached the bar and slid onto one of the bar stools, unsure of what to do. I cleared my throat, hoping to get Crow's attention, who still did not look over at me. He *was so* doing that on purpose. Ugh! Geez, what does a girl gotta do?

"Hey baby. You working tonight?" Great, I was a whore now.

"Please tell me you are. What I wouldn't do to have my hands all over you." There was a hint of humor in the voice, and something else about it, almost a familiar tone. I wanted to look over so badly, but I didn't want to show the guy a minute of my time.

Instead, I angled my face towards him and looked at black combat boots. "I'm taken, beat it." I looked back up to Crow but kept my body shifted towards the creep, who actually moved closer. My heart was hammering in my chest. Even that little act of bravery was enough to put me in a small shyness comma, and I wasn't sure I had it in me not to turn and run out of there screaming. Yeah, I was a demon too, but these guys had been in Hell a lot longer, and in fact, I didn't even want to be in Hell. I honestly didn't think I was bad enough to deserve to be stuck here.

How was I going to protect myself if this guy didn't lay off? What if Crow wouldn't help and something terrible happened here? Why hadn't I listened to Jax and just had sex with him like a good little Siren? At least then, I would be strong enough to kill a fly.

"You don't look taken." I knew that voice, or at least I thought I did. My eyes strained to look up, but I told myself it wasn't him. Kira, he's dead. My heart ached at the thought. I'd never get over Ian.

I shifted my weight forward. Maybe the guy would take a hint. The sound of a barstool to my left being pulled out told me the guy was there to stay. It almost had me shouting Crow's name for help. I needed to get out of there. Fear and nervousness were tingling every nerve in my body. My hands shook as I pulled out Cander's phone. Here's to hoping Hell had cell phone towers.

I scrolled for Jax's number. I needed him to come and get me before something awful happened. Sorry, Cander.

"I hear they have pretty thick waters in the Fifth Realm." The voice to my left said. He sounded so much like Ian, a swell of emotions bubbled up all over again. Do not cry, Akira. It's not him. Ignore this guy. Think of why you're doing this and wait for Crow.

I calmed my heart for a second and ignored the guy once more. The Fifth Realm supposedly was where I needed to go to save Cander. Other than that, I knew nothing of the Fifth Realm, so engaging in conversation would only leave my newness and vulnerability out in the open.

He chuckled. The sound of the laugh was enough to coat my body in goosebumps and my heart to stall. I pushed the call button. I was chickening out, but if I stayed any longer by this guy, I would have a mental breakdown at the thought of the love of my life. I hated this.

Before I could even get the phone up to my ear, it was snatched from my hand. "HEY!" I yelled as I turned to the problem to my left.

Except the word problem didn't even begin to cover it. "Holy. Shit."

His blue eyes engulfed my vision as a rush of static hit my ears. The need to pass out was overwhelming, given my delusional brain. *I'm seeing things*. I fumbled off the barstool and backed towards the exit. The guy could keep the phone. I really needed to get out of there now, I'd gone from lovesick mourning girlfriend/ murderer, to delusional lovesick mourning girlfriend/murderer.

"HEY!" A guy with blue hair shouted when I crashed into his table, spilling two drinks. I didn't even mumble sorry as my delusional mind turned Ian towards me and headed him my way. It looked like he was talking, but I couldn't hear anything. With one last glance, I turned and ran out of the bar.

"Akira!" I heard my name just as I slammed into someone's chest. I looked up as I stepped back, ready to run again. Ian. Or an Ian look-alike. Run!

"Akira, stop!" He reached out and grabbed my shoulders. For something that started as me seeing things, this was becoming too much.

"It's me! It's me! Baby, it's me! It's Ian!" I stopped my struggle to step back and gaped openly at him. It *couldn't* be.

"You only thought you killed me, Kira. The truth is that I used you."

Wait, back up. What? I frowned and took another step back. What the hell did that mean? He wasn't dead, and he…used me?

"Wow. Okay. Now just wait." Ian held out his hands and took a timid step forward, almost as if I was a wild animal getting ready to run. I was.

"You. You used me?" I didn't understand any of it. Cander even said I killed him. I had. I did. Except here he was, and he looked the same. Well, besides how much his ultra-good looks were enhanced.

"Baby, listen to me..." That name. I wanted to tear his mouth off. Instead, I clenched my jaw so hard it was only a matter of seconds before I broke some teeth.

"I thought you were dead! I heard Cander..." I was breathing like crazy now. I was going crazy. Crazy from anger. Insane from fear and confusion. I'd also started to stutter as black crawled at the corner of my eyes. "I heard him say I killed you. You're dead? Oh my gosh. No! This is a trick!" I looked around for people to jump out and start pointing and laughing.

Nothing. I was way past full freak out mode. Just as I started screaming for Jax, I blacked out.

"Akira, baby, come on. Wake up."

Pause.

"She's awake, just give her a minute to get her thoughts." Crow was talking to someone else, did I even want to know.

"No. Yes. I'll let her know." Crap, it was a phone call. Braving the unknown, I opened my eyes to see my dead or not so dead boyfriend in front of me.

I slowly got up from a small red couch, tucked in the corner of a dark room. "Where am I?"

Ian took in a deep breath. "We're still at the bar. We're in Crow's back room." I looked around and shuddered at the thought of laying down in a place so filthy.

I held up a hand to ward Ian away when he started to stand. "Who are you?"

He let out a frustrated sigh, giving the chair a disgusted look before sitting back where he'd been. Apparently, I wasn't the only one who thought this place was gross. "It's still me, babe. The way I started things off out there wasn't a good way to start."

"You think!" I snapped, pacing in the small room.

"Just hear me out, please."

"I thought I killed you. I thought you were dead. Everyone thinks you're dead!"

"Same could be said for you, babe."

"Don't call me that!"

A door opened before Ian could respond and in walked Crow. "Am I interrupting? Lovers spat I take it?" His dirty, greasy hair was more brown than black, which made sense to me now I knew he was a male Siren.

"Wow, you actually notice me now." All I got from that was a cheeky grin from Crow before Ian pointed at him.

"You're a Siren?" Ian sputtered out a laugh at Crow, who gave him a look of indifference and shrugged a shoulder. He was busy making three drinks.

It hit me a little too late what just happened, and then it made sense. The good looks, the charm, the fact that he wasn't dead. "Oh, my holy shit!"

"Was that an actual sentence?" Crow asked as he walked over and placed a drink in my frozen hand. I was going to kill that lying son of a bitch. I was beyond pissed. I slammed the glass down hard enough it busted sending shards of glass and liquid all over the wooden side table.

Ian stood, looking more than scared. "Akira, let me explain."

Oh my gosh, oh my gosh. I clenched my shaking fists and looked up to the ceiling to keep from strangling him. Okay, I'm eighteen. Way old enough to know not to throw a tantrum, but it was either that or kill him again. I took as much air as I could in.

"Ah, come on. The last time a Siren did this, my customers were out for a week." Crow spoke a second before Ian's warning. "Akira. Do. Not. Scream."

Too late. I let it all out. All my frustrations out in one huge ear-splitting scream as Crow and Ian put their hands over their ears.

I didn't give them time to recover or take care of the flames that burst out in random spots in the room or all the broken glass either. I lunged at Ian with all my might tackling him to the floor, claws out and all. "YOU WERE AN INCUBUS THIS WHOLE TIME!" I sounded like a demonic witch.

"Akira..." He struggled, managing to get on top of me, so I punched him right in the nose. Whatever my scream did clearly made him weak. I used my hips and rolled him underneath me as I straddled him and went in for another punch.

Ian grabbed my wrist before I could. "Baby, I still love you. It's still me."

Bullshit. Bullshit.

"HOW MANY!" I struggled to keep trying to beat the shit out of him as he got the upper hand and rolled me looking perplexed at my question.

I bucked widely underneath him. "Don't look at me like that you lying, piece-"

"CALM DOWN! It's not what you think!" He yelled in my face.

That only made me cry. He lied to me. He made me believe I'd been the only one when I was probably one out of thousands. And now he was yelling at me. "Just tell me the truth." I whimpered as I slowed my struggle. It was no use, he was too strong, and my muscles were nothing but a pathetic weak mess.

Blood trickled out of his nose, and his hair was wild, and even though he was clearly upset, his eyes were calm and understanding. It made him look older, and it only reminded me of how easy it was to fall in love with him. "The truth. When I found out you would be turning, I made a deal with the devil himself. The truth is while you were transforming into a Siren; I was transforming into an Incubus."

Ian's explanation was interrupted. "Only a Siren can make

an Incubus and vice versa." I'd forgot Crow was even in the room until then and made himself a new drink and put out my random rage fires. Ian shot him an enraged look, and Crow shrugged and gave us a look like he didn't understand why we were glaring at him.

"The truth was, no is, that I'm technically still a virgin Incubus just like you're hopefully still a virgin Siren. I turned because I was willing to give up my soul to be with you forever. The truth is I've been looking for you for weeks. I love you baby. Please don't be mad no more. I followed you through death and Hell. Please."

The truth was that my life just got a whole lot more complicated.

10

TRICKED

"Now that you two are done killing each other, let's go over the plan." Crow was on to his third glass, of whatever demon's drink, and sat us down at opposite sides of the room. Not that he needed to, I had calmed down and felt everything but mad and Ian, well he kept looking at me like I was tempting his demon side. Okay, maybe opposite sides of the room *was* good.

"Cander is in Asgret's realm, probably chained up and suffering as we speak. Before long lost *loverboy* here arrived, the plan was for me to escort you there and help you free Cander. Now it's safe to assume we have a tag along." He glanced over at Ian in annoyance.

"Damn straight, you do. She's not leaving my sight." Ian said, shifting in his chair. I wasn't sure what to make of him yet. All I felt was shock. I had more than enough guy problems to really make me believe I was acting on the Hellish side of a Siren and not the Ivy side.

"We have two days to complete this task since Jax called to inform me your presence is needed in the Ivy in three days exactly."

"Wait," I sat up, putting my new untouched drink aside. A lot more careful this time, I might add. "Jax called?" Why hadn't he come to get me? Was he okay? Was he mad that I left? He had to know where I was if he talked to Crow. Was he even concerned? Did I want him concerned? Geez, my head was in a bad place, and I wanted water, but sprouting a tail in here probably wouldn't help my problems.

"Who's Jax?" The question was laced with anger. I'd forgotten about his ability to read minds and an uncontrollable slideshow of what went down with Jax since the second I'd met him ran through my mind like a movie. I knew it was Ian doing it. By the time he'd watched all my thoughts and memories linked with Jax, his eyes were bright red, and he was raging like a bull.

"What the hell else did you do while I was looking for you, Akira? Do I need to read up on Cander too?"

I shot to my feet. "Stay out of my head Ian! It's not like I knew I was cheating on you! You were dead! At least that's what you made me believe!"

Ian also stood, heading my way. "Oh, that makes me feel so much better that right after I die, my girlfriend is out whoring around!"

"Seriously, Ian! I've gone through a lot since I've changed, and you haven't even asked me how I've been. You don't even know how hard it's been to stay around two Incubi and not have sex!"

"You don't think it hasn't been hard for me? I haven't fed once! Not a single time since I've changed!" He was only a couple of steps away, and I could feel the lust rolling off him.

"Oh, holy lovers everywhere," Crow said when Ian started to get closer. "You two can fuck it out later, but if you want to save your other boyfriend, we need to get this conversation on the right track."

At Crows talk of another boyfriend, Ian's eyes flashed red as he growled at Crow. Actually growled. Geez, I rolled my eyes to keep my sanity. This was not the reunion one would expect with a boyfriend back from the dead. Yeah, we were fighting, but that didn't mean under all the jacked-up crap that had happened since I saw him that I wasn't happy to see him alive. I definitely was. I'd missed him, I still loved him, and the sight of him had me in a puddle, but the reunion would have to wait.

I stepped back, taking a calm the hell down breath and sat down." Okay, carry on." I said to Crow as Ian shook his head in frustration and headed back across the room to sit.

Crow took a big drink while adjusting his sweat stained shirt before sitting down himself. "The Third Realm is next to impossible to reach unless you are a Siren or summoned."

This was starting well.

"Asgret is the Queen, you've already met Prince Jax."

I choked on the sour liquor while Ian sputtered out the word Prince, looking more than a little irritated.

"Yes. Prince." Crow confirmed. I already knew he was a Prince, but not of the realm where Cander was being held captive.

"Okay, so why isn't he the gatekeeper in that realm?" I asked, feeling the confusion in the air.

Crow sighed in annoyance as he twirled the black glass in his thick hands. How someone, so big and nasty looking could be a Siren was beyond me.

"Rumor has it that he switched because of a girl. See, Asgret's realm holds the evil spirits of the mentally unstable, succulent demons, and what we call Worm demons."

I shuddered at the mental image of a nasty grub looking demon. "Yuck."

Crow laughed. "I know what you're thinking, but they don't look like worms. They just have the name from their job. The Worm demons' job is to worm their way into the spirit's mind to keep them crazy and demented. They will try that on other types of

demons as well. Succulent demons are very similar, but they actually do look like worms. That's part of the reason it's hard to get into
the Third Realm. So, with that being said, you can see how Jax,
being the Queen's son, could get a little girl crazy. As a Prince, you
can claim the type of demon you want to be when you come of age."

"A Siren named Ariel was summoned to Asgret's realm one
day. The Prince took great interest in her apparently and vice
versa because on claiming day, he picked being a gatekeeper of
the Fifth Realm over being a Siren." Crow paused to take a
drink.

"Why that job? Why not a Siren to be with her?" I asked,
now totally enthralled in the story. So this was Ariel. I needed
to know more.

"Hmm, yes. Well, he picked that job because that's where
Ariel lived...with her husband, Cander."

"*Oh no.*" I gasped, feeling all sorts of emotions towards the
situation. Anger at Jax, hurt for Cander.

"Yeah. Oh no is right, and it gets worse. To become the gatekeeper, Jax had to challenge the current gatekeeper to a deadly
fight and win, which happened to be Cander's brother, the
former gatekeeper. He got his spot. You know what they say:
keep your friends close and your enemies closer. Naturally,
Cander would hate Jax for killing his brother, but somehow got
over it and befriended Jax. Well, until he walked in on Jax and
Ariel butt ass naked in his bed. Cander killed her and would
have killed Jax if he'd been able to."

This whole situation was not good. This entire situation was
beyond bad. Asgret had Cander. "But Jax and Cander live
together. Why would Cander hand me over so easily to Jax if
he hated him so much?" They seemed like good friends.

I'd almost forgotten Ian was in the room until he cleared his
throat. "I hate them both if it counts for anything." I could only
assume he said that because he read my mind on Cander too.

"I did."

I gave him an exhausted sigh. I just had guy problems left and right.

"That's where things get tricky. They live together, yes, because they are gatekeepers to Lilith's realm. I didn't understand why Cander would hand you off until I got the phone call from Jax. He knows you're with me, but I have him under the assumption that I'm holding you against your will. He thinks I'm feeding you lies that Jax is coming to save you for a ransom and that the tribe accepted you so he will be here in three days or you die."

Huh. "I'm so confused."

Crow drained the rest of his drink. "Cander needed Jax to extend the deadline, which is why, as you put it, he handed you over. How did you hear of the Ivy?"

I didn't like his tone of voice; it was like I could sense the bad news. "From my mother. She was the reason I decided to go through with the change."

"Okay, and if Cander's job was to get you through the transition, why do you think he hadn't given you that letter?"

"Umm...because he got summoned?"

Crow creased his brows in concentrated irritation. I felt like I was on trial. "Guess again. How about this. Who do you think made him follow through with that promise? The promise to get you through the transition stage?"

Ian inhaled a sharp breath and hung his head. His hands had started to shake, and when he looked back up, he was clearly mad at what he'd learned from brain raping Crow.

"I don't know," My knee bounced with impatience, and I just wanted Crow to stop the Q and A and get on with it. "Who?" I shouted in annoyance after thirty seconds.

Crow didn't answer as he made a drink, and I went back over the conversation.

"It was my mom. It had to be...she signed her letter with Siren love."

"Akira, your mother was mortal."

"No, my father is. I read her letter and I sav-"

Crow cut me off. "Akira, your mother is dead, and your father is alive. He didn't ever want you to go through the pain of losing someone like he had. He hired Cander and made a deal with him. If he made sure you made it through the transformation and gained a spot on the Watchers as the gatekeeper, he'd help kill and stage Jax's death. He also threw in your hand in marriage for assurance."

My brain could not keep up. "My father is a..."

Ian finished my sentence when the words didn't form. "An Incubus."

The rock-star life, the teenage fangirls every weekend, and the absence all made sense. But there was still a lot that didn't make sense, like my mom's letter. Also. If Cander was my betrothed, why would he leave me to have sex with someone else?

"So, what about this, then?" I said, pulling out my mother's letter with shaky hands. I was glad when Crow walked over to retrieve it because I didn't think I could walk.

"And why did Jax let me have Cander's "directions"?" I pulled out the paper and unfolded it to the last conversation we'd had. Ian walked over and took a look as Crow grabbed both letters and examined them like they held the world's secrets. For me, they did.

"Wow, Incubus love...really?"

Crow glanced at him before handing both letters back to me. "It's how demons sign letters...at least it is from the Fifth Realm. And Akira, you're going to need another drink before I get to this..."

I looked warily at my glass of black liquor. The alcohol tasted almost sour and didn't compare to a Mike's Hard Lemonade, but I shrugged and gulped the rest of the drink down so he'd get on with it.

"That paper is from the Third Realm. That letter isn't from your mom, it's from Jax."

"But my dad was the one who gave it to me? Well, kind of, it's a long story, I thought he gave it to me, and he did. But at the same time, he was in London...In a coma." None of that made sense. I feared the worst when Ian spoke up with slumped shoulders.

"Akira, I have to tell you something about your father..."

Crow, as usual, interrupted. "Let me guess; he's the one you made a deal with?" Ian nodded his head with an ashamed look.

"Some demons can pick up certain abilities. Jax being a Watcher, can change his appearance. Akira, I'm a betting man, and I'd put up a hundred souls that Jax has been posing as your father. Think about it. If he found out about Cander and Axel's plan, he'd need some way to assure you'd never kill him. Cander's directions are tainted. This last note is from Cander, but if there was ever a time he mentioned the Ivy, it wasn't him. Why would he want you to join the nunnery if he wanted you to kill Jax?"

"Wait, why did he make it known what was going to happen with Akira and make a deal to make me an Incubus?" Ian sat down by me. I was too caught up in the drama now unfolding in my life to take my hormones into account.

I was wondering about Ian's question as well. Crow acted like that was the simplest thing in the world, though. "That's easy. You're the backup plan."

"Where's Jax now?" I looked around in a frantic state. "That still doesn't explain why Cander was summoned. How do we get him out? What about my dad, is he okay? If that wasn't him the whole time, then where has he been? Why wouldn't Cander let me call my dad? I was tricked and...and. I... I'm confused. I can't breathe." I stood in a hurry to get the hell out of there. To where? I had no idea. I was hotter than hell and it felt like my skin was crawling.

Ian grabbed my arm, pulling me back down on his lap and wrapping his strong arms around me. "Shh. Breathe baby. Just breathe." I fell into him and curled into a ball, letting him hold me.

"It's the alcohol," Crow said, refilling my glass. I didn't think I needed anymore if it was causing this. Although I think anyone in this position would freak.

Ian softly ran his hands through my hair, making me feel better the more he held me. For a moment, I felt like I wasn't alone in the world. "You're not. I'm right here. I'll never leave you."

I felt the tickle in my throat and coughed which only hurt my pounding head more. "I need water."

Crow laughed and shook his head. "That is the last thing you need. What you need is to get laid." He said, sitting down a little too hard in his chair, making his drink spill over the sides of his glass. Ian tensed under me at his comment.

"I don't want to have sex just to have sex." This made Ian squirm. I could tell just being close to him was making him weak, but now that I was on top of him, I could only imagine how hard it was. I took in his scent, slid my arms up his chest, wrapped them around his neck, and hugged him closer. I never realized how much I needed him. Ever since he'd been in my life, he'd given me a hundred percent of him, so much that he followed me into Hell. I felt safe for the first time in days, and I didn't want to think of everything that just came to light or all the unanswered questions. I just wanted him to hold me.

"I will babe. I'm right here." Ian murmured into my hair. His breath was rousing my hormones.

Crow cleared his throat. "Alrighty then. I'm going to leave on that note, and we will finish this tomorrow." I didn't even hear him walk across the room but heard a door shut.

"I missed you so much, baby." Ian continued to run his hands all over me. "I didn't even know where I was until some blue-haired man found me wandering around in the desert a day ago and brought me here. I asked everyone about you, and when Crow heard, he told me to wait around, and you'd show up sooner or later. And then you were here."

I lifted my head and adjusted my legs around his hips, so I was still in his lap, but I could see him. This was not a good idea. Straddling a dead sexy Incubus was definitely a way to lose one's virginity. One side of his sexy lips curled up in a dangerous smirk. I couldn't help but think of the last time we had got this close as I traced his defined features with my finger. Felt his skin and lips pressed against mine. I ran both hands through his hair as he shut his eyes and let his head fall back. My mind flashed back to how soft his hair felt when I grabbed at it in need on his bed.

My thoughts suspended when I was flipped over on the couch, and Ian was on top of me. "Sorry about what's about to happen, babe, but thinking those thoughts has left me no choice." After that, he was kissing me and oh my God was it a kiss. There was no need to compare it. Not to Cander's or Jax's. Ian was the man I loved, and it was like he could kill me with a kiss. "No, but you can. You know how sexy that is?"

Rhetorical question, even if it wasn't, he was kissing my neck. He had his fingers in my underwear and in unexplored territory in a matter of seconds. I. Could. Not. Breath. "Ian." I gasped. "If you ...don't ...stop." The way he grabbed at my new body, breasts, ass and everywhere where I needed to be touched for so long was pure bliss. I couldn't keep my eyes from rolling back in my head from his searing touch and kisses.

"Baby, you're ready. I'm ready." He breathed just as heavy as he tore off his pants and was on to mine. When I was down to my bra and underwear, Ian grabbed his chest, and I feared the worst.

"Ian!" Fear and ecstasy made me sound like a dying whale. "Ian, what's wrong?" I cleared my throat as I grabbed his face making him open his eyes.

"Baby, you're the most beautiful thing I've ever seen. I just...I just can't believe you're mine."

I laid back down in a huff of emotions. "Oh my God, I thought I was killing you again."

Ian smiled like he was up to no good and trailed his hands up my body. "Babe, with what I'm about to do to you, you should be more afraid of me."

"We're going all the way?" I asked, feeling breathy again as he slowly rolled down my underwear. That was my answer. But did I want to give up my virginity?

"Ian?"

"Baby, you're ready?" He said it like a question but stopped his assault in my underwear and rubbed his thumb along my jawline.

"I...Well, I was thinking about how maybe we could do it the right way."

"Kir, I can read your thoughts, and I know you weren't thinking anything a minute ago. What is your deal with this? Why can't you just give me this?" He asked with glowing eyes.

Give him *this*? "You act like *this* is something I give away all the time. I just thought that-"

"That what, Kir?" Ian asked. The glow in his eyes was slowly dying down as he climbed off me. Now sitting on the edge of the couch, he rubbed his hand down his face.

I sat up and wrapped my arms around my knees, bringing them to my chest. "Maybe we could get married?" I offered thinking of how Cander and Ariel were married. Maybe they did it the right way?

"Seriously?" He asked with a raised voice. "We're demons. A Siren and Incubus. We're in Hell for fuck's sake, and you want to do things the right way?" He was starting to get madder by the second, and I didn't understand the big deal. He never pushed this on me before, so why was now a big deal?

"It's a pretty big fucking deal Akira! I loved you so much that I died to become a *demon* in *Hell*, an Incubus, I roamed Hell looking for you since I died. I haven't fed once Kir! I'm dying from lack of sex literally, and you want to get married before-hand." He stood somewhere in the middle of his rant and paced the room while I felt as small as a flea.

Ian didn't even give me a chance to explain before he threw on his pants. "Jesus Kir!" He walked towards the door and swung out, flinging a random vase off the side table. It shattered into a million pieces right as he stormed out and slammed the door behind him.

I bit my lip trying to hold in tears, but they spilled out anyways. I'd made a real mess of things. On top of that, tomorrow we would travel through Hell to the Third Realm. Fighting demons and God knows what else to rescue my betrothed. All with a man who loved me and died for me, and I couldn't even give myself to him. He was right. Every last bit of it was right, and man did I want, no need, sex. But, if I still had a chance to do it the right way, shouldn't I?

Where did he even go without a shirt? Was he really going to walk around the bar shirtless? There'd been no females in the bar earlier, but did that mean they wouldn't be there now? I stood in a hurry and got dressed, thinking of all the opportunities he would have and how I didn't want that. I wanted him to come back so I could explain and apologize. He was right; he did need to feed. God, I was so stubborn. I loved him. This was something I could do.

After putting on my shoes, I raced out the door, following the scent of stale beer and voices through a hallway to the bar. The bar was packed, and unfortunately...not with just males.

"There's my girl." The loud, slurring voice of Crow boomed as a hard hand slapped me on the back, almost knocking me over. I looked around, catching the top of Ian's head and a very slender hand on his forearm.

Crow catching my gaze reached out and grabbed my arm. "Oh man, Akira. I, you. I mean, stay and talk to me for a minute." *Oh hell no.* Did he think just because he was mad he could go out and slut around? Fuck that. I pulled my arm free, never moving my head from the spot in the crowd where I last saw that cheater. "Kira, have a drink!" Crow tried again as I started Ian's way.

Here's the thing. I'd looked in the mirror before leaving that back room and looking at the women here now. Ha. They didn't hold a flame to me, but most of them, well from what I could see, none of them were Sirens. As I neared Ian, I got a closer look at the situation. He was playing pool or trying to at least with another Incubus. I knew because of the hormones he was throwing off. He had black hair spiked and colored red at the ends and wore a tight leather black vest looking thing. He was heart-stopping, panty drenching sexy. *Two could play at this game.*

I didn't even look their way as I passed them. I brushed my long curly hair over my shoulders and leaned with both hands on the table's side, making an effort to keep one foot in front of the other so I could push out my ass. I knew I had caught mister black and red hair's attention and knew he could probably hear my thoughts as well, so instead, I didn't think. I made a show of tilting my head towards him, letting my blond hair fall on one side, blocking Ian. "Who's winning?" I asked in a voice more seductive than I thought was possible.

"Kir?" It sounded like a squeak. Wow, he just *now* noticed me.

I didn't budge as the six-foot, black-haired hottie made his way towards me. "You playing winner?" He asked me in a husky voice. It gave me chills. He was definitely experienced.

"Depends. Are..." I took a step towards him, running my

finger alongside me on the pool table. "...you winning?" He gave me a dangerous smile that left me breathless in a good way.

He glanced behind me, and I could feel Ian's heated gaze. I glanced back at him and made sure to throw him a sexy smile while I looked at the little slut practically crawling all over him. She had black hair, and although she was pretty, that's where it stopped. I almost felt sorry for Ian now. I really didn't have any competition.

I looked forward seeing my target had now moved closer, way closer. "If you're looking to make someone jealous," He paused, looking down at his arm and then my waist. *May I?* I'd forgotten about that ability. I bit my lower lip and nodded slightly. He slowly grabbed my hip and turned me fully towards him, pulling me in a little bit closer. "I am more than happy to be at your service." He finally finished whispering in my ear. I wiggled a little bit and giggled for effort.

I heard a thud.

"Hey!"

Then boot steps. I knew I'd got his attention, and it was all I could do not to laugh. My acting friend stepped away from me, winking before making his retreat.

I turned right as Ian reached me. "What the hell was that?" He boomed, no one really looked up or cared. I'm guessing a demon in here fussing and yelling was typical in Hell.

I looked down, my face getting red. I wasn't usually the type of girl to be like this, but he started it. "I came out here to tell you that you were right and that I was sorry. That I changed my mind, and that I wanted to, and then I saw you with...that girl." I stopped my babbling to catch my breath. Shrugging a little in embarrassment. "I just wanted you to know how it feels."

Ian breathed out, his nostrils flaring, and put a hand on my lower back. He'd never put a shirt back on from our earlier rendezvous, and I couldn't stop staring at his gorgeous muscles or the V leading under his pants. "Akira, I won't force you, but you gotta stop looking at me and biting your lip. That plus your hormones. Look." He turned my chin to look out into the bar. I immediately stepped flush against Ian and wrapped my arms around him.

Oh, holy Incubi and their ability to pick up hormones. I was like a piece of meat in a tank of piranhas. Why the hell did I leave that room? "Good question. Come on." Ian wrapped my hand in his large one and started pulling me towards the back room. I never once let my eyes leave the twenty or so standing demons with their deadly stares and glowing eyes. I just kept one thought playing throughout my head. I'm claimed. I'm claimed. My heart hammered, and by the time we made it back there, Ian was a mess.

"Kira, this isn't a joke. Do you think that door is going to keep them away?"

I didn't know what to say. I was sorry, I didn't think about that when I decided to play with lust. Crow ended up shutting down the bar to keep them out of the hallway and the back room. After a lengthy explanation of how Sirens were unheard of in that part of the Fifth Realm and how sexually frustrated that left demons lately, I finally understood why it had been so awful. Then I felt terrible.

Ian didn't push or come near me for the rest of the night. We slept on opposite couches, both lost in our thoughts, or at least I was in mine. Before I fell asleep, I snuck a look at Cander's "directions" wondering what he would have done if he'd been in that situation. I got my answer right before I drifted off to sleep.

I'd never have put you in that situation. If given a chance to hold you and be with you like that, I wouldn't have screwed it up in the first place. Dream of me, and I'll keep your mind safe. I'll see you soon and make everything okay. I promise.

-Incubus Love —C.

11

GOING THROUGH HELL

*J*ax must be the very definition of an evil genius. Ian being the backup plan was perfect. The night went by fine. Waking up to Ian and his gentle kisses however, was the total opposite. The air was so sexually charged by the time I talked Ian off of me, it probably could have killed an elephant.

As a matter of fact, it almost killed Crow, and he was close in size.

"Alright you two, all the customers have hard-ons, and it's nine o'clock in the morning." He looked half amused and half frustrated.

"You have customers at nine in the morning?" Ian asked.

Crow just gave him an irritated glance before turning to me. "You know you're going to have to have sex before your tribal ceremony."

I groaned inwardly. This was not a topic for first thing in the morning. "I still have to do that?"

"Do you still *not* want to kill?"

"Umm, yeah." I snuck a glance at Ian, who watched me like

he was expecting a different answer. I turned to Crow before Ian could piss me off.

Crow laughed. "Then, yes, you still have to do that."

"What did Pearl mean about going against my ancestors?" I finished zipping on my boots, trying to keep my hands busy. It still didn't help me with the shaking that I'd woken up with this morning. All my questions from last night were still there, and here I was hoping I wouldn't be too scared to travel through Hell.

We all started out the door making our way through the, no joke, crowded bar. Demons were so weird. "Your ancestors were..." Crow cleared his throat, "I mean, are, some of the deadliest demons around. Like I said, you just joined a nunnery."

After making our way outside, Crow cussed and muttered something about a map before vanishing back inside. That left me and the awkward situation with Ian. I dreamed about Cander last night. His face and how every time he looked at me, it was like he was glancing into my soul. I could see every memory of how he tilted his head and concentrated, or how his fingers felt on my skin. More than once I had to force myself not to open his "directions" to see if he had written something for me, or maybe was thinking of me. The whole situation was beyond bad.

"Kir, I can hear your thoughts," Ian said, tilting his head back to rest against the brick wall.

"I...I'm sorry?" What had I been thinking? Oh...Cander.

"You really like him, don't you?" He now had his eyes closed, and I took the opportunity to memorize every hard, sexy curve of his face and chest.

It was true that I liked Cander, he was infuriating, but even the little time we had together made me realize I did want him. Not that he wanted me back. He was playing nice now because he needed a savior, but he would undoubtedly be back to his asshole ways once he was free.

"But I love you," I concluded to him out loud and in my thoughts as I stepped closer and dared to touch his hard biceps.

He shivered under my touch and I stepped back, dropping my hands. I didn't need to put us in that situation again. "So, it will be me that gets your virginity then? He's not your boyfriend."

It sounded like a command, but even if it wasn't the way he said it, I was upset by the whole topic of it.

He straightened up from the wall and looked at me for the first time since we'd been waiting outside for Crow. "Akira, I'm not letting you near either of those guys. You're mine. I came to Hell to get you and...there's no changing it now. It's you and me. So you might as well get them out of your head." Ian said with flared nostrils.

I could do nothing but stand there with my mouth open, just waiting for a fly. Holy shit, did he really think that he could control me like that. You're mine? I'm not some object to be had.

"Especially Cander."

That's it. "One, you don't tell me what to do!" I took a step closer with a pointed finger. How dare he. "Two, I don't *belong* to anyone Ian!" I took another step closer, jabbing my finger into his chest. He seemed just as mad as me. "And third, you do not tell me I can't be around Cander. And, and what if I want him instead of you!" I yelled.

Whoops, that may have been too far.

I realized that was the wrong thing to say about a half a second too late when I was suddenly pressed up against the brick wall outside with Ian's hand around my throat and red eyes in my face. I choked and gasped as he continued to squeeze my neck tighter. I was sure I was going to die...if demons could die. I didn't know. But I was about to find out. Fear shot through me, and I wanted Cander to come to my aid, but I knew better than that. Even if he wasn't in the Third Realm, I bet he'd probably enjoy this.

"DO. NOT. EVER SPEAK HIS NAME AGAIN. YOU ARE MINE!" Ian yelled in my face. My windpipe was crushed, and I was slowly losing sight as my head felt on the verge of exploding. Was this how it was going to end? I tell Ian I love him, and he gets mad enough to do this to someone he loves?

The bar door slammed open along with Crow trotting out. *"Time to get your fiancé."* He sang out before stopping dead in his tracks, taking in the scene before him.

A second later, I was on the ground gasping, trying to get away from Ian as Crow held him back. It was like he was still gunning for me. I had no doubt now that he wanted me dead. My throat burned and more than once I tried to hold my breath to ease the pain in my throat, but my aching lungs wouldn't allow it. I really was in Hell.

"What's...?" My question of why Ian was still raging trailed off when I realized I didn't have much of a voice. I couldn't swallow, and the pain made my head spin. All I could do was breathe, cry, and sit on the ground. While Ian fought with every ounce of strength in his body to be released from Crow and finish the job. He screamed and roared, sounding more like a demon, rather than a man in love.

"Akira!" Crow yelled out, "Close your eyes, you're not going to want to see this!" I didn't want Crow to kill him.

"No." I whimpered, but it fell on deaf ears as Crow let go of Ian's arms and twisted his neck. Ian crumpled to the ground.

"I didn't kill him. Demons can't die from that. I just knocked him out for a minute. When you get a demon in a rage, there's no stopping it." Crow bent down and helped me to my feet. "I'm sorry Akira, I know you don't want to do this but damn it. You're a Siren now. You chose to live. So you need your strength. It's fucked up, I know, but you need to take in an Incubus's strength. I've never met a virgin before you and never in a million years a Siren one. I guess that is what's holding you to the Ivy, but still. If you want to do right by it, fine. Cander is your betrothed, do the mortal wedding thing when we get there and get on with it. As of right now, I don't know how much longer you're going to last... I'm not even sure you'll last to make it there." Crow shook his head and went over to Ian, dragging him up against the bar.

I was curious about a lot of things. The demon rage thing, how breaking someone's, err, some demon's neck couldn't kill them. But I couldn't talk, so instead, I walked over as far away from Ian as I could and sat up against the bar when Crow went inside. But not before he said when Ian woke up, he'd be okay. I couldn't trust it, though. I was hurt by his actions and mad, so, so mad. I broke down, the sobs sounded awful coming from my wounded throat. I didn't want Ian with us for the rest of the way. If we were going to save Cander, how was I supposed to deal with that?

I unfolded Cander's "directions" hoping for a shred of something helpful on what to do. Instead, I got the last conversation we'd had. I whimpered as I put it away, feeling alone and scared.

Ian awoke a couple of hours later, having no recollection of the purple bruises on my neck. I flinched from any attempt of his touch, and he kept his distance after giving up. Other than the bruising, my throat had all but healed from the red liquid drink Crow poured down my throat. I didn't know what it was, and I didn't ask, but at least I could talk now.

Crow had us suited up with weapons attached to belts and backpacks with food and water before leaving the bar. It seemed like we walked a good ten minutes pointlessly around the desert before I couldn't take it anymore. "Why don't we just black hole ourselves there?" I asked Crow's back. We walked in a screwed-up version of a line, Crow leading and Ian sulking about his actions behind me.

Ian projected a thought to me. *Black hole?* I ignored him.

"Think of Hell as a pie chart. Realm Five and three are on opposite sides. Realm Three is surrounded by water, which means lover boy will have to wait at the gates. Like I said, only Sirens can come and go freely, but we can't black hole ourselves or portal because it will kill us."

So what did that have to do with a circle chart? I was caught up in picturing Hell in my mind when Ian spoke up.

"Fuck that. I didn't come all this way just to-"Ian was now walking next to me.

Crow interrupted his rant. "What? You mean you came all this way to kill your girlfriend. How fucking noble of you. Shut up, boy, before I make you!" Crow said, looking back with red eyes. Wow. I didn't know we had that ability. Crow continued before Ian could throw a fit, "You don't have any choice but to stay behind. Incubi cannot read each other's minds. Jax wants to be the one to take Akira's v-card. I told him you'd be at the Ivy and out of Akira's range, so there wouldn't be any sex between the two of you. You play along and say I'm keeping Akira busy with bar duties, and he won't suspect a thing."

"The hell he's taking anything from her!" Ian shouted, kicking at the dry dirt like a three-year-old. I tensed at the situation and the conversation. Jax wasn't coming anywhere near me after everything he'd pulled.

Conversation ceased as I went over Jax's betrayal. Jax tricked me into thinking he was someone he wasn't. He was bad. Awful even. The fact that he had no conscience pretending to be my dad or faking a letter from my dead mother, was something beyond messed up. This guy would have got away with all of this if it hadn't been for Crow. It's no wonder this guy was from the Third Realm, his mind game played me big time.

Crow and Ian pointlessly bantered as we made our way across the cracked dirt. Every once in a while, my heeled boots would get caught in a massive crack in the dirt, and Ian would have to grab my sweaty arm to keep me from twisting an ankle. My outfit ensemble was just awful. I was a cross between a biker, cop, and college student. I looked like a bounty hunter gone bad.

"Okay, so I'll open a portal to the Ivy tunnel for you, just tell them you're there for Jax. If that doesn't work, tell them you're meeting Akira. Either one should get you in." Crow had pulled his hair back into a greasy pile as he spoke. "As for us..." He paused, taking off his backpack and motioned for me to do the same.

"Around this corner, or rather over this hill," I saw nothing but the same terrain we'd covered for the past five hours, according to Cander's phone. It had a supercharged, no dying battery. "We'll need to take to the water at a run. Transforming in the air is the only way you'll survive the current."

I gulped but nodded like I'd transformed more than once in my life.

"The waters are black, you'll have to use your hearing and senses to make it through the first couple of miles. Luckily, you have me. Just grab a hold of my arm and you should be fine. We'll have to swim as fast as we can, Hell's vipers live in those waters. One bite, and you will die unless we can get you to Cain and Elijah, Hell's healers in Purgatory."

Ian rubbed my back as I thought more than once about letting Crow go alone. And why I was letting Ian touch me. Ian ignored the latter of my thoughts but invaded the first one. "Why does she even have to go? Why can't you just go?"

Crow looked more than frazzled by the question, and I wasn't the only one that caught on.

He's hiding something. Ian's voice flitted through my mind, and I squeezed Ian's hand, dropping it just as fast but reassuring him that I agreed.

"Cander said for the girl to get him out, I'm just acting as a chauffeur. I won't be going into his cell. Now, remember the Worm demons. You make it through the black water, they are the next obstacle."

"Oh, great," I mumbled, taking a breath to calm myself down. Red flags were flying, and for some reason, I was getting an oh shit vibe when it came to this plan.

"The moment we break that water, we sing. Sing loud, concentrate on the steps you take and the words in the song. Singing or screaming to other demons is like nails on a chalkboard if done right. Once we cross through the red doors we're on to the next thing." Crow smiled with a distant look in his eyes as if lost in some memory. "You know how they say not to drink or eat in the land of Fae?"

This was a red flag. Yup, a red flag for sure. "Oh shit, fairies are real?" Ian was beside himself like Tinkerbell was going to fly up and kiss him. Geez, I really hoped that didn't happen.

Crow dished out one of the many annoyed looks that he seemed to have saved just for Ian. I couldn't help but laugh at my own miserable fate. This just keeps getting better and better.

"No! Fairies aren't real yah shit for brains!" Crow barked at Ian, making Ian's excited, almost boyish look drop. "It's just one of the many things that got twisted along the way. Humans got the Fimble demons mixed up with fairies, which do *not* exist. Fimble demons do, however. So once past those doors, we will officially be in the land of mind fucks. Don't make eye contact, not even by accident, do not accept anything...not just food or drink, nothing. Don't talk. In fact, once we cross those doors, it'd be best if you shut your eyes and hold onto my arm. Once we make it through that room, we get to the throne room."

Another throne room. *Fucking great.*

You got this, babe. I have faith. Ian whispered in my mind like he didn't just try to kill me. I threw him the memory, and he shrank away from me. I straightened myself up and pushed down my anger as Crow continued.

"You ask Queen Asgret for Cander, she releases him, and we get the hell out of there, the end." He finished in a rush and went through his backpack of stuff that I thought was pointless. I couldn't believe what I was hearing. We had to make it through the land of crazy, so I could *ask* permission to have Cander. *Oh hell no.* "There's something you're not telling us, and I'm guessing it's why you're so fidgety," Ian said. Puffing his chest and taking a step towards Crow as if he didn't just break his neck earlier.

Crow had been helpful, beyond informative, but that didn't mean we trusted him. This was Hell, after all.

Crow dropped his bag, muttering curse words before rubbing his hands nervously together. "There was a reason why Ariel was there in the first place. There's a reason why only Sirens can enter the Third Realm on their own accord."

"Figured you'd set us up," Ian said, dropping more than the usual sling of F-bombs. I was stunned speechless, not by Ian's F-bomb parade, but from Crow's betrayal. I guess there's no such thing as a decent man in Hell. Go figure.

"Hey! I've been nothing but helpful. I can just walk away and let her figure it out on her own." Crow shouted at the six-foot angry Incubus beside me. This wasn't good, and I needed Crow's help.

I stepped up, pulling Ian back. "No. Come on, Ian." Ian fell back beside me, and I turned to Crow. "Just tell us what the catch is."

He didn't even hesitate. "Scales." Crow caught our confused looks. "Asgret enjoys the taste of Siren scales. Getting one pulled is torture as you can imagine since they are part of your skin, but she also enjoys that."

I looked down at my tattoos. I remembered my transformation, how the intricate lines had raised running together before turning into scales that covered my breasts, and how my black tail shined with them.

"You knew, and you didn't tell us. What will happen if she takes my scales? Is that why Cander wants me to save him? Because she will take my scales? Is this punishment because he hates me?" I was all but yelling.

"Okay here's the deal, just because we're asking Asgret, or rather *you're* asking her for Cander, doesn't mean that's what she'll want. She usually keeps a Siren for a term, or rather until she's had a whole layer of scales, so she might be feeding off someone already. I'm not sure of the exact meaning of Cander wanting you specifically. I'd imagine he wants it to be you because if Jax has taken a fancy to you, Asgret will know and therefore not harm you."

"What happens if she captures me? I mean, isn't that a possibility? What if she captures me and then Jax will have both of us, because why wouldn't she right?"

I pushed away from Ian's attempt at comfort and walked a couple of feet away to get some space. It was still hard to believe this was my life...that all of this was real. Not too long ago. I found out that I was a Siren. From there my whole life has been an uncontrollable event that will not slow down or give me a second to breathe. I haven't even got my mind wrapped around the Siren part, not entirely anyway. Now I was going on some mission in Hell to save a guy who didn't even like me. I believe his words were something along the lines of, how he would rather *die* than touch me. So there's that. Jax was perfect, or so I thought, but he ended up being a mental case. Ian had changed since he'd turned. There was no denying that. And Crow...why was he being so helpful? How did he have all the answers?

What if everyone was crazy and evil? How could I trust anyone?

A great roar and rush of wind which made my hair go crazy had me looking back to see a demon portal had opened and Ian walking through it. Not once did he look back at me, and the portal disappeared.

"I know all this is messed up. You have no reason to trust any of us, but if you want to save Cander, then we have to leave now."

I turned back to Crow. "Honestly, I can't wrap my mind around any of this. Why me? I'm not even a full Siren or whatever you want to call it. I don't understand what's going on, and I have so many questions. I don't feel like any of this is real. It looks like we are in a desert, an endless desert. There's nothing here. No flames, no tortured souls, no mean looking red guy with horns and a tail. I feel like this is fake, like I'm going to wake up and this will all be a dream."

I looked around at the vacant cracked version of Hell. The atmosphere was hot and humid, and the sky was like a miserable cloudy day right before the rain. Then there was Crow. Not once could I imagine him being a beautiful Siren like I saw in the Ivy's Bessel. What happened to him, and how was he surviving? He was a good two hundred and sixty pounds and looked like he lived off a diet of cigarettes, liquor, and greasy foods. He was kind, helpful, and knowledgeable...but not once did I feel like he was going to grow a set of fangs and start killing people. Nothing made sense.

"Come on." Crow said, gently touching my back and nudging me forward. After walking in my stunned state of disbelief, I noticed that he held both our backpacks in his other hand.

"Right...here." I looked at him when he started to talk and then looked to where his finger was pointing to see that the whole scene around me had changed.

We were standing on a cliff, a very, very high cliff.

"Time to snap out of it, Akira, it's time to work." He thrust a water bottle into my hand, and I was all too aware of the next step.

"Crow!" He turned to look at me. It was time to confess. "I don't know how to do this. I've only transformed once..." I trailed off, looking at my shaky hands.

Crow nodded. "I figured as much."

"What? You knew! Then how do you expect me to change in the air then?"

All he could do was laugh. " That's why we brought the water. You pour it over yourself, and when you feel the tingling on your skin, you jump. Your body will know what to do."

The air was still as humid as before we were magically up on the edge of a cliff, and I stepped forward peering over the edge. I felt the drop of my stomach and the dizziness of my head just looking down at the angry waves crashing against the sharp rocks at the bottom. I stepped back just as a piece of the cliff crumbled towards the water. To say I was scared would be an understatement. I didn't want to do this. Nope.

I turned to say as much to Crow.

I was shoved hard off the cliff with nothing but a bottle of water in my hand and the roar of Hell's air rushing against me.

I screamed on the way down, waiting for my death, and surprised that the only shred of help was this stupid bottle of water. I unscrewed the cap and let the water fly up and hit my face as the sharp rocks below rushed closer towards me. The tingling started, but I wasn't sure if it would be enough since I hadn't undressed. I wasn't headed towards the black water below, but instead straight for the sharp rocks. I couldn't even breathe from the rush of the wind. I was mere seconds away from passing out and smashing into the jagged rocks. I could feel the heat melting my jeans off and my tail forming. Right as

I hit the lukewarm water headfirst between two massive boulders.

Even if I could process the fact that I was still alive, I didn't have time. The water seemed fine from the thousand-foot cliff above me apart from the waves hitting the rocks. Unfortunately, I now knew what Crow meant by the current. I was being pulled towards the belly of the ocean and into the depths of the sea. I desperately clawed at the rocks, but it wasn't enough. I was being pulled away, and I couldn't see anything. Not a single thing. My gills felt like they were on fire for some reason, and I was thrashing my tail as hard as I could, but it was useless. Thirty seconds in the water, and I was already tired.

Right after I gave up the fight and decided to let the current win, the sound of another form breaking the water caught my attention. A second later, a hand wrapped around my arm. I screamed as the hand tugged for me to follow. I stopped struggling, assuming it had to be Crow. Nothing else could be down here, right? At least that's what I told myself as the hand pulled me down. I wasn't sure if that was the way to go or not. I hadn't the slightest clue, so I helped Crow along as he guided me down.

Screams and pleads for help broke through my hearing the further down we went, and even when I tried to open my eyes, it didn't help since I couldn't see. The screaming became more desperate and louder the further we went down, and the hand on my arm squeezed harder. He was hurting me.

"Crow, that hurts." We were swimming faster now, and even with the bubbled sound of my voice, I knew that he could hear me. But for some reason he just ignored me and pulled me to go faster.

"Help!" The screaming from below us was more frantic, my heart raced, and my nerves told me to get away.

This seemed like a bad situation, who were the people screaming? I couldn't see them, or were they just voices?

Maybe they were people or demons that didn't make the swim and were trapped? Should we help them?

I knew Crow could hear them as well. I tried to get him to slow down, loosen his grip, and tell me what was going on, but he was a man on a mission. Doubt started creeping into my mind when the cries for help turned to demonic attempts to claim me.

"Mine." Hissed throughout the water.

I stopped swimming down and started pulling at the hand that held my upper arm. Something didn't feel right. This didn't seem like the plan, and I wasn't sure it was Crow that was holding me anymore.

I continued to struggle against the sharp fingernails digging into my upper arm when another hand grabbed my tail. I flinched away, but the hand still held on tight. "HELP!" I screamed, struggling against the grip that pulled viciously at my tail. It made no difference, and my heart was pounding hard with fear. I struggled uselessly against the hands on my arm and tail. *Oh my God, I was going to die.* This was a horror movie come to life. Wicked laughter filtered through the water at my screams for help.

I was running out of strength, putting all my effort into another swing of my tail, and the hand loosened. I tried one more time as I clawed frantically to get the hand off my upper arm. I was just getting ready to bite into it as a last resort while I struggled with my tail when yet another hand grabbed my hair. I screamed in pain. Another hand and more fingers grabbed at me, followed by another, then another. I was now horizontal in the water being pulled into the millions of hissing demons that claimed me as theirs. I thrashed to no avail and screamed but it fell on deaf ears.

I could sense the blood in the water the moment the pain in my side told me I'd been bitten. The pain made my head swirl, but there was no way to loosen their grip since they had a hold of my arms. There was no way of letting myself pass out. The fear and my screams wouldn't let me for some reason, and I wanted to pass out before they inevitably killed me. I stopped thrashing as more demons sank their teeth into my skin.

"AKIRA!" A familiar voice screamed, but I couldn't even yell back as a hand covered my nose and mouth.

I knew I was half dead...if not dead already, and this was only the first obstacle. I held my breath and stopped moving, which allowed the hands to scratch and bite at my body, sucking and claiming my blood.

Right when I felt the welcoming pull of my mind shutting off...a splash of water hit my face and I opened my eyes.

"AKIRA!"

Crow was hovering over me with a frantic expression, and beyond him stretched Hell's familiar cloud darkened sky.

"Holy shit." He breathed out in relief. I was scared to move for fear of the bites and damage I would feel on my body.

That's when I got a better look at Crow. It couldn't have been him who saved me because he was still in dry clothes like he'd never been in the water.

He helped me to sit up. "What happened?" I asked looking down at my skintight jeans and damage-free skin.

Crow shook his head. "I, I had no idea you'd be able to pick up an ability that fast." He studied my eyes more intensely. "Akira, what did you see?"

"I, what do you mean, how am I alive?" What the hell was happening?

"Akira, I was...umm. Well it doesn't matter what I was doing. You were looking over the edge, and then you stepped back...your eyes went white and then you went down."

I shook my head, "You pushed me off the cliff Crow!" I all but shouted. "Why the hell did you do that? And how am I back in my dry clothes? Where are all the claw marks and bites?" I yelled, taking off my jacket and throwing it down to look at my unmarked tattooed skin.

Crow looked down with a pained expression, scratching at his head. "Akira, you had a vision."

"But I could feel everything. I was there, it wasn't just some dream! All that actually happened. I, I don't understand." I said, sitting back down to steady myself.

"Demons pick up certain abilities based on their status, how long they've been here, and who they associate with. I don't know why you had a vision or what it entailed. I can tell you that whatever you saw didn't happen and that it was a vision. Your eyes went completely white, and you dropped to the ground. I've only ever seen one other Siren with the ability of visions before, and that was Ariel."

Holy shit.

I couldn't believe what I was hearing! I could still feel their hands and hear my screams. I could taste my own blood.

"Do all visions come true?" I asked with a shaky voice.

"That depends," Crow knelt in front of me to lift my chin. I let the tears fall down my face as my mind went over what happened.

"What did you see, Akira?"

I tried to talk, but all that came out of my quivering lips was a sob. Crow pulled me into a hug, and I ignored the stink of his shirt and greasy hair against my cheek. I welcomed the comfort as he waited for my response.

"My death." I managed to blurt out with more sobs. Crow stilled for a second before hugging me tighter.

"I saw my death Crow...I died."

12

ALL THE WORLD'S A STAGE

"There's always a way around a vision. Like for instance, I figured if I pushed you off the cliff you'd transform out of fear," he shrugged when I shot him a death glare. "But now that we know that's a bad idea we will jump together. Just hold onto me on the way down and instead of jumping off the front, we'll go off the side. Before we jump, we'll get naked and pour the water on ourselves as well. It will make for a faster transformation and there will be no foul-ups. You said they pulled you down...well we are going that way." He paused pointing straight ahead. "If you feel hands or anything bad, scream. Hold my hand, or arm or whatever tighter and we'll make it through together, okay?"

I nodded. "But what are those hands?"

Crow scratched at his head. "Those are some of the tormented souls you were wondering about earlier, and yes, they *will* eat us. I just didn't think they would be a problem. They usually aren't if you're not that far down. How did you get down that far?"

I thought back over the vision and wished for a moment Crow could read my mind so I wouldn't have to speak of my death out loud. "I heard someone else enter the water while I was trying not to get pulled away from the rocks. Then a hand wrapped around my upper arm and pulled me down. I thought it was you until the screams for help turned into them screaming mine." I shuddered at the feel of fingers grabbing my skin.

"Hmm. That doesn't sound good." Crow looked around us now like someone was going to appear out of thin air. "I don't plan to betray you or Cander, so that tells me someone else might be in play right now. Let's get going." Crow tugged off his pants.

I looked away and started to undress.

"Oh...and by the way. I might look a little different when I return to my original state."

I didn't say anything but wondered what he meant by *my original state.*

Standing awkwardly naked side by side, we poured the bottles of water over our heads at the same time. The tingling started, and I looked over at the black light shining from Crow, shit he was transforming before me.

"Crow?" I asked worriedly. What was going on?

Before I could freak about it too much, the light around him died, and I uncovered my face. The person who stood naked before me was not Crow, but a male model. My mouth opened in a shocked expression, but before I could ask what had happened, Crow laughed. "Come on." He said, entwining our fingers. Then we were airborne.

I didn't scream this time. Probably because I'd always felt safe with Crow. Also, now that he was in his true form...he was gorgeous. He shifted us for a head dive right when both our tails formed, and we broke the water with a sound of bubbles and nothing else.

"Akira, you okay?" He asked, and it didn't sound like we were underwater.

I squeezed his hand. "Yeah, let's go."

Crow took off through the water, and it really was like swimming against a current. I helped him as we went, having no doubt that my vision would have come true if it wasn't for him guiding me.

"I don't want to talk too much and attract any Vipers, but I've always wanted to show you my true self. Unfortunately, the longer you go without feeding, the more undesirable you become. Then at that point it's hard to get anyone in your grips if you look like I did. But if I was to move to water I could just stay in my true form long enough to feed and stay like this for a while. I guess I just didn't have any reason to get back into the water until you and Cander showed up. I owed Cander a solid, so here we are."

It was weird hearing Crow talk in a beautiful voice. It was even stranger letting him guide me through the dark waters. "How do you know where you're going?" I asked, worrying about the snakes and hands.

My answer was a laugh. "Just don't let go of my hand, and you'll be okay. Don't forget to sing, we are thirty seconds out. You know Sea Take Over My Heart, right?"

"Yes, is that what we're singing?"

"You betcha."

I found it weird that he had it down to the second when we would be there but ignored it. Only once in that thirty seconds did Crow squeeze my hand tighter, and I wasn't sure if that was to remind me or to reassure me that he was still with me.

My head broke the surface, and we sang the song that killed Ian as I took in my first look at the Third Realm. The Worm demons were no more than men and women in bathing suits lounging about on the beach we walked upon. Oh, and did I mention we were still completely naked? Some of the demons played volleyball, and some made sandcastles. Not once did we falter in our song. They never acknowledged our presence or acted like our song was hurting their ears. That part confused me. We'd only walked a couple of verses before two huge red doors appeared standing on their own with nothing holding them up, at the end of the beach.

You know when you get that feeling of being watched...that washed over me tenfold. Even though I didn't slow in my singing, I did look back. No one was watching us. It was almost like they couldn't see us, and nothing was following us, but I still couldn't shake the feeling. I looked to Crow and his bright green eyes that were filled with life. Before he transformed into his true form, they were dull and ugly. I sang, looking at him as I tried to get his attention. He nodded for me to look ahead as we both pushed open the red doors, still singing at the same time.

Level 2 completed. Now for the Fimble.

I looked down at Crow's tan, skinny feet, and the blue marble floor as we walked. Lively music, the most wonderful smell of food, and the sound of people laughing and enjoying life was all around us. I wanted to look up so bad. My mouth watered at the smell of food. I wondered when the last time I actually ate was, not that I needed it now. I guess I fed on souls.

Crow rubbed the back of my hand with his thumb, and I wondered again how he knew where he was going. If he was trying not to get caught in the Fimble demons' grips like I was, how was he looking up?

Questions swirled around us that I know were directed at Crow and probably myself as we passed through the demons' room.

"Care for a bite of ham? It's mouth-watering and dipped in souls, especially for Sirens?"

"Take my hand, and we will dance the night away."

"Please help me with this dress tie, it seems to have come undone."

"My child! Please, my child is missing! Please help me! help me!"

On and on the questions and tricks came at us. I never broke my stare and I never tripped as we made our way through the third obstacle. I should probably be thinking of what I was going to say to the Queen and all her shit. Instead, something black rolling down Crow's leg nearest mine caught my attention.

Blood. I could smell it was his blood, but it was black. Did a Fimble or Worm hurt him without either of us knowing? I started to ask Crow why there was blood rolling down his ankle and foot when a rush of wind from doors opening and the announcement of our names told me it was time to look up.

We had made it to the throne room. This was going almost...too easy.

Evil laughter flittered throughout the room. "Akira Black here to save her beloved.... how sweet." I looked up to see a frightful image, and the hand Crow still held got a squeeze. I squeezed his back in return.

There were Sirens all along both sides of the humongous mirrored throne room. Some dead, some alive and some in between that floated or swam in tanks of black, bloody water. In between the glass tanks of dead Sirens and those screaming for help, were glass bins with cut up human parts. I swallowed the bile and forced myself to look at Queen Asgret. I prayed we weren't too late to save Cander.

The Queen was hideous. Not a single thing about her was beautiful, and it served her right. At least this was the version of Hell I expected. In patches where she wasn't balding, white hair made up her head and not a single resemblance of Asian in her skin. Jax's dad must have passed down that trait. Missing teeth and more moles on her neck than anyone could count was just the beginning of her ugliness.

"Ah, and Crow. I see you've been bitten. How...perfect."

I looked over to see a bite on the upper inside of his leg closest to me. I gasped, hoping it wasn't a Viper. "Crow..." I said, feeling sorry and scared at the same time. He'd become a friend, he'd become someone I trusted, and he was a good guy. I mean, for crying out loud, we were both naked holding hands on a mission to save one of our friends. He didn't deserve this. He'd done this to help Cander.

"Akira, it's okay. I'll be okay." The handsome man beside me was nothing like the Crow I was used to, but that didn't make it any easier. He could have a great life outside the bar if he'd feed regularly. "I never wanted this life. It's time for me to move on anyway."

Before I could say anything, he leaned over and placed a gentle kiss on my cheek and let go of my hand as he stepped forward. "I trade myself to free Cander and let Cander and Akira walk safely out of this realm."

My heart dropped and the lump in my throat rose. "NO!" I yelled at the same time the Queen said, "Done." In a calm, mocking tone.

I pleaded with Crow even after Cander appeared fully clothed beside me. "Crow, you have to come back with us, please. *Please.*"

He shook off my arm and backed away, going willingly with the guards that pulled him towards a side door. "Take care of her Cander. And Akira...I wasn't even supposed to make it out anyway. That's why I offered to come. Take care of my bar!" He shouted before getting thrown into the side room, leaving Cander swallowing down his emotions with a clenched jaw.

So much had happened since I last saw him and the urge to run into his arms was intense. I stayed back though and gave him his space. I was all too aware of the Queen and the still screaming Sirens begging for help. I just hoped that she would portal us back and we wouldn't have to venture back through the realm again.

"Off you go before I change my mind." She said, as Cander took off his shirt and handed it over to me without a word. I took it, grateful not to be naked in front of a whole bunch of strange demons anymore.

"Portal us to the Ivy." Cander said in a harsh voice. I was afraid it would cause trouble, but instead she just laughed.

"Why would I do that for you?"

Cander smiled, *actually* smiled back at that witch. "Because Prince Jax is requesting our presence at the Ivy."

The Queen's smile dropped, and she squeezed hard at the arms of her chair. "Begone then!" She shouted. And not a second later, we were back on the beach in Miami.

And not a second after that, we were portalled back into our penthouse in Vegas. I had a major case of whiplash.

Geez, for the love of Sirens and Incubi everywhere, could someone please buy a damn plane ticket cause this portal crap was beyond trippy!

I looked around the lavish Las Vegas hotel penthouse. Everything looked the same. New, slick black and chrome modern design. I plopped down on the black leather couch as Cander paced like a madman in front of me. I felt like we were in the Third Realm for five minutes. I felt confused about how ungrateful Cander seemed, but maybe that was because of what Crow did. I felt a lot of things in that moment. We needed a plan for Jax. We needed-

"Close your eyes...I need to see what happened when I was gone without any blanks." I did as I was told and calmed my thoughts. Cander walked briskly over and placed both his hands on top of my half-wet head. His hands were hot, giving me chills. The moment I closed my eyes it was like a flash sequence of the events that took place, movie style for Cander, on the back of my eyelids. It felt weird having him poke around in my mind. Typically when he read my thoughts I didn't feel anything, it just happened, but this was like a hand squishing my brain. The moment it was over, I felt a cooling relief. Unfortunately, it didn't last long and I was greeted with Cander's red eyes.

"SON OF A BITCH!" Cander roared, turning around and flipping over the glass coffee table. The shattered pieces landed in front of me.

I wasn't sure what to do. Do I let him vent and get out his frustration, or do I break down and ask him what part of my time away from him made him so mad?

"We are so screwed it's not even funny!" Cander said turning around and kneeling down in front of me. His breathing was still ragged, and I could smell the anger in the air. It was like a dangerous turn on. *Grr*. Damn hormones.

"What part are we screwed about?" What I really wanted to ask was...Well, screw it. "When were you going to tell me the real reason for all this?" I stood and walked away as he turned and took up my spot on the couch, putting his hands in his golden hair.

No answer.

My turn to pace. "Okay, and I was this close to having sex with Jax." I paused, showing the little space left between my index finger and thumb. He just continued to stare as he rubbed his forehead. "And!! I have to be at the Ivy tomorrow!! Which happens to be where both Jax AND Ian are!"

Before I could finish my rant, Cander started laughing. Actually laughing. Did Hell freeze over in the short time we were away, or did I forget to grab the grumpy demon Cander? My thoughts only made him laugh harder until he calmed and stood walking over to me.

"Why do you think I was mad?"

"I don't know...there's a lot to be mad about." And that was true. Why would I assume he'd be mad about Ian? He acted like I was an annoying fangirl he just needed for sex.

"Listen." Before I could make my next round of pacing, in

one fluid motion and grabbed my shoulders. "This is going to be a lot, even more, to take in than you think you know. So, maybe you should sit down?"

Wow. Hell did freeze over. Instead of demanding or making me do something, Cander actually asked me. Hmm, nice Cander I could grow to like. I sat, trying hard to calm my heart that had picked up from his touch. *It's just lust Akira, nothing more, calm down.*

"I can still hear your thoughts." Cander taunted with his famous smirk. Which was just as irritating as it was sexy.

I sat up straighter pushing my hair off my shoulders while trying to show how unaffected I was. "And *you're* still an asshole, so get on with whatever you have to say. The sooner I get out of this demon drama and on with my life, the better."

He scoffed and shook his head. "Demon drama? You really think that once you get back to the Ivy you'll be able to live happily ever after? That you can just go back to the life you once had? To your friends? Tell me you're not that stupid."

His words came in the form of a lump in my throat and hurt in my chest. I let the tears gather in my eyes. Even if I didn't cry... it's not like he couldn't hear in my thoughts, how much I wanted all that. Him treating me like an ignorant child didn't help matters either.

"Yes." I had to clear my emotional lump from my throat to continue. It only made me feel more like an idiot.

"I did because that's what you said! Remember? Was it not you who said I would be able to go back to my friends and family? Back to a normal life once this was all over, or had sex? I don't know Cander. I'm hanging on by whatever little shred of hope I have left!" I stood up from the seat he'd just asked me to take and was inches away from him. "In the past week, I've found out that my dad is lying in a coma. A COMA... in some hospital overseas! I'm some Siren demon that grows a tail and can suck the soul out of people to survive! OH! And that's because I drown them...WHILE I'M A MERMAID! My super special demon power is to see the future, which I got from your ex-wife! Who you killed in a fit of rage all because she slept with the other Watcher that killed your brother and ruined your life! The same guy you wanted me to have SEX WITH! I CANNOT BELIEVE YOU CANDER! AND NOW MY EX IS BACK FROM THE DEAD, AND HE WANTS TO GET IN MY PANTS AS WELL! THE ONE DEMON I STARTED TO TRUST IN ALL THIS TURNED INTO SOME SUPER SEXY MODEL AND THEN GOT BIT AND SACRIFICED HIMSELF TO GET US OUT OF HELL! DID I LEAVE ANYTHING OUT?!"

I was breathing like a freight train when my fit was over and I felt no better. I took a deep breath in smelling his intoxicating scent and took a step back while bringing my hand up to wipe the tears. His eyes betrayed nothing, almost like I'd never even spoken. "Just...please." I didn't have the strength to even get my voice above a whisper. "Please tell me how much worse all this can get."

Cander cleared his throat. "Maybe it would be best if I just showed you. And before you ask, yes, just like I can view your memories...I can project any of mine to you. I think maybe that would be for the best. Otherwise, you won't believe it if you don't see it for yourself."

Seriously at this point it wasn't like I had an option. If it was something that I needed to know, I would have to go about it one way or another. "Will it hurt?"

Cander stepped forward brushing back a strand of my hair. "Not at all." And before I could stop him he put both hands on my head.

Suddenly I was in a different place, time, and state of mind. Canders, to be exact.

*A*xel wasn't just famous in the human world, he was one terrifying demon. Not many demons from the Fifth Realm messed with the traditional way of getting nutrition. But Axel always embraced his dark side, even before he was turned into a demon. Abel and I had made the decision to turn him together before he was killed. We knew he'd benefit the realm. Unfortunately, we didn't realize at the time just *how much* he'd benefit from it.

"So...are you finally ready for some revenge?" He'd just finished off some blonde groupie and threw her down to the cement floor. Not even bothering to wipe the blood from his mouth.

"Why do you think I would come to you for that?" Of course I was there for revenge. I just wasn't sure why I'd come to him. He was right. I just wasn't sure why, out of all the notoriously bad demons, he came to mind first.

Axel's phone rang before he could answer me. Clearly I was less than important because he took the call. "Yeah?!" His face relaxed under the female's voice I could hear from the other end of the line. "Oh, hey baby girl, I thought you were Liz. Your old pops is getting ready to go on stage." I scoffed at the term old pops. He looked thirty, but he was right, he was old as shit.

I paced around his dressing room looking around at the dead bodies, liquor bottles, and drugs littering the floor. While I listened to the one-sided conversation.

"Yeah, Bear...but you know boys don't know anything. Yeah. Yes, just don't even think about him. He's no good for yah anyways. Okay, you get some sleep and I'll see you in a week, kay? Kay. Love yah baby, bye."

Axel looked up from his cell, ending the call and picking back up our conversation. "Here's what I have to offer. I'll give you my daughter in exchange for your guarantee she makes it through the change."

"The wound from Ariel is still there, and you want to give me...*your daughter*? You think that's a good idea?" I asked, feeling a rage coming on. Axel was powerful but not as powerful as a Watcher.

Axel scoffed at my comment and finally started to clean himself off for the show that was supposed to start twenty minutes ago. Clearly, in no hurry since the crowd had entertainment, Axel opened a new bottle of Jack Daniels. "She could kill him for you, take his place..." He paused to let out a burp. "Then you get the fringe benefits. I'll sign her off to you in blood. A demon's mark, of course, to make sure I'm true to my word. If she falls in love with anyone before you, I'll go into an un-wake-able coma until the deal is done...Yatta, yatta, yatta. Jax is dead, Akira is your bride and partner. Deal?"

I didn't care so much for the girl, but if she would be Jax's undoing...then not just yes, but *Hell yes!* I headed for the door shoving the dead girl out of my way with the toe of my boot, careful not to get blood on them. "Deal."

I didn't even turn around but knew the deal was done when I heard Axel fall to the floor and grunt in pain. How very human of him to think I'd ever let a girl enter my heart after my bitch ex-wife. His daughter was a means to an end, nothing more and just to make sure... I'll hate her already.

Axel will fall and I'll undermine his deal when I never marry the girl. Unfortunately, I can't kill her if she's to take Jax's place. That's the dilemma I'm in right now. One gatekeeper, or Watcher, of a realm can't kill their partner. Not because it wasn't nice, but because that was the rules to the game. I physically *couldn't* kill him. Unfortunately, no one but a Watcher would know that. If I had tried to kill Jax that night, I would have ended up killing myself. So Ariel took on my rage. Not that she didn't deserve it, stupid whore. Sometimes I think...

*T*he feeling of lightheadedness took over and then I was back in my own body, staring up at the one guy that planned to hate me. Planned to leave my father in a coma. Who started all this. Threw me into all this. Swore to hate me, and for what? All to use me to kill Jax? I was nothing but a tool. Cander was back to looking more and more like his true self...a demon.

And my father.

I remember that day. I'd broken up with the first boyfriend I'd ever had because I found him kissing another girl at a football game. I was *heartbroken* and needed to hear his voice. Liz let me call even against her better judgment, or that's what she said. She was right. How would I have known my father was sucking the blood out of some girl's neck he'd just killed? And making a deal to marry me off like I was cattle for trade.

"Listen...I know you hate me right now," Cander said kneeling beside the couch.

I sat up, trying to straighten my dizzy mind. "Then why? Why even show me?!"

He slowly made his way up to sit on the couch as if any sudden movement might set me off. Well, he was right to be cautious around me. Stupid asshole. My blood felt close to boiling. I was so pissed. This is the life I'm now stuck with because of him!

"I needed you to hear the truth Akira! I know you hate me and that's fine. I know you have no reason to trust me now with what I put you through but believe me, things have changed. And even though this may still seem like some half-assed scheme to get you to kill Jax...it's more than that now. I never realized you'd be stuck in this Ivy mess. Akira you may think they're the good guys but trust me, they're not! They are no better than the demons in Hell, maybe even worse! They are a society of drones. They look peaceful and walk around their fancy Bessel, but the truth is that every Siren you saw there is trapped. They can *never* leave unless they are told to, and only then to feed. Do you really want to live your life under someone's thumb? After I got to know you, well after I first laid eyes on you in the restaurant, I knew it would be impossible to hate you. Not because I'm in love with you though. Don't get this twisted.

This isn't a declaration of love. I couldn't hate you because you were so innocent in all of this. You reminded me of myself before I was turned. I hated that I pulled you into this. So I vowed to keep an eye on you and honestly help you through the transformation. About the marriage thing...I never thought that far ahead. I didn't know when I would get summoned, and Jax was a last-minute idea to keep you safe. I knew somehow you'd become important to him too, at least I hoped you would. And if that happened you would be able to save our asses. And then you went off and joined the Ivy, which was never planned. Getting you pulled from the Tribe will mean war if we show up tomorrow and they accept you."

We both took a moment to let what he'd said sink in.

"You actually care?" Would he even tell me the truth?

Cander's brows sunk low. "I'm here. *Right here*. Isn't that enough proof? I do want Jax dead...but I wanted you to know the truth also, and now you do. So if you help me." He paused and reached over grabbing my hand. I tried not to think too much about it. "I will help you."

This wasn't the deal a girl with a super-hot guy holding her hand wanted to make, but this is all I had. As fucked up as it was, if he was willing to help...sure. Why not help kill the bastard that fooled me?

I looked down at his warm hand that covered mine. I felt safe with him. With Ian back, I didn't need any more confusion, but I did need someone I could trust and I felt that with Cander. I looked up into his golden eyes and knew he had been staring at me when our eyes met like he'd never looked away. His words played over in my mind. *This isn't a declaration of love.* Was this lust then?

"Deal." The word left my lips, and my memory flashed back to the deal that dad made with Cander, and I temporarily panicked. Would this deal hurt? I closed my eyes, waiting in fear.

I felt a wind pass through the room that hadn't been there before. I held my breath waiting, but there was no pain.

I jumped and my heart spazzed when Cander's other hand lightly cupped the side of my face.

"Deal." He whispered back.

Nothing happened other than the feel of Cander pressing a light kiss on my forehead, and a tickle on my back-right shoulder. I opened my eyes as he dropped his hand from my face.

He looked up at me and shrugged. "You can make a deal without pain...if your intentions are good." There was a wicked gleam in his eyes. I wasn't sure what to make of it so I thought back to more important matters, as I cleared my throat and scooted away.

"My dad and I aren't close but... I've never seen him like that. So...*so careless*. I mean he's a demon... He's the reason why I'm like this. He's the reason-" I stopped and took a much-needed breath. "Really...you're both the reason I'm in this mess." I looked away, feeling a thousand memories of my dad and myself come to mind. In the memory Cander showed me it was like he could care less about me. Was that how he really felt? He had to have known Cander wouldn't be loyal to his deal, and now he's in a coma. Although for him, a demon, the only one affected by that would have been his band members and me. My dad acted selfishly. The way he killed that blonde and threw her to the ground. Like she was nothing. It was disgusting.

I stood and moved to the window that overlooked the city,

not caring that Cander was probably listening to my every thought. I needed time to process things. My dad never loved me. At that thought I felt a sharp pain in my chest and I tried to take a deep breath but it didn't remedy it. So why should I marry Cander and fix this mess? This was my dad's mess, not mine. My annoying conscience spoke up again, and if I was a demon, why the hell did I keep hearing these voices?

Because your father is still your father, you love him. Save him. I grabbed at my head, maybe I could squeeze the little buggers out. This voice crap was insane.

The hell with your father, show him the same mercy he showed you. He never loved you. He would have drained you eventually like that poor girl in his dressing room. He killed your mother. He's a demon.

No! I shook my head. *Stop it! I remember!* I replied back to the voices in my head. *I remember he never missed a holiday. Dad and I together on Christmas morning in Colorado. We went every Christmas just so there was a guarantee of snow on the ground. We'd sit in our lodge and drink hot cocoa after presents and watch the snow fall down. Or the hours of Monopoly or Wii we would play growing up when he was home. He cared when he was around.*

Dads are supposed to protect their little girls. Maybe it was Jax acting again as my dad during that memory of Cander? Could it work like that? I needed to find out.

You'd only find out your father is a heartless demon, one of the worst in his realm to be precise. He's known for his kills. Usually demons leave their kills for the lower-class demons to finish off and make out to be the work of a careless murderer. Or something believable to the humans. Axel doesn't...he wants the world to know of demons and evil. He thrives on it.

This voice. This wasn't my usual conscience. When did my voice of reason start knowing stuff I never knew? And sound so...sinister? My head throbbed painfully. The only balance I had was my hand on the cold window. What was happening to me?

You found out you're no better than your murdering father.

My headache had gone from throbbing to stabbing pains.

No! I'm better than that! I'll fix this, all of this! I'll fix dad! I'll fix this Ivy mess! I'll do all of it! I'll fix everything!

A round of pain to my chest and then to my head hit me hard and I almost crumbled to the floor in pain. I needed water...that's what this was. It had to be. Just breathe through it Akira, breathe through the pain unless you want to sprout gills. The glass wasn't doing anything to hold me up anymore. I dropped to my knees, holding my head so the pain would dull maybe.

That's because you are a weak... "NO!"

Simple-minded, evil product of Axel and... "I SAID NO!"

Your mother would have hated this, hated you... "THIS ISN'T MY FAULT!"

Oh, but it is...

More pain. I couldn't breathe through this. I needed water. I was dying without it.

Haha, stupid girl. You're not dying because you need water, you need sex, and now you'll do it because you're evil. Cander doesn't love you. Jax doesn't love you. Ian never loved you, and neither did Axel.

If I could just get more air into my lungs maybe I would be okay. It just felt like I was suffocating. The black was seeping in and taking over.

I can't pass out every time life gets hard though.

I squeezed my eyes shut and shook my head. *Fuck this voice!* I'm a demon! I'm Akira fucking Black, and I will not falter to my feelings anymore!

I stood on shaky legs. I hadn't even realized my ears were buzzing until it started to subside. Then a voice so loud it felt like I was standing next to a freight train broke through.

"AKIRA!"

Ouch! I put my hands over my ears. "Cander what the hell?!"

I realized I was taking some time to think but damn, did he have to shout in my ear!?

Cander's frantic look told me he'd been trying to get my attention for a while. *Whoops.*

"Damn it Akira! DAMN!" He threw off his leather jacket, and before I could figure out what he was doing I was pulled into a bone-crunching hug.

I muffle talked into his shirt. "I can't breathe."

He squeezed me a little tighter against his hard, warm chest before letting me go. "What the hell was that?" He asked before making me sit down on the couch.

"I need water...and I have no idea. My thoughts are jumbled and going crazy in my head."

He looked sexy with his frantic breathing, sweat, and tight black beater. I looked away.

"First off, you weren't having thoughts. I couldn't hear a damn thing. Second...you were having some mental fucking break down and I couldn't snap you out of it!"

I wasn't sure how to respond to that. I opened my mouth and then shut it. Cander didn't hear any of that? What did that mean?

The sound of something hitting the hotel room door pounded throughout the space. Giving my temporarily calmed heart, a heart attack. Cander and I both looked at the door.

BANG!

What the hell? I jumped at the sound and grabbed my chest with a shaky hand. *They're coming for you.*

I looked at Cander as he also jumped to his feet. "Time to go." The terror in his voice made my heart rate pick up but I was too scared to move as Cander ran to get his jacket.

BANG! BANG! BANG!

Ha, only a matter of time now, you unloved piece of shit.

"Who is it?" I asked Cander. I stayed glued to the couch's arm while leaning away from the door.

BANG! It was like the world had slowed down, I could only hear that wild banging on the door and my harsh breathing. I zoned out and could only see Cander talking as he stuffed his pockets with crap.

This was it.

I was going to die. But I had no idea by who...or why? I had started to shake, unable to help it.

Breathe in. Breathe out.

BANG!

I was now panting in fear.

BANG!

Breathe in.

BANG!

Breathe out.

HA, HA, HA. Only a matter of time now. Only a matter of time now. Only a matter of...

"DOES IT FUCKING MATTER?" Cander's yelling broke me from my trance and I could hear again.

Whoever it was had made progress as the wood started to splinter.

I was in full panic attack mode now.

BANG!

Cander held out his hand for me to grab but was obviously done waiting. He grabbed and hauled me upright from the couch suddenly as the door was hit harder. BANG! BANG!

Oh my, go-

CRACK!

I knew whoever it was had gotten through. Not by the door hitting the back of the wall, but by the look in Cander's eyes as they met mine. He didn't even look at our intruder as she spoke. His look said everything. Namely that there was no running now. Whoever this was, we would have to face them.

"Great, I was worried I'd miss you. I don't believe I've had the pleasure."

Cander, who had me in a death grip by the shoulders facing away from the door, cussed and swallowed hard before turning me around.

I looked at the most beautiful woman I'd ever seen. She smiled, and Cander introduced her.

"Akira this is our Queen." He let go of my shoulders and moved to kneel beside me with a bowed head.

She stepped forward smiling, and my heart still hadn't calmed. Queen? As in Queen of Hell?!

"Nice to meet you, Akira."

The world was moving in slow motion again, and it was fair to say her beauty was frightening.

"You can call me Lilith."

13

GAME PLAN

*S*o, Hell finally caught up to us.

"So you're the one, Miss Akira Black. You're the one causing all the problems." She wasn't done. Her fire red hair sparkled in the fancy light of the hotel room. She wore a breathtaking silk floor-length gown that trailed slowly behind her. She also had on bright red Stiletto heels that matched her hair, and chandelier diamond earrings. The men she came with were dressed in tuxedos, and I wondered if we'd pulled them away from a red carpet somewhere. Even though she looked gorgeous...I was well aware we were in some type of trouble by the unmistakable glare on her face. I'd never felt more worried in my life. She paced back and forth in front of the large glass window as she lectured Cander and me who sat on the couch. Every time she switched positions, her long black dress would catch on a broken piece of glass from the coffee table, and my ADD would kick in.

A sideways glance from Cander showed more than annoyance, but I was never one to listen. "Queen Lilith, it's not that I don't want...I mean." Geez, how do I even put this?

"I want to be a demon. I just don't want to kill."

Did I really just say the words, I *want* to be a demon out loud?

Her shrill laughter broke through the awkward, dense air around us. "You just don't *wanna* kill, huh?" She laughed some more before turning to her two hired hands, "She doesn't want to kill!" They started to awkwardly chuckle as well, even though it was clear they weren't sure if they should laugh or not. I would have laughed at the situation myself if I wasn't busy trying not to freak out.

"ENOUGH!" Apparently the time for giggles was over...and I think her henchman not only jumped out of their skin but may have shit their pants by the terrified looks on their faces.

"Akira...my new trouble stirring, unclaimed Siren. I have a way for this to work in everyone's favor." Before she could even turn her bright eyes back to me, Cander was on his feet.

"NO!"

Holy shit did he really just say no to a Queen of Hell? "No, I will not let her make a deal with you!" Umm, apparently he did. And then repeated it for good measure. *Yup, we're dead for sure.*

Lilith turned, giving both of us her full attention. "Cander. Sit."

Almost like a dog, he sat down right away. I looked over but his face gave nothing away. Had she mind controlled him?

"No you silly girl. I didn't mind control him. He just knows better than to mess with his Queen. Now. Time for a little history lesson. And before you get all up in arms about your time limit, just know my faithful servants have not only concealed our whereabouts but have also paused time. So no harm...no foul."

I was trying to figure out how they could actually pause time when I caught onto the fact she could also read my mind. *GREAT*! I might as well start speaking everything out loud so no one misses out on a single thought. *Geez, why the hell did I only get the-*

"Lilith, please go on." Cander said before I could finish my thought.

She smiled the whitest smile through her red lips and turned looking out to the Vegas strip as she began her story. "Once upon a time there was a little girl. She was told to stay out of the water. She was told not to follow her brothers into the water, but Pearlesiona was not one to sit out *just* because she was a girl. I liked that trait. I liked that trait so much that I decided to save that little girl amid drowning. Not only had I saved her life, but I also offered her the chance to become one of my subjects along with immortality.

"Which always comes at a price. *Always*. She would need to sacrifice the thing that she loved most dear to survive the night. I gave her one night to complete this task. I told her that upon completion I would arrive and take her to a new life, a new world. She told me it was her brothers that she loved dearly. Pearl, all of eight years old, assured their blood would be an easy task. If I hadn't seen it in her eyes, I would have stayed around to make sure she actually completed the task."

She walked over and sat down where Cander sat our first night of Q and A, and it seemed like that was a lifetime ago.

"Up until this point in time, there was not a Siren line. There was an opportunity in the fear I witnessed during this...accident, and I knew I needed to take advantage of it before another realm got the idea. So as Pearl was to be slicing into her own siblings, relishing and bathing in their blood. I performed the necessary ritual to complete her change back in my realm. I remember her hair and those bright round eyes. Her pale, smooth skin dotted with specs of crimson blood and her beautiful smile when she saw me approach. I remembered thinking then that she would be one of my favorite daughters. Not because she was the first of a line, but because of her wickedly evil nature. She was a natural and I never suspected a thing."

"I would create the ultimate water demon, and I did. However, there were side effects that I did not anticipate. Their creation was not like my Succubi demons who could produce their own race from a bite, furthering their line. Pearl was to be the only one, and I didn't give her reproducing venom. I didn't think I needed more than her. But as the days unfolded, she became less and less evil, and more...depressed. It was *outrageous*!" Lilith flicked out her wrist and snapped, creating a lit cigarette to appear in her hand as she crossed one perfect leg over the other.

She took a drag and continued talking around a puff of smoke, "She was the first to *ever* break a demon deal. See Pearl had never killed her brothers! She had lied to me. She must have killed some sort of animal to get the blood splattered on her face. I'm guessing she told them to run or hid them somewhere. So she saved them, but without reproducing venom she had no way for them to be like her. So very annoyingly mortal like she used to be she...she prayed out, and who other than the great Apollo answered. Most likely because he saw the opportunity for their side. With Pearl's creation the Chosen was in an uproar, and it was *thrilling*! I once again tipped the scales with her creation. Unfortunately in the game of Heaven and Hell...the scales still need to be balanced. *So they say anyways*. Apollo came down in all his stupid glory and melted the demon seal off her back. The deal brokered along the lines of him not only making her brothers immortal, but also making them into Sirens. Or at least from what I could determine." Lilith brushed back her hair from her shoulder as her eyes flashed red. Before I could even think of what the Chosen was or who Apollo was, she continued.

"He gave her his light, creating the Ivy Tribe and the ability for *MY* sons and daughters to create Pearl's line. Since she didn't have reproducing venom, Apollo gave them the ability to transition from tail to legs and reproduce naturally. So...an Incubus with a human, like who I assume your mother was, can create a Siren. If the human makes it through the pregnancy that is. Apollo made a deal of his own with Pearl and her brothers. As the leaders of the Ivy Tribe they would have to solemnly swear to only feed enough to survive, but never kill. It would be against his light. But they needed a way to ensure that the deal wouldn't be broken, so the test of the scales was created. That fun pool trick you had to endure. From there the Siren's scales would reveal their soul and allow them into the Ivy Tribe. It would also help in furthering their line and it gave more power to the side of light through Apollo."

I couldn't figure out how this deal she was going to propose was supposed to help me. From everything she said, the Ivy didn't seem so bad. Even knowing my mother's letter was a fake, I mean, killing was the whole thing I was trying to avoid. So would it be so bad to join them after all?

Be a nun, and never see your boyfriend again. The annoying voice came back. This time with only a slight sharp noise like the wind up of a camera. I shook my head to get it out.

Cander just frowned like always, but it was Lilith who answered the question in my head. "Because you don't have a pure soul. The black and white scales answered that. You also have more than one problem at this point. The Ivy would never take you under normal circumstances, but say they did, you would just be locked up and drained of your power. Plus you didn't continue your transition all the way, meaning you only have a couple days to live. They most likely have your boyfriend captured. You also have a Feenbler demon attached to your soul, undoubtedly one you picked up from the Fae demons. You have a lot of issues and no help...which is where I come in." At her last statement, two things happened.

The first, Cander jumped off the couch and away from me

like I was a leper while drawing a huge ass knife like he was about to lop off my head. The second...Lilith laughed at this display so much she had to wipe away tears. I didn't know what the hell a Feenbler demon was, and I didn't feel anything on me. I looked down and patted my belly to be sure nothing was on me. For good measure I even looked up and all around me. I know she said soul but I wanted to make sure I couldn't see anything. Cander acted like I was about to hulk out and kill him. All this combined just made Lilith laugh more, and even her Henchmen chuckled. I'm just glad I could provide entertainment, all I could do was sigh and add it to my shit list.

I stood ready to throw my anger at anyone I could. "Seriously Cander, what the hell are you going to do? Kill me?! And what the hell is a Feenbler demon?"

I didn't feel anything "attach" itself to me when I was going through the realm. It was annoying that I had picked something up during the rescue. The whole thing did seem entirely too easy, so maybe that's what I got for wishful thinking.

Lilith, done with the comedy, stood up and wiped at the edges of her black eyeliner while checking herself before composing her facial features. "Sit."

I sat, slowly, but gave Cander a death glare for good measure. He put his knife up, running his hands through his hair pushing it back before looking at me and cussing.

"I will help you with your demon problem if you agree to a deal." A deal with Lilith sounded worse than bad, but I wasn't sure I had a choice. I looked to Cander for help who came back over to the couch, sitting as far away as he could from me while rubbing his temples.

"What is the deal?" I wanted to make sure I wasn't signing anyone else's death warrant.

She sauntered towards us now, and it wasn't until she got closer that I noticed a huge black snake slithering alongside her high heels. *Where the hell did that come from?* Her Henchmen made their presence known as well by stepping up directly behind the couch. If I wasn't already on edge, I definitely was now. We were boxed in.

"A simple deal. You kill Pearl's brothers and bring her to me. In exchange, I will get rid of the demon attached to your soul and make Ian one of my higher-ranking demons, which will ensure his safety. Doing that will also get him out of the way for you to marry Cander. Once that is completed, the deal Cander and Axel made will be complete and everyone will be happy." She was now directly in front of us, so close that her pet snake who was camped around her ankles, shot its tongue out in lazy intervals that touched Cander's boot. I didn't understand how he looked so unaffected. I was barely keeping it together having that huge thing near me. On top of that, Lilith radiated pure evil and as much as I wanted to squirm back...we were trapped.

"What's the catch?" Cander said in a low dangerous voice. I didn't know where he got his fearlessness from...but I wish I could death stare a Queen of Hell like him.

"Catch? *Hmm*..." There was a twinkle in her sharp green eyes. "I guess that would be Akira's precious *friends* and *familiar*." Upon seeing my shocked and confused face, she explained. "*Liz*."

Familiar? Was that Spanish for family?

"You have my friends and Liz." It wasn't a question...I knew she probably did. All I could do was say it out loud, barely above a whisper, and let it sink in. I should have expected something like this. After all, she was still evil, even if she was claiming to help us. I should have known better, all evil villains pulled this type of shit in stories. I never had a choice from the moment she broke through that door. I would have to make a deal with her whether I wanted to or not.

She smiled. "You're right...you never did. But just think, this is a good thing! I will hold off your transition until you get what

I want done. And that also gives you a little more time!" At this point her snake gave up assaulting Cander's boot and was making its way up her perfect body. Which looked like she enjoyed a little *too much*. I wondered how the snake could even climb her silk dress. I shook my head to concentrate and stop worrying about the snake.

I felt itchy from my nerves. This was all a lot to take in. Alex, Kay, and Liz were all tied up somewhere and in danger. And it was all my fault.

"And...I will even ensure you have help in taking down Pearl. You will need me. You will both have Ian and Jax to deal with, which Pearl has probably shifted to her side by now, and then you have the Kuppa demons. It will be a lot, and who am I if not a gracious Queen? I will help you in any way I can. Don't think of your little friends as my captives...think of them more like incentives."

Cander clenched his hands, and I could tell he was feeling just as frustrated as I was. "I thought they only intervened with attacks on the outside to the Tribe. The Kuppa demons shouldn't be a problem if they let us in the front doors?"

She raised her chin, letting her snake slither around her neck. Up close, its nasty black scales shined so brightly they almost looked wet. "That will all be explained and dealt with after the seal is on you both. Time is running out. Deal or no deal."

I almost wanted to laugh even though none of this was funny. It was a lot to take in and Cander and I were *way* in over our heads. Kuppa demons? Really? I looked at Cander. Other than the pounding of my head, shot nerves, and a million questions...there wasn't much else I contributed to an argument. We were literally caught between a rock, being the metaphorically evil Queen in front of us, and her henchmen behind as the hard place.

He swallowed hard and shifted his hand almost like he

wanted to reach out and grab mine. I took a slow breath in anticipation, I could use his comfort. But Cander and I didn't have that kind of relationship and I swallowed down my disappointment as he dropped his hand. He must have thought so too. As much as I loved the thirty second struggle of Cander opening and closing his mouth with no sound coming out...we needed to get this going.

No more thought. I stood, holding out my hand like a dorky car salesman. "Deal."

She smiled and glanced at Cander ignoring my outstretched hand as she petted her snake. I slowly put it down and looked at him.

"I hope you know what you're doing." He stood too, giving me a hard look with a shake of his head. "Deal."

As soon as he said it, a white-hot pain slapped so hard across my upper left shoulder blade that I thought the blistering temperature would reach my heart. I arched my back grabbing at my shoulder right as my knees gave out. My whole body throbbed and as much as I tried to claw at it, my hand couldn't get close to where the heat radiated from. It was like my shoulder had turned into a stove top. It was then I realized I wasn't the only one screaming in pain. I looked up from the tile floor to see Cander on all fours, fists closed, and bright red eyes staring right at Lilith's knees. Just when the black started to dot my vision, and my screams were too horse to continue, the pain stopped and evaporated like it had never happened. I looked up at the Queen while trying to stand on shaky legs.

She clapped with joy. "Excellent!"

"YOU BITCH!" Cander roared and charged her full force. I scampered back around the couch as Lilith's men rushed towards him. *Cander no!* It didn't matter how fast they were though. Right before Cander tackled her, she flicked out her wrist, and he flew back through the air hitting the far wall. Glass rained down from the picture he crashed into before he landed hard on a side table that busted under his weight. Other than my scream when he fell, there was nothing but an eerie quiet.

This was it. I was going to have a full-on blackout from the fear thinking of what she would do to Cander for his attack. It was clear she had less than pure intentions from the pain we'd felt, but it was too late. We made a deal with the Queen devil herself and now we would probably die because Cander was an idiot. But instead of getting mad or punishing us, she just stood watching as her men pulled Cander up by his arms. They braced him into a standing position and held him up. They stood quiet and blank, awaiting her command. I lowered my shaky hands from my mouth and grabbed the back of the couch for help.

"When you arrive you will be greeted with a couple different scenarios." She took her time looking between both of us as she talked. "But one thing is for sure. They will want you on their side. They will try to fool you into believing they may not accept you and ask you to go through the Acceptance Ritual. This ritual will be a Q and A...and you will *not* be able to lie. They will do this to find answers. Only by performing this Ritual are they allowed to use Apollo's truth serum. They might even try to find out what power you yield to use it for their advantage. All the Ivy Tribe will attend and "*vote*" to see if you are worthy to enter their Tribe. And since we already know they want you for your power, it's nothing more than for show. So, play along. It doesn't matter what you tell them, or if they find out anything because it will be in vain. They will also have you believe up to that point that they just openly let your friends in the Tribe temporarily out of courtesy to you. But once you are a member you have to kick them out. This will lead us to a hopefully tearful goodbye and you will have to watch them go. This is one scenario, *and* the one we hope happens."

"But if I have to tell the truth after I drink this stuff, won't they find out the deal and plans we made?" I was getting nervous about this plan and wasn't entirely sure I could pull it off.

Looking unconcerned she held up her hand. "Don't worry about that. I will block this conversation and anything else I give you before you leave."

She walked over to Cander who was still struggling in and out of consciousness, his head bobbing up and down. She petted his hair like a dog. Watching her pointed black finger-nails run through his hair had my nerves on edge. I gripped the couch wanting to rip her hair out for touching him. I reigned in my emotions best I could but it was still hard to see.

Lilith's voice entered my mind as she continued her assault on Cander's hair. *The rest of the plan will be leaked into your mind, for we need Cander's genuine reaction to play the part.* As she snapped her fingers and spun around, Cander broke out of his stupor and shook the guards off with a growl. He now fully stood on his own.

She made her way to the door. "I will be sending the rest of the plan into Akira's mind, and she can fill you in." She looked directly at Cander, who's only response was red eyes and clenched fists. "Just know that I will be sending help with this plan. Have Akira get Pearl alone while you take out the broth-ers. Then you both portal here with Pearl. You will be done with our deal...your seal will melt away, along with your friends and...*Liz* being free. Although, I would have to guess that the best time to kill Jax, will be at the Ivy since he will be there as well. And remember, you know nothing of any of this, you are still new and just escaped Crow's bar."

I could tell our time had run out with all of this but I still had questions. I pushed away from the couch and turned in her direction. "Wait Jax and Ian can read minds! And I found out about all of this before Ian went to the Ivy. He could have told them all of this! Why do you think he won't betray me?"

Lilith turned slightly. "One...with that demon attached to your soul they will not be able to read your mind anymore. Cander could for a while because he is your betrothed, but since this conversation, I see it has cut off all forms of mind read. I can and will always be able to because I am your Queen. Ian would not have told them that you were no longer at Crow's bar and on a rescue mission because he loves you and knows Jax is the enemy. I have it on good authority that he will do anything to win you back. I have a feeling Pearl probably already struck a deal with him using that to her advantage. She is smart, evil, and tactical. I don't know what this deal will entail but gauge his reaction to the plan I will send you. Like I said he will do anything to get you back, so as you can imagine him making a deal with her wouldn't be so farfetch'd."

I took a step away shrugging off my leather jacket. The room was growing hotter. It was either that or the panic making my blood pressure rise. "And what happens to the Ivy Tribe after all of this? To me? You said my transition is extended but..."

"But it's more complicated than just having sex. You either need to embrace the light or the dark in you by the time you return here with my delivery." Lilith now fully turned, giving us her back. "Remember not all evil is as bad as you think." And with that she was gone, along with her men and nasty snake.

"Shit." It was the only thing in my mind to say until a second later I was brain slapped with "the plan." I reached out and grabbed onto the kitchenette counter to hold myself steady.

Cander started to walk over to me but took a step back suddenly like he'd just remembered I had this thing in me. *Stupid Feenbler demon*, and on that note, *stupid plan*. This was not going to work. Well, I had to hope it *would* work, because I had everyone that I loved and cared about on the line. Along with Lilith sending me the plan was three distinct scenarios that could play out. They played like a video in my head. It was creepy and cool at the same time.

"I don't know what she sent you, but you have to tell me so we can go over it." I rolled my eyes and made it back to my jacket while trying to reach behind to feel this demon seal on my shoulder. When I couldn't feel anything I gave up and put my jacket back on. Not for the chill but for comfort and as a way of distraction. "Cander I can't do that." I sighed.

He threw his hands in the air in an overly dramatic fashion. "It's me and you Kira! Not you and demon Queen Lilith! We know she plans to betray us somehow, so maybe following her plan *isn't* the best way to go about things." He growled as he walked towards me with a dangerous gleam in his golden eyes, and I knew that meant he was trying to use his powers. I sighed and ran a hand through my now dried hair.

"Stop with the powers. I need some space to evaluate things for a moment. Maybe make a list-" Writing things down always helped me put things into perspective. "And before you tell me we don't have time...we do."

"*No...we don't!*" He growled.

"*Yes...we do!* What is this? A game to you?! My friends and family have been taken! On top of that we have to follow through with this plan because of our deal. I'm going to have to deal with Ian and Jax when I get there too, which I don't know how to freaking handle!"

Cander closed the distance between us now and grabbed my shoulders, gentle but firm at the same time. "*Exactly.* Listen, I can help you with what you're feeling...but I can't if you don't tell me what you're thinking. This damn Feenbler is screwing things up! I'm not used to not hearing people's thoughts." I raised an eyebrow at this but let him continue. "I know what you're going through..."

I couldn't help myself. "You've had three men trying to have sex with you?" He smiled and the red in his eyes shut off. I was glad because it made it a little more bearable to look him in the eye.

"Do you want to be a Watcher?" He shook me lightly as he asked, and I knew the time for joking was over.

I opened my mouth to answer but I wasn't sure what to say. Being a demon, or rather a Siren, at this point wasn't a choice. It was either that or death. But the decision was to be a light Siren or a dark Siren. It was really a choice of morals at this point.

"I don't know." And I didn't.

Cander released his grip on my shoulders. He grabbed my hand and pulled me around before forcing me to sit down on the couch. "Then tell me. Tell me what you're thinking." He ran his hand through his hair. I could tell that meant he was frustrated. "Because I'm going to need you in this one hundred percent if we are to follow through with this deal *and succeed*. You're going to have to open up and choose a side. I know this is difficult. I know this has been a blur of events, and there is a lot to account for, but we don't have a lot of time. The little time you do have is a hell of a lot more than most demons have when they turn. Still. Decide. You have to."

I knew that much was true. It wasn't like I was trying to be difficult, but this was a big decision.

So I did what he asked.

I told him my thoughts on all of it. About him, Ian and Jax, as well as my friends and family. What I was scared about if I went to the light or went to the dark side of my demon. We talked about what the light would even be like without Pearl. Neither of us had been part of that world to know who would lead the Ivy next if the appointed leaders were gone. We didn't know what the implications of our actions would be from the Chosen when we disbanded their system. I told him how I felt nervous and unsure about marrying him and becoming a Watcher. I'm only eighteen and the thought of being with him made me wet...but it was just lust. Would those feelings go away after we had sex? And did love even exist in Hell? I told him how I'd feel if and when my dad was to wake up, and how I wasn't sure if I ever wanted to see him again. Above all, I was mostly confused about there being a good and evil demon world.

I hadn't realized I had kept so much in until it all came out. And even though it was a lot, Cander sat patiently through it all. He put away his gruff attire and answered my questions the best he could. He discussed things with me and didn't rush me. It helped a lot and talking to him made me realize I'd never opened myself up to anyone besides Kay and Alex. We talked for what seemed like forever. The city lights shined in through the darkened penthouse, and we let that be our light. We were both aware time was slipping away but we also knew that once we stepped into the Ivy Tribe, our lives would change irrevocably. After all our talking, Cander left to replenish the minibar. I went over everything in my head, walking into the bathroom to examine my tattoo as I thought.

One...I knew Ian and I wouldn't work. Not just because if I picked the dark side I would be married, but even if I was to pick the light he could not be in that world. So upon entering the Ivy, I would put thoughts of me and him out of my head from now on. Two...I guess between life and death, being a Siren *was* the best option. So no more death talk. I knew that I would have to embrace a side and quickly. Three...if I wanted my freedom and still be able to see my friends I would have to pick the dark side. That would leave me to finish Cander's deal that he made with my dad and kill Jax. That would make me a married woman with the job of a Watcher in Hell.

I thought back to when Cander explained about the Watchers and the Chosen.

"Think of them as the council members of good and evil. Heaven and Hell must be balanced. It's only when they become *unbalanced* that the scales, as Lilith put it, are tipped and the end times are triggered. They are unbalanced now, but to what side we aren't sure of yet and that's because Lilith and Samuel created twins. Dream Walkers named Blake and James. One on the side of dark, and one the side of light. To balance this problem it was only fair to allow the Chosen to procreate, but in doing so it tipped the balance yet again. The Chosen's offspring resulted in a girl being born. This girl will have to choose a side to balance it out. This is a lot to take in and I'm summing this all up for now, but just know you will learn what you need to if you choose to be a Watcher. The Watchers are under the lead of Anock, the Prince of Hell. With a chance to steal a win for the dark Anock has made it his life's work to marry this girl and make her a Queen of Hell. Our job, well *my* job, is to get her at any cost. On top of everything else we have going on."

In remembering Cander's explanation, he made it seem like it was the easiest thing to contemplate. But all I got from it was Cander was the bad guy in the story and if I chose that side, I would be too. He went on to explain that the Chosen was the opposite side of the Watchers. Instead of a council of demons, they were a council of top-ranking angels. When humans thought of Gods or famed Olympians, they were really no more than the leaders on the Chosen council. After I got caught up on the fact that Apollo, the sun God, was not a *God* but an *angel*...I dorked out on all the other mythology. Cander had to pull me back to Earth to concentrate on the topic at hand. Reminding me that we could have that discussion at another time and that I would learn it all later.

I went to work french braiding my hair back into something manageable. I realized all the Sirens in the Ivy left their hair down and curly but if I was going to be carrying out a kidnapping of a high-ranking leader of the light Siren community, I needed it out of my face. I scoffed and went back to my thoughts. Three, if I am honest, I was leaning towards the job of a dark Siren, and I couldn't deny it might have something to do solely with Cander. If we disbanded the light Sirens' leaders, and if the rules changed when new leaders were appointed, I was free to see my friends and family. That was literally everything I wanted. I could pick them, but could I pick them knowing that I couldn't kill...knowing I would leave Cander and my dad's deal unfinished and leave him in a coma for the rest of his life.

When I was finished with my thoughts, my hair braided, and I was refreshed, I stepped out into the living space to find Cander waiting for me. He was back to drinking a beer, which I had again asked him why he drank it, which his answer was to chuckle. He looked like he had time to clear his head as well. He looked confident and less rattled.

He went right into going through the plan we went over earlier in the night, and I knew my life was about to take another turn as soon as we left this penthouse. "So, after you make it through the question ceremony with Pearl and the rest of the Ivy I will be asked to leave, and I'll cause a scene." He was going over the plan, or the part of the plan that was a lie since I couldn't really tell him was a lie because of what Lilith showed me. I couldn't tell him that he was wrong, and that's not how it would go but knew I needed to let him think that for the time being. I hated lying, but her plan was better, and she also showed me that if I let him in on the plan, it would fail. That flittered into my mind when I decided to tell him the truth earlier in the night. I'm guessing she put that seed in there, to begin with. So, lying it was.

"Exactly. Then you will kill the brothers, while I get Pearl alone." I reached back and messed with my braid, trying to make it seem like I was concentrating on that so he wouldn't see I was lying. Which him killing the brothers wasn't a total lie...he would have to kill them.

"The only variables in this are Ian and Jax. Jax will reveal working with her if he defends her during all this, and he will be quiet. If Ian made a deal for you with either Pearl or Jax, the other end is most likely to kill me for you, so I will have him to contend with. And all that isn't the only problem, we will need a big enough distraction to pull away the members of the Ivy so they aren't involved, or they will come to their leaders defense. There are thousands of them and only two of us." Cander drained the rest of his beer, tossing it on the already glass littered floor and opened another. I felt sorry for the maid.

I cleared my throat. "That's the part where Lilith's plan comes into play." I walked over and leaned against the back of the couch to face Cander. He was leaning against the backside of the kitchenette counter. "She will be sending a distraction, her plan doesn't clarify what. It looks like an army almost, but either way, something to start attacking The Kuppa demons. Which thank you for letting me in on the giant squid creatures, as if I wasn't already freaking out." He rolled his eyes and gave a half-smile. It made my heart skip, and I quickly went on before I could think any more about what that meant.

"Anyways...So while we are saying our goodbyes, this attack will be launched, making Pearl send out her Sirens for the defense. Lilith's plan is to act as if her attacks are trying to break the glass to The throne room. Sirens will panic and flood out, not only to defend their home but to get out just in case the glass breaks."

Cander gave me a look, "That glass is created by angel magic. There is nothing that is going to break it and if I know that...then The Tribe will know that. They aren't going to flee. They know they're safe."

I thought about this and replayed the fake plan she sent me. "I don't know, she seems to think that whatever this purple powder, which I might add is weird that there would be a dry powder in water but whatever, that her demons are trying to coat this glass in...will, in fact, break the glass. The video plan, whatever she sent me, shows the glass cracking as it floats down and touches it."

Cander pushed off the counter with his back and stood fully, squinting his eyes. "Holy shit! She got a warlock's powder."

"Umm, right. I'm just going to lock *that* question away and the fact that you are way too much of an excited evil henchman and continue on." I ran my sweaty palms down my skintight jeans. Lying had a horrid way of making my sweat like a pig. "Anyways, as I was saying. They all flood out to do their thing, and for good measure like I said, Lilith has demons behind the demons attacking, holding light Siren hostages." In this scenario, it's an all-out light vs. dark Siren war, and it was crazy to think that Cander was okay with that, but yet again I had to remind myself what he was...what we both were. Fortunately for all the light Sirens, the real plan was more convert and less warlike. At least I hope that was the actual plan. Knowing that Lilith plans to betray us, I couldn't help but wonder if her real intention was to take down the Ivy, like in the fake plan she sent me. This was all a confusing mess.

Cander flipped a knife around on his palm, making it spin in circles as he started to pace, I wondered how in the hell he managed to do that without stabbing himself. "That would create the perfect distraction. Alright. From there, I do my job, and you do yours. There's only one problem."

He stopped in front of me, and I went back to messing with my hair thinking maybe I should put it back down and back up. Something to distract him from knowing I was lying. "What's that?"

He tucked his knife in a holster before squaring me a look in the eye. "Your boyfriends. If you kill Jax, you become dark, whether you want to or not. Ian isn't going to let you out of his sight...and I'm going to be busy with the brothers, which are immortal by the way. It's not like I can pull out a gun and shoot them, I'm going to be busy squaring off with them, and Pearl isn't going to sit idly by and let her precious brothers be attacked, and watch the Ivy go down. And Jax isn't going to let you hurt her, and Ian is going to be rushing you out of there or trying to kill me. So then what? Or did Lilith not show you that part of the plan?"

I gulped; he knew it was a lie. His eyes warmed to their gold, and he leaned into me, his lips a breath away as he reached up, pulling my busy hand from my braid. "She did." I inched my head back; I didn't need his distractions right now, and I had no doubt he could kiss the truth out of me. He followed slowly closing in, and my body sang from his nearness, but time was running out, and he knew it and he didn't have time to get it out of me. "Cander we need to go. She did tell me that part. I know what to do, just trust me." At this I side-stepped him and shook out my shaking arms and hands. I could hear his sigh and a beer bottle skipped across the wrecked ground somewhere to my right. It was still pretty dark to see.

Before I could get far in my retreat, his warm hand wrapped around my forearm, and he pulled me back in one swift move. My back slammed into his chest. Encircling his arms around me, so I was trapped, he leaned his face down level with my hair. I closed my eyes, shivering as his warm breath tickled my neck. I took a shaky breath in, soaking in his nearness. "You're lying. I know you are." His voice was rough with need as he brought his hand up, roughly grabbing my chin before kissing my neck with strength and perfection. I gasped and held on to his arm that held my chin, suppressing a moan.

I wanted more but knew it wasn't the time. Before I could get a word in as he was making his way down the side of my neck to my collarbone, he continued. "and I guess that's what you need to do...for this to succeed." He stopped, dropped his hand, and turned me around, and I looked up into his gold eyes. He leaned down and gave me a gentle kiss, his eyes flashing white, causing just as much impact on me as his sexual assault. I couldn't help but close my eyes. "But just know I'm sincere when I say my feelings have grown for you. He kissed me again. "Not just Incubus feelings." And again. "And come hell or high-water, Akira Black, I'll fight for you."

14

THE BUILDUP

"Just, I don't know. Go for a swim for a bit until I figure out what the hold-up is." Cander said before backing away from the rock while pulling out his phone. Apparently, the rock opening into the tunnel trick wasn't going to work for us this afternoon. Funny since we were motivated to go in and kick ass and then BAM, rock blocked.

I looked to the waves crashing against the small beach and the golden light of the sunset as it reflected beautifully off the water. It was truly a sight. I looked back at Cander, he was clearly busy yelling at someone on the phone. He wasn't paying attention to me, so what could a little swim hurt? Peeling off my way too tight clothes, I laid them next to my new weapons that Cander had graced me with. A thrill of excitement ran through me at the thought of turning. This would be my first time trans-forming on my own in the water. Would I be able to see clearly like I had with Crow? It hadn't seemed like the waters in Hell had salt, would the salt hurt my eyes? What if there were sharks in the water?

A deep laugh from over my shoulder had me covering my

privates and spinning around. Cander stood with a way too amused look on his face. "You're a demon, and you're worried about *sharks*?"

"Well *yeah*. Sharks are like super strong, fast, and twice my size. They could chomp me before I even have a chance to swim away. Demon or no demon."

"Yeah, that's kind of the point, Akira. Use your demon powers and send them away."

I thought about it. "So, like sing?" I shook my head. "We're running out of time to save my friends and family, this was a stupid idea anyway."

"Actually. It seems like the magic in the stone needs to be reset anyway, so...yeah, we got time."

I scoffed looking over to the large rock. "The magic has to be reset? Like a Wi-Fi password?" I laughed, unable to help it as Cander plopped down in the sand.

He picked up a shell and examined it before tossing it in the water. "Laugh all you want. You're part of this world now, so it's better to learn about it rather than laugh at it. One of these days you're going to be out here on your own and you will need to know how to survive." He paused, concentrating on the hand I had covering my breasts before running his teeth over his bottom lip. "Put on your clothes or get in the water, you're tempting me."

I looked to the water wondering how I could scare away a shark. Yeah it was a stupid fear, but sue me, I'd only been a Siren for a short time now. "Do we really have time for me to swim? How will I know when to come back?"

"I'll summon you." Cander lifted an eyebrow. "Unless you're too chicken."

Damn him. "Fine. I'll swim, but I thought you couldn't hear me or talk to my mind with this thing attached to my soul?"

Akira, your vagina is showing. Cander's taunting voice entered my mind. I yelped, realizing I had moved my hand away to put it on my hip. Heat rushed to my cheeks and I immediately turned and rushed to the water. It wasn't like he hadn't seen it before, but still.

I slowly made my way into the water not once feeling like it was too hot or cold, but the perfect temperature. The tingle ran through my body and I quickly sank down, holding my breath before diving under the water. The last thing I heard was Cander laughing. No doubt at my vagina showing. I could feel my tail, scales, and gills form but no pain came from it, just like when I transformed with Crow. The water was also crystal clear and the salt didn't affect my eyes. *Hmm...This Siren thing is actually pretty cool.*

Being that Cander and I were only in a small bay area, I would have never imagined to see such colorful exotic looking fish this close to the shore. I floated in the water remaining still as I watched them all with awe. I explored and twirled in the water with a simple swish of my tail, continuously looking back to keep the shoreline within my sights. I loved swimming underwater with my tail, it made me feel euphoric and enchanting.

"I AM A MOTHERFREAKING MERMAID!!!" I shouted in the water, scaring away a school of silver-colored fish swimming past. It made me giggle more. This was amazing! Why did Sirens have to be created by a demon for evil? Sirens could actually do so much good for the humans if they weren't trying to eat them. What if Sirens could form aquatic survey teams to help stop humans from drowning? Instead of assisting them in drowning. They would be heroes!

Thoughts swirled around about the craziness of the Siren life as I explored. A beautiful blue shell caught my eye and I headed for it. Right as I went to touch it a shocking warmth spread through my body that had my hairs standing on end with goosebumps. The feeling of being watched fell over me and my heart started beating a little harder. I looked around but saw nothing.

Hmm. That's weird.

I shrugged it off until a swish through the water from somewhere behind me sounded. I turned around fast. But only a trail of bubbles left in whatever creature's wake remained. I knew it was time to go, that was way too freaky. I stayed still a beat longer trying to figure out if my fight or flight would kick in or if I was just imagining things.

"I swear to God if there is a freaking shark in here." I muttered out loud before turning back to my shell. I would pick it up then rush back to Cander. I didn't want to stay in the water too long just in case but I always had a weird obsession with shells. This blue one would be perfect for restarting my collection. I mean, as a wanted killer, it wasn't like I could just go and gather all my old stuff out of my house.

Another swish in the water shot panic through me.

This swish was a lot louder than the first and put my heart in my ears, thumping loudly. And even though I was afraid, I was rooted in my spot. Before I could even think of moving a sharp pain slashed down my tail and forearms. I cried out in agony dropping the shell before looking down to see spikes protruding out from my tail and arms. They looked like curved blades made from bone. *What the?* I needed to get out of here! Was my body making these things come out because I was scared? What if something was hunting me?

A bubbling sound in the water too close to my left shoulder stilled my muscles.

I knew something was behind me so I turned extremely slowly, unsure of what I would find. Unfortunately, what I found just happened to be a shark. Three times my size and slowly stalking towards me. An animalistic growl broke free from within me before I could control myself. The rumble was feral. It didn't sound like me at all, but strangely felt natural at the same time. Suddenly I wasn't scared anymore, I was pissed.

I let the feeling take over my body tenfold hoping the anger would keep me alive.

The shark, which I was pretty sure was a tiger shark, continued to stalk closer. I knew it was preparing to charge. I floated as still as possible letting my growls increase to show dominance. If it charged...would I be able to grab its jaws and hold it back from chomping my ass? Even though I still didn't have the strength of an Incubus, I would have to try. I now had blades at the ready. I could just cut him up with my tail and arms if I had to. It was hysterical that I'd never fought a day in my life and now I was just supposed to fight a shark? In the words of Alex...child, please.

It's time. Cander's attractive voice entered my mind, startling me.

Bad timing. I thought back but no answer came. The shark's tail started fluttering hard back and forth. I knew that not only was I out of time to come up with a shark killing plan, but this asshole demon attached to my soul blocked Cander from hearing me back.

Forever alone, and now you will get eaten for it. The demon on my soul hissed in my mind. Real fucking convenient for that little shit on my soul to pipe up when it suited him while ruining my telepathic life.

I can't hear you...but if you're in trouble do the creepy shriek-hiss-yell thing that Sirens do. Cander said, this time with impatience.

I did remember when I screamed both Crow and Ian flew back. That had to be it. As if I had a sixth sense, I could feel something at my back. I looked carefully over my shoulder to see a second shark stalking me from behind. *Fucking hell.*

Big mistake. Apparently, you aren't supposed to look away.

I could feel and hear the water's displacement, signaling that the shark was charging and I was out of time. The scream that came out was from fear as the shark's nostrils and sharp teeth were seconds away from me. It sounded like the loudest nails on a chalkboard shriek I'd ever heard. As I screamed the water formed a barrier around me in waves that seemed to push the sharks back. I could feel the power radiating from me like a dark cloud, capturing everything in my screams path. As they were pushed back from me, sharp black claws formed from my fingers. I only glanced down for a second to take in the change. I felt powerful, invincible, and the only thing I wanted to do was give chase and devour them as they would have me.

Before I could even think about what I was doing, I shot towards my prey.

*M*y hands sunk into the sand as I popped my head out of the water. My mouthful of fangs retracted back into my jaw as I swallowed the leftover blood. Cander stood on the shoreline, looking sexy as hell in his all black biker outfit, with his arms crossed and eyebrows raised. "I take it you had a good time?" He asked as I waited for the tingling to stop and my legs to form.

I was still coming out of whatever haze I'd gone into, which was like a drunken blur, after the shark incident. My legs finished forming and I stepped out of the water, looking down at the blood mixed with water trailing down my naked body. I stood on the shoreline watching the weird blade things absorb back into my skin and my claws go back to my usual looking manicured nails. I resemble something out of a horror movie, yet every time I changed it felt like the most natural thing. The demon life fits me. It just sucked that it did.

"You killed a shark?" Cander asked, pointing out to the water. I looked back to see a shark bob up to the surface and ride the gentle waves.

I cleared my throat from the weird feeling of my gills closing. "I think I killed two." I looked back to see another dead shark pop up next to the first.

"HOLY SHIT, KIRA!! What did you do?" Ian's voice broke my concentration off of my kills and brought me back to reality. I looked over to the rock where he stood staring at me with his eyes bugging out of his skull. I sighed.

Before I could say anything Cander took a step towards me, crossing his arms again as his eyes turned red. "She did what she had to do."

Ian looked between Cander and me before shaking his head and walking up to grab my hand. "Come on, the ritual is about to start." He started pulling me towards the rock as it opened. I stumbled still getting used to being on my legs, as well as keep up with him. "I'll take you to your room to get ready." Ian looked back at me, staring openly at my bouncing breasts. I put my free hand over them as I yanked my other hand free from his.

"*I can walk by myself, Ian*!" I hissed. I felt irritated and annoyed just seeing him. It was clear the feelings I thought I felt towards him...wasn't love.

"Yeah?" He slowed and fell back into step with me as we entered the tunnels before looking back to Cander, who followed with heavy footsteps. "Then I'll walk *with* you."

I rolled my eyes, really not in the mood for the boyfriend part of this plan. "This, she is *mine* shit, has to stop! I'm not going to put up with you acting this way forever!"

Ian turned his red eyes on me but before he could say anything, I continued. "I mean it, Ian! If you want us to go back to the way things were, or even have a chance at a relationship with me, this obsession stuff needs to end!"

Ian scoffed. "I thought girls liked that possessive shit."

"They do when it's with a guy they actually want." Cander said from behind and I tensed as Ian turned around heading towards him.

"You have something you want to say, asshole? You realize that's *my* girlfriend? MINE!"

Cander walked up meeting him and irritation shot through me at the alpha display. "We don't have time for this!" I yelled as I crossed my arms, turning my naked butt to the guards at the vaulted door.

I sighed. If Alex and Kay were here they would be eating this shit up, but unfortunately, *this shit* was what was stalling their rescue. So I wasn't amused.

"And she's my *fiancée!* By my count that makes her more *mine* than anything." Cander growled with red eyes stepping even closer to Ian as his muscles flexed. Power filled the air raising my arm hairs and I had to give it to Ian for holding his ground, because when I glanced behind me Cander's power even had the guards shifting in fear.

"I will do whatever I have to for her to be mine!" Ian growled back with a tensed body. I could tell he was trying to expel some power but it was nowhere near Cander's level. It was almost embarrassing to watch.

Cander glanced over Ian's shoulder catching my eye and I just shook my head. This wasn't the time. The look he gave back confirmed he picked up on my thoughts. All without even hearing me. Soulmates much?

"Now is not the time for me to teach you a lesson, *little boy.*" Cander warned in a low, rough voice before shoving Ian out of the way with his shoulder and heading towards me.

I turned, heading for the door before either of them could catch up to me. I needed to stay focused on my friends and family. There was *a lot* that could go wrong with any of these so-called plans Lilith hit me with, and I didn't know what would happen if I failed. I had people to save. Guy shit came second.

As soon as we made it through the doors with the slam of the vault behind us, a red-headed, small framed girl with the freakiest eyes approached us. She bowed her head before draping a white silk robe over my shoulders.

"Akira Black, please follow me." She said in a timid voice.

I looked back to the guys and Cander nodded. Ian just shifted irritably, clenching and unclenching his fists. I sighed in annoyance. I would just have to ignore Ian. I turned back to the girl who led me to a room off to the side of the tunnel before the Bessel entrance. I could hear the busy everyday chatter of the residents inside, and I wondered if they would all be at this Ritual thing like last time.

"Where are you taking me?" I asked as she opened the door, bowing her head once again while waiting for me to enter.

"The council requests for you to be presentable. Apparently there has been some...incident before your arrival." She said staring at the stamped silver floor.

I walked into a dressing room. It was equipped with clothes, full-length mirrors, and a vanity with a counter full of supplies to get presentable with. I turned to her as she entered the room closing the door softly behind her...the quiet set me on edge. It was either that or her trippy purple, star-shaped eyes. "And how do you know there was an incident?" I asked, not letting her out of my sight as she laid out a sheer white floor-length dress that would not help much in covering my bits.

She took in my stance. "I'm not here to hurt or trick you, Miss Black. Pearl has assigned me as your servant." It wasn't lost on me that she evaded the question, but I was stunned by what she said.

"Servant?"

"Yes." She said holding up both her wrists that were decorated with black tattooed rings around them. "I am a Succubus demon, one of Lilith's daughters. I was caught trying to break a friend out of here. Instead of death, Pearl likes to keep anyone who trespasses against her as a prisoner." She cleared her throat. "I mean servant."

I couldn't believe what I was hearing. What bullshit! "Does Lilith know about this?"

The girl nodded before heading over and running a bath. "She allows it as long as Pearl keeps us fed. As long as my mother's realm is fed, which gives her power, she could care less. I'm one of the millions she's birthed, and out of those, there are hundreds of us here trapped and never once has she *ever* tried to free us."

"So, she doesn't care at all?"

"It would seem that way." I got the feeling that I'd struck a nerve, but she still held politeness in her voice.

"Those tattoos on your wrists. Are those what bind you?" She glanced at them before going back to adding bath salts and oils to the water.

"Yes. No one can pass the vaulted doors with these marks. They were made from a Magical and are unbreakable."

I swallowed, feeling emotion for this girl. I needed to get her out of here. They *all* needed to get out of here. I needed to give Pearl to Lilith. I needed to free the Ivy. It just made my plan more cemented in my mind. *I could not fail.* There was more than just my friends and family on the line now.

"What's your name?" I asked in a more receptive tone.

"Fasive." She answered before turning back to me and bowing her head again. "Please allow me to get you ready. There isn't much time."

I looked to her then to the water. "Won't I just sprout a tail?"

She shrugged. "You might since you are still young. But if you do, it's okay. Either way you will need to be cleaned." She made a show of giving my blood-stained body a once over before looking at the bath.

I shrugged off the robe letting it fall while I headed for the clawed foot bathtub. It was clear I was going to have to get used to being naked from now on since I was a Siren. Fasive stepped aside letting me step into the water, and I sat quickly even though the heat of the water stung. My tingling started and I held back a frustrated sigh while closing my eyes. I wasn't in the mood to turn. I really just wanted to wash this shark blood off me and get this over with. *Don't turn. Don't turn. Don't turn.* I looked down to see my legs still there and I wiggled my toes as the tingling died down.

"Looks like you're getting the hang of controlling your transformation." Fasive said before tilting my head back and pouring a cup of water over my hair.

It felt weird having someone else bathe me. "Is this normal?"

"What do you mean?"

"I mean...does everyone have servants?" I asked, feeling weird calling her a servant.

"Look down." I did as she said as she soaped my back. "Just the important members." She answered.

"I didn't realize I was important."

She spoke so low I almost didn't hear her as she moved to my arms. "You're more important than you think."

---

*C*ander

"What took you so long?" I growled out trying to keep my temper in check towards my last-minute help.

James scoffed, pulling in his wings while stepping over the dead guard. "Sorry, your *oh holy demoness*, but some of us are actually doing important work these days."

Strife and Envy stood back, still cleaning the black blood off their knives, ignoring the banter.

It was my time to scoff. "Like stealing Mikayla. You know I summoned Blake. Why the hell are you here?"

James shrugged in his Watcher uniform. *How the hell did he have a Watcher uniform?* "I was bored, and Blake is a little tied up at the moment...you could say. Anyways. I also don't know what you're talking about."

Envy stepped up beside James, her pink hair that was cascaded over her right shoulder was speckled black with demon blood. *"Yeah, yeah.* Either way, when we get Cander and Akira out of this mess, you know Anock will have us hunting Mikayla again. And you also know we are all team Blake. So your evil ass better not have hurt him." Strife walked up, taking Envy's hand before kissing her cheek.

James took in the demon Watchers from Fellen's Realm of emotions with a disgusted look on his face. "Does Jax know you shit-heads are backing up Cander and trying to kill him? Also, please! I'm the good brother, remember?"

I didn't catch the girls' response as I looked around. No one had seen us take down the Ivy's guards, and it almost seemed too easy. Although the Ivy did always have weak security. I hadn't planned for Akira to be taken to get ready but it worked out. After she left, Ian pissed and moaned before stomping off somewhere, which gave me time to put *my own* backup plan into motion. If we were going to take out that little shit, Jax, the Ivy's council, *and* steal Pearl, we needed help. Akira was too new to her powers and if it was just up to her and me, we'd fail. We just had to play this plan out the correct way for Akira to be the one to kill Jax. *I couldn't.* Strife and Envy being Watchers themselves couldn't. Shithead James could, but then that left us with a Fated on the Watchers, and that shit didn't help the first time when Blake was in Hell. James down there would be a fucking nightmare. James *was* a fucking nightmare the two days he *was* there.

I zoned back into the conversation to see Envy and all her pink hair and attitude getting into James's face. "We know you have her. We saw you and Blake *both* leave with her! Also, nice job trading Blake for Ander, by the way. You really are a piece of shit to lock up her guardian angel."

James's wings broke free and I knew it was time to intervene. "Enough! I don't know how much time we have. You all know enough of the plan so we can counteract Lilith's betrayal. It worked out that I saw the real plan, or we'd be dead, but Akira doesn't know that I know. Let's keep it that way and stay hidden. When you see her head this way that's your cue, James. I'm counting on you so don't screw me on this."

James scoffed. "I'm an angel, *remember*. My inner light-"

Before he could finish whatever idiotic thing he was about to spout, Strife interrupted by laughing as I once again cut them all off with a rush of power. "We don't have time for games! If we don't do everything perfectly, down to the last second, Lilith will have our asses. Got it?"

James cracked his knuckles while the girls nodded their heads.

James pulled back in his wings once more as he took a step towards me. "And if things go south?"

Strife and Envy knew what was on the line if we fucked this up, but I still didn't appreciate the concerned looks. "Then you take your cube and get Akira and the girls and leave. Did you find where Lilith has her friends?"

"Yeah. But there's something you need to know about that." James ran his hand through his hair. "Akira's familiar is there."

I thought back to the last demon who ever had one. It didn't surprise me that Axel would have tied a Magical to Akira but how the hell wasn't I able to pick that up? And if that was the case, how did it got captured?

"It's a cat that her friends kept calling Aldus Snow. They have no idea it's a witch." He said shaking his head in disbelief.

"Witch or warlock?"

James scoffed. "The aura was purple. Witch."

"Her friends...I picked up they were humans, are they?"

"From what I can tell."

"FUCK!" I turned and grabbed my hair. I was hoping that

her father roped in a guardian angel as a hail mary but that was obviously out of the equation. I didn't think Akira had known about her familiar if she didn't know about who she was or what her dad was. But how had the familiar kept itself hidden this whole time?

Familiars were witches or warlocks that were attached to another demon via a deal. Like supernatural bodyguards, and they could take the form of anything. But they still had a human body. They could only stay in their familiar form for so long, so how the hell did that thing stay hidden? Was it Akira's security? Or the housekeeper? If the familiar died, so did Akira. It was as much attached to Akira's soul as that annoying demon she picked up when rescuing me. So this was a huge fucking problem.

I shook my head from the thoughts when I realized I was getting crazy looks. "Lilith knows too. She even taunted Akira with having her familiar and I didn't catch it. Fuck!"

I turned again facing my backup. "So now we have two problems. I just don't understand why the familiar would let itself get taken. It has magic."

Envy sighed. "Well, if the familiar has grown an emotional attachment to Akira, it probably cares for her friends. It might be able to get itself out but not them. Either way, we have to speed this up. With our Queen dead, we can't leave our realm unprotected for too long. And now it seems we have another problem to deal with, so we need to hurry."

"Right." I nodded, thinking of the shit storm we were heading into. Akira couldn't know. Not now at least. This would distract her more.

I turned down the tunnel to the Bessel. This was my last chance to rid the world of that motherfucker and maybe get the girl. It was now or never. I looked to my team and they nodded while pulling their weapons.

"Let's get this over with."

15

THE QUESTION

I leaned over and whispered so that the guards behind us couldn't hear. "I have a plan."

Fasive looked shocked but reigned it in. "I thought you were trying to get *into* the Ivy. What do you mean a plan?"

I glanced back only for one of the guards to growl at me to keep walking. I let out my own growl in response. When did I become a prisoner?

"I can't explain everything right now, but I want to help you. Can I trust you?" I asked a little louder to be heard over the commotion of the Bessel up ahead. It sucked I was being paraded through the middle of their city wearing nothing but a sheer white dress that showed everything. *Everything.* I'm guessing that was the point because Fasive took time decorating my naked body with shimmery glitter paint and stuck white and black jewels on my tattoo. She also put them in my hair. I felt like a glitter Goddess, and if I wasn't about to be kicking ass, this would have been beautiful. Unfortunately, it was just more humorous than anything.

"You can." Fasive said with a small nod before looking back to the floor. I let out a sigh of relief because I could hear the truth in her words. Even though I hated her looking down at the ground, I was glad I got her to walk next to me instead of behind me. In the short time we'd known each other, I had been trying to show that she should be treated with respect.

The members of the Ivy stopped their activity as soon as we entered the Bessel, leaving the place abnormally quiet and extremely awkward. There were hundreds of Sirens in here, most giving me looks of hate while the others gave looks of lust with roaming eyes over my exposed body. My heart raced in my chest and I squeezed my hands tight at my sides trying to calm my nerves. I hated being shown like prized cattle. Plus, what would happen if they decided to fight us to save the council? There were a lot of them and only Cander and a very naked me. Well and there was Ian...but we didn't know if he'd been corrupted yet. So he was a wild card that was better left alone for the time being.

Raise your head and be confident. Our plan will work, and also, you're looking fucking delicious fiancée.

As soon as Cander's voice ran through my head, my heart skipped in my chest, and heat rushed through me. I just hoped he couldn't see how his voice affected my body. I also wasn't even going to think about how much I liked hearing him call me that. I looked up to see him standing at the entrance of the Dome next to both Jax and Ian. He looked like he'd been pulling at his hair. It was both sexy and fun to look at but it also gave me a sign that he'd had his hands full with the guys at his side.

Jax wore what looked like a black military uniform and gave a half-ass smile when he saw me. Before I knew everything he did to me and found out that he was evil incarnate, I probably would have been tripped up by his sexy lips. All I really wanted to do now was tear them off and shove them up his ass. Ian was wearing jeans and a tight black shirt and was doing nothing but shooting red eyes at the other two males to his right. All I could do was sigh.

"Guy problems?" Fasive whispered as we got closer.

"Too many to count girl."

I could tell she wanted to laugh but she curled in her lips inward instead. No matter what happened with this Ivy mess...I knew I'd found a friend in her, in just the short time I'd known her.

Cander stepped forward and the other two guys followed suit, leaving me immediately overwhelmed by the male testosterone in the air. It quickly faded when I locked eyes with Cander's whose were full of lust.

"You ready?" Cander asked in a husky voice, and the double meaning wasn't lost on me. Was I ready for the ritual? Was I prepared to help take down the Ivy's council and kill Jax? Was I ready for him? There was a lot I needed to be ready for, and honestly, I really wasn't. At this point I was just going with the flow and it was too late to turn back now.

I nodded, unsure if I could keep my voice steady.

"Fasive." Jax nodded in the way of greeting towards the redhead.

"Asshole, nice to see you again." She said only sparing him a small glance and sarcastic smile before looking back to the ground. *Oh yeah, she is so on the friend list.*

"You know him?" I asked her.

"We used to date." She said looking up for a second. "That was before I realized he was an asshole."

I snickered and was glad for the break in the tension. Unfortunately, it only lasted for a second before the doors opened. I realized the hundreds of Sirens in the Bessel must have only been a portion of the Ivy because the Dome was filled to the brim with spectators. Sirens spread out on both sides of the walkway, sitting in stadium seating that went all the way to the thrones where the council sat. I swallowed before taking a deep breath. Cander was right, no more hiding.

I raised my head in a show of confidence, right as Cander spoke into my mind once more. *You got this. Remember the plan.*

"Akira Black, please continue forward." Pearl's voice echoed throughout the Dome. I could hear her voice as if it was right in front of me even from being as far away as I was.

"Well here I go." I muttered right as Fasive whispered good luck and stepped away. Apparently, this part I had to do alone.

The guards followed me up to a raised platform in front of the council before rudely shoving me down and telling me to kneel.

Apparently, Pearl's little show was a huge deal because she was dressed in an extravagant pearl-colored gown mixed with lace and pearls that was long enough that the train laid over the steps leading up to their seats. Her brothers both wore light blue tuxedos that looked like bad 80's prom attire and I had to cough to cover up my laugh. Good Satan, they looked horrid.

"Akira Black, you were here exactly three days ago. At that time you did not pass automatic entry into the Ivy. Do you know why that is?" Pearl asked sitting up straighter in her throne while lifting a finger to her chin.

"Because my scales and gills were not the right color." I said straining to keep the sarcasm at bay.

Coughing in the crowd to my left caught my attention and I glanced over for a second seeing Cander and a super tall blonde guy next to him covering up a laugh. He obviously wasn't a Siren if he was blonde and it made me wonder who he was.

Pearl cleared her throat and I looked back at her irritated face. "You did not pass automatic entry because you do not hold pure light within you. With that said, after much delibera-tion...we decided maybe we were a little *too* harsh." She stood using the arms of her throne as support. "Maybe it's time to give the evil-hearted Sirens in this supernatural world a chance." She looked around eyeing the crowd as murmurs started throughout that she quickly silenced with a raised palm. I wanted to roll my eyes. We were all demons, but yeah, sure, let's think there's pure light in us.

"Apollo, our savior and mentor, has given us a solution for this very problem. The Acceptance Ritual. In this ritual, you will drink a truth serum and we will perform a series of questions. Easy, *simple questions* that I'm sure you will have no trouble passing. And if you do pass, then that's it, you're in. Simple *and* harmless. We at the Ivy believe in second chances. We believe in the potential of good in demons. There can be a better way. So that is why, Akira Black, we are giving you the chance to enter into this Ritual and become a member of our great society. So...do you accept?"

"Yes."

"Excellent!" She said while clapping her hands before sitting back down. It was so obvious this was all for show. Lilith really did have it down to exactly what would happen. This whole thing was almost irritating. If she was powerful enough to predict the future, why couldn't she have simply come down here and got the job done herself?

A rumbling of the floor had me looking down to see an opening. The floor slowly separated and a stone altar rose up in front of me. Once in position, a glass vial tube with a shiny yellow liquid so bright I almost had to cover my eyes rose up from the stone.

These people really had a thing for the dramatics.

"Drink." One of the brothers demanded once all the rumbling quieted.

I was nervous about drinking it, but with a shaky hand I took the warm glass container. I lifted it, prying out the cork lid quickly before I chickened out. *Here's to hoping this doesn't taste like cat piss*. I looked to Pearl right before I lifted the tube to my lips and drained the hot, tasteless substance down my throat.

Instantly feelings of nausea and dizziness came over me. I dropped the vile letting it shatter unintentionally on the stone altar as the warm liquid seemed to slide down and touch every inch of my insides. I reached out and held the altar while closing my eyes and willing the feeling to subside. Cander never told me if I could die, but I wondered if it was a possibility now with how bad I felt. I really hoped this shit was approved by the FDA.

"Now," Pearl spoke with a smile in her voice. When I opened my eyes, there were two versions of her intersecting back and forth. I closed my eyes again to help my light-headedness.

"I just have one question for you. To love or to lust?"

I looked up and laughed feeling extremely confused by the question. "That's the question? I don't understand." I slurred out.

Snap out of it Akira. Remember the plan!

Cander's voice boomed in my mind and I put my hands up over my ears. I shook my head to try and snap out of it like he said, but it wasn't working.

"Yes! Will you choose to be a light Siren that *doesn't* murder and can *love*, or will be you choose to be a murderous demon forever lost in Hell with your lustful ways. *To love or to lust Akira?* That is the question."

"I don't want to kill." I said looking up at her.

Pearl smiled. "Well, then this is a pretty easy question then isn't it?"

"Why not both?"

"Answer the question!" She yelled and I straightened up. I watched Pearl as she made her way down from her throne. Her brothers escorting her down the stairs. The dizziness was fading and I was starting to be able to function once more. Behind her throne stood Jax and I wondered why he would stand up there. One of Lilith's possibilities flashed through my mind. The one where Jax *did* make a deal with Pearl to accept me into the Ivy so I couldn't kill him. That had to be the one that was playing out.

She's just giving you a pointless question. Remember, she's going to accept you either way to honor the deal with Jax.

Cander said into my mind. I looked over at his intense face, but not before catching Ian's smirk from where he stood behind him. I also caught Fasive's worried face looking between them. Something was about to go down.

Or she made a deal with Ian, and you guys have this all wrong. The demon on my soul said.

Between the serum, Cander, Lilith's plan, and this little shit demon, I was going to have a brain aneurysm.

"I SAID ANSWER ME!" She screamed, bringing my attention back to her approaching form.

Intense pain shot through my head with another round of dizziness. Before I could stop them, the words flew from my mouth echoing throughout the vast space. "I CHOOSE HELL!" I screamed and the wooziness faded.

A wicked laugh came out of Pearl, almost like she knew I would say that. "And why is that? Why are you wanting into the Ivy Tribe if you want to be a murderous whore?"

"A murderous whore who's a virgin?" I countered back as another round of punishment hit me. This time in the form of a cough accompanied by a splatter of black blood covering my hands. Apollo wasn't playing around about this serum.

Pearl and her brothers were now right in front of the altar. "So, to love or to lust?"

"To love." I said as everything started to fade. Pearl's laughter filled my ears as I looked over to see Cander fighting his way to get to me.

Cander screaming my name was the last thing I heard.

I startled awake, sitting up fast with my heart beating out of my chest. The dimly lit room I was in spun a bit before righting itself. My head felt like someone had repeatedly hit it with a baseball bat.

"Headache?" An amused voice asked.

I looked over to see the blonde guy I had seen earlier in the ceremony sitting next to the bed I was in. He was wearing the same black, weird looking uniform I saw Jax in. It immediately put me on edge.

"Who are you? Where is Cander?" I remembered seeing him rush the guards before passing out. *Shit*! *How long had I passed out for*?

"I'm James. Cander went to intercept the bomb from coming into the Ivy." James scoffed before rolling his shoulders. "It was supposed to be my job to stop you from letting the warlock in, but you can see how that worked out."

"Bomb?"

He shook his head before standing up and moving around the room. It was then that I realized I was in a huge bedroom. "Yeah, you know. The bomb that you were going to bring in."

I scooted to the edge of the bed, glad to see I was back in my regular clothes that I had laid out on the beach before my swim. "I wasn't letting in a bomb. The warlock had dust for me to throw on Pearl's door, to lock her inside until we..." I stopped talking and my heart sank when I realized what I just revealed. I had no idea if this guy was a friend or foe.

"I'm here to help you and Cander. Along with some of the other Watchers."

"Oh." I said still feeling unsure if I could trust him or not. I looked around for Fasive but it was just him and me. I moved to the vanity since he was blocking the door. "Okay then. I need to get to Cander."

"Nope." He said while running his hands through his hair.

He had the same hair as Cander. Longer on top and short on the sides.

"What do you mean...nope?"

"You and I have a date with Jax." At that he rolled his shoulders again and two enormous white wings grew from his back.

"HOLY SHIT!" I yelled stepping back into the vanity to get away from him.

"You're a mermaid and an angel surprises you?"

"I. Umm. Yes?" I mumbled before straightening myself out.

He scoffed and opened the door for me.

"I don't understand what's happening right now. Did I die?" I looked down and patted myself to make sure I was real. I felt real.

James sighed before shutting the door again. "Listen, we don't have the wonder twins for very long before they have to return to their realm. If you want help killing Jax, I can help you but we don't have a lot of time."

"But you're an angel. Aren't you supposed to...you know?" I asked raising a hand to his wings, then pointing to myself.

He laughed and the sound clenched my lady parts. *Eek*. This was not the time to add more guys to my list. "I'm not going to kill you. I'm not technically a full angel, but none of that matters. I'm here to help so let's save the Q and A for later, okay mermaid girl?"

I nodded. "Umm, yeah. Sure." This time when he opened the door, I pointed for him to go first. Cander may trust him but that didn't mean I did. How did I know that he wasn't on some super-secret mission from Heaven to wipe us all out, and I was his first victim?

He laughed before stepping out into the tunnel. "I'm *not* going to kill you."

I followed him still unsure about the situation. "Why are you in a uniform like Jax?"

"I borrowed it from my brother. Now. After you passed out Cander kind of lost his shit and since I'm not technically supposed to be here, I had to bail. I waited for things to calm down and when they did, Pearl announced there will be a welcoming party for you in an hour. That doesn't give us a lot of time seeing as you slept for 20 minutes of that."

"Shit!" I patted down my leather jacket to feel for the knife Cander gave me in the inside pocket. I had half an hour to trap Pearl and kill Jax. The reality set in and my hands started to shake.

James looked over catching me at the start of a freakout. "You ever kill anyone before?"

"Does it look like I go around killing people?" I asked sarcastically.

He scoffed. "It looks like you stepped out of a modeling catalog."

We were right before the entrance to the Bessel when James turned fast grabbing my arm before pulling me into a random room. "HEY!"

"Shhh!" He hushed before turning me around to see Cander tying the warlock's hands together behind his back with black rope. The warlock mumbled and grunted from behind his gag. Two girls in the same outfit as James and Jax stood close behind watching Cander tie the man up. One had dark skin and bright blue colored hair that was shaved close to the scalp on one side and long on the other side that was curly and had braids. The other girl had the same hairstyle, but hers was bright pink, and her skin color was white. The crazy thing about them was their bright orange-colored eyes and lips. It was trippy.

James stepped back from me pointing to the girls. "Akira, meet Envy and Strife. Envy and Strife, Akira. Blue is Strife. Pink is Envy. There, now girl power and all that." The girls glared at him while I just shook my head in confusion.

"Go team!" James said throwing up his hands.

"Shut up man." Cander said working the rope.

James sighed, pulling out a knife that he flipped in the air repeatedly. "*Sorry, sorry*. I'm just getting a little stir-crazy right now. Don't we have a Watcher to kill?"

"Does it look like I'm baking cookies, dick? This fucker was hard to take down." Cander said. He caught me looking, so I walked up and pointed to the poor man. He looked like he'd taken the beating of his life.

"Ugh. That was supposed to be the help for the plan." I said unsure of how fucked we were now.

Cander looked up, his gold eyes glowing with irritation. "You mean the real plan you never told me about? The plan that had *this* asshole attaching a bomb into your hair and resulting in the Ivy blowing up? Along with us in it."

I stood there and thought about it. "The plan that Lilith showed me just had him handing me a powder that was supposed to seal Pearl inside her room. Why do you think he would attach a bomb to me?"

"Because I saw a glimpse of what she showed you when we kissed before we portalled here. I'm guessing the demon on your soul can't block everything when you're distracted." Cander said as he stood.

"Lilith made it clear that if you were to find out the real plan, it would fail." I countered as the worry started to set in. "She even showed me the outcome of what would happen if you found out. We would fail and Pearl would kill us."

Envy stepped up beside Cander. "Cander explained to us that you felt pain after the deal, you have to know that she was planning on betraying you. Did you not consider that is how she was betraying you? Feeding you false images and scenes to secretly play out her own plan. Lilith couldn't give two shits less if you bring back Pearl alive or not. She's never hidden the fact that she wants to see this place burn. Instead of the possibility of you two failing, I can see now why she would want to make sure that the Ivy was destroyed while she had the chance. She's been after Pearl ever since she made that deal with Apollo."

"That doesn't make any sense. Why now? You're telling me she couldn't have just sent a warlock down here before and snuck a bomb in herself?" I asked.

James nodded. "Akira's right. If that evil bitch wanted to blow this place up, she would have done it before now."

Strife walked around the room before kneeling down in front of the warlock that still laid on his stomach, watching us through the gag. "There must be something we're missing." She said pulling on the warlock's black hair for him to look up. He screamed out in pain through the gag from the position she had his neck in.

"Envy...maybe it's time to work your magic on him?" Strife asked looking at Envy, who gave a wicked smile and stepped forward right as Strife picked the man up by his hair and flipped him onto his back. The man grunted and cried out. I was just blown away that someone so small could flip a whole man over by his hair.

Cander walked over standing next to James and me as we took in the show. "Do we have time for this?" James asked, looking between the scene and the door.

Envy smiled as she stood straddled over the warlock, that now whined while trying to struggle away. "There's always time for this." James just scoffed in response before rolling his eyes.

Envy sat down hard on the man's lower stomach, causing him to cry out again. She reached out and undid his gag quickly grabbing his chin before leaning forward to stare into his eyes, as her own started to glow.

"Tell me what makes you envious, little one?" She whispered in a sultry voice as her nails grew and turned into black claws like mine had. They pierced his face and tiny rivers of red blood poured out down his cheeks and onto his neck. The warlock stayed utterly still with a glazed-over stare. It was clear she had him in some type of trance.

"The Siren." He answered.

Envy looked over to me then Cander with a confused face before looking back at the man. "Which Siren?" She asked.

"The one in this room."

"Why?"

"Her power."

I looked to Cander, and he glanced back with a frown. It was clear this was news to him.

"Why?" Envy asked again, squeezing his face harder.

"I want to be Lilith's favorite...but she is her favorite." He said before coughing and I looked down to see Envy had now wrapped her other hand around his throat. His confession confused me, I couldn't be the demon Queen's favorite. I'd only met her once. Plus, there had to be a lot of demons more powerful than me. Although Crow had said something about my visions being special.

"Why?" She continued.

"Because Akira's mother had a guardian angel." This answer caused the room to still.

"Doesn't everyone have a guardian angel?" I asked in a low voice to not mess up Envy's process.

Cander leaned over. His lips were so close to my ear that his warm breath tickled my neck. "Only the important humans that can change the course of history."

I looked over staring at him like he'd grown two heads. "So?"

Cander just licked his lips and crossed his arms facing the interrogation again.

Envy eased up on squeezing his throat. "Are you envious of Akira's light then?"

The man laughed and it was evident by the look in his eyes that his trance was breaking. "Her powers."

"Who was Akira's mother? Why does Lilith favor Akira?" At this question, Envy went back to squeezing his neck.

"Dark Nephilim." When he went to continue, Envy interrupted by slamming the man's head down against the ground. "LIAR! The only light and dark mixed are the Fated." Envy screamed in his face.

"Akira's grandparents were Magical and Nephilim. Lilith needs Akira's blood with Apollos serum in there."

Cander stepped forward now standing over the man. "Then why were you going to blow her up?" He asked.

"The charm would have saved her."

The door flew open behind me, giving me a small stroke as I jumped away and flew into James.

Fasive rushed in her eyes wild. "It's time! Pearl's in her room and the brothers, Jax and Ian are in the throne room. I think they may have seen me and I couldn't use my power to get out of there, so you need to go!"

I looked over at the sound of a crack to see Envy standing up with the warlock's head in her hands while his blood poured out of his head and squirted out of his body. It was the first time I'd ever seen a dead person, not counting Ian, and nausea immediately rushed over me. I turned watching Envy toss the man's head before she licked her hands.

Holy shit, what had I gotten myself into.

A hand on my shoulder broke me out of my sickness and I looked up to see Cander. "You ready to become a Watcher?"

"And be evil?" James asked before getting hit in the stomach by Strife.

"And be a powerful fucking Siren?" Envy added.

"And be married to his sexy ass?" Strife chimed in pointing to Cander.

I looked around the room, and I knew my fate was sealed. There was no turning back after I walked out of this room. This wasn't one of my books, shows, or favorite movies. This was real. Life and death, and I had people to save. So was I ready?

I looked over to Cander wiping some blood from his cheek. "Count me in."

"*A*kira, wait."
        I turned to see Cander hanging back in the room as Strife, Envy, and James followed Fasive out.

"Yeah?" I asked, taking in his intense stare.

Cander stalked slowly towards me as soon as the door shut, leaving us alone. The air was immediately filled with his powerful lust. He stepped into my personal space before backing me up against the wall. "What are you-"

"Shhh." He whispered while raising my chin. My heart hammered in my chest with nervousness as he brushed back my hair. I fought the need to close my eyes at his comforting touch. "Are you sure this is what you want?"

I sucked in a breath trying to control myself when his own breath tempted my kiss. I looked down at his full, sexy lips. "Is this what you want?" I countered.

I barely got the words out before he grabbed my shoulders and kissed me hard. My body sang better than any Siren's melody from his mesmerizing lips, need rushed through me. I wasn't sure what brought this on, but holy demons, I didn't want it to stop. I reached up grabbing hard at his hair and pulled him closer as his hips rolled into me and I moaned into his mouth. This kiss wasn't like the one where he fixed my arm, which clearly worked. This...this was fucking ecstasy, desire, and pleasure, so intense it made me dizzy. I throbbed with need, and my blood tingled with the power he was feeding me. I'd never before seemed so sure of anything in my life until this moment. It was clear that he was my opposite that fit me like a glove. Even though we found each other through some messed up demon deal, it felt like we were made for each other. Cander's bite to my lip, drawing blood, brought me out of my thoughts and fueled my desire more. Right when I went to grip his erection he pulled away with wild eyes and messy hair.

"If you fuck like you kiss Akira Black, you are never leaving my bed." He said in a husky voice. "I would do anything to continue this but we have to go. I just wanted to give you a little power boost and make sure you knew what you were getting into."

I cleared my throat and looked down to hide my blush. "Right. Okay. I'm ready, and I know what I'm getting into." I paused, taking in some much-needed air before staring into his captivating eyes. "So does this mean you're going to keep the deal with my dad and marry me once I become a Watcher?"

"We made a deal Kira...and I plan to keep it. You're stuck with me now." He chuckled and the clench to my lady parts only made me realize how soaked I was. *Great! Hopefully I wouldn't go full Siren over him, making me wet.*

"You know I can't fight, right?" I asked as he ran his thumb over my bottom lip, wiping away the blood.

"I figured that out, but you did just kill two sharks."

Unable to help myself I grabbed his hand and pushed his thumb into my mouth, sucking on it, while locking my eyes with his. What I wouldn't do to have this be something else instead. I twirled my tongue around his thumb while I continued to tease him.

He sucked in his breath, his gold eyes glowing with promises as he pulled out his thumb. "*Fuck.* You know playing with fire will get you burned little girl?" He growled before grabbing my throat before applying pressure. Was it fucked up this was turning me on more? "You also know I'm not going to go easy on you the first time, right?"

I chuckled seductively. "I was hoping you'd say that." I

glanced over to the door feeling our time was running out. Cander and I had gone from enemies to slightly fucked up soon-to-be lovers. I wasn't sure how that had happened, but I wasn't complaining. If I had to be honest it was always him from the very moment he busted into my birthday dinner with his red eyes and bad attitude. With the uncertainty of what was about to happen, I just hoped I wouldn't lose him now.

"Ready?" I asked when I realized I had zoned out, only to be met with his intense stare.

"For this?" He paused with a wicked gleam in his eyes as he grabbed my hand and kissed it while opening the door. "Hell yeah."

16

THE PARTY

"*P*earl will be along shortly." One of the brothers said upon our entry into the Dome. It had been transformed in the short time since we were last in here to a grand party with decorations and fancy tables.

I leaned over to Fasive. "How the hell did they transform this place so fast?"

"They have a warlock on call." Her whispered response made the others in our group tense up. It was clear having a warlock present, and on Pearl's side, was a bad thing.

James clapped his hands together before rubbing them and putting on a brilliant smile. "I didn't know this was a party, but I'm glad I came." He grabbed a champagne flute off a nearby table, pretending that Cander's friends were just here to celebrate my recent change to the Ivy. Pearl's brothers, Jax, and Ian sat around a circular table that was the closest to the thrones. It looked weird to see them all sitting together, and my awareness spiked that we could be facing off with Ian as well as the brothers and Jax if, for some reason, they had converted him.

The brothers glanced at each other, suspicion in their eyes

before looking at James. "What's a Fated doing at a party for a Siren?" The brother to the left of Jax said.

James chuckled. "What, just because I'm a Fated I can't celebrate with a longtime friend?" He asked, looking back to me and I got the hint to play along.

I stepped forward next to him, touching his arm for a second before dropping it. "James and I go way back."

The brothers scoffed at this. I wasn't sure if they bought it or not. It really didn't matter if they did though. We were running out of time before this place would be filled to the brim with Sirens. Time was of the essence, so this small talk shit would have to end soon.

Ian rolled his eyes before downing a glass of champagne and standing. "I can attest to that. Before I ever knew about this world James was a frequent visitor to the Black residence. I just never knew what he was."

I wanted to squint my eyes in confusion but Ian's hard stare told me to agree. It also told me he was trying to speak into my mind but it wasn't working. I was kind of glad for the asshole demon on my soul. But it made me wonder...why was he confirming James's fake story? Maybe he was still on my side?

"Thanks for saving me from Crow, asshole" I said to Jax, playing along like I'd been tied up in Crow's bar this whole time.

Jax looked shocked. "What do you mean save you?"

I rolled my eyes. "I went looking for Cander, and Crow locked me up in his bar!"

Jax scoffed before standing and looking to the brothers that also stood. Ian took a step back and immediately the room filled with Cander's power, who had stepped to the other side of me.

"You can drop the act Akira." Jax laughed. "I know your plan." His intense stare with his cat-shaped pupils were intimidating enough on their own that I almost took a step back. I held my ground instead and clenched my shaking hands into fists at my side.

"We know *all of your plans*." Jax said, pulling out a knife and pointing it to us.

The brothers laughed creepily together. "Did you really think that once you were part of the Ivy, you would be able to kill?" The one to Jax's right said.

My heart skipped in my chest. Lilith said it wouldn't matter if I joined the Ivy, that it wouldn't affect anything. Had she lied about that too?

You dumb bitch, you actually thought Lilith would keep her word. Deemmoonnn. What part of that in your tiny, and I mean super small brain, don't you understand? The demon hissed in my head.

Cander stepped forward, cracking his knuckles. "I don't know what the fuck you're talking about, man. You or these creepy-ass douche-bags."

Jax laughed at this. "OH! My bad!" He put his hand on his chest, feigning surprise. "So, you're not trying to have Akira kill me to exact revenge for killing your brother and fucking your wife? Which I might add was an *amazing fucking lay*. I mean, the shit she could do in bed! Did you know we were fucking before you guys even got together? I guess you could say I was her...dirty little secret."

A deep, feral growl erupted from Cander and I looked over to see Envy place a hand on his shoulder, trying to calm him. A growl rose up in me as well at Jax taunting Cander, but I held it back. The guards that I didn't know were in here, came out of nowhere and now approached slowly, their harpoons aimed towards us. I looked back to see more at our backs. We were surrounded. I could also see Ian making his way towards our group as he backed away from the trio of crazies ahead of us.

Before Cander could respond, Jax continued. "Damn. That means I didn't have to trick Akira into joining the Ivy? You mean I didn't have to pretend to be her father and get movie star boy to become a demon?" He stepped forward, stalking towards us but a flare of Cander's power made him stop in his approach. "I didn't have to write a fake letter from her mother, and make a deal with Pearl?"

A growl erupted from me, followed by my arm spikes unleashing. I released the power I felt from within, directing it towards Jax, who stumbled back a step looking shocked. "*Aww.* Baby Siren here has some power!" He said with a laugh looking to the brothers that laughed as well. Fuck them. I grabbed the knife under my jacket but stopped before pulling it out, deciding instead to hold on to it and have it ready.

"Enough of this!" Cander's rough voice broke through my growls. It was clear they knew the plan the whole time, so what was the point of us sitting here chatting. We needed to get on with this before the tribe showed up.

"*Okay, okay.*" Jax said, throwing up his hands. "I'll stop, but I just have one question. Now that she can't kill, how are you planning on getting your revenge?" Jax lifted his knife, pointing to James then Ian. "Angel boy and the movie star are the only ones who can kill me now that Akira is bound to the Ivy rules. I mean, I've always known about the Ivy and their inability to kill, but I just thought that was like..." He paused, looking at us like we should know what he was trying to say. "*You know*? You can't kill, and if you do, you get a slap on the wrist sort of thing? I didn't *actually* know that the serum they make you drink, from the almighty Apollo, *actually* stays your hand!? It's crazy, right? Who would of thunk it?" He flipped his knife in his hand, catching it with precision.

I swear my heart dropped into my stomach. We hadn't known that. Lilith never said anything about it, so if that was true, that meant I really couldn't kill Jax. I wouldn't become a Watcher. I wouldn't save my friends and family. My evil dad wouldn't wake up and...I looked over to Cander, not wanting to face reality. We would never be together.

Cander caught my eye and must have been thinking the same thing. Panic was on his face like I'd never seen before. Tears I didn't know had formed threatened to break free, and I felt James put a hand on my shoulder. I looked over to see his heartfelt face.

How had we failed so fast? Was this really it?

"Actually." Ian stepped forward, now giving Jax a hard stare. "Akira isn't part of the Tribe. You aren't the only one that can make deals."

What?

Jax tilted his head and narrowed his eyes. I spoke before he could continue his evil villain monologue. "Ian, what did you do?" I stepped forward, unsure of the wrench he might have thrown into our plans.

"Five minutes." I heard Strife whisper at my back. Shit, we were almost out of time. I looked to the guards that still stood positioned in a circle around all of us.

Ian looked over with a frown. "Akira I'm sorry. I told you, you are mine and I meant it. If you joined the Ivy, I wouldn't ever be able to be with you, and I couldn't have that."

"Damn, this is a party after all." James said at my side, dropping his hand from my shoulder. I ignored his banter because this wasn't the time to joke. This could make or break us.

"What did you do?" Cander growled. I could see his muscles tensing at my side.

"WHAT I HAD TO!" Ian yelled, throwing his arms up in the air. "It was clear no one knew about the serum not letting the Ivy kill. So when I found out, I made a deal with Pearl." At this, the brothers stepped forward with deep frowns. It was clear this was news to them as well. "If I promised to kill Lilith after my powers form, Pearl would give Akira a messed-up batch of serum and reject her from joining the Ivy."

The room quieted, and everyone stilled to the point I was sure they could hear my heart beating out of my chest.

So, I wasn't in the Ivy? I looked to Ian unsure of what this meant.

Jax's and the brothers' laughter brought me out of my confused thoughts. "*You* kill Lilith?" Jax asked laughing loudly while holding onto a chair for support before wiping his forehead with the hand that held the knife. "Oh damn, that's hilarious!"

Ian growled, stepping forward while pulling down his shirt from his shoulder to show us a black circle on his back. "It's true! I would do anything for her and anything to be with her! Including killing Lilith!"

Jax looked at the tattoo, then to James. "And how do you feel about retard over there saying he's going to kill your mother?"

I looked at James shocked at the news. He just shrugged. "More power to the little guy."

Jax scoffed, looking towards me. "Still...even if you can kill, *which* none of us know for sure until you get into that pool and we see your scales, you would still have to have Cander's knife. You do know who Cander really is, don't you? I mean, if you were going to kill for him, I would have to assume you would know his true identity?"

I glanced over to Cander wondering what Jax was talking about, but he wouldn't meet my eyes.

"Stop it!" Cander yelled, making me jump.

The guards stepped forward some more, but before they could get too close, the brother to the left of Jax yelled. "Bar the doors and announce the party is canceled. Go protect Pearl and keep her locked in her room!" The guards looked to each other then backed away as the brothers made their way to sit on their thrones.

"Well, that was easy." James whispered at my side.

"We always love hearing a good Bible retelling. Go on." One of the brothers said to Jax, who laughed evilly, before grabbing some champagne and taking a drink. *Bible retelling*?

"You know it was your mother who corrupted him." Jax lifted the champagne glass to Cander even though he was looking at James. "That's why they both ended up in her realm."

"What the hell is going on?" I yelled, losing my patience. The itch to kill was growing by the minute the more I held the knife inside my jacket. I was ready to kill this evil asshole...if he would just shut up.

"You see. If that thing you are holding is in fact the knife, which I doubt since it was hidden far within my mother's realm...you would be suffering the side effects of it as we speak. I mean, even without the knife, doesn't Cander just make you want to kill things?"

I had no idea what this asshole was talking about, but I wished he would get to the point. I looked to the pool wondering if I really needed to get in there to prove Ian's story, or if I could just trust that when it was time to slice Jax's throat I would be able to do it.

"Akira." Jax said, and I looked back when he whistled like a dog. "Pay attention, baby girl. You are standing next to the notorious Cain from the Bible."

My initial anger at being called to like a dog faded into confusion. "His name is Cander," I said with annoyance, looking to Cander. Who still refused to meet my eye but continued to stare and fume at Jax like an enraged man.

"*Wrong!* James's mommy poo influenced Cain to kill Abel, his brother, because she wanted to make them both demons in her realm. She had a thing for them I guess. *Anywho*. When they both came down to Anock's Realm, his magical healers took Cain's mark off of him and made it into a knife. You know the protection mark. They turned it into a killing knife. The knife would be the only weapon capable of killing a Watcher. It was hidden for a while, until I got it of course. The only thing left for him to do was change his name. It also helped not having two Cains in Hell, I mean, that shit was confusing. Unfortunately, everyone still knows him as the demon of murder."

My mind flew back to Cain and Abel in the Bible. I knew one brother had killed the other, and that was it. Obviously, I never went to church growing up. I can see now why they prevented that from happening, but it did make me a little dumb on these things.

"Is this true?" I asked Cander, err, Cain.

"Does it matter?" He snapped back. My anger grew and the knife in my hand heated.

"Not really asshole, but it would have been nice to know!" I yelled back, pulling the knife from my jacket, exposing it for everyone to see.

"Is this the knife?" I asked, holding it up in the air.

The sound of a glass flute shattering on the ground came from Jax as he stood and took a step back putting the round table between us. "HOW?" He asked.

Cander laughed. "It wasn't that hard. I knew once Akira had Ian at the lake, it was time to get the knife. So I went and killed some of your mom's guards and left my signature in her throne room. I knew she would summon me. Being summoned is the only way into the back realm past the throne room. So I came back and set Akira up and had her play along with your little plan for a bit while I searched for the knife. I had a strong feeling she wasn't going to sleep with you. I didn't exactly know you were planning on joining her to the Ivy. I just knew that you had *some* plan to stop me. I found the knife at the last second and had Crow trade his freedom for mine and gave it to Akira." Cander shrugged like he wasn't the very first murderer in history.

Jax's face grew redder by the minute, and the brothers

stood from their thrones. "It doesn't matter! We still don't know if she can kill! What's to say you have your new little murderer fight me, only at the last second, she isn't able to finish the deal? Huh? What then?" Jax looked manic and was slowly backing up towards the brothers.

"And what about our deal, you little shit?" Jax asked, looking to Ian who then looked to Cander with a clenched jaw. "You made a deal with me! You can't break deals, remember? You kill Cander, and I will let you become a Watcher?"

Cander's eyes went red beside me and I knew there was no protecting Ian now. If Ian had known Cander was the demon of murder would he have made that deal?

"We still have a deal." Ian said, facing Cander and flexing his muscles as he cracked his knuckles.

James and the girls scoffed beside me, and unfortunately, I couldn't help but agree. Ian's obsession with me had gone way too far this time. If he took on Cander, there was no way he would live to see his deal through.

"SO GET THE KNIFE FROM THAT WHORE AND KILL HIM!" Jax shouted.

My temper flared and my arm knives came back out as I stepped in front of Cander. I would like to see Ian try. The blade in my hand was sweaty but I gripped it hard, waiting to see what Ian would do. I felt Envy and Strife getting restless at my back and I knew the time for talking was over. Finally.

The moment Ian's red eyes turned towards me...I knew that son of a bitch would pay.

How dare he say he loved me, then turn around and listen to Jax like a whipped dog. Let alone make a deal with the same demon that impersonated my father and almost bound me to the Ivy in the first place!

I saw the red flare from behind my eyes and knew that my eyes were shining red. The loud rustling at my back left told me James's wings were out. The time for play was over. I knew they all had my back. I wasn't dumb enough to think this wasn't going to be a shit show, but it didn't matter. Time was wasting, and Ian sealed his fate when he sided with Jax.

"You want this knife, asshole?" My demonic voice was loud and the creepiest thing I'd ever heard.

I laughed, feeling the euphoric joy of getting pay back on the son of a bitch who wrapped his hands around my throat.

"Come and get it."

---

*C*ander

Akira stood in a fighting stance, holding my knife in front of us all. The very people that could take down everyone in this place and not blink an eye. Protecting me, an all-out killer...and some of the most notorious villains in history at her back. James, who was a psychotic angel responsible for the apocalypse. Envy, who converted Hitler, and Strife who was responsible for World War I. Yet she stood protecting us. Even though she wasn't at full strength, and had no knowledge of how to fight, or even who she was protecting. Her ass in those tight black leather pants was sexy, but her demon voice was the turning point to the hard-on that I was now sporting and clearly on display through my tight jeans. This would be an uncomfortable fight. I willed myself to calm down with the reminder I would be fucking that ass when this was all over.

I couldn't believe that little fucker Ian actually, sort of, saved us from the deal we made with Lilith. It didn't surprise me though when he turned right back around and fucked us when he sided with Jax. Seeing Ian's red eyes trained on Akira darkened my skin without me trying. I wasn't sure how she was going to take my true form, but he'd brought my demon out when he threatened my girl. I ripped out of my jacket as my dark blue skin transformed, and my claws broke free.

"James, protect Akira and help her take out Jax. Strife and Envy, we have the brothers and Ian. *Kill them*." I growled right as Akira let out a demonic roar and rushed towards Ian. Before I could worry about her taking Ian on, James flared his wings catching Ian in the stomach and sending him flying back over the tables. I watched as Akira changed course, rushing towards Jax. She darted over tables and jumped over chairs like a demon-possessed, never letting her eyes break from her target. Seeing James at her back I knew she was protected, and I took off for the brothers determined not to fail her. The sound of doors slamming open and shouts erupting had me looking behind us to see the Ivy's guards rushing towards us.

"WE GOT THEM!" Envy shouted, pulling out her double blades as Strife pulled out her Katana.

I focused back on the task at hand knowing even if there were a hundred guards, those girls could take them. They were legendary for their fighting skills and if I didn't have a task to complete, I would have liked to watch the show. I wasn't sure what demon skill the brothers had taken, but it clearly wasn't shit. They ran as soon as they saw me changing and I wondered why Lilith even thought this was going to be hard for me. Adrenaline pumped through my veins at the thought of killing again. I needed it like a drug addict needed their next hit.

Right as Akira approached Jax...she dropped to the ground. *Fuck.*

"WHAT THE HELL?" James shouted, grabbing the knife and standing over her in protection. Jax would try to kill Akira before she could wake up, and James couldn't kill him or we'd be fucked.

I looked over to see the brothers running for an exit, before looking back to see the girls kicking ass. Envy impaled a guard on his own harpoon right as Strife ripped another's heart out.

Jax laughed, bringing my attention back to Akira as I

approached them. "This is the girl that was supposed to kill me?"

I ignored the taunt and picked her up, backing away. "Stall him!" I shouted to James before taking off for the pool. "And don't use the knife!"

"My pleasure," James said in a demonic voice with glowing red eyes. He clearly stole his brother's powers, switching sides again. I just hoped he hadn't fucked Blake, wherever he was.

I kissed Akira's forehead before lowering her into the water and letting her go. "I'll be right back, Kira."

I watched her float down in the water for a second, knowing she would be safe in there. Sirens could breathe underwater, and the pool was spelled to be bottomless. When she awoke from her vision, she would be in Siren form and just swim to the top. Thankfully from my little time married to that two-timing bitch Ariel, I actually learned something. The lights surrounding Akira confirmed she was transforming and would be fine. I took off for the little shits before they could leave.

I pushed aside tables and chairs, letting them fly out of my way as I closed the distance to the brothers. My anger and excitement grew. "You really thought you could get away from me?"

"Please! Please don't kill us!" One of the brothers begged.

"We will do anything!" The other said. "Even a deal!"

I growled in response, rushing my power towards them.

"I don't make deals with cowards."

I woke with a start, opening my eyes to see my black hair floating in front of me in the water.

Where am I?

It only took a second for awareness to hit me, and I sucked in water from the shock and looked down and all around to see

I was in mermaid form floating in the water. I just came out of a vision that I didn't have time to figure out, so I would just have to re-examine it when it was over.

How the hell did I get in the water? The last thing I remembered was running towards Jax.

Jax! Fuck! I shook the sleepiness from my eyes and darted up in the direction my senses told me that air was located. I pushed my tail hard, and relief hit me when I saw the rippled surface of the top. I was in the pool in the Ivy. I didn't know how or why I was in here, but I was. As I swam up, I looked down to see my white and black scales. Ian *had* told the truth, he'd stopped Pearl from joining me to the Ivy. But it still left me back to where I was in the first place, an unclaimed Siren.

I broke the surface and wasn't prepared for what I saw.

Strife stood by the edge of the pool ripping through an Ivy guard's throat with her elongated teeth at the same time she ripped his arms from their sockets. The guard's black blood flew into the water, and I barely held back the bile rising in my throat. I floated back, looking around to see James with Jax up in the air in a choke hold. His white wings and red eyes looked freaky. My nerves rose when I realized I couldn't see Cander or the brothers.

The sound of a grunt from Envy broke my concentration, and I looked up to see Ian had punched her in the nose and they were squaring off.

"SING!" Strife yelled. She swung out her sword in a circular motion slicing three guards entirely in half at once. Their top halves slid off the bottom halves of their bodies while black blood squirted into the air.

"Me?" I asked. Unsure of what she meant.

"YES!" She screamed in frustration. "Lure Ian into the water and kill him, damn it! Do something!"

"But won't it affect everyone?" I yelled back.

"Just do it!" She yelled before screaming out in pain as she took a harpoon to the shin.

I sang, zoning in on Ian's face. This wasn't the Ian I thought I'd fallen in love with. Turning into a demon had brought out his worst qualities and made him crazy. I needed to undo what I'd helped to create.

After the first verse Ian turned to me mid-fight as the red died down in his eyes.

"KEEP SINGING!" Strife yelled, fighting off more guards as Envy ran to help her.

I sang more as Ian shuffled to the pool and locked eyes with him as I willed him to swim to me. I floated back away from the edge taunting him in. He slowly sat on the side of the pool before lowering himself to me. I thought back to the pond and wondered if this was how he looked when I accidentally drowned him the first time. I sang louder, feeling the power in my song and continued to float further back as Ian now swam towards me trying to keep up. He was still in his clothes and shoes, with that weight along with his pathetic doggy paddle he wouldn't last long.

I swallowed and sang out another verse as the reality of what I was willfully doing, hit me. I was killing him. I was singing him into a trance until he drowned, and this time it was on purpose. Could a demon die by drowning? I faltered in my song, trying to figure out if this could kill him? Could *I* kill him? He was going to kill Cander. He was even willing to fight me for the knife. Did I want to kill him? No, I didn't want to kill anyone but he wasn't giving me a choice. There was no choice in any of this. I would have to kill. My temper flared, and I continued my song.

"YOU'RE GOING TO HAVE TO RIP HIS HEART OUT TO FULLY KILL HIM." One of the girls yelled, but I stayed focused on Ian.

The blue eyes that had once made my heart flutter, now

made me sad. I watched as he started to sink further down. The water was currently right under his nose as my trance still held him but his muscles were starting to give in, making him slowly sink more and more. I looked at his perfect movie star good looks and swallowed hard. He should be on the big screen, and yet here he was, drowning again because of me. Was he conscious underneath all this and screaming for help? Or would he die peacefully in this trance until I ripped his heart out?

I glanced up at the last second before Ian and I sank beneath the surface to see Cander screaming for James to stop as he rushed towards him. He grabbed the knife before James could give the killing blow to Jax. I finished the song and watched Ian convulse in the water, his trance turning into fear as he reached out for help. I needed to make a decision and I didn't have time to think about it. I shot away from Ian as his eyes rolled back in his head, and he sank down into the water. I needed to kill Jax before someone else did.

Breaking the surface I jumped out naked and rushed towards Cander. Jax shuffled back after taking a kick to the gut from Cander before lunging back at him. James was shouting something at me, but I couldn't hear yet from the static that filled my ears from my near kill. Luckily, I managed to catch the knife he threw at me though. Cander turned in time to dodge another punch from Jax, and during the commotion, I ran alongside his huge demon back to sneak around and attack Jax.

Hearing rushed back to me all at once as Cander turned away, exposing me at his back unintentionally, right as Jax swung out with sharp claws aimed directly for me. I had no time to move away. Right as the claws were about to pierce my neck, a piercing scream penetrated the air as Fasive pushed me out of the way and took Jax's massive demon claws herself. I landed hard on my right shoulder with a thud and crack to the side of my head.

I looked up to see Fasive laying on her back, holding her throat as she coughed up black blood that also squirted out of the open wounds on her neck. I rose with new resolve as anger tinted my vision red and my body shook with power. Her pained eyes swung to me as Jax stood over her laughing.

"Look what happens when you get in the way of a Watcher, Fasive."

I took advantage of his distraction and slammed the knife down hard at his back. Opposite of where his cold black heart was, and with how long the knife was, I had no doubt it pierced it. His demonic screams brought out my own demonic laugh. I didn't know how good it would feel to get revenge.

"How does it feel to be stabbed in the back, motherfucker?"

---

*C*ander

My beautiful, demonic Goddess did it. She fucking killed him in the most poetic form and it brought black tears to my eyes. Unfortunately, there wasn't much time to celebrate. She had to complete the full change to demon *and* Watcher and all within the tiny amount of time that Jax's heart still beat in his chest. And we couldn't do it for her, but only walk her through it.

"Akira, listen to me!" I begged as I shook her shoulders to snap her out of it. She was still laughing like a maniac and if she didn't get with the program, he would come back to life. "You have to carve his heart out, and you need to eat it! Now!" I yelled, gently pushing her to the ground. I pulled out the knife handing it to her as I rolled Jax over onto his back, giving her access.

"NOW AKIRA!" I yelled in a frenzy, hoping it wasn't too late.

She laughed some more before going silent and dropping

her head, and with her cascade of hair, I couldn't tell what her eyes were portraying. "Akira?" I asked, shaking her shoulders. She was a dark demon now, and she would be hit with blood lust, but we didn't have time for her to feed the usual way. She needed to eat from him. Unfortunately, when demons turn, they don't behave precisely how you want them to.

I felt Strife and Envy walk up behind me, and I glanced back, looking around to make sure there weren't any more threats. "How the hell do I snap her out of this?"

"Umm." Envy said, her eyes going wide as she looked towards Akira. "I don't think you have to."

The all too familiar sound of a chest cavity breaking brought my attention back to Akira. In one motion, she punched a hole in his chest and ripped out his heart. She shoved it into her mouth and ripped into it with her serrated demon teeth. We all watched in shocked silence as she ate his still-beating heart, and her final transformation took place.

Fuck...she was the most beautifully evil thing I'd ever seen. Her red shining eyes turned molten silver with a beautiful red ring on the outside. It was trippy and I loved it. Her hair transformed colors and would continue to from now, based on her mood. Apparently, she was still feeling dark because her hair changed back to the black color it had been after she'd killed the sharks.

A feral scream pierced the air when she finished the heart, and we knew she was starting her transition to a Watcher now. She would be the first Siren Watcher *ever*, and her power would be something even Pearl couldn't rival. As her tattoo grew, she transformed right there on the tiles outside of the water, tail and all. Her spikes grew out of her black tail and glowing arms. I knew when the transformation was completed because she zeroed right onto me.

Her power grew in the air as her silver eyes started to glow.

Once a demon zeros in on a kill after transforming nothing

or no one could stop them. I thought it was adorable that she felt she could take me, but also knew it was dangerous for everyone else in this room, even Strife and Envy.

Akira growled at me, before licking her lips.

I readied myself and looked back to the girls.

"Run!"

17

POWER GRAB

*P*ure power flowed through my veins like I'd touched a live wire. But unlike a human that electricity would blow right through and fry, this power circulated through me, it was one with me. I was *alive*.

I was *powerful*.

I was *more*.

Well...I was *more*, until I had a two-hundred and fifty-pound demon on top of me.

"I will own you!" I threatened, trying to wiggle out from underneath him. I wanted to embrace the power and kill everything and everyone in my path, but instead, I was being held down.

"AKIRA!! We have to leave! You can own me later!" The blonde demon that held me down yelled. He looked familiar in a way that made my body ache with need. I knew him from somewhere, but whoever he was, it wasn't really important.

I *needed* to kill.

I *needed* blood.

"She doesn't hear you, she's still in a rage." A female voice said to my left. I huffed, bringing my knees up to get him off, but that only resulted in someone else holding down my legs.

I felt rage like I'd never experienced before, so strong it made my head pound. I screamed using my Siren power to take out the ones holding me down.

This just caused the asshole on top of me to laugh. I quieted down when I noticed the beating vein in his thick neck. "Akira quit it now! We have shit to do! You just need-"

I sank my fangs into his neck before he could finish and drank deep. "OWE! FUCK AKIRA!" I don't care what he thought I needed...I *wanted* his blood. Lust, safety, and strength filled me so much that I moaned. When my prey tried to move away, I latched on harder, resulting in him hissing a sound of pleasure. Apparently, I wasn't the only one liking this.

"Jesus, save it for the wedding." Someone said, but I was in too much bliss to care. As the warm blood flowed down my throat, it slowly replaced the rage with a lust so deep I couldn't stop myself from rubbing against him.

Him?

Cander?

Cander!

I broke free from his neck, reality slowly crept back into my senses. What in the actual fuck? Was I just drinking Cander's ...blood?

Cander's gold eyes shone bright with desire. I blinked. I was confused at what was going on as I swallowed the remaining blood in my mouth.

Awkward. Even more awkward that it tasted good.

Cander slowly climbed off me, and I noticed all the scratches and bite marks all over his arms and chest. Then I looked down to see me, naked. Cander cleared his throat, gaining my attention as Strife and Envy stood beside him, watching me. "Feel better now?" He asked.

As I stood, my muscles ached painfully, so no, I wasn't

feeling better. I went for a general answer instead. "Umm. I guess." I cleared my throat and tried to gather my thoughts. Jax was dead. I remembered killing him and eating his heart, but the rest of what happened was a blank. So I had chosen a side, and I was a Watcher.

"Did I do that to you?" I asked Cander, who threw some clothes at me.

"I've suffered worse. I had Envy search through the rooms to find you some clothes. We have to get moving, so hurry."

I looked around to see the entire stadium-sized Dome filled with dead Siren guards as I got dressed, which was a bit hard to do over the half wet, half-dried blood that caked my body. I swallowed hard when I saw Fasive lying dead on the ground with her vacant eyes staring up to the ceiling.

"The brothers?"

"Dead." Cander said, holding a hand over his bleeding neck. It looked to be slowly healing as less and less blood trickled out from under his hand. "But James is gone." He paused and looked to Strife and Envy, who seemed pissed. "And he took Pearl with him."

"WHAT?" I yelled as I finished tying up my hair. "We need her in order to save my friends and Liz! What do you mean he took her? Like he went to save her for us, or like he went rogue and just...fucking took her!?"

Envy walked over placing her thumb under my eye, I started to flinch back until I realized she was just wiping blood from my face. "After you raged out on Cander, we decided to go capture Pearl. When we got to her hall, the guards were already dead, and her door was open. We ran into the room to see James disappearing into his cube with Pearl unconscious and tied up. We are guessing he went rogue."

His cube? I shook my head. I would save that confusing question for later.

"FUCK!" I yelled and was shocked to hear my demonic

voice. I cleared my throat and took a deep breath to calm myself. "What are we supposed to tell Lilith now?"

Cander stepped forward. "Seeing how she didn't really want Pearl in the first place, but your blood filled with the serum, I'm guessing it doesn't matter that she's gone."

"I highly doubt that she is going to be happy, even if that *is* her real plan. We made a deal, remember? This seal on our back is from the deal we made saying we would bring her Pearl and kill the brothers! If we don't honor it, what will happen to my friends and family? We can't just show up empty-handed!"

"I know that Akira, but I think you forget about our limited fucking time. We have to figure out how the hell to get out of here before the whole tribe finds out what happened and attacks us!" Cander said, grabbing at his hair in frustration.

That didn't make sense. The Ivy was physically unable to kill, so they wouldn't be able to kill us. Still, I guess going against thousands of angry Sirens, whether they could kill or not, could be bad. "Fine." I said, already concluding in my head that there wasn't any point staying here in the aftermath of our death capade.

"Not fine." A new voice said, startling us all to turn around.

A man in a bright gold gladiator looking suit, equipped with a blinding white sword, stood in front of the councils' throne. His long blonde hair hung loosely tied back, and his expression read relaxed, but his muscles were taut and looked ready to attack. He was huge. The size of a freaking giant, and how long had this guy been standing there?

"Oh shit." Envy said, taking a step back, and I looked over to Strife, who held an equally worried expression.

Cander, however, looked annoyed. "What brings the great Apollo to a demon den? Come to check up on your lackeys?"

Holy shit, Apollo?! Like, the mother freaking Apollo sun God? Wait, no. He's an angel. Oh...yeah, I could see how that would be bad. I continued to freak out in my head as I glanced down at my bloody self. He was probably going to kill me first.

Apollo laughed, bringing out his sword and leaning on it. "Oh, Cain. You never fail to amuse me." He paused, looking over to me and my heart stopped. "I see you added a new member to your team. Doesn't surprise me you eventually took out Jax, little shit had it coming."

I looked over at Cander in confusion. *Umm.* Why were they talking like buddies? Was he not here to kill us?

Cander stepped forward slightly in front of me. "We don't want any trouble. Let us leave."

Apollo laughed, standing up straight to swing around his sword like a baseball bat. I gulped so loud Strife looked over and rolled her eyes. "I can *tell* you don't want trouble." He stepped down the stairs making his way towards us as he looked around at the carnage and the floating Incubus in the pool. "I mean the way you took all the guards out it was clear you didn't want any trouble. I understand why you took out the brothers. Of course, I'm no fan of *any* demons, but those guys were just the worst."

"Wait. You were here the whole time?" I asked, unable to help it, even as Cander gave me a warning look to be quiet.

Apollo stood by the pool now, poking his sword into Ian, making him bob up and down. I cringed thinking of how much of a shitty person I was. "No, I just showed up. But I do have a one-way looking glass into this place whenever my serum is used." He paused the poking to look at me. "So, thank you for that. And the show. It was quite amusing."

Before Apollo could get any closer to us Cander spoke up, pausing his advance. "What do you want?"

"I don't want anything. But I do need someone to lead the Ivy now that you unfortunately took out the previous rulers."

"It was the Fated on *your* team that stole Pearl." Envy said, rolling her eyes before putting her hands on her hips.

Apollo scoffed. "James is on *no-ones* team if you hadn't noticed, but that's beside the point. I need someone to rule now, and I think I have the perfect team."

When he turned back to look at Ian in the pool, I spoke up before losing my nerve. "Why do you even care? This is a tribe of demons?"

He turned away before poking Ian again with his sword. He was like a little kid. Well, if the little kid was ten feet tall and looked like a very sexy gladiator. "I understand you're new, so I'll explain. This tribe of demons has decided to join together so that they wouldn't kill. They were made demons against their will. My job is to protect the Almighty's humans, so put two and two together. I could just kill them all but...There is a balance between these things. So, to sum up. I can't. There has to be an equal balance of demons to angels, and if this is the only work-around, I'll take it."

Apollo turned around and walked back to the thrones before turning around again to face us. I was pretty sure we all took a collective sigh when he put some distance between us. "Now. Jupiter and Laken, it's time to work."

Huh?

A flash of bright light had me covering my eyes, but it only lasted a second before it calmed back down, and I was able to see again. On either side of Apollo stood two ordinary-sized angels. Wings and everything. I looked over to Cander to see him grip a dagger at his side, while Strife and Envy did the same.

"Jupiter, please clean this up," Apollo said to the male angel to his right. Jupiter stepped forward and began shooting light out of his hand that evaporated the dead demons and blood wherever it touched. I gulped, hoping he didn't decide to shoot the light at us.

"Laken, please raise the Incubus and Succubus. They are

the new council." The female angel with purple eyes and matching wings stepped towards the pool.

Was he talking about Ian and Fasive? I looked around, but everyone else here was a Siren.

Cander cussed under his breath. "No! No! No! Are you really going to raise that little shit to lead the Ivy? Are you fucking kidding me? He's not even a Siren!" Cander growled at Apollo, his eyes turning red.

"It makes my job easier. Pearl and the brothers were given the power to convert their own people when they became Sirens. Sirens still need to feed on your kind to be turned in the Ivy. Especially these, they don't complete kills, so they're not as strong. The Ivy's Sirens need power boosts every so often. Pearl and the brothers were given special powers to take care of their members, but now that they're gone, they will need someone in their place. Instead of just gifting another Siren or Sirens, these two shall do fine."

Apollo appeared behind us in a flash of light that had us turning around and Cander drawing his blade, aiming right at him. I readied myself for a fight right in time to see Apollo stab his sword through a Siren guard crawling towards us that we hadn't seen.

He turned back to us, rolling his eyes before looking at the angel shooting light. "Jupiter, you aren't focusing on your intake. Push more from the base of your power!" He shouted towards the male angel that clinched his jaw in anger before going back to work. I just stood there, unsure of what the hell was happening. Apollo took in my confused look, scoffing before placing a hand on my shoulder. My whole body tensed as I stood utterly still, watching his other hand spin his sword point down casually on the ground. "Interns from the academy. These two are set to join the Chosen soon, so I broke them out for a field trip, but obviously, Athena's little meditation sessions aren't working."

Athena? The academy? Jeez, my head hurt.

He spoke like we were old friends, but I couldn't do anything but swallow and hope he didn't drive that sword through me. Cander's growls interrupted Apollo before he could continue, and I looked to see him glowing red. Like his whole entire body. I'd never seen that happen before, that must be bad. Uh, oh.

"Remove your hands from her. Now." He growled in a deep demonic voice I'd never heard before. I looked to Apollo then back to Cander in a very uncomfortable showdown.

Apollo raised his hands in defeat, stepping back and laughing. "Calm down Cain. I'm just trying to connect with the newest Watcher. You know we're buddies, right?" He asked before flashing away in another bright light that had us turning back around to see him again on the thrones.

The sound of coughing from the pool and a shocked gasp to our left had me looking to see Ian climbing out of the pool and Fasive sitting up holding her neck.

"They can bring people back from the dead?" I asked in shock.

"Correction, Laken can bring *demons* back from the dead. They were never alive, so technically it doesn't count. But yes, Laken is our newest intern to the angel of death, Samuel." Apollo answered, even though I wasn't talking to him.

Ian looked at me as he climbed out of the pool then to Cander, who stood at my side. I looked away, wondering what he saw and what he remembered from me trying to kill him.

"Approach me, Incubus and Succubus. You will now be the new leaders of the Ivy."

It was clear by Fasive and Ian's faces that it was the last thing they wanted to do. Instead, Ian started to make his way towards us, at least, until Apollo's voice boomed across the space.

"YOU WILL APPROACH OR GO BACK TO YOUR DEATH!"

I looked to Fasive, who sighed, looking to us before slowly making her way towards Apollo, who looked like an avenging angel with his gold wings spread wide. I wanted to say so much to her now that she was alive. Mainly, thank you since she saved my life.

Ian and Fasive stood before Apollo, while Cander, Envy, and Strife continued to give each other looks like they were having a silent conversation.

"We need to go." Cander said, leaning over and whispered in my ear.

"You're free to go. No one will stop you." Apollo said not even looking at us.

I watched as Ian and Fasive were made to kneel before him. I wondered what would happen to them and the Ivy, but we didn't have time to stick around.

I looked back one last time to see Ian and Fasive surrounded by a white light before Cander pulled me from the room.

Cander and I stood outside my Hollywood mansion. When I asked Cander why we were here, he said that he had James do some recon work and that he'd found out this was where Lilith was keeping my friends and Liz. Kind of poetic that everything was coming to an end where it had started.

"Akira, there's something you need to know before we go in there."

I turned to Cander biting the inside of my lip to keep my emotions in check. I was a badass demon now, sure, but if things went wrong and Lilith decided to kill them...I wasn't sure

I would be able to handle it. So if he was about to say something overly emotional, I would bawl my eyes out.

"James found something out when he originally came here, and I want to give you a heads up. Maybe try to lessen the blow."

"Yeah?" I nodded impatiently, waiting for him to continue. What could be so important that it warranted stalling our rescue mission.

He sighed. "Your housekeeper isn't who you think she is. She is a witch...and your familiar."

I waited for him to say something else, but just he continued to stare at me like I was about to lose it. I stepped back from him and laughed. "Liz? An actual witch? Like with a pointy hat? After everything I've been through since meeting you...seeing mermaids and angels I guess it doesn't surprise me that witches are real. But why do you think she's a witch? And why is this something we need to talk about right now? I can deal with that later...if they make it out alive." I leaned forward, grabbed his wrist and started to walk. "Let's go."

He pulled back on his wrist, stopping me in my tracks. "Akira, she is your familiar. Meaning she has promised to protect you. It also means she's your cat."

I laughed louder this time. "My *cat*?" He was definitely making shit up. "You think that the woman who raised me is a witch? Yeah okay, that kind of makes sense...but you also think she's my cat?"

"Akira, it's not funny. I'm not making this shit up! Have you ever seen your cat and your witch-"

"Liz!" I corrected.

"Fine. *Liz*, in the same place together? No. You probably haven't." He concluded without even hearing my answer.

I scoffed. "Aldus Snow is a male cat, Liz is a female and- "I paused, trying to get my thoughts straight. "AND, I thought we didn't trust James!"

Cander growled in frustration before taking an intimidating step towards me. "Why would he lie about this? Besides, familiars can change into *anything* to stay in disguise to protect their charges. Hell, if she chose it, she could have become a houseplant for all you knew. I'm guessing she chose a cat so she could be close to you at all times, and a male one to throw off anyone from guessing she is a witch!"

I flinched, taking in the implications of it all. Cander was right. I had *never* seen Liz and Aldus Snow in the same spot or together *ever*.

"Fine." I said, shifting impatiently. "We will deal with this later. Let's go."

"Yes, but you need to know that a familiar will tie themselves to the soul of the one they protect."

"Meaning?"

"Meaning if she dies...so do you."

I sighed. "Great, now I have two things attached to me and a snowball's chance in Hell of saving myself. Can we just go and get this over with." I turned away, heading back for the house.

Was I ready to fight? No. Did I think I could win? No. But it wasn't like I had a choice now.

"Wow. No thank you, Cander, for the information. Nothing?" He grumbled as we walked to the front door.

I shook my head in disbelief. "Yes, thank you for the information. Sorry I don't seem too receptive, but this is kind of a serious moment right now."

Cander ignored me as he opened the front door, and my heart stopped at the sight. The house I grew up in was in disrepair. The entryway was wrecked with broken furniture scattered in pieces all over the marble floor. Holes were in the walls. The entryway chandelier was broken and hanging by a thread from the ceiling.

"Holy fuck." I whispered with my heart in my throat as tears sprang to my eyes. It was apparent they beat the holy living shit out of Liz. Either that or she put up one hell of a fight.

A stream of bright red blood smeared across the floor heading in the direction of the basement caught my attention. I gulped down the fear rising within me.

"They aren't dead yet." Cander grabbed my clammy hand and led me forward to follow the blood streak as I stumbled along.

Alex, Kaydence, and Liz were in this mess because of me. They were captive to a demon Queen of Hell, and being a newly turned Siren wasn't going to do shit in saving them. Even Cander was no match for Lilith. Walking along my torn up house, I knew there was only one thing to do when we faced her. I would give myself up if I had to. Hopefully that would be enough to save them.

"Ah! There you two are!" Lilith exclaimed as we followed the trail of blood to my home theater. I looked to see Alex, Kay, and my cat all tied up in the back row of chairs with Lilith's goons standing over them. I looked over to Cander then back to my friends and cat. So Cander was telling the truth.

Lilith walked to us before surprise filled her expression. "You chose a side I see! Congratulations!" Her joy was rehearsed and it made it hard to stop the red glow of my eyes.

"Your son took Pearl." Cander explained, watching Lilith's snake make its way over to us.

Lilith tsked, walking over to me calmly before petting my head like a dog. "I know. It's too bad that you weren't able to complete my task but I guess since you still got rid of her...I can go easy on you."

"AKIRA!"

I heard Cander's scream a second before Lilith threw out her hand and blasted power at him, knocking him into the movie screen. I heard the shatter but didn't have time to look before Lilith's snake shot forward and sank its fangs into my neck so fast, I barely had time to register what was happening.

The scream that came from me was inhuman, and not in a demon way, as I fell to the ground. The pain was so extreme light dotted my vision. I transformed into my Siren form without warning. My tail flopped hard against the ground as I struggled to pry the snake off, but it was no use.

"That will do, Maliki." I barely heard Lilith say before the snake unhinged it's jaw from around my shoulder and slithered back to her. I whimpered on the ground while trying to hold onto consciousness.

Lilith laughed and I looked up to see her snake pouring my blood out of its mouth and into a glass container Lilith was holding. "I know you figured out my real plan, but I still didn't think you were stupid enough to try and break a demon deal. I fully expecting you to bring Pearl to me. Yet she is not here." I felt a tingle on my back shoulder blade. "But since I'm feeling generous and was able to get what I needed, I will lift the deal from you. Just this once though. But let this be a warning...the next time you disobey me, it will be your last."

My head lulled from the snake's venom and I let it fall hard to the ground, I no longer had the strength to hold it up. I strained to look around from my position on the floor wondering if my friends and Liz were still okay.

"They will live. For now." Lilith's voice brought me back to look at her. She turned and then her goons, snake and herself disappeared into a puff of black smoke.

The loud mewl of a cat was the last thing I heard before I gave into the venom.

"*S*o, we won't ever see her again?" The muffled sound of Kay talking brought me slowly out of my dreamless sleep.

I stirred, immediately recognizing the soft hands that stroked my forehead.

Opening my eyes I was surrounded by the ones I loved most. I couldn't hold in the sob that escaped me. "You're all okay." I gushed, sitting up and rushing into my Abuela's arms. She held me tight as I cried and let the past three days of emotions out.

"Of course we are, mi nieta." I heard Alex's hushed voice whisper to Kay that the term meant my granddaughter, and I laughed before pulling away from her warm embrace.

"I am so sorry." I looked at each of them and noticed Cander leaning against the wall by my closet watching the show. "I didn't mean for any of you to get hurt." I sniffed and went to rub the tears and snot when Kay shoved a tissue in my hand.

"We know that, sweetie. Cander caught us up on everything, and for the record O.M.G! You're a freaking mermaid!! That is *so cool*!" I blew my nose as I sat back in bed.

Alex stepped forward, leaning over and kissing me on the forehead, which produced a growl from the back of the room. We all laughed.

Well, not Alex. His eyes went wide and he stepped back like I had the plague. The scene only made us laugh more, even Liz.

Alex leaned over from a safe distance and whispered. "*Umm*, is he single?" I shook my head and busted out laughing again. God, I had missed them.

"Side note. Abuela is a freaking shapeshifter!" Kay said, making Liz scoff as she stood up to straighten her usual outfit.

"I am a witch!" She declared.

The room silenced until all our held back laughter busted

out again. Liz just shook her head before kissing the cross around her neck and muttering prayers.

"Also, I love the hair. It goes with the whole demon-mermaid thing." Alex said, sitting in Liz's spot with a cautioned look at Cander.

I leveled Cander with a look that said to behave. "Thanks. I hate that I got you all involved in this."

Kay took my hand from the other side of the bed, sniffing up tears. "We thought you were dead. *Everyone* thought you were dead."

"Well, not everyone." Alex countered. "A lot of people thought you were on the run for killing Ian."

I sighed. "I *did* kill Ian."

"Ten bucks! I knew it!" Kay shouted, holding out her hand. Alex rolled his eyes and took out his wallet.

"You guys seriously bet on if I killed Ian or not!" I shouted.

Alex sighed. "Hey we were locked in a cage for two days, there wasn't a lot to do."

My head dropped with guilt until Alex lifted my chin. Then immediately dropped it at Cander's approaching footsteps.

Alex looked to Cander. "Dude, I bat for your team. Chill. But also don't." He paused, looking Cander up and down in a way that even made me blush. "That demon growl is pretty sexy."

"Uh...hello." I said, feeling super awkward.

Alex's face turned the color of lava. I looked at Kay. She looked at me, knowing what he was about to say so we joined in. "OH MY GOD! I DID IT AGAIN, DIDN'T I!" He exclaimed, and then immediately crossed his arms when he realized we copied him. "I don't say that phrase that much!" He pouted. Kay and I died with laughter.

Cander just rolled his eyes, clearly unamused by us. "Now that Lilith has your blood we need to get back to the mansion. There's no telling what kind of shit she has planned. We also have to figure out what we're up against now that Ian is in charge of the Ivy. You know he isn't going to let you go that easy." Cander said, reaching for my hand.

I pulled the blankets back and scooted to the edge of the bed as Liz came in with tea for everyone. My eyes filled with tears and I swallowed hard, trying to keep them in. I didn't want to leave them. They were my family.

"Tea first, then leave." Liz announced, pushing past Cander to set the tray on my coffee table. When Cander went to open his mouth, Liz lifted her head and gave him the best stare down he'd probably ever received.

I wasn't shocked when he grumbled something under his breath and went back to leaning against the wall in silence. I laughed under my breath that the big bad Cander was told what to do by a little old lady.

We all moved to the sitting area as Liz began to pour our tea. "This next part, you will have to do alone Akira." Her serious tone brought back the silence and my gathered tears. She forced a teacup into Cander's hands before sitting and pouring herself a cup.

"I have been with you from the moment your mother found out she was carrying you in her womb. She came to my home in the woods on a stormy night. I remember hearing the thunder crash before a frantic knock sounded at the door. I opened it to see her standing there with a tall man. He had onyx hair and silver eyes. I knew he was a guardian angel from his aura, but was confused as to why he would expose himself to the one he protected. And why the pair would be knocking on my door."

She paused in her story to take a sip of tea, and the clanking of the tiny teacup against the glass saucer pulled my attention to her shaky hands. Before I could say anything, she continued. "I had my home warded against any visitors that intended to do me harm. I knew they weren't there to give me trouble when they were able to walk in. It was the angel that spoke, explaining how the demon that Jade carried had to be born, and that they needed my help. Most of the demons born do not survive, this is known. To ensure that you were born safely, I became your familiar. Meaning my soul would attach to yours and help to strengthen it. As a witch, I am doomed to Hell for my demon blood. But due to my duty and sacrifice, her guardian angel gave me this cross that would allow my soul to arrive in heaven when my time comes."

I took a big drink of tea, trying to digest everything that was being said. "So, my mother knew my father was a demon?"

Liz leaned forward, placing her teacup and saucer down before brushing off the lint from her dress. "She knew. She also knew she would die. Akira, your mother worked for the Chosen."

Shock and anger flooded me, and I let the frustration out through tears. "So I was just a job to her?" I asked, my voice rising as I set down my cup. No. This wasn't right. "Liz, I have the letters between her and my dad! They were in love!"

She looked at me with sadness. "She could have loved him for real, but he was a target for the Chosen." I looked back at Cander who walked up and gripped the chair behind me. He looked down and shook his head. It was clear he didn't know this part of the story either.

"So what then...why did they make her get pregnant by him?" I asked, wiping angry tears away.

"I don't know that part of the story, and I wasn't meant to. We are almost out of time. You go now with your demon, and I will be here when you need me." Liz looked to Alex and Kay with a heartfelt smile. "I will protect them, but this part you do alone. You are woman now, and it's time to live your life."

I stood. "Just leave? Leave you, Alex and Kay? The only family I've ever known? And now I have more questions about my mom than I did before! I'm confused, and what if Lilith comes back?" I felt fear rising within me as I took a step away from them.

Kay and Alex looked to each other as they stood before coming over to wrap me in a bear hug that pulled a sob from my throat. "I don't want to leave you guys!" I cried into their shoulders, and the shaking of theirs told me they were crying as well.

Alex looked up and stepped back, giving Kay and me a moment. How was everyone okay with how fast this was moving? "Don't go having tons of demon babies and not sending me pics, okay? I also want pictures of any sexy demons and angels." She said with a tear-filled smile, before kissing my cheek and stepping back.

I didn't understand why everything was moving so fast. "I don't understand why I can't stay for a while if this is goodbye, why can't I stay?!" I shouted at Cander and Liz, who remained silent as Alex stepped forward, wiping the tears from my eyes.

"Promise not to wear flip flops with skinny jeans *ever again*." I laughed, but he shook my shoulders and continued. "If any demon, angel or otherwise says one negative word against Gerard Butler-"

"I know, I know. Kill them on sight. And the flip flop skinny jeans thing was one time!" I laughed through more tears at his serious face.

"One disastrous fashion choice of a time. Now, moving on. And what do we say when we have a bad day?" He quizzed. My throat choked up and I sounded like a dying cow, but answered anyway; with what was supposed to be our soon to be college motto. "Tequila o'clock, ticktock, and socks so they don't knock." I finished bawling into his shirt while he rubbed my back.

"That's our girl. Now go down there and be a badass mermaid in Hell." He lowered his voice and raised his eyebrows. "And for the love of God or Satan...or whoever, *please girl*, go have you some hot demon sex."

I laughed and gave him a huge hug.

There would be no planning college parties in our joint apartment, where we had wine mixers or studied for our exams together. I looked to Kay, who rushed over in another collective hug with us. Alex and I wouldn't attend any of Kay's runway shows in Paris, where we planned to get extremely drunk. Go to the top of the Eiffel Tower. Meet a mime...and then kidnap said mime. No trips to Australia to find all our dream husbands. There would be no watching Liz and Alex fight over decorating my wedding, or battle over baby names. Those plans would be on them to complete now, without me. There were so many other things I should be there for, but I had chosen my side. I realized to live... an extraordinary piece of me had to die.

I stepped back from them and wiped at my tears.

"I summoned them." Liz said to Cander.

"Summoned who?" I asked, clearing my throat.

Cander sighed but didn't answer me. A second later two figures in black cloaks with hoods that hid their faces, appeared in the middle of my room.

I stepped back, alarmed.

"Mi nieta, I will always love you. Remember you are special, loved, and wanted." Liz said, stepping back as the figures walked towards Alex and Kay.

I took a step forward to block the figures. "Cander what's happening?" I asked frantically.

He walked forward and took my hand, pulling me back from Alex and Kay but didn't answer. I started to pull away until I heard Alex speak.

"It's okay, Akira. We love you." I looked back to see him and Kay holding hands. Tears streamed down both their faces.

"Always," Kay said as the figures got closer.

"What the hell is going on!?" I shouted, trying to pull away from Cander, who opened a demon portal in my room. I looked back to see skeletal hands lifting out of the sleeves of the hooded robe heading to touch both Alex and Kay.

"NO!" I shouted as Cander grabbed my hand and pulled me towards the portal. "NO! STOP!" I screamed.

"You don't need to see this, Akira! Come on!" Cander shouted with one last pull that sucked me into the portal.

The last thing I saw was the skeletal hands touch Alex and Kay's foreheads before they fell to the ground.

18

PLANNED

I learned a couple of things. *One*, Cander could read my mind once again. He said Liz had pulled the demon from my soul. That all sounded complicated and scary, so I didn't ask any questions on that. I was glad to have the little shit demon gone, but now I was back to having Cander reading my mind. *Two*, his bike automatically went back to the weird white tree, which could be at the mansion or generally wherever he wanted it in Hell. When I told Cander that it didn't make any sense, he said that it was spelled by the twins to go wherever he wanted it to appear - and to stop worrying about his bike. The last thing I learned was that, no, my friends weren't dead...just their memories wiped, which was equally as bad. Yes, they were alive, but not to me.

"So, *all* their memory, from the time they were born until now or just the memories that included me?" I paused, taking a moment to run my hand over the hard, cracked ground that I currently knelt on. "And why would Liz betray me...us, like that?"

Cander looked over to me from where he currently leaned against the tree. "Just the memories they have of you, the twins would have just filled it in with someone else. Liz just did what she was supposed to do. Familiars are high ranking Magicals, right under the council of magic; she is a high ranking Magical. I'd only ever heard talk about her but had never met her. Supposedly, she was on the council a long time ago. She is probably one of the strongest living witches around. Now, if I *hadn't* been there, I don't know. She might not have reported it, but Magicals are obligated to keep the peace between angels and demons. They are the mediators between the two sides, with the main goal of hiding reality from humans. She most likely saw me and felt obligated to call and get a memory wipe."

I just raised my eyebrows at him as I looked up. If he thought that explanation did anything to answer my question, and not confuse me more, he was wrong.

"There's a lot to learn, but Liz did what she had to. Now get up, we have a lot of shit we need to cover. You're a Watcher now, and you need to be inducted. You need to learn about your job. I mean, we have people waiting to get into our realm, and the time for messing around is over. Anock is going to have our asses if we don't get back." Cander believed that was a good enough answer. To whatever the hell Magicals were. To the council of magic. To the unasked question of how did his explanation make any of this alright. It didn't, and my friends were gone. All the memories and life we had, now it was like it never happened.

Cander walked over to me and knelt in front of me, before reaching out and lifting my chin. "Akira, I know it sucks, and it may not seem fair-"

I took my chin back in defiance and stood, taking a step back from him. "It *isn't* fair, Cander! They wouldn't have told anyone! You know that! They would have died for me before they let anything happen, and I would do the same for them, and look at how I betrayed them!"

"It *is* fair! That's the way of things. Do you think you're the first supernatural who had to walk away from friends and family once they were thrown into this life? News flash, Akira, you're not! I know it sucks, I know you miss them, but it has to be done *to all* humans that find out." Cander stepped into my space, grabbing harshly at my chin that I tried to jerk away from him, but he just gripped it tighter. "I'm not the villain in this story, and where we are going, you'd do well to remember that."

He leaned forward, giving me a surprisingly gentle kiss before removing his hand and walking back to his bike. "Now, let's go."

I shed the last of the tears that had gathered in my eyes and wiped my face. I felt numb, and maybe it was from the whirl-wind of events that had taken place so fast, but it also could be that I hadn't been warned that was going to happen. My leg wrapped around the bike and Cander took off, while I continued to think. I knew he could read my thoughts, but I didn't care. He'd been pretty respectful of my thinking space and hadn't commented on my thoughts so far. I watched the dry ground pass by us, still in a trance-like state. *It just wasn't fair.* He could go freely between Hell and Earth because he was a Watcher, so that meant I could. I thought I'd be able to visit my friends and family, never thinking that they wouldn't be a part of my new life. I mean, yeah I was a demon in Hell and Alex would go to college, Kay would continue to model, but still.

Another thing that pissed me off was my absentee father. Why was he allowed to roam Earth as a demon, yet everyone else was in lockdown? Why was it okay for people to remember him, and my life and friends' memories were wiped as if I had just been gum stuck on the bottom of someone's shoe?

The sight of Crow's bar coming up fast made my heart hurt more. My friends were gone, and I would never get them back, and the one friend I did make in Hell was most likely dead, and Cander was just rubbing it in.

Cander? I asked, directing my thoughts at him. I was mourning my friends, Liz, my human life, and he wanted to rub salt in the fresh wound of Crow sacrificing himself.

The bike shut off, and Cander got off looking at me with annoyance. "Would you just stop. Stop acting like I'm trying to break your evil little heart. Suck it up, babe." He grabbed my hand and pulled me off the bike, as I sucked some much-needed air into my lungs.

Welp, might as well add this to the miserable Adele song/slideshow of shit images that would be circling my head for eternity.

We passed the bikes as we walked in, and a fleeting moment of terror stopped my pity party. "Holy shit! Who's taking care of the bar?" I asked Cander. His only response was to scoff. God only knew what the hell was happening in there. It was probably trashed. Knowing Cander, he was probably going to add to it, *shit* probably steal something. Like he took my friends' memories.

Cander let go of my hand harshly with a growl. "God, you're infuriating woman!" He walked ahead, wrenching the door open with unneeded force, and I chased after him.

"You were supposed to be taking care of this place!" I all but shouted, speed walking to keep up with him. I wasn't a complete idiot to know he wasn't at this bar because he saved my life, dealing with Lilith, and honoring his deals. Still, I guess I was really shouting at myself too. We both should have also thought of Crow.

"And he did."

It took a second for my eyes to adjust from the blinding desert light to an extremely dark bar, but I knew that voice.

"Crow?"

*A*fter my uncontrollably loud scream of excitement and me rushing into Crow's still handsome arms, Cander's possessive growls wrenched me out of Crow's embrace, and brought my attention to the fact that I had knocked out all of the customers.

I looked around with pursed lips and a guilty conscience, "Oops."

Crow laughed, going back behind his counter, as I made my way back to Cander.

"I didn't know you and Crow got that close?" He asked.

I rolled my eyes. "This guy saves your life, and *you* aren't that excited to see him alive again?"

Cander put his hand on my back, kicking a green-scaled demon on the ground out of our way, as he steered us to an open seat. "That's because I knew he'd be fine."

"No, he *hoped* I'd be alright. You're lucky I was back in my Siren form, or I wouldn't have been able to fit through that hole, man." Crow said, pouring three shots of black liquid.

I gave the liquid a look of disgust, remembering the sour taste of the last stuff he served me. Crow scoffed, "Just drink it, princess, or we're not friends anymore."

I snorted out a laugh when I heard Cander say something like, we can't have that, before lifting his shot glass in the air. I picked up mine as Crow lifted his as well, clinking our glasses together in a toast.

"To new friendships, sneaky back doors, and gay men!"

"Cheers," Cander said with a laugh. I was confused by the last part but downed my shot, the taste was pleasurable and went down exceptionally well.

I set my glass down carefully compared to Crow and Cander's slam of theirs.

"Okay, explain," I said.

Crow laughed, pouring us all another round. "You want to tell her lover boy, or do you want me to?"

I looked to Cander, who dragged a hand down his face, and it wasn't until then I realized how exhausted he looked. "When I made that deal with your father, I realized I would need to get my mark, the knife, for you to complete the task. The only problem was the knife rotates randomly between Hell's Queens to keep it out of Watchers' hands. I thought I was screwed when it was time for me to enter your life and have the knife ready for you because I found out it was in Jax's realm. I can portal in and out of *any* throne room in Hell, but the knife wouldn't have been in that room. It would be in the back realm, which I couldn't go into unless I were a Watcher to that realm."

Cander paused to take a shot, and I followed suit, thinking about how good the liquor tasted. "I remember coming here the night before I went to retrieve you and having a drink with Crow in the back."

Crow spoke up now, taking over the story. "Yeah, I also remember you being a little more than frustrated after seeing Akira with her fuck boy for the first time."

"Fuck off, man," Cander grumbled, making Crow laugh.

"Why would you be frustrated after seeing me? Why does everyone hate Ian?" I asked, feeling a little defensive about my past relationship. I mean, yeah, he was an asshole now that everything had boiled down, and we found out how obsessive and crazy he was...but still. I hadn't known that *back then*. He had been a different person before he'd turned, yeah a little obsessive maybe, but not crazy... yet. He'd been a movie star for shit's sake. I would say that I was doing pretty well at the time, I concluded in my head, taking the bottle from a laughing Crow and pouring myself a drink.

"Do you really need to ask why everyone hates him? Do you not remember him trying to choke you out?" Crow asked, and Cander's eyes flashed red. "Anyways." He held up a hand and a look that said that wasn't the point. I drained another shot, feeling my muscles relax and my head hum happily.

"Being a bar owner, I hear a lot of talk. The talk was, well, the rumor was that Queen Asgret took those that are her equals in Hell, or those she couldn't kill, into her torture room attached to her private bedroom. Once I shared that with Cander, we came up with a plan." Crow explained, and I noticed that even though he was back to his handsome self, along with an amazing voice, he still talked the same and sounded funny. Like a rambling older man. The thought made me giggle, and before I could lift another shot to my mouth, Cander grabbed my wrist and lowered the glass.

"Easy, babe. Let's save getting wasted for after the tour of the mansion." He chuckled along with Crow. "We wouldn't want you getting lost and ending up in Remarose's room of death."

Crow shivered, acting scared or disgusted, I couldn't tell, but it pulled a laugh out of me all the same, and I realized I was drunk. *Great.* My first night in Hell and I was sloshed.

"Wait!" I shouted, grabbing my shot glass back. "I thought you said I couldn't get drunk!?"

Cander laughed, taking back the shot again and shooting it before I could. "You can't get drunk on human alcohol, but you can get drunk on distilled blood."

Distilled...blood?

I slowly sat back down before I looked from Crow to Cander, who just looked back, expecting me to freak out. "I-"

I thought about what I wanted to say, but really what was there to say? I had killed Jax and ate, literally ate his heart, and then bit and scratched Cander vying for his blood like he was my own personal juice box.

"Okay." I sighed, pushing the bottle away, feeling more sober than fifteen seconds ago.

"Anyways." Cander said, "I'd known how to get out of

Asgret's back realm ever since Jax told me a story when he was trashed one night, but I wanted that secret of how to get in and out of the back realm to stay hidden. So if I were summoned, I would have to find another way out. Crow conceded to help me. The night you were crying and wailing over Ian, who, by the way, was innocent."

I looked to Cander in confusion, interrupting him. "What do you mean?"

He laughed. "Don't kill me." He said, as he held up his hand and I could tell by the shine in his eyes that the alcohol, err, blood was getting to him.

Crow stepped back, hugging his bottle of black goodness. "Uh, oh. I don't like this already." He said, and I rolled my eyes at the two of them.

Why did they always think I flew off the handle?

"Because you do," Cander answered my thoughts.

Whatever. I thought back to him with an irritated sigh.

"So...I was the one who let the dark-haired girl into Ian's house. As a matter of fact, I drove her there."

I opened my mouth, then closed it. I repeated that a couple of times, trying to figure out if I was mad, impressed, or shocked.

Instead, I laughed. "*You*?" I pointed to him, grabbing the nasty blood bottle and poured another shot. Fuck it; I needed a drink. "*You* are the one that started the whole thing, and because of *you*, I discovered the water and Ian drowned. I *killed* him!"

Cander lifted an eyebrow, not impressed by my reaction, err...non-reaction. "You would have killed him either way; he had it coming, the little shit. It's just too bad that Jax made that fucking deal with him, and he's still in my way."

Cander looked to Crow and the bottle that he was still cradling in his arms, pointing towards it. "More."

Crow walked over with caution, looking at me like I was a

ticking bomb, as Cander snatched the bottle the men had been favoring over my bottle.

"Cander! I thought my heart was breaking!" I yelled, and Crow flinched back about to cradle his bottle again. I shot him an irritated look. "Quit it, or I *will* scream."

"Okay, okay," Crow said, lifting his hands.

"Well, I had to fucking do something. You were about to give that prick your virginity, and I still needed time to get the knife. I saw the bimbo on the cover of a magazine with him a while back and persuaded her to follow Ian. Then I kept her sexed-up and happy in my hotel until it was time to use her as a backup plan." Cander shrugged as my mouth dropped.

"Are you shitting me?! You were *fucking* Summer?" I yelled, feeling my eyes tingle, as the room tinted red. That stupid, *beautiful*, bitch was literally messing with every guy in my life.

Cander scoffed. "She was food. Chill." He turned to dismiss me as he reached behind the bar, grabbing a bottle with green liquid.

Crow sighed, right as I was getting ready to lose my shit. "Just hear the rest, Kira. Remember me? Crow? I thought you wanted to know how I'm alive and in the flesh."

I sighed. Crow was right. The red died down in my vision, and I poured another shot.

"Kir-"Cander tried to warn, but my growls shut him up, and he conceded with a sigh. I was in Hell and if I wanted to get shit faced, after all the *shit* I just went through, I would. Plus, he literally put me through my first heartbreak so he could steal a knife.

"So, while you were crying over Ian...I went and murdered every single thing in Queen Asgret's throne room. Captive, guard, or otherwise, and I left them all in a pile and signed my name." He paused, running a hand through his hair, as my eyebrows touched my hair. *Holy shit.* "See, when someone above your station summons you, you are obligated to go in good faith, and I knew she was going to summon me to her back realm. She would be pissed at what I'd done and want revenge, but Lilith would never let me die, so I knew I was fine either way. I mean, if she brought me to her throne room, I could just portal myself out, so I knew she would bring me to the back, and if the rumors were true, it would be to the torture room."

Crow stepped forward, replacing my bottle with a fresh one, and I temporarily wondered how demons paid for their blood. *Hmm.* Crow cleared his throat, bringing me back to attention. "The night he was summoned, he called me. Told me about you, about the spelled "directions" he left you, and Jax. He said he would be summoned soon and that I needed to trade myself for him, and I would need to bring you with me so that the Queen would surely let him walk. He told me how to get out of the back realm to escape."

My mouth dropped. "So, you knew he was going to be fine the whole time?" I asked Cander.

Cander cleared his throat with a roar from the green liquor. Whatever that was, it was strong. "I gave him the way out, but it was Cain and Elijah that *ensured* he got out. The snake bite wasn't planned."

"How did you get the bite healed? I thought you said we would die if we got bit?"

Crow shook his head in dismay. "We *will* die if we get bit by a Hell Viper, but being a Siren, when I traded my life for Cander's, the Queen planned to keep me alive and eat my scales. So she called Cain and Elijah. They are dark Magicals, and Purgatory's gatekeepers. They are known as Hell's healers. While Elijah was healing me Cain leaned over and said, consider it a wedding present. At the time, I had no idea what the hell he was talking about." Crow chuckled. "I'm guessing he was talking about you two, and then they said to run. I did, while they distracted the Queen. The rest is history, and I'm back, baby!"

Crow brought up his hand for a high-five, and I laughed, meeting my hand with his. "That is so crazy!" I said, turning to Cander. "You planned the whole thing?" Shock ran through me at how well Cander had planned it.

Cander shook his head. "I never planned for Jax to trick you into the Ivy. I knew he was planning something, but not that."

"Well, it worked out," Crow said. A grunt from one of the customers on the floor had us all looking to see the demons starting to gain consciousness. "*Eww*. You two better jet before you have thirty pissed off demons after you."

Cander laughed. "Yeah, man. We don't want her job to be any harder than it's already going to be."

I ignored that little bit of information, remembering everything that Cander and I'd gone through the past three days. "What about when you had us chased out of your bar the first time I was here?" I asked.

"That was Asgret's lackeys," Crow answered.

I sat straight, still confused. "So, why didn't they take him then?"

Cander laughed. "It was supposed to be an ambush. Crow warned me when we came in, so I asked some pointless questions to act like I was there for a reason."

"What does that mean?"

"It means, originally, I was there to leave you with Crow and get ready to be taken. But her guys were there, so we had to switch directions. I left the spelled note with you at the hotel and was just going to leave you there. But you'd need a way into Hell, and I figured Jax would be the key. Crow couldn't leave the realm so I just had to hope Jax would bring you here, and with my note and bike, I could get you the rest of the way."

"Hmm," I said, still reeling from all the information. I looked at Crow, who was now busy cleaning and doing catch-up for the day.

"Wait," I said, pausing Cander in standing up. "If everything is done then...does that mean my dad is awake?"

Cander sighed, pulling out his phone. Crow marveled at the largest phone in history, "Man, I want one of those." He said.

"What's so special about it? You don't have one?" I asked, making Crow laugh.

"No, *no one* has a phone. No reception. That thing-" He pointed to Cander's phone. "Is special, for Watchers *only*, and is spelled by the twins never to die and pick up the shit from the human realm." He scoffed, grabbing our glasses and dipping them into soapy water.

I watched as Cander turned it on and googled my father's name, before clicking on a live news report. I scooted closer as we both watched a doctor in front of a podium, behind him was my dad's band as the press shouted question after question at them.

"So, does that mean he will recover?"

"Again, we aren't sure if this means he will even wake up, but brain activity increasing during a coma is a positive sign of recovery." The doctor answered as flashes of light hit his face.

I sucked in my breath at his answer. I became a Watcher, Cander saw that through, so why wasn't my dad awake?

"There were reports that Akira was sighted visiting him at the hospital, is that true?" Another reporter asked the doctor.

The doctor shook his head. "I am not sure of that answer, as I'm not in charge of security in and out of the room. All I can answer at this time are questions in relation to the health of my patients."

Before another reporter could ask a question, Cander flipped off his phone and shoved it in his pocket at the sound of another demon waking from my Siren scream.

"Why *hasn't* my dad woke up? I thought the deal was done?" I asked Cander, feeling confused.

Cander sighed. "You don't remember the whole deal, do you?"

I thought back to when Cander showed me the deal made in the nasty room backstage of my evil, drunk father's dressing room.

"She could kill him for you, take his place..." He paused to let out a burp. "Then you get the fringe benefits. I'll sign her off to you in blood. A demon's mark, of course, to make sure I'm true to my word. If she falls in love with anyone before you, I'll go into an un-wake-able coma until the deal is done...Yatta, yatta, yatta. Jax is dead, Akira is your bride and partner. Deal?"

"Getting married?" I asked.

Cander nodded, standing from the stool.

"But that wasn't a necessity; he just said he would add it in on good faith or something."

"It's all in the wording girly, everything he said before Cander said done. That's the deal. So, I guess the only question for you love birds is ...when's the big day?" Crow asked.

I scoffed. "Does it even matter, we're in Hell?"

Cander stepped into me, grabbing my waist before slamming me flush against his hard body. The smell of liquor fanned my cheeks as he smirked. "What's wrong, Kira? Am I a little too much demon for you to handle?"

I bit my bottom lip to stop the smile.

"You wish." I said before I decided to kiss him.

"Then." He leaned forward, sucking my bottom lip into his mouth before biting down on it. He stepped back and looked towards Crow. "I guess as soon as possible."

19

INITIATION

*T*he outside world of Hell went from blinding light to pitch black in an instant. It was as if someone had flipped a switch. There were no stars. No moon. Just endless black, and if it wasn't for the headlight on the bike, I was *sure* we'd be screwed, but Cander never even flinched when it happened. I guess he was used to it, but I felt like I was in the twilight zone. The realization that I was in Hell at night seemed a lot scarier than being here during the day. Thoughts of *Dante's Inferno* slammed into my mind. I glanced around, half expecting to see flames or demons eating humans or people stuck in the ground still alive. Thankfully there was only the tiny spotlight from the motorcycle. If there *were* those things around us, I'd rather not see.

A dot in the sky suddenly grew to a million specks in the sky as we got closer to the biggest mansion I'd ever seen in my life. I soon realized they were stars as I looked up to see the moon off in the distance. When I glanced back, it was like a black hole. It was as if the moon and stars in this place were only over this mansion.

The twins spelled Purgatory to have stars and a moon. Anock said it was a must for his realm to have stars for Mikayla, Cander said into my mind.

Who's Mikayla?

The one we're seeking. I'll get to that later, for now, let's just concentrate on learning the mansion. You have a big day tomorrow.

Cander parked his bike under the tree and stretched with a huge yawn. "You're immortal now, like me." He explained as I got off, and we headed for the double doors leading into the mansion. "We normally don't need sleep, food, water, or human things, but it's been a while since I've fed, and my energy is drained."

He opened the door, and I stepped into an air-conditioned room that looked like a sitting room. It was extremely formal, with chaise lounges and dark polished furniture. Dark wood floors with fancy antique carpets accented the space. When the door closed behind us with a loud creak, I looked back to see them shut. They seemed completely different from the small patio doors they had been before. Now they looked like huge, ten feet tall doors that looked way out of place in this room. I turned in a circle taking in this bizarre room while Cander watched. I looked up to see that the ceiling held a black diamond chandelier. Massive gold-framed paintings that featured demons killing angels decorated the walls.

"If we are ever summoned to the throne room, you will come to this room, then go through those doors," Cander said, pointing to the massive doors.

"But we just came through there, and it wasn't a throne room?"

He walked over, putting his hand on my lower back and steering me towards an average-sized door, which I thought would lead to the rest of the mansion. "This is called the drawing room. It's confusing, I know, but let's just stick to the basics and work our way up. I'm throwing a lot at you, and it's going to take a while to learn it all. We'll go through the basics tonight, feed, get some rest, and then tomorrow you will get prepared for the Watcher initiation."

I bit the inside of my cheek, already feeling overwhelmed. I followed him through the door into a long hallway full of doors, and it looked like the same hallway I was in the day I woke up here naked. "This looks like the mansion hallway we were in the first time I was here."

Cander sighed. "That's because it is." He stopped walking and pointed to the doors. "This is Purgatory. It is a realm in Hell ruled by Prince Anock, who happens to be the Watchers' leader."

I nodded, taking it in.

"When humans die, they come here." He started to walk again, going up to a door and opening it, showing me inside.

I sucked in a shocked breath. Inside the dimly lit room resembling a meat cooler, humans hung upside down by their feet. Some still alive and being bled out by a naked, green-skinned demon with horns and red eyes. Some had long been dead and skinned, only their meat hanging from hooks. I put a hand over my mouth and stepped back, looking at Cander as he shut the door.

"You can see what happens to the humans who wander into this room." He said, starting to go into another room before I put a hand on his arm, stopping him from opening it.

"Wait." I paused, swallowing my nausea. "So, there are humans here as we speak wandering the mansion?" I asked, turning around, but I could only see one hallway, which didn't make sense.

"Purgatory is a mansion to keep humans meandering around confused until Anock decides which realm they belong in. Then it is *his* gatekeepers, Cain and Elijah, that usher them where they belong. But this mansion is also where all the Watchers live." He explained and grabbed my hand to walk again, and I looked around at the fancy pictures hanging on the wall. They were all portraits of people, but none that I recognized.

"Why don't we live in our realm, or quarter or whatever," I asked.

"Realm." He corrected, then stopped walking when two young, stunning girls came out of a room laughing and talking. They both looked intrigued when they saw us and walked over. One of the girls was dressed in nothing except leaves held in place with twine around her tanned, toned body. Her long curly blue hair complimented her high cheekbones and perfectly shaped lips. The closer they got, the more I could see her yellow vertical eyes and patches of shiny blue scales on her skin. I looked over to the other girl as I shuffled closer to Cander. She was a super tall knockout dressed as if she just came from a dinner party. She had a long black evening gown that opened in the front to show her white patent peep-toe heels. In contrast to the other girl who looked like she stepped out of a *Tarzan* movie, this girl's skin was almost blinding white, yet worked with her long black curly hair and bright red lipstick. Unlike the other girl, though, her eyes looked normal. For all I knew they could be the mean girls of this place, but they both looked friendly enough

"Andronomean. Remarose." Cander said to them in greeting as they smiled back, taking me in. The strong smell of roses hit me, and I could tell it was from the girl with black hair.

The girl in the black dress stepped forward and put out her hand. "I'm Remarose, but you can call me Rose for short." She said, and I held my breath at the strong rose-scented perfume. Lord, this girl could dial it down a notch, but now the nickname made sense.

I smiled and shook her hand. I needed to start on a good note here. "Akira," I said.

The other girl followed suit and held out a hand that I took next. "It's awesome to have another badass woman on the team.

Oh, and you can call me Andy." She said with what sounded like a slither at the end of the word team. I thought the nick-name Andy for a girl seemed a little weird, but more than that, I had a feeling she might be some type of snake demon based on her looks and accent. If that was the case, I *really* wanted to be on her good side.

"Are you guys Watchers too?" I asked, causing them to laugh.

"They wished, but no. We are both permanent residents here at the mansion. We are on the defense side of the mansion, and in return, Anock keeps us fed." Rose said.

"How'd everyone hear the news so fast?" Cander asked, pinching the bridge of his nose, and I took it that he was irritated.

Andy scoffed. "How do you think?"

A door shut, drawing my attention down the hall, and I saw two approaching males. Identical males at that, well, other than their hair color. One guy had brown, and the other had blonde. "Speak of the devils, and they shall appear." The blonde one said in a sing-song voice.

"Well, I see you're still looking a hot mess since we last saw you." The brown-haired one said to me, and I looked down at my borrowed clothes, blood-stained blonde hair, and dried blood-covered body. Eek. I was a mess. And why had my hair changed color again?

"I don't think we've met," I said cautiously, looking to Cander, who laughed.

"That's because we were in our true form. I'm sorry about your friends." The guy answered back, and I swallowed hard, feeling the emotions creep back up. So they were the ones that Liz called. "I'm Elijah," The brown-haired demon said.

"And I'm Cain." The blonde-haired one said.

"We're the gatekeepers for Purgatory." They said together in a weird creepy, monotone voice that gave me chills.

"Umm...hi." I said with an awkward wave. "So, what kind of demons are you guys?" I asked, looking to Rose, Andy, and then the guys. I felt like I was in Kindergarten all over again. When silence fell over the hallway, along with eyebrow lifts and awkward stares, I knew I'd performed some big no, no. Before the silence could swallow me whole, I continued like I didn't realize this was awkward. "I'm a Siren." I finished, looking over to see Cander snort and shake his head.

"Wow."

I looked over to him and hugged myself. "Shut up," I said to him under my breath.

Cain finally broke the silence with a laugh. "Oh, girl, you have a lot to learn." I could feel my face getting hot, and I glanced nervously at the girls, who didn't look mad, just amused.

"I'm an Arachnid demon," Rose said. I wanted to ask if that was a spider, but instead nodded and said, "Oh." Like I knew what the hell that was.

Andy pulled back her hair from one side of her shoulder and pointed to her scales. "I'm a Viper demon or snake." She said and lifted her chin, giving me a hiss. Her forked tongue shot out of her mouth, and I swallowed hard.

I tried to reign in my terror. "That's cool."

The silence took over again, and I wasn't sure I had any more dumb things left to fill it with, so I was thankful when the girls waved their goodbyes and continued down the hall.

"So, now that you're here, we can start planning the wedding!" Elijah sang, clapping his hands and jumping a little with excitement.

Jeez, the word really *does* travel fast. I chuckled. "I guess."

Before I could even get the words out, Cain shoved Elijah towards the wall, getting in the spotlight. "Right. We were thinking about something red! It would pair well with the blood fountains and, of course, the dinner table. We will have distilled blood on tap, *of course*, but our spelled alcohol will be there, along with fresh blood. The color will be needed to help the flower arrangements pop." He paused, looking over to Cander. "I told Anock, we would *not* be having Queen Mandra's sacrifices, burnt or charred nasties, like the last get together. I mean, a lot of us like to eat the skin and seriously...who brings a burnt crispy human and slaps them on the table to eat like a barbarian."

Elijah nodded in agreement. "Those Lava demons have no class."

I blanched and took a step back. Oh dear baby hellhounds, they were talking about eating people for the wedding dinner. It probably was a good thing *not* to ask what kind of cake they planned.

"You gave Blake so much shit about having to dress and prepare Mikayla for Anock, and yet you are all over us about this wedding," Cander said in annoyance.

Elijah rolled his eyes. "Well, whatever." He said, making me laugh. These two were a mess. "This is a wedding on *our* turf, and if it's here, it's going to be fabulous. I mean, we are in Hell, but that doesn't mean we can't be classy bitches. The gardens are perfect. We figured while she's going through her trials, we will be getting everything set up. Another thing we were thinking-"

Before he could finish, Cander interrupted. "And that's our cue." He grabbed my hand, tugging me forward. "You all can talk about that shit later. She needs to eat, and so do I." As I was getting pulled away, I looked back to the perplexed look on the twins' faces and snickered.

"It was nice meeting you guys," I called, and Cander growled for me to come on. It only made me giggle more. This place was a lot to take in, but so far, the demons I met were right up my alley.

*C*ander explained that we would finish the tour tomorrow and led me down a flight of concrete stairs. I stayed quiet to gather my thoughts as we went along. I wasn't juvenile enough to think we weren't going to have sex. I knew we were, but it just felt...rushed. Well, I wasn't sure if it was that or the fact it seemed more business to him than romance. He kept referring to it as eating. I mean, I guess that was *what* it was, but still. Tiny lights flickered on as we walked, illuminating the stairs for us, and I loved how they were red. The lights made it look scary, almost like we were walking down into a dungeon. Maybe we were?

Cander dropped my hand and walked off when we got down to the bottom, leaving me alone to check out his space. The décor had gone from a fancy White House looking mansion to a bachelor pad, as I made my way into the living room. His area had an industrial feel to it. Concrete floors with black metal and dark wood designed furniture. He had all the usual things you would find in a living room and a fully stocked bar. Thank who the fuck ever put that in there. I heard losing your virginity hurt. If that were the case, which I doubted from my more than ready to go body, I would need some painkiller in liquid form, so I headed for the bar.

Right as I reached for a bottle filled with black liquid, a flash of skin caught the corner of my eye, and I yelped almost dropping the bottle as I turned to see Cander shirtless. And yeah, the view was amazing.

"HOLY SHIT, you need a bell! You scared the hell out of me!"

Cander scoffed, pointing to his neck. "I highly doubt that. You might even have more Hell in you than I do seeing how you almost ripped my throat out."

I let out a nervous laugh cringing. "Yeah, you might be right.

Sorry about that." He looked down, and I murmured, not sorry, before turning my back and snickering.

"What was that?"

"Hmm? Nothing."

He scoffed, and it was hard not to laugh. It was fun messing with him. "You coming?" He ran a hand down his face again, and I took it as his tell for being tired, it was also clear that our happy drunk buzz from Crows' bar was sadly wearing off.

"You want a drink?" I asked, holding up the bottle.

He shook his head before turning around and walking back into a hallway. "If I'm not buried in your tight pussy soon, I'm going to find someone else to feed off."

Okkaayy. How the hell did he manage to both piss me off *and* turn me on at the same time? Wow, I had issues.

I placed the bottle down on the bar and hurried behind him, watching the hard muscles in his back flex as he walked, while subtly wiping the drool from my mouth. The memory of how good his blood tasted slammed into me as I followed him. I realized I wanted to do it again, but I shook the thought away as we walked into the biggest bedroom I'd ever seen. It was much larger than my old bedroom at home, and *that* was saying something.

"Wow," I whispered, taking in the entire space while Cander watched with heated eyes. It followed the same theme as the rest of his place, except the décor of his bedroom held hints of BDSM from the hanging metal chains, whips, and floggers on the wall. I walked over to them, only ever seeing this stuff in *50 Shades of Grey*. Fuck, I was so screwed and in way over my head if this was any indication.

"Hopefully," Cander said, his breath stirring my hair as he whispered, making me shiver, from that, and the heat of his body close to me. I took a calm-the-fuck-down breath, trying to play it cool, even though I wanted nothing more than to turn around and wrap myself around him. I decided to continue my exploration, doing my best to both entice and ignore the six feet worth of delicious demon at my back. Cander moved closer to me and now had a hand on my hip, his thumb slowly circled and teased, and I bit my lip to keep from moaning aloud. Okay, maybe I wouldn't be able to ignore him for long.

Curiosity got the better of me. I slowly reached up, trailing a shaky finger down one of the metal chains and wondered if he planned to use any of this stuff on me. I didn't get very far before Cander's hand shot out, grabbing my own and holding it in place on the chain. He went flush up against my back, his erection pressing erotically against my ass, making me gasp.

Before I could move away, he nuzzled his nose under my ear, pushing my hair out of the way before kissing my neck, slow and soft. I struggled to hold in my erratic breathing even though I was about to have a stroke.

"Would you want me to use these?" He asked.

I wasn't sure, but the realization that he was reading my mind as I went through this added to my nerves because I was bound to think of some dumb shit. Turning my head, I arched my back, pushing my chest out, and pushed my ass further into him. It felt like heaven. "Can you not read my mind while we do this?" I taunted.

His hand that held mine on the chain dropped, and he now had both his hands grabbing my hips, keeping me in place while grinding into me. The feeling was so erotic and pleasing. I reached out, grabbing the chains on the wall to steady myself and couldn't help but grind back into him. Fuck, I wanted him! So...so *fucking* bad.

"Fuck." He growled.

Another grind and I was throbbing, panting, and ready to be fucked.

"I can feel how wet you are already." His low, sultry voice sent goosebumps along my skin. I ignored him as I melted with pleasure.

Before long, we were both gasping as the friction built between us. I turned my head, connecting my lips with his. The action ignited us further, causing him to slam me into the wall as I released the chains, crying out before I gripped his hair tight with one hand. At the same time, I used my other hand to hold his hand tight on my hip. The wall gave him more ability to grind harder into me, and I moaned into his mouth, unable to help it anymore.

Don't stop, don't fucking stop. I let my thoughts scream as pressure continued to build when Cander's lips broke mine and moved onto my neck. He kissed my neck like a man starved. It was clear from his breathing he was getting pleasure and power just as much as I was, and we weren't even naked yet.

You aren't getting off yet, sweetheart. He tried to pull away, and I reached back, holding onto him, forcing him to stay against me as I bit his lip so hard blood gushed into my mouth.

Mmm, you taste good. I let my thoughts scream. I released his lips when I felt my fangs grow so I wouldn't hurt him but still held him in place, pushing back into him. *Bite me,* I begged. *Do it.* I ground harder against him, and I heard him suck air through his teeth as his forehead rested on the back of my head and my hair stirred from his heavy breaths.

"Akira, if you don't get on that bed, I'm going to take you right here." His lustful voice sent thrills through me.

"Take me then," I whispered, not wanting the bliss to end, but then in one quick motion, he stepped away, releasing my hips, and the loss of his body had me grunting in frustration.

"Bed. Now." He growled.

I turned to see the glow in his eyes burning so bright I had to look away. I swallowed, more than ready for the bed. *Fuck yes.*

I slowly walked over to it looking up at the massive mirror on the ceiling above the bed, while Cander poured us wine from a corner table I hadn't yet noticed. He walked over, offering me a glass as I stared at his huge erection that was straining against his pants, which didn't help calm my rapid heartbeat. "Drink, it's spelled, it will help."

I gulped the sweet red wine down quickly in one go, loving the instant buzz in my head and relaxation in my muscles. A little bit of wine dribbled down my chin, Cander reached forward and wiped it away with his thumb, staring deep into my eyes. "Better?"

I laughed. "Yeah, a bit." I sighed, letting go of my nerves. "Now what?"

Cander swallowed down his wine in one swallow, placing it down next to my glass on the nightstand. "Now we get cleaned up, I decided as much as I need to fuck you, I would rather not do it with that asshole's blood on you. I only want one man's scent on you, and it's mine, and *only* mine."

Aaaaaand, my heart was jackhammering again.

I followed him into a side room that led to a bathroom with a sauna tub on one side, and the other had a waterfall shower. An enormous floor to ceiling, spiked mirror sat in the middle, and I cringed when I saw how messy I looked.

Cander scoffed. "Stop it, you're beautiful, and you know it." I watched through the mirror as he slowly prowled up behind me like a predator, eyes trained on mine. I released a shaky breath as his fingers slipped under my shirt, lifted it, and slowly pulled it off. That's when his eyes broke away from mine to concentrate on my breasts. I felt another flood of wetness in my panties. He licked his lips before wrapping his arms around me from behind, only to trail his hands painstakingly slow down my stomach to unbutton my pants. Fuck being bashful, I released my bottom lip that I had been biting and let out a moan as my eyes closed and my head fell back to his shoulder.

"So fucking sexy." He whispered as he pulled my tight jeans down past my hips, just enough for him to trail a finger through my soaked center, and I gasped as he slowly pushed two fingers into me. He only left them in for a second before pulling them out, and my eyes flew open.

"You're such a tease," I whined, watching as he laughed while pulling my pants down and off. I turned around completely naked and super nervous as I reached for the button on his jeans with shaky hands.

"Your turn." I wasn't sure why I suddenly felt nervous again, but I did. As much as I was ready and wanting him, my nerves wouldn't go away, and I just hoped I wouldn't be like this every time I saw his God-like body.

I pulled his zipper down before grabbing his pants at his hips and tugging them down. His hard erection sprang free, and my mouth dropped, but I picked it up quickly and looked away bashfully before he could see me gawk.

"Okay, you ready?" I asked as I turned towards the shower that I had no freaking idea of how to work.

Before I could get too far, his warm hand wrapped around my wrist, giving me pause. Pulling me back towards him, he grabbed my chin, staring deep in my eyes. I suddenly felt like I was drowning, and not a single drop of water was on me.

"Kiss me."

I stepped into him, wrapping my arms around his neck right as our lips melted together and my breasts crushed against his hard chest. We both moaned at the same time from the incredible feel of our bare skin touching. It was like we were made for each other. The tingling, the power, it felt like nothing I'd ever felt before. It swirled around us in the air like magic. He breathed me in as he pushed his tongue further into my mouth. My power fed him and tingled back into my body as I pulled his bottom lip into my mouth, feeling high on power and lust. We were in sync, and I never even opened my eyes as I felt him walk us back towards the shower.

I ran my fingers through his soft, luscious hair as I felt a spray of warm water hit my back before he grabbed my ass, lifting me. I wrapped my legs around him as his cock aimed hungrily at my entrance. I opened my eyes while breaking our kiss and saw the same *want* reflected in Cander's eyes.

"I hadn't planned to do this here." He breathed, before setting me down gently, and I tried to ignore the disappointment that spiked through me. "But ...you're so *enticing* and *mesmerizing*. You don't even have to open that pretty little mouth of yours. Your Siren calls to my demon." I stepped back into the water as Cander matched my steps, running a hand through my hair, helping to get it wet. His intense stare with his smoldering eyes, kissable lips, and sculpted body called to me. I *had* to touch him. The pull to feel him was enough to knock me over. I reached out, feeling the scruff on his chin before moving to feel his smooth chest as he continued to wash my hair and body.

"And these fuck me eyes." He cussed before turning me to face the shower wall. Every second he was in contact with me, I was bathing in immense pleasure, and I moaned as his hand curved around my ass before squeezing it. "They are going to make it hard to stop fucking you once I start." I was panting as he massaged the soap lustfully, and slowly into every inch of my skin, taking his time at my breasts. I couldn't help the noises coming out of me, and from his harsh breathing and shaky hands, I knew he was beyond control at this point.

"I want you," I whispered as I turned into him, not giving him a chance to stop me. I grabbed his cock and slid it next to my pussy rubbing against it.

"Fuck it." He moaned before lifting me so fast I barely had time to wrap my legs around him before he turned us and my back slammed against the wall, water cascading down both of us now.

I grabbed his face kissing him with all my power as he pushed the tip of his hard cock up my center before stopping.

"*Yes!*" I cried, wanting it further. I wiggled, grabbing hard at his head, trying to force him in but yelped when he stepped back from the wall with me in his arms and slapped my wet ass.

"No!" He growled as he stepped out of the water and walked us back into the bedroom. "I want to taste you first."

He threw me back against the fabric headboard in one quick move, I hit against it with a thud and looked up to see his eyes swimming with hunger. *Holy fuck, yes!* A yelp flew out of me in surprise when he grabbed my ankle, pulling me towards him as he climbed on me like a man possessed. His lips slammed against mine painfully, but my body still flooded with desire all the same, and I gripped hard at his biceps as he situated himself over me.

"I want you so bad. I don't want to wait anymore." I whined as he pulled back to make his way down my body with his mouth. His lips and tongue alternated between licking and kissing me. I closed my eyes, a moan escaping me as he pinched one nipple while his tongue was assaulting my other nipple. Fire filled my veins, and I writhed against him wanting more. The motion causing him to growl, and the vibration against my breast in his mouth almost had me getting off from the pure pleasure.

"Cander," I warned, trying to move his hand down to my aching cunt. I needed a release, and God was he proving to be the man to do it, so why wasn't he giving it to me.

Fuck me! I begged in my mind.

He pushed my hand away, kissing down my belly.

"I need every inch of you." He answered as he ignored my pleas.

I looked down, watching as his skilled mouth played havoc on the sensitive skin under my belly button. He moved his way further down as I shivered in anticipation. A slight panic went through me as his mouth hovered over my throbbing center about what he would think. I'd never had a guy go down on me before, and I didn't know if I looked or smelled okay down there.

"Shh." He licked right up my center, and my heart stalled as I cried out in pleasure. "You're overthinking things, just relax." He whispered against my clit. Another moan broke free, and I obeyed, letting my head fall back against the pillow.

My mouth opened in shock seeing how sexy it was to watch him go down on me from the mirror on the ceiling. I was only able to look for so long before my eyes slammed shut, my back arched, and a loud moan tore out of me as his tongue slipped inside me and a wet finger slid in my ass. I never thought I'd want that or that it would feel good, but it did, and even though I had my eyes shut, they hurt from being rolled back so far.

Fucking shit, if this was what Hell felt like I wanted to be this bad always.

Cander laughed against me, the vibrations making me gasp before he continued to nip, lick, suck and bite at my pussy. His steady hands moved to squeeze and massage my breasts at the same time. My heart was beating so hard I was afraid I would die from it, and a scream tore out of me that sounded like he was murdering me as my legs suddenly shook from the intense orgasm he ripped out of me. I gripped Cander's hair pushing his face further into me as I rode him through my pleasure. I didn't care if he couldn't breathe. *I never wanted it to end.*

"*Oh, my God.*" I moaned as he licked me clean when I finally released him, feeling complete bliss.

"It's not over yet." He huffed, climbing off the bed, pulling me up with him.

I watched as he stroked himself, and my mouth dropped open. It was the sexiest thing I'd ever seen.

"Fuck me," I begged, opening up my legs.

"Do you want this?" He teased in a heated voice. I nodded, licking my lips before I could stop myself.

"Get over here then." He demanded, and I obeyed, so fucking ready for his hard cock to be pounding into me.

I got up slowly following him to the front of the bed as my cum slid out of me, coating my thighs, and I watched his eyes go to that spot before he licked his lips again.

"Get on your knees."

I kept eye contact as I slowly knelt in front of him. His cock aimed right at my face had me licking my lips again. He turned, giving me the most amazing view of his ass as he reached down underneath the bed. He pulled out a metal chain with a black leather collar on the end, followed by rope and a black silk blindfold.

"Do you know what these are for?" He asked, and for the sake of not looking like a complete idiot, I stayed quiet and shook my head, eyeing them with a mix of terror and excitement.

I watched as he clipped the end of the metal chain into a small metal ring that was fixed into the concrete floor right in front of my knees that I hadn't yet noticed. "This one." He paused, looking me up and down. I bit my lip to keep quiet, intrigue making me want to know his plans. "Goes around your neck." He leaned forward, brushing my hair back behind my shoulders before wrapping the collar around my neck and buckling it snug.

As soon as he finished buckling the collar, I looked up right as Cander reached forward, pulling my hair hard, and making me scream in pain. I reached up, trying to catch his wrists to make him release me, but he wouldn't.

"AHH!" I screamed as he pulled me, trying to get me to stand up by my hair. When the chain restricted me from standing, I cried out again.

"See." He said before finally releasing my hair.

I whimpered in pain as I dropped his wrists to rub my hair. I wanted to cuss him out! What the hell would possess him to treat me like that? Before I could open my mouth to do just that, he bent down and kissed my head, massaging and petting my wet hair back where it hurt. It was clear we were doing this BDSM thing, and now that it had started, I was seeing a side of Cander that I hadn't seen before.

"You won't be able to move away from me now, however," He paused, turning around and picking up the rope next, and I wasn't sure if I was down for this like I had initially thought. "We can't have your pretty little claws aiming for me again. So this..."

He walked around me, dragging the rope slowly over my breasts, making me shiver from the course material on my nipples. "Will help. Put your hands behind your back, and grab your forearms."

"And if I don't want to?" I challenged.

"Then you will have more pain than pleasure." He said from somewhere behind me. I took a deep breath in, wanting to do whatever I needed to do to get the pleasure I wanted.

"Okay," I whispered, causing him to chuckle.

"Good girl."

He slowly tied the rope tightly around my wrists and forearms, so that I was stuck in that position and helpless to his commands.

"Cander?" I asked when I no longer felt the rope moving.

"I'm here." He said with a chuckle from somewhere behind me. I panted, flinching when I felt his finger slowly trailing down my spine and then suddenly stopping, He held it there for just a second before pulling it away and spanking me hard. I screamed in pleasure, oddly finding it arousing. The inconsistent mix of nerves from anticipation, pleasure, and pain was thrilling.

He came back into my sight with what looked like clamps. "Nipple clamps." Twenty genius points for the virgin. "These will keep those fucking gorgeous breasts busy while I occupy your mouth."

Heat flooded to my core as he put the first one on, causing me to scream from the bite of pain. He leaned forward, grabbed my chin, and kissed me so expertly that it stole my breath. It distracted me from the pain temporarily before clamping the other one to make me whimper. "You will behave, or I'll tighten these." I bit my bottom lip and nodded. Fuck I would so behave if that was the case.

"First, I'm going to fuck that pretty little mouth of yours, and then I'm going to fuck *you*." He growled. "If I didn't want those sexy as fuck eyes staring at me while I shove my cock down your throat, I would blindfold you." He stepped forward, rubbing his dick against my mouth, the precum from the tip now coating my lips. I jutted my tongue out, licking the tip of his cock, not even thinking twice about what I was doing. I wanted it, I wanted him, and I immensely enjoyed the sound of his shocked gasp. I'd never gone down on a guy before. Even though it was foreign, pleasure still shot through me as I tasted him, and I wanted to do it again, just to please him. I strained against the ropes hating that I couldn't touch him.

"Open." He demanded, and the moment I did, his hard cock slammed into my mouth as he grabbed hard at my hair. The initial shock made me gag as he pulled my head back slightly. Before he could push back into my throat, I swirled my tongue and sucked hard as he groaned and started to fuck my mouth. His sounds of pleasure were enough to undo me. If this was the reward for being tied up and letting this gorgeous demon of murder fuck my mouth, I would take it.

"*Fuck, you're fucking amazing at this!*" He moaned, causing my wetness to double and run down my thighs. I needed to touch him. I pulled again at my binds, but they wouldn't budge. Next time I was going to touch him, and there would *sooo* be a next time.

He continued to thrust in and out, his moves getting frantic before he grunted and a rush of his cum filled my mouth, which I quickly swallowed down. He finished his release and then pulled my hair, forcing me to look away from his still hard, pulsing dick even though all I wanted to do was retake it.

"Now you're about to be properly fucked, Akira Black."

I licked my lips, cleaning up the last drops of his cum. My high started to die down, making me realize the nipple clamps were still on me as he untied my arms and unbuckled the collar. I reached to remove them, but he stopped me.

"Those stay on."

I stood, raising an eyebrow at him before walking forward, grabbing his cock and stroking the smooth skin, euphoric to finally touch it. I moaned, and he mimicked the noise as I squeezed harder.

"And if I don't want them on?" I asked with a sly smile as I watched his eyelids flutter.

"Then...this will happen." He grabbed my arm, throwing me over his lap as he sat on the bed. His hard cock rested under my belly while he held both of my wrists easily in one hand, and before I could think, his firm hand slapped down against my ass. I quickly realized this time was punishing, unlike the pleasure I felt last time. He spanked me again, causing me to cry out.

"You." Cander murmured as he paused his assault to massage my aching ass, making me moan. Unfortunately, it evaporated quickly with another scream of pain. "Can have pain...or pleasure, Kira."

I whimpered, bracing for his hand again, but instead, he pulled me up and pushed me onto the bed. "Get on your back and lift your legs."

My heart raced as I scrambled back on the bed before lying down.

"I'm *starving*." He growled, and it was the only warning I got before he swung my legs over his shoulders, and his cock slammed painfully into my body. I screamed, and my blades erupted from my forearms. I breathed out harshly, and never once did Cander slow down but roughly shoved into me *instead*. I opened my eyes, willing myself to relax, and I noticed trails of black blood racing down his arms from where I'd stabbed him with my demon claws.

He dropped my legs quickly before leaning forward and kissing me deeply, slowing his thrusts. "If you say this is too much, I will only fuck you harder until you learn...do you understand?" He asked, and it was hard not to be pissed. As far as first times went, I didn't think he was going to be a wuss, but fuck, he could be a *little* gentle.

"Yes." I grounded out, before looking away as tears gathered in my eyes.

I heard him scoff, and he stopped still deep inside me. "I need to feed, and I'm drained. *You need to feed*. Do you feel the power you're getting?" He grabbed my chin, forcing me to look at him. "Do you feel the tingle?" He asked, pushing further into me, more than I thought possible, and it suddenly felt good. "Do you feel the pleasure?" He rotated his hips, and this time I moaned, realizing it *was* pleasurable. I looked up at the mirror and watched his ass flexing as he pushed into me with skillful thrusts, my breathing started to pick up as the pain evaporated. Watching him fuck me was the biggest turn on I'd ever experienced.

"Now," He ran his tongue along my lower lip, and I captured it with my teeth, sucking it into my mouth as I ground into him. He pulled away, breaking our kiss with a concentrated look. "Bite. Me."

His thrusts sped back up, causing me to growl in pleasure as I looked at the throbbing vein in his neck. "With pleasure."

I heard him suck in a breath at my vicious bite. I loved the feel of his hot blood running down my throat, and his power filling me like never before. A sudden orgasm rushed through me at his moans of pleasure and pulsing cock deep inside me, and I released my bite with a mix of screams and growls.

I wanted *more*!

"FUCK!" He screamed as I bit him again on the other side of his neck but pulled back when I felt the nipple clamps tighten.

I guess I wasn't a good girl anymore.

"Get on your hands and knees." Still trying to catch my breath, I licked my lips, looking at the delicious blood racing down his tight pecs and abs. I pulsed again and realized I wasn't even close to being done with him.

"Do you want me to fuck you harder this time?" He asked in a low voice that promised pleasure. I got on my hands and knees before looking back at him as he pushed his hair back from his face.

"Yes, please."

A stinging that pulled more pleasure than pain raced across my ass, and this time I wanted to feel it again. I screamed in ecstasy.

"You never ask for what you want, Kira!" He growled, and I looked back to see his gold eyes had turned red, and a devilish desire raced through me. "You demand it!"

He reached forward as he mounted me from behind, and I shivered as the clamps tightened while he rubbed a cold liquid against my anus. "Cander?" I asked cautiously.

"Just relax, its lube." *I got that*, but he knew my question without me having to ask. Was he going to take me up the ass without asking first?

"Can-"A sudden pressure pushed against and into my ass and I screamed before grunting through the pain.

"It's just a butt plug. It will enhance everything. Just *breathe*." He said before placing a gentle kiss on my ass, and then a blindfold fell across my eyes. I laughed nervously, feeling only pain but ready for the pleasure. The high that I felt told me I was just getting warmed up, and we were in for a long night. I wanted to turn the tables, and for every pain he gave, I was going to give back.

I felt him position his cock at my entrance, making me squirm in excitement.

"I'm not moving until you demand it, baby girl." The nickname sent thrills through me, causing my heart to skip a beat.

I gripped the blanket as I licked my lips.

"Harder, now!"

The last thing I heard that night before passing out was Cander's soft whispering voice saying,

Welcome to Hell, baby girl.

Welcome, indeed.

20

SHOCK

"*H*OLY SHIT!" I gasped.

It wasn't every day you woke up to the gate-keeper twins of Purgatory standing over your bed watching you sleep.

"What the hell are you guys doing?" A wave of dizziness hit me as I sat up in bed, bringing the sheets up to cover myself.

"We are not that scary," Cain said with a flare of attitude while setting a breakfast tray down on my lap. The intense and delicious smell of chocolate chip waffles hit me, and I looked down to see a stack of them along with coffee, bacon, and eggs making my mouth water. I rubbed my eyes, looking at the tray, and then to the twins.

"Thanks?"

Elijah made himself comfortable at the foot of the bed, crossing his legs in front of him criss-cross applesauce style. If I weren't still trying to calm down from getting the shit scared out of me, I would've found his cute little kid mannerisms funny.

"Pshh." Cain hit Elijah, making him scoot over. "We get you your *favorite* breakfast foods, and that's *all* the thanks we get." How did they know this was my favorite?

"Sorry." I took in a deep breath. "You just startled me awake is all." I reached for my fork, no longer able to ignore the mouth-watering smells coming from the tray. "Where's Cander?"

"Well, we have a full day ahead of us getting you ready for your trials tonight, so eat up, and don't worry about him. He had some business with Anock today." Cain said, reaching over and stealing the coffee from my tray.

"HEY!" I shouted, but it just caused him to laugh.

Cain took a sip giving an overly dramatic sigh of content-ment before putting it back on my tray, all while I watched with my fork in the air frozen mid-bite. Un-freaking-believable. Can't a girl have her own coffee in this place?

"Oh, chill. We are going to be around for a *long-time* sister, so you best get used to us now."

"True." Elijah agreed. I scoffed before taking a bite of my food, *finally*.

The explosion of flavor in my mouth had me closing my eyes. *Fuck*, when was the last time I'd eaten? This was a close second to sex at this point, and that was saying something. Cander said I didn't have to eat now that I was immortal, but if the food was always this good here, unnecessary eating was a *must*!

I took a drink of coffee, pleasantly surprised that it was just to my liking, with a touch of vanilla creamer to it. "I thought Cander said I didn't have to train for this thing last night after I accidentally opened up that portal."

"Umm, no. You *need* to train because you accidentally opened up that portal. I'm guessing he was being sarcastic. You're lucky Cander is a Watcher and was able to close it." I continued to eat while listening to Elijah's explanation and overly dramatic hand motions. It was mildly amusing. "You literally opened a portal during your big O! Which is *super hilar-*

ious, by the way." He paused for him and Cain to laugh at my expense.

Okay, so what?

I may have accidentally opened up a portal when I was in the middle of having the most earth-shattering orgasm of my life, so sue me. How was I supposed to know I could do that?

"You are one powerful bitch!" Cain said, causing me to sigh.

"I had no idea I could even do that!" I argued, watching Elijah reach over and steal a piece of bacon.

"We could tell! The alarms sounded, and we busted in here. Imagine our surprise to see you riding Cander's face, reverse-cowgirl style, and screaming OH GOD, OH GOD!" Elijah said, laughing between his horrid imitations of my screams.

I hid my molten face in my hands, the embarrassment of it all coming back to me. There I was, coming on his face when this giant black hole opened up by the bed, along with wild winds and a roar so loud I couldn't hear. I screamed and jumped off Cander, who closed it with a wave of his hand while laughing his ass off, only to turn around and see the twins watching it all in shocked amusement.

It was an interesting end to our night long sex session, *that* was for sure.

"Okay, okay. We'll stop teasing you so you can eat. Now that you're eating for two, you'll need your strength for portal training."

Coffee came out of my nose, and eggs flew down my windpipe. What in the actual fuck did he just say? If it weren't for Elijah coming over and slapping a hand on my back, I would have keeled over my eggs.

"Eating for two?" I asked.

What a *not* so funny joke. Did they not realize that last night was the first time I'd ever had sex?

"Oh, we realized it. What *you* don't realize is that supernatural pregnancies happen a lot differently than human ones.

How do you think Anock has over a thousand hell spawns?"
Cain asked.

Anock had a thousand what? I shook my head in confusion.
Who was Anock? And did he just read my mind?

"Wait, you can read minds?" I asked Cain.

"Well, duh, we both can. Usually, all Watchers can. You just
didn't get that power. Anyways, that's not the point. There is
only a certain limited number of supernatural beings that have
ever been able to get pregnant, and it just so happens you're one
of them."

I set my tray aside as a slight buzz of panic filled my head.
"Oh my God! You're serious!? Or you think you're serious!?" I
got up from the bed, not caring about my nakedness as I walked
over to a dresser with my clothes Cander showed me last night.
I looked down at my flat belly before putting on my bra and
scoffing. This had to be some hazing the new demon joke.

"We don't think *we know*, and this *isn't* a trick. We could
smell it on you as soon as we came in this morning. So while
you were sleeping, Elijah used his magic to look inside you and
confirmed it."

I blanched. "He did what to me!"

"Oh chill, it's just a little spell like X-Ray vision. It's harmless, but the point is you're going to be a mama demon, so
congrats, girl!" I couldn't see which one of them said that as I
put on underwear, but the cockiness in his voice proved he
believed it. Either that or he was an excellent actor.

I wasn't sure what to say. I opened and closed my mouth
more times than I could count but stopped when I realized
nothing was coming out. The shock was taking over my vocal
cords. Five minutes awake, and I'm told I'm pregnant after only
one night of sex. *One!* This was a joke, it had to be. Instead of
responding, I continued to put on the Watcher's uniform
Cander had set out for me.

"She's in shock." I heard one of them whisper, and I looked

over my shoulder to see them both eating my breakfast. I rolled my eyes, turning back around. "Well, we told her. It's not up to us to make her believe it." I heard them continue.

"I can hear you."

"Oh." They snickered as my patience quickly evaporated. "Well, *anywho*. We both thought it would probably be best not to tell Cander about this little speed bump until after you complete your trials." Cain said as I walked over and sat on a stool to tie up my boots.

"Okay, so say I really am pregnant, and this isn't all just some play a trick on the new girl. *One*, why would it matter if I told him or not? I mean, if you guys could tell this morning that I was pregnant, what makes you think he hasn't already discovered it this morning also? *Two*, how the hell could you tell I was pregnant the morning after having sex for the first time? Supernatural pregnancy or not, that sperm would be nowhere near any of my eggs yet. *Three*." I paused, standing up as I forgot what three was, or just didn't have anything else to add.

Before I could open my mouth to continue, a robust masculine scent of sweat, blood, and leather from somewhere in the living room assaulted my senses. My vagina suddenly throbbed, a line of drool slipped out my mouth that I didn't even have time to wipe before a wave of dizziness hit me so hard, I almost collapsed. I sat down right as Cander walked in, covered in sweat and blood. His uniform ripped in various places, and my mouth watered at the strong scent of his blood. He looked like he just came from a battle against every demon in this place. It was the biggest turn on, and my fangs started to grow before I shook my head, reigning in my weird hormones.

"Told you." I looked over to see Cain and Elijah on the bed, giving me a, we told you so look along with pursed lips and hands on their hips. They told me I was pregnant, not that I suddenly had a super scent and an extreme urge to fuck at the smell of Cander's blood. I had no answer for the dizziness, and I had no idea what all pregnancies entailed. Still, all the things I was experiencing were probably just me being a new demon.

"Told you what?" Cander said, running a hand through his sweat-drenched hair as he paused midway to our bathroom. "Shouldn't you have her training already?" He asked the twins.

I forced myself to look away from the tear in his shirt and instead into his sexy-as-fuck eyes. "Umm...yeah, well, Cain and Elijah were just telling me an interesting story." I began, looking over to see their eyes widen with a frantic look.

Cain hopped off the bed, and Elijah followed. "Akira, don't," Elijah warned with a panicked look, and I smiled. I got them. They *must* have been joking if they didn't want me to tell on them for pulling a prank.

Cander turned towards us now narrowing his eyes as he took in the situation. "What's going on?"

"They think I'm pregnant." I blurted out with a laugh while pointing to the guilty parties.

My laugh quickly died when two things happened in a flash so fast I barely caught it. Cander turned as white as a ghost before throwing the nearest thing in his path. Unfortunately, that thing just happened to be Elijah, to the other side of the room. His overly loud gay scream and blurred body flew past my face, and I stumbled back, landing on my butt back in the chair, trying not to laugh as he then went for Cain.

"No! Easy! Cander calm down!" Cain yelled out like he was talking to a rabid dog. I pursed my lips to keep in my laugh, Cander *did* kind of look like one. And so what if he was beating their asses, serves them right for joking about something like that. Pregnancies were not a joke!

Cain's hand lit up with a swirling ball of purple light that he threw, hitting Cander. Which only made Cander pause briefly in his attempt to kill him. He was furious that they would joke about something so serious, or he believed them and wasn't happy about the situation. Either way, when I took in the seriousness in both men's eyes, my laughter died. Cander's eyes were bright red, and he was breathing like a freight train. I stood, needing to calm this situation somehow.

"Cander, calm down." I started. "They are just joking, and shame on them for such a shit joke, but is that any reason to throw Elijah?" I looked over at Elijah, climbing back out of the rubble that used to be our dresser. Lord, give me strength.

Cander turned his red eyes to me temporarily before making his way cautiously towards me. Seeing him approach me with red eyes raised my anger. Hell no, if he thought he was going to come at me like that, super great sex or not, he had another thing coming.

"Akira, be careful, he's in a rage," Cain warned. I heard him but kept eye contact with Cander as he stopped right in front of me, looking me up and down like he was sizing me up to kill. I stayed still remembering how much hell I caught when Ian was in a rage. No matter how much being threatened pissed me off, I didn't want a repeat of getting choked.

Cander dropped to his knees, his face inches from my vagina, startling me. He leaned forward, taking a deep sniff before grabbing my ass and pushing my vagina into his face. Ugh, this felt good and all, but the sniffing was *super weird*, and we had an audience.

As quick as his little sniff my vagina activity started, it ended, and he pulled back as if it bit him before getting back onto his feet. He turned and let out a demon growl so big that it filled the room. It was a roar filled with pain, fear, and sadness, and that scared me.

"Umm..." I looked to the twins and then to Cander's pacing form, as my hands started to shake in fear. He was acting like what they said was true, but that couldn't be right. None of this could be right. *Right*? "Oh, God." The sudden anxiety and fear of the situation hit my stomach. I bolted for the toilet slamming the bathroom door behind me as I threw up my breakfast. Unfortunately, it did not taste good the second time around.

Once I'd thrown up everything and my stomach calmed down, I freshened up before heading out to see the twins gone and Cander on the edge of the bed staring intently at the ground.

"Cander, it's not true. There's no way-"

"You're pregnant."

"*I* just don't understand why Cander reacted that way?" I said, watching intently for a person in a different color shirt other than white to come by. We learned the hard way that I can open a portal just fine, but where it opened...that was a whole other thing entirely. The first four times I *did* manage to open one, that much was apparent by the alarms going off in the mansion. The only problem was that we hadn't been in there when I was trying to open them, but out by the white tree. After I accidentally swallowed a random demon up into God knows where, Cain and Elijah brought me back into the mansion and through a door that led to more desert. This was a different desert. Honestly, this shit was hella confusing, but *this* desert, unlike the desert outside the mansion, had people wandering around like zombies and wearing all white.

They explained I wouldn't be able to move my portals out of here because it was a realm all to itself and that this was the perfect place to practice. The goal was to portal one of these zombie people to where Elijah stood a football field length away. I also learned that Cain and Elijah were very protective of the white-clothed zombies, and when I called them zombies, they got mad.

"For the last time, they are just people who have died and

are waiting to see what realm they belong to. That is so disrespectful of the dead, and there are no such things as zombies."

After Cain's hissy fit, I decided to focus on opening the portals and not teasing him anymore. But *whatever*, they were still zombies. I mean, I watched one of them run into another, then they fell in a pile, and more zombies fell on top of *them*, and before long, it was just a pile of useless zombies. *Also, it was freaking hilarious*. They also said that if I got one of the more frantic zombies in regular clothes that ran around screaming for help weaving in and out of the slow zombies, I got a hundred points. I wasn't sure what the points led up to, and when I asked, they just said I would get a surprise if I got to a thousand, so that was my goal for the day.

So far, I'd accidentally managed to suck Elijah up into a portal. We lost him for a good twenty minutes before he portalled himself back. Before we could ask why his clothes were burnt, he grumbled, not another word before limping back to his spot, which had me laughing so hard I almost pissed myself.

"Because these trials or initiation, *whatever you want to call it*, are dangerous. Watchers are supposed to be the strongest demons in Hell. This test is designed to push your limits. Only the strongest make it through. There have been demons that have died during the trials trying to become a Watcher. Yes, you're a gatekeeper but to be a Watcher and be accepted by Anock...you have to pass this. There is no backing out either. You have to go through with it, and Cander knows that. He's scared, for you *and* the baby."

I looked over into Cain's concerned expression. "That's why it is so important you get this right. You will have to portal to every realm in Hell and retrieve a key, except for the King's Realm and Jax's Realm. You could see how going to see his mother would be an issue after you killed him. Anock was gracious enough to let that one slide. Once you get these keys, you bring them back, and you're home free."

"That's it?" I asked. It seemed way too easy.

Cain scoffed. "Did you not see Cander when he came back today from hiding those keys in all the realms?" He paused, pointing to a frantic woman running around calling for someone named Dave, while my heart shrunk, and not for the zombies. If he came back looking like he'd fought for his life and that was just to hide them, what the hell would I return looking like when I went to retrieve them.

"Exactly," Cain said, answering my thoughts. "Now concentrate. You will have to be able to portal yourself back here and we don't have a lot of time." I took a deep breath before letting it out slowly and shaking out my hands.

I *could* do this. I *had* to do this, and Cain was right. Maybe it was the insanity of all this, or perhaps I was trying to ignore that I had a growing demon baby in my stomach. Still, the fact was, I hadn't been taking this very seriously, and it was time I started.

I watched as she ran from person to person crying out. Given how fast and hysterical she was, there was no way I was going to be able to get her. So instead, I would focus on the slow ones for now. I zeroed in on an adorable little boy with short brown-black hair and big round brown eyes. My heart broke for this baby. Why did the young have to die? Not him, I didn't want to hurt him accidentally. I looked over to see a woman that looked like a stuck-up bitch. She was perfect.

Raising my hands how they taught me, I closed my eyes and called for my power. It always came in the form of tiny tingles along my skin, and I knew it was ready. Opening my eyes, I looked from the lady to Elijah. I wanted her to go to Elijah, so I concentrated on where she was going, instead of where she was now. *Breathe in. Breathe out.* I grunted in concentration as I threw my hands out, imaging where I wanted a portal to go. I almost closed it in shock when it appeared where I wanted it. Holy shit, I did it! The woman slowly meandered in with a blank stare and not a care in the world where she was going. Right as I closed it, to open one by Elijah, the frantic woman still screaming for Dave tripped and fell into two more zombies. *Bonus*. Looking at Elijah, I threw out my arms, aiming for them to reappear there.

A huge black hole ripped open and out walked the zombies and one frantic zombie right next to Elijah. I closed my hands and dropped my arms, letting the tingling of my powers die down. I hadn't heard anything Cain was screaming until my hearing came back full blast, telling me I must have been concentrating pretty hard.

"OMG YOU SEXY MERMAID PREGNANT BITCH *YOU DID IT*!!" He shouted, picking me up and hopping up and down while I laughed and struggled to breathe.

Cain put me down when I gasped for breath. "Okay, now do that about a million more times and a lot faster."

"Deal, but won't that drain my powers for tonight?"

"I wouldn't worry about that. I'm sure Cander is planning on giving you a boost before you leave." He said with a wink, as I concentrated on another zombie.

"Wait, you never told me how many points the normal zomb-"I paused, wincing before correcting myself. "I *mean,* people are." I bit my lip to keep from laughing at the angry face he was giving me.

"The white-clothed people are 10."

"WHAT! That's not fair!" I whined.

Cain laughed before snapping his finger for me to look ahead. "Back to work, bitch. We still have to tour the realms."

*A*fter what felt like five hours in that hot ass sun moving zombies, I finally got it down well enough to switch our practice location to the white tree outside of the mansion. When I got done moving the other people where I wanted them, I practiced portaling myself. After that, I did both simultaneously, before eventually mastering opening a portal to Earth. I was glad that I was learning this ability and even mastering it, but the closer we got to my trials, the more frantic and irritated I got. The image of Cander coming back bloodied and tore up kept replaying through my mind. I *couldn't* fight. I didn't know *how* to fight. What if I had to fight my way out of a bad situation and died. Not only did I have myself to look after now, but I had my baby. That thought was still a foreign concept that didn't seem real yet, so I tried not to think about it during training, but it reminded me how much I had to lose.

"So there is one King, one Prince and seven Queens of Hell, which makes up the nine realms. You will not be going to the First Realm, which is the King's, and you will not be going to the Third Realm, Asgret's Realm." Elijah said as we walked over to the tree.

He opened a portal, but before we went through, he stopped me. "We are going to the Second Realm, Queen Mandra's Lava Realm. This is the first one you will go to after it starts. Pay attention to your surroundings while we are here, and do so quickly. We are only giving you a sneak peek, but remember, to portal to a place; you have to have been there. So absorb what you need to, and fast."

I sucked in a shaky breath, feeling nervous. I mean, we were getting ready to step into a mother freaking Lava Realm. "Will I meet the Queen while we're there?" I asked.

Cain shook his head. "No. All the Queens will be at the ceremony with Anock awaiting your return. You will be given complete reign over their realms to find these keys, and they are not to be there to help in any way."

He shoved me forward to walk towards the portal. "Then how the hell am I supposed to find a key in a whole realm?!" That was a bunch of bullshit!

"You will be assigned someone to assist you with finding the keys, but they can't help you out of trouble, and they can't portal you. They are only there to help with the clue for that realm and be your tour guide. Nothing more."

I sighed. This was going to suck ass.

Both Cain and Elijah grabbed my wrists as we stepped through the portal together, and I was glad they did, so there was no chance that I would get lost in the middle of nowhere. The feeling of weightlessness came over me only for a minute before we stepped out into some type of throne room that was a million degrees. The air was so hot it hurt to breathe. It was also huge, like Asgret's throne room, but this had glass walls giving you the perfect view of the lava that poured down them from the other side. I stared straight ahead at the throne, which was surrounded by a lava ring, with a background of, you guessed it, *lava*. Along the walls held charred bones in some type of decorative pattern. Before I could ask any questions or take any more time to look, Cain was pulling me back to a portal that one of them must have opened.

"Okay, enough viewing. Now you know where the lava realm is, time to head to Realm Four the Revenge Realm." I strained to take any more detail in that I could as he continued to walk and talk. The glimmer of something blinding me for a split second stole my attention to the throne, but before I could look further, he tugged me forward. "The Revenge Realm was once Queen Eiseth's Realm, but she has recently passed away due to some...unfortunate circumstances. It now belongs to Queen Balli."

No sooner than we reached Elijah, the portal sucked us in

once more, and nausea hit me, but I managed to hold it in. I'd heard that throwing up was one of the symptoms of pregnancy, but this was a bunch of bullshit. How was I supposed to concentrate if I was sick all the time? Queen Balli's Realm of Revenge looked like an actual horror movie. Bright red marble tiles made up the floor and leading up to the throne featured black statues that had moving eyeballs. The throne had flames licking up the back of the chair, and above it, hung a chandelier made of bones. The longer we stayed, the more chills I got in this place, so I was glad when we headed for the next realm. I repeated them in my head to keep them straight, lava was two, three was the crazy realm, and four was revenge.

"Next stop is Realm Five, which is your realm, the Sexual Realm. Queen Lilith runs it, although you probably already know that." Cain said, and I scoffed. Yeah, I knew all about that crazy bitch, and her snake that almost bit out my throat. I swear if she weren't my Queen, I would kill that huge nasty thing next time I saw it.

We stepped through the portal to a throne room filled with orgies. *Eeek and Ewww*! Thank God Lilith wasn't here, but her loyal subjects were, and everywhere you looked, someone was getting fucked, sucked, or railed on. It was massively awkward and as horny as I was all the time, this was just *sooo* uncomfortable and disgusting. I looked over to her green velvet backed throne to see her asshole snake on it.

I turned away. "Okay next realm." At this, the twins laughed but must have agreed because Elijah opened a portal.

"Okay, next is Realm Six, the Realm of Emotions. Queen Fellen ran it, but Mikayla killed her, so they are currently awaiting the King to pick another from his harem."

"A Queen from a harem? Realm of Emotions? Like, where Strife and Envy are from?" I asked right before we stepped through.

"Exactly." Elijah was the one to answer me this time as we all stepped through to color Hell.

It looked like a rainbow threw up, and I blinked at the bright colors, squinting my eyes. *Dear baby puppies! Did they have Lisa Frank down here? What the hell?*

The black marble-tiled floor of this throne room reflected all the wild colors of the spotlights pointing down from the ceiling. The walls twirled on their own like a bad hippy trip lava lamp, and every single thing here was hard to see. The throne was clear glass but hollow, and the inside swirled with a cloud that turned different colors. This place should be called the mind-trip realm instead. *Eesh.*

"Okay, this place sucks. Let's go to seven." I said, feeling like I was about to puke again. I *really, really, really* did not want to look for a key in this place.

The twins laughed, and we stepped back into the portal, walking out in front of the mansion. "Ta-da!" Elijah said. "Realm Seven is Purgatory, and your last stop before you will make your way to the drawing room to present your keys."

"And that's all there is to it!" Cain announced like this was going to be a cakewalk.

I took a shaky breath, telling myself I could do this, I had to do this. Reaching down, I placed a hand on my stomach and looked down. I just hoped I didn't kill us in the process.

21

TRIAL & ERROR

*A*fter portal practice I met Cander at our place, which I found out was just *his place*. He showed me to an adjoining space connected to his, through the living room, and it had pretty much everything his room had but was more girly. I even had my own bedroom. When I asked why we had two bedrooms, he said that he'd told me that this wasn't going to be a loving relationship from the beginning. He said he wanted me, but the marriage was just about finishing the deal. He also made it clear that he wasn't going to mess up this time and get attached like he had the last time. Whatever that meant. Sex this time was different too. He seemed distracted and would barely kiss me. He lasted just enough to give me power, then pulled out and threw my clothes at me.

I wasn't sure what I did to make him act like that, and it just kept getting worse from there. On the way to meet the twins, who he said would be escorting me down to the table of royalty, he wouldn't stop asking me if I was okay or if I needed anything. It didn't make any sense and fueled my anger so much that I accidentally raged out on him two times, almost killing a small white cat and three goblin looking things in the hallway. He wanted to know if I was okay? If I needed anything? Oh, I don't know-how about a caring fiancé? How about having sex with some feeling, care, and emotion to it instead of just fucking someone only to feed? When I calmed down, right before we got to the drawing room, he said it was probably just my hormones, and I lost it again, this time slashing and clawing down his face. I probably would have killed him if Cain and Elijah hadn't come along and put me into some invisible box. After that, Cander walked away with a roar so loud it shook the floor.

The twins calmed me down with some weird blue swirling light that felt amazing. It relaxed my muscles and put enough calm over me enough that I stopped raging and trying to kill everything. I was still pissed about our separate spaces, or maybe it was about me marrying someone who pretty much said it was just for business? Or perhaps it was because he now acted like sex was nothing to him after our first time, and all the things he said and all the things I felt, only to act as if he only cared about the baby. Was everything leading up to this fake? All the things he said. All the growls when someone touched me, or the caring attitude?

After they finished getting me ready I looked like *Xena, the Warrior Princess*, and there was nothing left to do but sit in the drawing room and wait for my trials to begin. I put Cander out of my mind as much as I could.

"What is the point of the Watchers?" I asked, breaking the silence.

Cain looked over from where he sat, scoffing at me. "I thought Cander explained all that."

"He did, I mean to an extent. I guess he just didn't explain everything."

Elijah and Cain started in with just as much as Cander had said the first time. It only confused me more, but it was still better than thinking about my other frustrations, and if this was to be my life, it was best I understood it.

"Why can't Anock just take this girl? Why did he trust this Blake guy, who she was Fated to be with?" I sucked in an annoyed breath, playing with one of the two battle axes they'd given me. "It seems like a lot of this could have been avoided. I mean, our job is to make sure Hell wins the curse of the apocalypse, right?"

Elijah nodded, taking a sip of his martini, that he had magically made, before answering. "Yes, a lot of this *could* have been, but Blake and James had to pick a side. Good or evil. The balance was still..." He paused, looking at Cain. "Sorry, my brain is a little fried today from you and your future hubby's assaults." I smiled, holding back a laugh, yeah...he'd taken a beating today. *Oops.*

Cain sighed, snapping his fingers for his own martini to appear in his hand. "The balance *was* un-balanced with their birth, but you can't just have supernaturals running around without being claimed. To be fair, they each had to pick a side, and James picked the Chosen while Blake chose the Watchers. Anock thought it was better to keep Blake close to keep an eye on him, so he made him his guard *and* a Watcher. Blake wouldn't have been a disturbance in our plans to take Mikayla if he'd never gotten his memory back. There is a long back story we can't possibly tell you all in one night, but we lost her either way. Now we have to get her back. In the meantime, the Watchers still have the job of grabbing *other* potential women on Earth for Anock to mate with and add to the Dark Nephilim Army."

"*Hmm*...So why do you guys have magic, and none of the rest of the Watchers do?" Before they could answer, my mind flashed back to how they appeared in my bedroom to wipe my friends' memories. "And why do you guys look like the Grim Reaper and don't need a portal to appear on Earth?"

Cain and Elijah both looked to each other before sighing. Cain walked over, putting his hand on my shoulder before sitting next to me. "I see now that Cander never told you who we are."

"Not that it matters," Elijah added grumpily, and I could tell I'd hit a nerve. I mean the first night in the hallway, they didn't say what they were like Andy and Rose had, but they *did* make it seem like I shouldn't have asked.

"We have magic because our mother was a Magical."

I looked to his sad face then to Elijah's. "So Magicals like warlocks and witches?" I asked.

"Yes." Cain laughed, shaking his head before looking away. "Our mother was a witch. Not a very powerful one but a witch all the same. And our father..."

He paused for so long that I wasn't sure if he was going to answer. Elijah stood and made his way over to lean against the arm of the couch in front of us. "Is the King."

"The King? As in, like Satan or the Devil?" I asked shakily. If that was the case that would make them-

"The Antichrists, according to the Christian Bible," Cain said, answering my thoughts.

My mouth dropped, and a rush of fear coated my arms in the form of goosebumps. I'd been around them this whole time. It was weird to think of them like that, though. I mean, we were *all* demons. I knew that, but they just didn't fit the bill or what I would imagine as the King's sons. My nerves calmed down after thinking it through.

"Oh," I said, unsure of what else to say.

"Yeah, oh," Cain said.

"But if you guys are real-"I stopped when they both gave me a deadpan expression. "I mean, born. Wouldn't that have made the balance uneven, or are you saying that Jesus isn't real? But that still wouldn't make sense because Jesus was human, and you all are...well not, so if he is real, then the balance would still be more to Hell, right?"

They both watched as I rambled on, and I couldn't take sitting down anymore, so I paced while gathering my thoughts. This was all a lot to take in! I mean, holy shit! I was getting an exclusive on what humans would kill to know firsthand! I never went to church growing up, and it probably stemmed from having a demon father and a witch nanny. However, I still knew enough about the Christian religion. Now with what I knew and what was real, it was mind-boggling.

"Listen, this is not what you need to be focusing on right now," Elijah said, standing and stopping my pacing.

I ignored him. "But if you're so powerful, then why can't you guys just snap to wherever Mikayla is and take her?"

He sighed before putting a hand on his hip. "Because that's not how it works. We can go to someone on Earth who summons us or is dying and predestined for our realm, but that's it."

Cain stood to shove a purple drink in my hand that had a little umbrella in it. I looked at it before I took the glass. "I'm pregnant, *remember*? I thought pregnant women weren't supposed to drink." I asked, feeling weird referring to myself as one. I still didn't feel like one.

"*Psh*. You are also a demon, and since Cander and Anock appointed us as your new baby physicians, we say alcohol is fine." Elijah said, forcing me to sit back down by my axes and take the drink. I looked over to the sharp axes before taking a sip. It tasted like grape soda. That was another thing that cracked me up. They expected me to have the knowledge to use those axes, and it was *hysterical*. I'd most likely end up axing my damn leg off before defending myself with one of them.

"So when we get Mikayla back, and Anock marries her, and we have a super army to win the apocalypse, we win? So what's so bad about Hell winning if it's like this? This isn't so bad." I said, looking at potentially two of the scariest demons here and holding back a laugh at their prissy demeanor and harmless martinis.

Cain shook his head. "You aren't getting it. Hell will completely take over Earth. Demons, the King, and all the Queens will be unleashed and have free reign over the humans. There are gatekeepers like us, not to keep Hell in, but gates made by Heaven to keep stuff out. Angels and other demons, or worse the demons from the King's Realm."

"But from what I saw so far, I mean, we all have our demon forms, but it seems like we are all decent when in human form," I argued. It seemed weird to me; Cain and Elijah were demons in Hell, and they didn't want Hell to win but wasn't that why we were all fighting? For our side to win? If Heaven won, weren't we all supposed to die?

"You just aren't getting it. Humans are like a necessary bug in the animal food chain. It keeps all us supernaturals busy running the system and keeping things in line. We demons need to eat, and only tortured humans go to Hell. Angels need to protect humans on Earth. Magicals need to keep angels and demons in line. And all of it works like that forever. The Almighty got bored and threw a kink in the chain by creating that curse, the apocalypse. Now activated, there's no stopping it, but maybe with Mikayla, Blake, and James, there can be a decent outcome. Maybe it can be righted again. If Anock gets Mikayla, it's over. No more balance. No more Earth." Elijah said. "There are a lot worse demons out there that you have yet to see. If Hell wins, it will be chaos, bloodshed, and mayhem. Your friends and everyone you've ever known will end up in one of those scary-ass rooms."

"So you don't want Anock to win? Your very own side? On the opposite side of everything, what if Heaven wins, won't we all die?"

Elijah and Cain stood taking a step back against the wall as the sound of drumming started from behind the door. "Or... what if it just stayed like it was now?" Cain asked, avoiding my questions.

Before I could answer, the drumming got louder, and I stood and faced the doors. My nerves and heartbeat picked up from the unknown. I was nowhere near ready for this. I just hoped I could portal to these places, let alone explore and find keys in them.

"I guess it doesn't matter," I said with a sigh setting the drink down and grabbing the axes.

I looked over to Cain and Elijah stepping up on either side of me. It did little to ease my fear of meeting the fallen angel Anock and going through his trials to join his team.

"Oh, it matters," Cain muttered as the doors started to open.

My sweaty hands tightened around the axes as I first took the smell of sulfur, and then the sight of smoke drifting up to the star-filled sky from in between the snarling demons by the doors. The drums continued to beat loudly in a ceremonial rhythm that reminded me of a tribe of Vikings. It felt like my heartbeat was matching them in terror. Right as the doors slowly opened, Elijah leaned over and whispered in my ear.

"You wanted to know why it would be bad for Hell to win the apocalypse? Well, you are about to experience that answer firsthand."

*O*kay, so Anock *was* scary, but also *super hot*. Even though his enormous black angel wings were intimidating. The way his tanned skin stretched over his tight muscles was pure perfection. So much so that the guy hadn't even bothered with a shirt. Thank whoever the fuck for that. He had honey-colored eyes, high cheekbones, thick lips, and sexy reddish-brown hair that hung loosely around his face. He was what Alex and Kay would call, *super yummy*. I almost wondered if his angel side enhanced his looks. Like James, he held a little more beauty to him than even the sexiest demons.

"It's nice to meet you finally," Anock said with a confident smirk. He situated his hands together in front of him on the table. He was in the middle of, who I assumed were, each of the Queens of Hell. They all sat in front of me at a long black table made out of what looked like black tree branches. Behind each of the royal members stood their gatekeepers, besides Cain and Elijah, who stood next to me. I glanced over to see Cander standing behind Lilith and the sight of her and her evil ass snake that almost ripped out my throat, had a low growl forming in my throat. I looked back to Anock before I made a fool of myself and attacked my own Queen.

"It's nice to meet you as well," I said, straightening my back to show confidence and putting all the other thoughts out of my mind. I could tell this was a sink or swim moment, and obviously, I was here to swim the shit out of this.

Anock chuckled before grabbing a wine goblet in front of him and taking a drink. He looked over to his left and down the table to where Lilith sat. "And how do you feel about your newest gatekeeper?" He asked her.

My heart sped up in anticipation of what she would say about me. That warlock had revealed that I was important, and we found out it was because of my blood, which she now had. She needed me, but I wasn't dumb enough to think that made her like me.

Lilith raised her chin, and avoiding me altogether, looked to the Prince. "I believe she and her son will serve their purpose well."

I gasped. She knew I was pregnant, and that I was having a boy. My eyes flew to Cander, but he just stared forward like I didn't exist, so I looked to Elijah, who jutted his chin forward to look back at the table in front of me. Apparently, everyone knew about this other than me. I'd only been here for two days! Shit! I'd only been pregnant one day!

"Yes." Anock mused. "I had heard from the twins we were expecting another soldier for the army. Two Watchers reproducing should have a potent outcome, indeed. Now that we know she is one of the limited ones capable, she will be next on my list if she survives the birth." He spoke so casually about my fate. I almost thought he was joking.

Lilith chuckled, petting softly at the snake's head. "Of course. However we can further the army. You are welcome to have as many babies with her as possible." She paused, finally looking to me with a wicked smile as I struggled to breathe. "Who knows? She may even be the one to make another dream walker?"

The word dream walker jolted my mind back to the conversation with Cain and Elijah. That was why Anock wanted Mikayla. She could make more dream walkers, and they were the ones that could win the apocalypse. My hands started to shake so bad I almost dropped one of my axes, but thankfully both the twins reached out and wrapped their hands around mine steadying them. I looked once more to Cander, his eyes locked onto mine this time before looking away quickly. It was just long enough for me to catch his anger. Was this why he'd been acting so different lately? Had he known I was going to have to get pregnant by Anock next?

"And how do you feel about that, Akira Black?" Anock asked, stealing back my attention.

I steadied my breathing before answering. "I will do anything I need to serve the realms," I said through clenched teeth. I would say what they wanted to hear for the sake of my neck. That didn't mean I agreed, hot fallen angel or not.

I can see why Cander's anger at my pregnancy went a lot deeper than just me participating in these dangerous trials. He was going to have to share me with Anock. At this point, all I could do was follow along and play the game, but I would find a way out of this.

"Now," Anock said. "There are seven keys that you will need to find. One key in each realm. You will be given a limited amount of time in each realm to find them, one hour per realm. Once you see a purple flash of light fill the sky above you, that is your thirty-minute warning. To find these keys, you will have to work quickly and expertly make your way through these realms with the help of a key finder and one clue. Finding these keys is more than a game."

I sucked in a shaky breath as I listened. Anock continued, "It's about showing that if we send you into one of these realms for whatever reason, you will be able to complete your task and come out alive. My Watchers are the strongest demons in Hell and have all proven their worth in these trials, and now it is your turn to prove yourself."

The more he spoke, the more I shook. It was clear we were approaching the start time, and I wasn't sure I could do this.

No backing out now, you got this. Cain said into my mind.

I looked at him, slightly nodding, looking back to Anock as he spoke again. "The flash of blue light in the sky will mark your start and your end. If, for any reason, you portal back to this spot without all the keys, you forfeit your right to be a Watcher...along with your life."

It was clear he paused to let this sink in, and I wasn't sure I could feel my limbs anymore. I didn't know that. I didn't know that if I didn't succeed, I would die. I looked down the table to all the Queens and their mixed stares of taunting smiles and vicious glares. Some looked evilly amused by the fact that I might die, but half of them looked pissed for some unknown reason. Above an orange-skinned Queen stood Envy and Strife, and I couldn't stare too long at their pitying faces. It was clear that they were scared for me, and that didn't help at all. Although, if they could make it through, maybe I could too?

"You are going to be given a guide to help you figure out the clues. At the request of your fiancé and fellow gatekeeper, I have decided to show leniency towards you based on your condition by allowing a friend to help you. But this demon is in no way to help you portal, or survive an attack. You have to prove that on your own. You are responsible for portalling both you and your guide. Cain and Elijah have set a certain color to you so we can trace your portals. Your helper has a certain color as well. Once you arrive with your keys and have been checked to make sure there are only your colored traces, you will finish and be an official Watcher."

"Bring in the helper!" Anock yelled, and Elijah stepped forward, waving his hand.

In the blink of an eye, Crow appeared with a martini shaker in his hand. "I was fucki-" He paused mid-sentence lowering the shaker and doing a three-sixty. Crow looked around at the audience of demons, the twins and me, then to Anock and the table of Queens. He then dropped the shaker and ran over in front of Lilith, immediately dropping to the ground in a bow. I had to give it to him, for someone who had no idea what was going on, he recovered quickly. "My Queen." He exclaimed. I continued to hold in a laugh at his display. Thank God they gave me Crow.

"What a wonderful way to show praise to your Queen." Lilith purred, looking over the table to where Crow still bowed with his head on the ground. "And such a fine thing at that." She looked behind her at Cander. "Make sure he's greatly rewarded for his help in this little key finding thing." She said.

Cander nodded. "Yes, Your Highness."

I wanted to roll my eyes but held back since Anock's eyes zeroed in on me during this whole scene. So much so that I fidgeted under his glare.

"ENOUGH!" He shouted. "Rise and go to Akira!"

Crow stood and made his way towards me with a concerned stare.

"Now. I will give you five minutes to collect your thoughts and say your goodbyes, and then Cain will light the sky."

Cain nodded, and just like that, all the demons behind us cheered. I looked back to see tables magically appearing with scraps of human parts and pitchers of blood. In an instant, they were tearing at the tables, fighting, and even though we were outside, it was so freaking loud I stepped back, wanting to cover my ears. I looked back at the table where all the royalty sat with their feast. I was glad this was one big celebration for them, while I fought to find some stupid keys. *Not.*

"Akira." I turned to see Cander walking towards me. He glanced at Crow at my side before looking back at me. "There's a lot you still don't understand yet."

"Awkward," Crow said, backing away towards the twins. I rolled my eyes.

"Like if I make it out of this alive, I'll be a common whore, passed around to make babies?" I asked, dropping the stupid axes and crossing my arms.

Cander growled before running a hand down his face. "Just listen." He stepped closer, and I almost moved away, but intrigue stopped me. "I'm sorry." He said, running the back of his hand gently down the side of my face. It felt like Heaven to have his caring side back, but I tried not to show how much I liked his affection. "After I found out, I thought it would be easier to handle all this shit if I pushed you away, but I can't go through what we went through today. When we get back-"He stepped closer, giving me a gentle kiss on my head before stepping back. "We will figure out how to handle all of this."

I sighed. "Okay."

"Hey, Crow!" He shouted, and Crow jogged over.

"What's up, man?" Crow greeted, and they clasped hands

before Cander pulled him in for one of those weird guy hugs, but instead of letting him go, he held him close. "You let anything happen to her or my son I will personally see to it that you are tortured for all of eternity down in the King's Pits." Crow gulped, and Cander released him quickly, making him stumble back.

"Got it, man, of course," Crow said, and I cringed, feeling sorry for him. There was probably a good chance that something could happen, and if it did, Cander should know Crow well enough that it wouldn't be his fault.

"Get ready," Elijah said, walking up, and I looked back to see Cain now standing in front of the table.

Cander's fists clenched, and he leaned forward, whispering in my ear, causing me to shiver. "Be the bad bitch that killed two sharks and ate an evil Prince's heart out. You got this."

As soon as he said that, he and Elijah stepped back, and a flare of blue light lit up the sky along with the drums starting again while a horn sounded. Loud cheers and growls filled the air again as the demons celebrated the start of the trials.

I grabbed both axes in one hand as I pointed to open a portal to the lava realm away from all the spectators. Before I opened it, a piece of paper floated down from the sky in front of us, and Crow jumped up and grabbed it.

"Lightning makes glass and glass holds lava," Crow said, reading the paper. I grabbed his hand and opened the portal concentrating on the lava covered throne room.

Crow squeezed my hand in support.

"Let's go find some lightning."

22

SINK OR SWIM

"*W*hat the fuck!?" Crow exclaimed as we stepped into the lava realm.

I rolled my eyes. "It isn't *that* bad." I spun in a circle taking in the empty throne room. The rush of lava flowing on the other side of the glass made a low gurgling and bubbling sound throughout the space. "I'm just glad I did it right."

Crow laughed, pulling out the paper, and reading it out loud again while I searched for a door. "Okay, it says, lightning makes glass. I've heard that before, so that's right." I sighed, feeling extremely overwhelmed. I grabbed his arm, pulling him to follow me as I spotted a side door further down. I just hoped it didn't open into a wall of lava. Crow continued. "And glass holds lava." I looked over to him as we stopped in front of the door.

"Well, technically, I would think lava could melt glass, but this glass is still holding it. Maybe the key is here in the throne room? This glass is holding the lava outside."

I looked over to the note, then back at the room. "Yeah, I mean, I guess that's right. Okay, you take that side, and I'll look over by the throne." I pointed to the opposite side of the room.

"It wouldn't hurt to look, but for some reason, that seems too easy."

"Right." Crow took off to his side as I headed to the throne. This all did seem a little too easy. I mean, they said to explore the realm, not to just portal to the throne rooms. If that were the case, this shit would be super easy. Yet, Cander showed up all banged up, so it had to be difficult.

Right as I reached the throne with my concentration on the ring of lava floating and bubbling around it, Crow yelled out. "AKIRA!" I looked back to see Crow backing away from some demon cats with red spikes crawling out from a small hole in the wall. They growled and hissed angrily, and even though they were the size of an average house cat, I wasn't dumb enough to think they wouldn't fuck us up.

I looked at my axe, trying to figure out if I could take all twenty of those little shits. There were too many of them though. I would have to get pretty close to swing the axe to hit one. At that point, those things would probably jump all over me and rip me apart.

"RUN!" I shouted, taking my own advice and bolting to the door. The metal handle burned my hand so badly that I screamed and immediately let go of it. I barely managed to open the door as Crow ran up next to me. I was able to open it the rest of the way with my axe before grabbing his hand and running through the dark tunnel. The temperature cooled about twenty degrees the instant we were inside. I looked back to see the cats sitting in the doorway of the throne room hissing and growling at us.

"Shut the door!" I yelled, watching to make sure they weren't chasing us. I was grateful for the burning torches that hung in intervals on the wall; otherwise, I probably would have busted my ass.

"Forget it." Crow slowed his run, and I followed suit. "It doesn't seem like they're following us."

"So," I said, catching my breath and looking around. "If that key is in there, we're fucked unless I can take those things out one at a time."

Crow scoffed. "Those things are pretty tiny, but even with that, you'd have to get really close to them."

I stepped away, lifting my axe. "That's why I said to run."

I watched as a black bug that looked like a beetle scurried past us on the wall, and I shivered in disgust before I could stop it. "Eww. So gross."

"Yeah, I never understood the need for bugs in Hell." Crow said with a laugh.

"*Anyways*, let's go. Maybe we can find something out there that will make more sense for this key crap."

Crow ran his hand through his hair before shaking his head. I looked over to his muscles bulging through his tight black T-shirt and looked away before he caught me. "I don't know why the hell they picked me for this, but I promise I'll help as best I can."

"We'll finish this, don't worry about that."

* * *

Cander

I couldn't stand to look at Anock's smug face, so I walked away from the table and into the mass of demons fighting, clawing, and fucking each other. I stopped at a table when I noticed one of Anock's daughters, Alexis, at a table in her demon form eating the skin off of a human arm. I watched her for a second, the stress taking over my headspace. Would that be mine and Akira's son in a few years? The twins didn't want me to know about Akira being pregnant but felt it necessary to give that information to Anock via mind speak while they were off training her.

I showed up to deliver the newest batch of human mates for Anock with Envy and Strife and was ambushed. Anock asked what I planned to name the baby, and I remember my body automatically filling with dread. I knew it would only be a matter of time before he found out. I was stupid to think I'd be able to keep her hidden away until she gave birth. The whole purpose of our job was to find women for that bastard to rape and impregnate. Then my future wife gets knocked up after our first night together. A demon getting pregnant was extremely rare, so for Anock, a Watcher getting pregnant was like his golden opportunity. I knew there was nothing I could do to stop him from having her. After the shock, then came the anger. Envy and Strife attempted to calm me down, but after I killed half the lower demons in the mansion, they eventually gave up and disappeared.

I was going to have a child, after all these years being alive, and a son at that. I watched as Alexis transformed back into her human form, standing naked covered in blood next to her meal. Being only five, she still had some of her baby fat and was adorable, but as a demon, she was dangerous and, most of the time, uncontrollable. Anock had thousands, maybe even tens of thousands of these dark Nephilim for his army. He had only ever taken a liking to her and let her roam the mansion. The rest are locked away in a room, only getting fed enough to survive and wait there until the final battle. I felt sorry for them, and a lot of the time, I wondered if I was the only one. Anock talked about my son being part of his army, but I would die a thousand deaths before I let him throw my son into that prison. We didn't even know what demon he would be or what powers he'd have.

"Hi, Uncle Cander," Alexis said, walking over and bringing me a baby's severed foot. My stomach clenched, and I leaned down, taking it from her before tossing it on the table behind us.

"Hi, little cat. What are you doing out in this mess?"

She sighed like she was just so overwhelmed with her little life. She probably was. "Daddy didn't feed me today, so I was hungry." She shrugged.

"Where is Candance?" I asked, referring to her nanny.

"Oh." Her tiny bottom lip jutted out. "I ate her."

I blinked as my mouth opened then shut again, trying to find the words. "Hmm. Well, maybe-"Before I could get another word out a hard slap to my back about knocked me over, and I looked up to see Chort, a Watcher from the Ninth Realm.

"Hey there, asshole, whatcha picking on little kids for?"

Before I could answer, a hiss had me looking back to see Alexis had turned back into her cat form. I stood and faced Chort, as she ran off into the crowd. "Man, nothing just trying to make sure she was good."

"Yeah, congrats on the dad title. Sucks you have to give your girl up, though." It's common sharing women, having orgies, or multiple women in your bed, but most of Anock's women didn't survive.

My fists clenched along with my jaw. "Yeah." I dragged a hand down my face letting out a sigh. "It's pretty fucked up. I was hoping to take her far into my realm and hide her, but his fucking lackeys found out."

Chort was a pretty good guy, even though he came from a fucked up realm. The Ninth Realm was one of sorrow, and a lot of the realms were messed up, but his almost topped them. People known for struggling to get past their pain in their own lives were thrown there. It was wailing screams of sadness and moaning cries throughout the realm, and it didn't matter how powerful you were, it sucked all the happiness out of you the moment you were there. The demons there were especially hardened to emotions from the nonstop crying they heard around the clock, making them meaner and more robust fighters. It was always hard to look Chort or his partner in the eyes because I swore every time I did, I saw the tortured pain of what they had become.

Chort scoffed, shoving a cup of black blood in my hand. "Fucked up doesn't even cover it, and I would know." I gulped down a good bit, glancing back to the table to make sure I wasn't needed. Lilith stood up against Anock in a way that said I would be on guard duty by his door tonight. I growled and downed more blood. "Looks like you're going to need this more than me." He said, reaching over to a random table and refilling my cup.

"I just wished I knew how she was doing, man."

"Yeah, I bet. I can't believe they made her go through with it pregnant. I mean, if Anock wants her so bad, why risk it."

Another growl, along with my power flaring up and erupting out of me before I could help it, made him laugh. "Easy killer, I'm on your side."

We stood in silence as I took in the celebrations around us. I was sure I would still be pissed, her being pregnant or not, that I couldn't be the one to help her through this. Akira had become important to me. Even though I wouldn't fucking let it turn into something as serious as love, it messed me up all the same. She was mine, and I wasn't there to protect her. Anock even made sure to rub it in, by having me gather the keys and hide them in some seriously screwed up places. I didn't doubt her skills in the water, especially after taking on two sharks alone, but on land, she had none. Jax was a right time, right place kind of thing. So far, every time she's raged out, it was nothing more than kitten scratches that made me hard more than anything.

A purple light lit up the sky, signaling she only had half an hour left in the lava realm. I downed the rest of my blood and looked to Chort, watching him sway on his feet, apparently deep in the liquor. I grabbed his shoulder and steered him back through the crowd to his partner. "Come on, man, let's sit by our charges so I can get to your level."

———————

So, we'd found the key. Unluckily for us, it just happened to be on a rope dangling over a pool of lava from a cliff surrounded by spiked lava cats. Oh, and once we stepped out of the cave, the whole area was filled with pools of lava with only a small walkway of mazes in between all of it only big enough to walk single file. I managed to stop one cat that rushed us when we first stepped out of the cave. I was balancing between two pools of bubbling lava because I didn't have a choice. It was either that or backing into Crow, essentially knocking *him* over into the lava, and possibly falling in myself. So I ended up swinging the axe broadside like a bat and knocking the little fucker right into the lava. That's when we learned they not only survived the lava but could swim through it like pros. It swam to the other side of the pool with a hiss and left us alone.

Above the lava hanging at odd angles and by random limbs, were who I guessed to be the people who belonged in this realm. Some were alive and screamed as their skin boiled over the hot magma. Some were so close to the lava they were nothing but charred skin, while others had long been dead, probably from the loss of blood to their upper extremities. The heat mixed with the stench of death smelled so bad I felt like even the sweat I wiped away smelt like it. I'd probably gagged about ten times trying to hold back my nausea. There were also random bolts of lightning shooting down every so often from an empty black sky throughout the realm. Those and the lava pools were the only light we had.

Thankfully, there was a little more walking room around the lava where the key hung, but then we saw the cats.

"Okay, so use me," Crow said, making me scoff.

"Like what? You get chased through the realm by demon cats while I scale a flat-faced cliff with an axe, which by the way, is fucking impossible. Then I get the key and somehow get back down? Oh, and then hope you hadn't died along the way." I pointed to the lava. "I mean, I don't know about you...but I highly doubt being immortal or not, that I'd survive falling in that."

Crow sighed. "What other choice do we have?"

I looked to the cliff, cats, and then the lava. There had to be something we were missing. There was a sheer cliff that lava bubbled up against. Somewhere above was an overhang for the rope to hang with the key. I paused in my thinking.

"WAIT! What if we knock down the key?"

"How? And when it falls, how are you supposed to catch it?"

I nodded, still trying to think it through. "I don't know, but what if we use the cats?" That cat earlier fell into the lava and popped back up.

Before I could finish the thought, Crow interrupted. "But what does any of this have to do with the clue. It didn't have anything to do with finding the key, so maybe the paper had something to do with how to get it?"

"Fuck!" I yelled, grabbing at my head. A purple flash of light lit across the sky, and my heart raced at the warning. "FUCK, FUCK, FUCK!" I spun in a circle grabbing at my head. What the fuck was I going to do?

Crow grabbed my shoulders, shaking me out of my freak out. "Okay, stop! Just listen!" I stared into his worried green eyes and took in a slow breath.

"Okay...reread it." I said, moving his hands off my shoulders with my shaky hands. If I failed at the first key, not only was I a pathetic demon but also one who had signed the death warrant for her own baby.

"Lightning makes glass and glass holds lava."

I grabbed the paper and read it over a couple of times to myself. "Okay, so that lightning that keeps flashing makes the glass that holds back the lava. So what if-"

I paused in excitement as the idea formed. "Okay, we need to find that glass! The lightning is making it, so we find some and put it over the lava!"

Crow nodded, "Yeah, and how do we get the key down, and what about the cats?"

"If the glass covers the lava, I could get the metal on this axe hot enough to throw it up and cut the rope. The rope falls, and we get the key! I mean, the rope is already frayed. I'm guessing from the heat, but either way, that has to be it!"

"And the cats?"

I looked over to them calmly sitting by the cliff. "I don't think they are going to mess with us if we don't mess with them. They only seem to give chase or attack when we get too close to them. I think they were put there as a distraction to make us think we had to climb the cliff."

"Right."

Lightning cracked through the sky off in the distance, and I took off running. "Come on!"

It was hard to run and keep my balance given the little ground between the pools, but I managed and only stopped when I came to an empty pool filled to the brim with huge, sharp slabs of glass.

Crow caught up, and we both looked at the pieces.

"It's going to take the two of us just to move one." He pointed out.

"I know, but what choice do we have, come on." I put my axe in the holster on my hip before walking over and grabbing a big one from the top as Crow grabbed the other end. We lifted it and started walking with Crow looking back over his shoulder.

"So, since I'm walking backwards, carrying a large sheet of glass on a tiny walkway for you. If I fall into this lava and die and you and Cander don't name the baby after me, I'm gonna be pissed."

I chuckled as we moved along as fast as we could without falling in. "Okay, I will consider it."

"Psh. Consider it? You better name him Crow for his first, middle, and last name, Kira, or I'm haunting your ass."

We got to the big pool and laid down the piece, both of us catching our breath. "Okay, so let's test it before we carry any more of those pieces."

We picked the glass back up again, and as we dropped it into the pool, lava splashed up and almost hit my leg. The glass bobbed and floated on top of the fiery lava but floated nonetheless.

Crow grabbed my arm. "Come on. We're running out of time."

After getting the pool filled the best we could with odd pieces where they almost formed a barrier, a thought hit me.

"Fuck!"

Crow sighed. "What now?"

"My weight? The glass floats on the lava, but won't it just sink if I step on it."

"Damn it. I didn't think of that." Crow cussed, grabbing hard at his hair. "The cats!"

I sucked on my lips in frustration. "What about them?"

"Okay, hear me out." He said, pointing to the cats. "They have spikes, and the key has a loop."

I waited for the big reveal when he reached out and shook my shoulders in frustration. "Put a cat on there, chop down the key so it will land on a cat, and then get it from a cat. They are probably small enough not to sink the glass."

I scoffed, shoving his arms away from me. "And how the hell do we do that, Crow? What am I supposed to do? Just go up to one and say, excuse me mister demon cat, I know you want to kill me, but could you do this one favor for me?"

I turned away from him and his dumb idea before I pushed him into the lava. The hopelessness of the situation hit me, and tears burned my eyes. I sniffed them back, too pissed off to cry.

"No, but I can," Crow said, and I turned to him, putting my hands on my hips, getting ready to lay into him. Before I could, he continued. "I can talk to animals." He shrugged as my mouth dropped. "That's my power."

---

*A*fter the most awkward time watching Crow, a six-foot sex God looking demon, get on his hands and knees and meow to a herd of cats, our plan eventually worked out. I seriously needed one hell of a drink.

I opened the portal back in the throne room to the revenge realm thinking of the creepy frozen statues with moving eyes. "Why the hell didn't you tell me you could talk to animals!?"

Crow grabbed my hand, and we started towards it. He shrugged nonchalantly. "It just never came up." I narrowed my eyes at him as we stepped into the portal and stepped out into the empty throne room of Fourth Realm.

"What?" He asked. "It never did."

I willed myself not to develop the power of shooting lasers out of my eyes and tried to calm my temper. "Are you shitting me?" I walked away from him, circling the statues with a watchful eye for the key. I pointed to the other row of sculptures on the other side of the aisle. "Start looking. I don't want to be behind like before." I said in anger. A statue of a guy getting his face melted off gave me chills, and I surveyed his space quickly. "How about when I got my power? You could

342 | THE IVY TRIBE

have been like, yeah seeing the future is cool, but I can talk to animals." I paused, looking under a statue's dress. No key. Damn.

I looked to Crow, who rolled his eyes at me. "Or! Or here's one! How about when we got to the lava realm, and we're getting our asses chased by demon cats!! Hey Akira, don't worry, I have the power to talk to animals. I can calm them down, or better yet ask how to get the key!"

After giving him a stern bitching we both finished our survey of the sculptures and met at the throne. Crow sighed. "I'm sorry Kira...I just wasn't thinking. When I'm around you I get a bit distracted, I'm sorry." He grabbed my hand and squeezed, looking deep in my eyes, and I knew he meant it. I could tell there was more to me distracting him, but I dropped his hand and put it out of my mind. "Okay, you're forgiven."

I walked up to the throne, circling it but keeping my distance from the flames that licked up it. "So, there's nothing here that I can see, but there's a door over there." I pointed, and we headed towards it.

Before we could get to it, a flash of white above us caught my eye, and I looked up to see a paper floating down. I'd forgotten about the clue. Face meet palm.

Crow jumped up and grabbed it, reading the clue aloud. "Revenge is a dish best served cold, but only after melted."

I groaned. "I have no idea what that means. Do you?"

Crow raised an eyebrow, shaking his head. "Not a bit, but maybe we will just stumble onto the key like we did last time. The clues seem to be about getting it, not finding it. So let's start there."

We reached for the door simultaneously, and Crow seductively laughed when I pulled my hand back. "Afraid to touch me?"

Even though he was playing, I scoffed as the deep timbre of his voice had me clenching my lady bits. I was obviously hungry. "Quit that shit," I growled, going through the door before he could and gasped in surprise.

He laughed but stopped when he got a look at what I was seeing. "Is that a mother fucking dragon?" He asked before his jaw dropped.

My eyes bulged, and I took in the entire scene. "And is that a mother fucking castle?"

The sound of a door slamming behind us had us both jumping, and I looked to see that it was hanging in mid-air in between two trees. At least it hadn't disappeared. We stood on a grassy hill on a sunny day, staring off in the distance at a colossal dragon guarding a castle. My sanity cracked wide the fuck open.

I busted out in a fit of laughter, and I couldn't stop. Crow looked over at me like I had lost my marbles, and I still couldn't stop, even when I had to wipe tears from my eyes.

"Okay, okay," Crow said, shaking me, and I settled down, taking a big gulp of air and pointed to the scene.

"Can you talk to dragons?" I asked, feeling so fucked it wasn't even funny, well, not anymore anyway.

Crow shook his head, his eyes wide like saucers. "I have no idea. I didn't even know dragons existed."

"Fuck." I sighed. "Let's get this shit over with."

I took off down the grassy slope with Crow by my side. This was such a weird realm compared to the last one. Hell, there were even birds chirping. It was so non-threatening that when a butterfly flew up into my face from the grass, I flinched back like it was going to bite. It just felt too weird.

"So, from all the talk you hear at the bar, you've never heard of this place?"

Crow shook his head. "No. I mean so far, this seems like a sort of paradise. I'm not sure anyone even exists in this realm."

I looked around, noticing the lack of tortured souls. "But

that doesn't make sense. The realms run on souls, so Purgatory has to be sending people who deserve to be here."

I stepped over a random log, watching Crow do the same. "I don't know. Maybe they're in the castle?"

"Yeah, maybe. But what do you think the paper means?"

"I think I have an idea about that. Queen Eiseth was famous before she died for all those tarred status in her throne room."

I thought back to what the twins said. "The Queen that died, right? Cain and Elijah never said how, they just said there were complications."

Crow scoffed, wiping the sweat from his forehead. "That's because they killed her defending Anock and Mikayla, or so I've heard anyways. But the point is those people were famously bad on Earth. For example, Countess Bathory, and some guy named Hitler. I don't know them because I was down here before all that, but apparently, she took them in and tarred their asses, and those are the statues in the throne room."

My mouth dropped. "Wait! Like they're still alive? Their eyes move!"

"Exactly." We slowed down, and Crow grabbed my arm to follow his lead and knelt in the tall grass as we were almost at the castle. He lowered his voice, as well. "But they are tarred, and they are in the Fourth Realm because of revenge, that was their punishment. Tar is hot, and have you ever heard of the saying revenge is a dish best served cold?" He asked, and I nodded.

Crow pulled the paper from his pocket and handed it to me. "Revenge is a dish best served cold, but only after melted. So what if all the people are in the castle and cannot get out because of the dragon. Maybe they are in there living their best life. I mean the saying, served cold, refers to serving revenge when least expected or well after the argument's heat has cooled."

I squinted, trying to keep up but still didn't understand.

Crow sighed in frustration, taking back the paper and shoving it into his pocket. "So if people are in there, their revenge will come in the form of getting tarred alive and stuck in that position for all eternity."

"Okay, that makes sense, but that still doesn't tell me anything about the key," I argued.

"We need to get into the castle, and if I'm a betting man, I'll bet we need to see someone get tarred to figure it out."

I gulped, looking back to the castle.

"That's if there *are* people actually in there, and your theory is right."

He grabbed my hand, and we stood as the dragon raised its head to look at us. "And that's if we can get past this dragon."

The dragon let out a roar so loud that the ground shook, and if Crow hadn't been holding my hand, I would have fallen back from the forceful stench of its breath rushing at us. We stood still only for a heartbeat, watching to see what it would do. I knew we were screwed when it took a step towards us. Only I was half distracted when something fell from it.

"Did a piece of its chest fall off?" I asked Crow, who narrowed his eyes and tried to get a better look at it. The dragon took another step, and the same thing happened with its face.

"I don't..." He paused, concentrating on the dragon, and I looked back and did the same. Something was off about it. Another step showed it hobbling, and another piece came off. "Wait a minute," Crow said a hint of terror in his voice that chilled the blood in my veins. I looked at him as he pulled me back.

"Is that-" Before he could finish, I finally saw what he saw as the dragon neared.

And here I thought this was just a typical fairy tale scene.

"Dead bodies?" I asked.

The dragon no longer interested in pursuing us slowly, let out another roar and charged.

"RUN!" Crow screamed and pulled me not back to the door, but to the castle, as the dragon gave chase. Its massive body consisting of corpses shook off and fell to the ground. I looked back to see dead bodies shedding off the dragon as it ran.

We approached the castle, and Crow opened up one of the enormous doors. At the same time, the dragon's foot, encased with dead bodies, crushed the cobblestone behind us. I was half shocked and half relieved when the door opened, but we didn't think about it too much as we ran inside, slamming the door closed behind us.

I panted, trying to catch my breath as I put my hands on my knees, leaning over for support. "Holy-"

"Shit!" Crow finished.

"Excuse me, madam." A posh accented voice said.

I looked up and immediately lurched back, my backside hitting the door we just came through. "FUCK!" I screamed, looking at the very, very dead butler in front of me holding a silver tray. A meat cleaver stuck out from where it was wedged in the top of his head, blood still coated the side of his head that took the brunt of the blow. It was all down the side his neck and all over his black and white tux. He tilted his head to the side in confusion and looked at me and then to Crow.

"Can I offer you an hors d'oeuvre?" He asked politely, bringing the silver tray closer to me. It held a tiny glass bowl full of eyeballs that still had the stems on them, a criss crossed pattern of chopped fingers and rolls of skin.

I gagged, putting my hand over my mouth as Crow stepped up beside me. "No, thank you." Thank God he could talk because I sure as hell couldn't. I glanced behind the butler, taking in the rest of the scene as Crow continued. "We're looking for a key." He said.

I looked away from the scene of dead people walking

around in evening wear as they conversed and went about their business like we weren't here. I brought my attention back to the butler in front of us. "Ah, yes. Medusa is expecting you."

A laugh started to bust out that I covered with my hand as Crow glared at me.

"Right this way." The butler turned and walked off.

I leaned over to Crow as we followed. "Did he just say Medusa? As in the actual mother freaking Medusa?" I whispered.

Crow maneuvered us out of the way of a lady eating her entrails. I quickly looked away, yup this realm sucks ass. So far, it topped the list. As in, I'll take the weirdest things you'll see in Hell for 500, Alex, please kind of weird.

"The very one," Crow whispered back as the butler led us through the kitchen. It sucked so bad that all I could do was concentrate on his feet. Even then, the blood and guts we walked through were hard to miss. "I heard she retired some time ago but had no idea she ended up here."

"Retired?" I asked.

I looked up in confusion, and Crow nodded. "Yeah, she used to be a Watcher in this realm."

"I didn't know you could do that?"

Crow scoffed. "You usually can't, but she ended up in the King's harem, and he took pity on her."

I wasn't sure what to say, so I stayed quiet. The butler led us to a throne room. Again, these people and all their damn throne rooms. I rolled my eyes but stopped when I saw Medusa on the throne. I quickly looked down, too afraid to find out if the rumors of her were true or not.

I heard Crow chuckle, and I looked over to him in confusion. "You're an immortal dummy. You can look at her. That party trick only works on humans."

"Well, I'm not about to find out!" I whispered back in anger.

The beautiful voice of a young woman calling my name had me in a trance. Automatically I looked up, forgetting how I had just planned to not look at her. It didn't matter though her voice was pure beauty.

I blinked.

"Akira Black the newest, or soon to be the newest Watcher." She paused, looking to one of her snakes and petting its head affectionately.

"Oh my." She laughed. "I have a feeling we will be the best of friends."

23

THE HUNT

Cander

"STATUS!" Anock yelled at Cain.

The realm quieted down to hear the fate of my future wife. I'd checked my phone every five minutes up to this point like an obsessed fool. There were only two purple flashes so far, telling me she was almost through finding the second key in the Fourth Realm.

Cain set down his martini and stood to address the crowd. "They have obtained the first key and are almost done finding the second." He said, sitting down, crossing his legs prissily before picking up his martini.

I rubbed at the headache starting to form. Anock had made me hide the key with Medusa. The one who was responsible for tarring the prisoners in that realm. She threw up a black tar, trapping them in place, like her cement trick with humans. After attempting to peel her off me, I watched as she walked over and placed it onto one of her servants' heads, and then proceeded to throw up on them. Even I didn't know how to get that shit off. When Eiseth had been alive, she would just melt it with a flick of her wrist, but that was a power Akira didn't possess.

I looked up from the edge of the table, where I sat alone as Elijah approached. "What the fuck do you want?"

Elijah gasped, putting a hand on his chest, feigning offense. "Well, exxccuusssee me. I was simply just coming over to see if you were doing okay. I mean, it's not every day the demon of murder becomes a baby daddy."

I slammed my cup on the table, flaring my power in anger. "Why the fuck did you tell Anock?"

Elijah pulled up a chair next to me, and I growled in annoyance. Why were her trials taking so long?

"Well, first off, did you forget that he's the demon of minds?" It was rhetorical apparently because he rambled on. "Second off, that and only that was the real reason he ditched the other realms. She would have had a real chance at losing that baby if she went to those realms."

I swallowed the last of my drink before handing Elijah the cup. "Whiskey," I demanded.

He took it and rolled his eyes. "Oh, sure! Use me for my powers, but be mean when I want to be a friend."

I growled, wanting to snap his head off his body.

"Okay, okay." He snapped, and a glass of spelled whiskey appeared.

"Why is this taking so long?"

Cain walked up laughing, and I growled again. I wanted peace and fucking quiet. If these assholes were around and something happened, Princes to Hell or not, they were getting tore the fuck up. "It's just because you're worried about her."

"Holy fuck!" Elijah exclaimed, standing up so fast that his chair fell back. I stood too as a quiet filled the space. I looked down the table to see that all the royals were fine, but they were standing around looking at something on the ground that I couldn't see.

I stumbled past Elijah and Cain going around the table and stopped in my tracks, taking in the scene before laughing my ass off. I wasn't an idiot to know that I had half of the realm looking at me like I'd lost my damn mind, but fuck if I wasn't proud.

I looked at Medusa's dead body again, trying to hold back another round of laughter. The words, TRY HARDER, were carved into her naked torso. Medusa was the King's favorite, and I'm sure Akira, in a pregnant rage, probably got pissed she hid the key and killed her. Judging by the gaping hole in her chest, she ate her heart out as well. Akira left her adorable scratches and bite marks on her, and I could see it all now. This was fucking great! Akira was getting fucked so good she wouldn't know what hit her the minute she and my son returned.

I ignored Anock's annoyed growls and went back to my chair.

"That's my girl."

***

J growled at Crow's annoying jabbering, as I strung the second key on the chain around my neck and tucked it back down in between my boobs. "Like I have said for the millionth time." I pointed and opened a portal as the dragon rushed us.

I grabbed his hand and stepped through into our throne room in Lilith's Realm. "We didn't have time for her bullshit!"

Crow stepped away and grabbed his head in frustration. "There are going to be consequences for that, Akira! She was the King's favorite! It was known not to touch her! Listen, I know you're having horm-"

I turned and flared red eyes at him. "I swear on every demon in this realm if you say hormones, I will kill you myself."

"See!" He growled and took a step towards me, "You're acting irrationally! Why are you yelling at me if it wasn't for that!?"

I took a step closer, matching his challenge in anger. "I wasn't acting irrational, Crow! This is me and my damn baby's life on the line! Untouchable bitch or not, I had ten minutes, and she was playing games! And I'm yelling at you because you keep bringing it up like I fucking had a choice!"

I hadn't expected him to grab my face hard and slam his lips into mine. Was I hungry for him? No, but I was fucking starving in general. And now shocked by the rush of emotions that hit me with the force of a hurricane. My mind swirled only with need. "Fuck!" I gasped as he reached down and cupped my pussy. I only needed one thing. How had I not realized how hot and sexy Crow was before? How good he'd feel? So strong, sure, and fucking amazing.

"AKIRA!" I gasped as something cold and wet splashed my face, forcing my eyes open that I didn't even realize were closed.

Crow stood in front of me, holding an empty wine goblet with a concerned look. "Okay. I don't know what the hell kind of vision made you do that-" He pointed to my hand still firmly cupped around my pussy. "And as awesome as that was, we have to go. I got the next clue!" He said, shoving the paper at me as I removed my hand, still reeling from the vision. I took the paper from him, still dazed, as I stepped away from Crow. That's the second damn time I've had that vision. The first time was during the fight at the Ivy, and it was clear that this was going to happen if I didn't stop it.

"I keep having the same vision that we hook up," I said, feeling the heat rush to my face as I looked down from his piercing eyes only to notice the bulge in the front of his pants. Well...this was awkward.

"What do you mean you keep having them?"

"Just like I said, Crow. The first time was during the big fight at the Ivy. You showed up, and we started to hook up right then and there. This time we were here, but every time we fight beforehand and then start to tear each other's clothes off."

I cleared my throat and looked to the clue, not wanting to hear his response. I wasn't the cheating kind, and this didn't seem like a life or death vision. So why did I keep seeing it?

"Fucking in life gets you fucked in death." I looked around the throne room. Last time I was in here, it was full of people having sex everywhere in piles on the tables, couches, and beds that lined the aisles. Now they were all gone. I continued to look around, spotting the side door like all the other realms so far had had.

"Another one that doesn't make any sense." I shook my head in frustration and headed for the door.

"Akira, we need to talk about what you saw."

I snorted in frustration. "No, we don't." I opened the door, looking into the biggest torture chamber with the most vilest things happening that I'd ever seen. I stepped back into the throne room, shut the door, and threw up right beside it.

I felt Crow's hand rub my back, and I moved away. "Don't!" I said, stepping away from him, the vile door and my mess.

He sighed. "What did you expect, Akira? This is Hell."

Tears pricked my eyes, and I didn't want to cry, but I didn't want to go back in there. "I don't know, Crow!" I wiped hard at them in frustration and turned away from the door. "I didn't think I would see a whole room of people getting raped and tortured!"

"I know, I know, it's not what anyone wants to see, but you know as well as I do, we have to go into that room."

"WHY!?" I yelled. "This is so much stupid bullshit! Demons were in there, butt fucking a screaming man on his knees covered in blood! Where in the fuck is there supposed to be a key in there!? Everywhere I looked, someone was getting raped to death!" I fought off another round of vomit.

Crow walked over, pointing to the door. "Those are rapists getting what they deserve!"

That was...well...I guess that's what Hell was for, right? Justice served to the evil people of the world. Hearing or thinking about it, though, and actually seeing it were two very different things. I was in no way ready to go back in there, and what would happen if they saw Crow and me? Would they string us up too?

A flash of purple lit the throne room, and I let out a hysterical laugh, followed by more tears. I walked numbly to the door, flinging it open and motioning for Crow to go in first.

"Then lead the way," I said, feeling sick again, now just purely off the sounds as I followed closely to Crow's heels.

"They aren't going to mess with us if that's what you're worried about." He said when I grabbed the back of his shirt, closing my eyes and letting him guide me.

"I don't want to look," I mumbled and ran into his back when he stopped suddenly.

He turned around towards me, and I opened my eyes, looking up at him. I willed myself to ignore the things in my peripheral vision. "Figure it out Akira, because this is the job. This is your damn realm that you will be guarding. This room," He grabbed my chin and forced my head to look out over what was happening. I stifled a cry. "Is where you will be a lot of the time."

He let go of my chin, and I glared at him in defiance. "You don't have to like it." He said with a soft voice and understanding eyes as he rubbed my arms in comfort. "You just have to find a way to ignore it. That's what I do."

"Just ignore what's happening right now?" I asked in disbelief. "Like it's nothing!" The sound of a gurgled scream had me
glancing to see a giant purple-colored dick getting shoved into a
man's mouth with his dislocated jaw hanging down. I swallowed the bile and looked back to Crow and then pulled out my
phone, looking at the timer I had set. We'd wasted forty
minutes.

"It doesn't matter," I said, deflated. "There's no way we're
going to find this stupid key in twenty minutes."

Crow narrowed his eyes and shook me. "Woman, I am
mother fucking Crow. We will find this key even if it kills me!"
He declared. "Now toughen up buttercup. It's time to get out of
this shit show."

I sucked in another upset breath and nodded, he was right. I
could at least try, that way when I did die, I could say I tried.

"So as much as I hate to say it, I think the key is here somewhere. It may just be on or near one of these sections."

"Fuck."

"Seems to be the theme of the day in this room." I glared at
him, and he flinched back, throwing up his hands.

"Okay, bad joke."

I couldn't believe my eyes. "There," I said, pointing to a
statue of a giant concrete snake. The key hung on a rope around
the snake's neck.

"Well, that's fucking easy," Crow said.

"Agreed."

We walked to the snake, and I acted on Crow's advice,
ignoring everything that was going on around me.

A white tag hung from the rope by the key that read.

Sorry for taking your blood. Now we're even.

"You think it's a trick?" Crow asked.

I laughed, reaching out and snatching the key off of the
snake. I half expected the damn thing to come alive and try to
kill me, but nothing happened.

Walking back into the throne room, I threw out my hand, ready to head to color land. That's what I decided to call Envy and Strife's Realm since it was just a crazy, psychedelic land of color.

Crow jogged up, grabbing my hand right before we stepped into the portal. "We need to talk about all of this."

We stepped through.

"SHIT, that's bright!" He exclaimed, and I laughed.

I headed to the throne as he caught the next clue. "Don't bother with it!" I yelled. I heard him scoff but kept walking.

"Why?" He asked, and I looked back to see him following.

"Because right before Cain, Elijah, and I, portalled out of here during my tour, I saw something shiny in this colorful cloud inside the throne." I pointed to it, still seeing it shine.

"It says, a glass case of emotions, hehe, signed Cain." Crow rolled his eyes, and I laughed. Only Cain would put in a movie reference for something life or death.

"Yeah, so it's in here."

Crow laughed. "Okay, but how do we get it out?"

I looked around, only seeing swirling colors and things that made drugs look like a joke.

"I have no freaking idea."

Crow crumpled up the letter and threw it to the ground. "Cain fucked us with his stupid idea of humor!" Crow roared, and I was shocked to see his anger for the first time.

I looked to the crumpled note and picked it up, straightening it out.

"Give an emotion to get a key." I read, flipping over the paper to see Cain's silliness on the back. I held it up to Crow. "You just had to flip it over," I said in frustration, walking back up to the throne and touching it.

The red cloud that swirled around the other colors broke free and floated to my hand. I lurched back in surprise, and it drifted back into the cloud. Hmm, that's weird. I put my hand back down, and this time yellow floated up, but again I moved my hand away.

"Crow, I think each one of these colors in the cloud represents an emotion."

"Hmm." He put his hand down, and once again, the yellow came up, but like me, he moved it off the glass before it reached him.

"I think you're right."

"So...that's easy," I said, thinking of an emotion I could afford to lose. I thought of greed and put my hand down. I watched as a dark, ugly looking green swirled up fast aiming for my hand, I held my hand still on the glass and watched as the green seemed to inspect my hand. Apparently, it wasn't the right emotion, and it soon returned to the other colors.

"Which one did you try to give up?" Crow asked.

I shrugged. "I thought of greed."

"I hate that guy, by the way. He's a complete asshole. The only thing that helps is how Elijah sings Creed songs to him when he comes around."

I scoffed but looked back to the throne, trying to concentrate on an emotion. Maybe hate? I could afford to lose that emotion. I mean, who likes to have hate in them? I put my hand back down as Crow continued.

"Get it? Creed sounds like Greed. And it's bad music, and Greed is a bad guy." He laughed out loud at his terrible joke before nudging me in the side. "Eh, eh?" I glared at him in response, trying to concentrate. "It's funny, right?"

"I'm trying to concentrate," I said through clenched teeth. I watched as a bright red shot forward towards my hand and held my breath, hoping it would take it. But, like the others, it went back.

"UGH!" I yelled in frustration, taking back my hand and stepping away in anger. "Why won't the stupid thing take any of these emotions?"

Crow sighed. "I'm guessing it probably has to be a good emotion, like happiness or love. I mean this is Hell, I could see how that would be a requirement for this realm to take the good stuff."

"Shit." I cussed, trying to think. Was there anything good as far as emotions that I could afford to lose? I continued to think as I watched Crow try and fail with a light blue and bright green.

"What were those?"

"Sadness and jealousy." He said with a sigh.

What emotion that was good could I afford to lose? A purple light flashed throughout the throne room, and my heart sped up with worry. Happiness? Love? Lust? Joy? Pride? Amusement? Gratitude? Inspiration? Every single one I could think of I felt would have dire consequences to losing. I mean, is this just for the key, or would I have to give up an emotion every time I came here? Would this one emotion be gone forever or merely for these trials?

"I'll do it," Crow said, and I turned to him.

"Do what?"

"I'll give up something big like love or something."

I hated even to hear him suggest that. "But wouldn't that go against the rules?"

"Not necessarily, they said I couldn't help defend you from danger, and that I couldn't portal you. It's all in the words girly."

"Okay, but not something bad, like love."

Crow scoffed. "Why would it matter? This is Hell, why do I have to keep telling you this? I don't need love to eat and survive, and I've gotten on fine without it up until now."

I looked at the throne. "Do what you want then."

He chuckled. "I will, don't worry."

I watched as he placed his hand on the throne, and at first, nothing happened. I started to wonder if I was going to have to

THE HUNT | 359

do it, but then pink and red shot out from the cloud and twirled together like a dance before making their way to his hand. I held my breath. I didn't understand his logic for wanting to get rid of such a strong emotion but kept quiet.

The colors slowly came up, and almost like a cat rubbing against someone's leg, the colors rubbed against the glass in affection. Crow looked to me in confusion, and a second later, he fell through the glass.

"GRAB THE KEY!" I yelled in fear at the chaos of colors and everything going on as I pulled on Crow's arm to get him out.

"Got it!" He said standing up and just like that the glass covered back over the throne's seat.

I grabbed the key from him and went to work, putting it on the necklace. "Come on. I'm not sure how much time we have." I started to walk before I realized how much of a bitch I was being, even for being on a time crunch. I turned into him and gave him a huge hug and a small kiss on the cheek.

"Thank you, Crow. I know you gave up a lot." He pulled me away and laughed.

"You're welcome, now let's get out of this shit. It feels like I took five hundred shrooms."

I laughed, feeling happy as I opened my last portal. I realized then just how much that emotion meant to me to have.

We stepped through Purgatory, and instead of a welcoming party, we were greeted with all Hell breaking loose, literally.

My smile dropped as I watched Anock tear a black horned demon in half with a roar.

"What's happening?" I asked in terror, watching a head fly past me.

"Someone-" I jumped and let out a yelp as Cain appeared to my left. "Killed Medusa, so the King decided to let some demons out of the Pit as a form of punishment."

"I tried to tell her not to," Crow said, and I growled.

"Well, I got the keys now what?"

"Now, get out there and help us, *Watcher*," Cain said before disappearing.

I looked over as Crow cracked his knuckles. "It probably wouldn't be so bad if you hadn't left that message."

I scoffed. "I was in a rage!" I yelled. As a demon cat, this one all black instead of red, rushed me with green eyes. I pulled my axe and landed it down hard on the back of its neck, slicing its head off.

"Yeah, well, next time, learn to control yourself," Elijah said, appearing out of nowhere.

"Where's Cander?" I said in fear when I couldn't see him through the battle.

Elijah laughed. "You're worried about the literal demon of murder? He's fine. He just sent me to make sure you were okay."

I took out another cat, glad none of the bigger stuff was coming at me yet. I needed to learn how to fight.

"Yes, you do!" Elijah grunted, taking the force of a demon about to bite my head off.

"WAIT!" I said, as an idea hit me. "Elijah, can you separate all the Pit demons from all the others?"

I looked over to him finishing off another demon by tearing off its head. Eww.

"Ugh, yeah. Why?"

"Just do it!" I screamed, praying to whoever this would work. I concentrated on building energy. I was going to need a shit load for what I was about to do.

"TELL ME WHEN!" He yelled.

I concentrated on what I needed to do, taking in the tingling power.

"NOW!" I yelled back.

Elijah let out a roar of exertion, all of a sudden, a group of demons stood on one side. Cain and Anock stood on the other side with all the regular looking demons behind them, if that was such a thing.

I yelled, creating a portal moving it over the Pit demons and didn't close it until they were all gone. The roar of the portal evaporated, followed by silence. Everyone turned to me, and I didn't have time to explain, or even show them the keys before the last tingling left my body. Before I knew it, I crumbled to the ground and shut my eyes.

24

HEATED

Cander

"YOU COME ANY CLOSER, AND I'LL BREAK YOUR FUCKING NECK!"

My demon was struggling against me, wanting to break through. Those fucking idiots! Why would Cain and Elijah allow her to do something so stupid? Every single influential leader and Watcher was in this place. So why would she think that we hadn't thought of doing that? We had, but no one can portal to the Pit other than the King. The demons he released from his realm had to be killed, not portalled away to where ever the fuck they went. Plus, it would take an extraordinary amount of power to do that. The kind of power she shouldn't even have. I wasn't sure it was something *I could have pulled off*, yet she carried my child and decided to try it carelessly anyway. No regard that she could have killed our baby, and yet no one thought to stop her. The twins could have read her mind, but when I asked them, they gave me a bullshit excuse. They said they were busy mind communicating with Anock about a plan, fighting, *and* trying to talk out loud. They said they didn't know what she had planned, which was a bullshit excuse, and they knew it.

As soon as I'd seen her open that portal, I ran. I ran to stop her, hold her, *fuck I didn't even know*, but I can't remember ever being that scared in my life. She can't die because she's immortal, but she could have killed our baby. Somehow, when the twins checked, he had lived through it, which was a surprise for everyone. It told me we had a strong son. Cain, myself, and Elijah portalled her back into my room, setting up a triage of sorts. I haven't moved from her side since. I've been continuously feeding her energy and draining myself, but she still hasn't woken up. Even though the twins say she will soon, that her mind is fine, it still scares the shit out of me. Now Anock has the fucking balls to show his face here. It's just as much his fault as any. If he had contained those demons well before she returned, none of this would have happened. Instead, he was having fun, along with all the Queens. They were taking their time with their kills instead of coming up with a plan to get them back to the Pit or kill them faster. He was supposed to be the fucking demon of minds, yet he spouted some bullshit that he couldn't control Pit demons. I didn't believe him.

Now he comes in here and says she didn't get the last fucking key to his little game, but he would let it slide. Then when he didn't take the hint that I was on edge. He flexed his power and told me she sent the demons throughout all the realms, and it was utter chaos. That she would be punished accordingly. Yeah, over my dead fucking body. And now here we are, me hovering over her and him stalking in the doorway.

"Leave," I warned. Anock thought this was a game. It wasn't, no part of this was amusing. Yet he still stayed testing my patience. I looked back to see him leaning against the door with his arms crossed and a smug look on his face.

"You know that even after this little marriage ceremony, she will still be mine?"

A huge rush of power built as my demon claws started to form. I wasn't going to be able to hold back from attacking him for much longer, and the fucker knew it. She would never be his.

"No," I growled. "*She is mine.*"

Anock let out a laugh before pushing off the wall and stepping closer. I let my power fill the air as a warning. Prince or no Prince, I wouldn't let him get near what was mine. I tried to step away from her for a day. I attempted to distance myself and act like she was nothing, but I couldn't pretend anymore, she was everything to me. In my entire existence no other female came close to knocking me flat on my ass like she had, and I wasn't going to let her go now.

He brought out his wings and flexed his powers, but I wasn't impressed. I had watched Blake pine for Mikayla from the shadows as she ran around with Anock down here. Blake allowed Anock to have her during the day, and he got her at night, but that wouldn't be me. I wasn't some pussy Anock could waylay. I was the demon of fucking murder. The baddest son of a bitch around, if he thought he could take my girl...he had another thing coming.

"Take another step, and I'll rip them off."

When his eyes flashed red, I let my demon free as I stood from the bed. I took my first step away from Akira since she'd passed out, which made my anger rise even more. Even being an inch away from her when they needed me was enough to make me go into a rage. I made my way slowly to the front of the bed, blocking her from his view. "Come near my wife and child...I dare you."

Unease and danger filled the air, and I could feel my demon wasn't going to hold back from attacking much longer if he stayed near her.

"You'd take me on? Your leader? You may be the demon of murder, but do you really think you can take on the demon of minds?" He took another step, and my demon growled as my fangs formed.

"You can get fucked if you think you're having a baby with her or adding my child to your army."

He laughed. "And how do you plan to stop me?"

Before I could respond, Akira's weak sounding voice broke through the chaos. I turned around watching as she opened her beautiful red and grey eyes. The sight killed my anger in an instant.

"Cander?"

———

*A*nock left slamming the door, and I didn't have any idea what was going on. Cander was transforming back from his demon form. It didn't take an idiot to see they were having some type of fight. I just didn't understand the details. I remembered the demons from the Pit and saving everyone. Was that why Anock was mad?

"I take it he's mad at me?" I tried to talk the best I could, but I felt like I got hit by a semi.

Cander walked over with a concerned look on his face, and I could see the worry lines etched into his forehead. When he just kept staring at me like that, I started to get worried.

"What?"

Cander leaned down, kissing me before gently laying down next to me. Had Hell frozen over? Was that what happened when I portalled all those demons? Must be, because not only was he acting super nice, but he also brushed back the hair from my face. He literally cuddled with me when not too long ago he was throwing clothes at me after sex and pushing me away. So, yes, apparently, I have the power to freeze Hell over.

"I'm sorry." He whispered into my ear before giving me a soft kiss on the neck. Butterflies erupted in my stomach, and I sighed, loving the feeling. I liked this Cander, *this Cander was* the one I could keep around.

"I feel like a piece of shit for the way I acted towards you." I turned my head to look at him. "I thought I was going to have to give you up to Anock, and I wouldn't have a choice. So I pulled back from you, but fuck that." He leaned over, kissing my neck again.

I opened my mouth, unsure of what to say but didn't get very far in voicing my opinion before his lips were on mine. I moaned, enjoying the rush of his power flowing through me.

I pulled back. "Cander, we need to talk about stuff." When I looked into his gold eyes full of heat, I knew it was pointless, and I also knew I didn't really want to talk when he gave me that look.

"Fuck it," I whispered, grabbing his face and pulling him back down on me.

I wanted a whirlwind of uncontrollable lust, but it was clear from the way he was giving me painstakingly slow kisses that he had a different idea.

I slowed my movements and closed my eyes, letting the feel of his strong, sinful hands give me pleasure.

"Cander," I whispered.

His lips scorched a path of kisses back up to my mouth before he pulled back. "What, baby?"

Fuck, I loved it when he called me that. I held in my smile while my heart tripped in my chest.

I reached up and brushed his hair from his eyes. "Don't ever pull away from me again."

He frowned in concentration, staring deep into my eyes. I saw the world there, my world, my perfect, fucked up world, and I never wanted it to end. He reached down between us and caressed my stomach that held our child. "I won't ever let you go again."

His lips slammed into mine in a delicious frenzy. After that, we were out of control, and even though I wanted it rough, he only gave me a little force, but I could tell he was holding back. I was okay with it because he cared for our child and was not just fucking me but also connecting with me. Every pass of his lips along my stomach made my heart squeeze a little more. Every heated stare and gentle touch he gave me promised always. He was mine, and I was his, and I knew as we made love for the first time, that would never change.

"Can we all just stop for five seconds?" Cain asked in a prissy tone, throwing his hands up in the air.

I huffed in impatience. "You say *we* like I even have a choice here. Every time I open my mouth, *you all* shut me down."

I watched in the mirror as Strife raised an eyebrow. "Uh...no way sister, gay boy one and two are the ones shutting you down. I agreed with you and Rose that you should have your hair up. You're probably going to get hot in all of that anyways."

Elijah scoffed, coming over with a different tiara, testing it out on the top of my head. "*Pleeaasse.* You already know we will make sure the temperature is perfect. Who do you think we are?" He looked back to the room. "I say half up, and half down, her neck is too long, and with the strapless dress, it will look funny if it's completely up."

I reached up, grabbing my neck. *Was it too long?* Geez, talk about slamming someone's confidence on their big day. These two were insufferable when it came to planning.

The wedding was in four hours, and I stood in the middle of the twins, Rose, Andy, Strife, and Envy, as they all tried to figure out my hair. It took us almost three hours to decide on a dress, which involved me standing in my living room as Elijah and Cain magically dressed me with an array of dresses. We, as in Cain and Elijah, eventually settled on a black strapless, princess styled gown. The bodice was tight with a mix of lace and satin that flowed down through the tulle to the bottom. It was so puffy I had no idea how I was supposed to sit down in it. After my hair, they told me I would dress and, lastly, given makeup. It was enough to make me dizzy. I was just listening to everyone argue, and it confused me more. I sighed,

Baby, I can hear you stressing, just ignore them. Cander spoke into my mind making me smile.

Are you spying on me on our wedding day?

Before I could hear his response, Cain came rushing towards me, waving his hand in the air like a madman. "Oh no, you two, don't!" He snapped, and a tickling feeling entered my mind.

I gasped at the weird feeling, as I stared up at him in his annoyed stance, tapping his foot.

"What did you do to my head?"

Cain scoffed while Elijah laughed. "I blocked him from your mind until you get to the aisle. He cannot see the bride!"

I laughed, putting a hand on my stomach. "Well, I think we're a little too late for traditions, and it's not like he can actually see me."

"Even so." He snapped his fingers, and a sparkling glass of champagne appeared. "You need to get prepared and not be lovey, gushy, mind-reading while you get ready, that can wait."

I shook my head in annoyance. "Whatever. Okay, I say hair up." I looked around the room at everyone, eyeing each other in awkwardness while drinking their champagne. They clearly didn't think that my hair should be up. Probably because of my long neck. Psh, whatever, I just wanted to hurry up and get the day done. Cander had said he had a lead on what Lilith may have needed my blood for and more information on my mother. Not to mention, my dad, which I still needed to sort that out mentally. This fighting about what I was going to look like on *my* wedding day had gone on long enough.

The arguments around the room erupted again, and I zoned out, wishing I could just talk to Cander. The only good thing about today was that I'd be walking down the aisle to him. I needed to be in a good mood for him, well and the baby, and *not* stressed. I mean, this was my mother freaking wedding day. Although thinking about it, would my wedding day if I'd stayed mortal be any different. I took a sip of champagne as I thought more of how Alex and Kay would most likely be just like Cain and Elijah, and everyone else would be Liz balled into one. The thought made me giggle.

The room quieted, and Envy walked over, putting a hand on my shoulder. "Are you okay?"

I looked around to realize everyone held concerned looks. I guess I had zoned out for a while. "Yeah." I cleared my throat of the sudden emotions. "No. Well, I mean, *yeah,* everything is fine." I turned around on the little black stool, facing the room, trying to figure out how to explain what I was thinking and feeling. "I was just thinking of how much this is a shit show." When the room's energy deflated along with shocked and sad faces, I threw up my hand before they could interrupt. "And I appreciate it." I paused, wiping the sudden stupid tears that had formed. "Because this is exactly how it would be if Alex, Kay, and Liz were here." I took a deep breath in trying to get the thickness gone from my throat and smiled. "So everything is okay, perfect actually. I realize a lot of you don't know who they are, but they meant a lot to me, so thank you."

All at once, I was being smothered in one giant hug of crying men *and* women.

"Pregnant lady can't breathe!" I gasped, trying to get out of the group hug.

They all laughed, stepping back as Cain placed a loving kiss on my forehead. "Oh, hush bitch, you don't need to breathe anyways, you're immortal, *duh*." We all laughed again, and I was guided back onto my stool as Envy shoved my champagne back in my hand. The mood instantly lifted in the room, and I felt a thousand times better. Shit, this hormonal pregnancy stuff was no joke.

"Now you just sit here and let us prepare you for the wedding. You just focus on drinking those nerves and memories away with that champagne. You are stuck with us, girl, so dry those tears." I let out a sigh of relief before taking a sip of my drink.

They were right.

"Now, about this hair." Elijah started again, holding up the tiara.

A laugh burst from my lips before I could stop it. *"Fuck."*

Cander

I straightened my jacket in the mirror before grabbing the hair gel.

"I only have about five minutes. Walter is only projecting me as a favor, but who knows what that asshole is doing to my body, so I would rather not be gone for too long anyway. Plus, Mikayla still isn't back, and I need to be there."

I sighed, turning towards Blake standing there in his black Watcher's uniform caked in blood. "And you know James will be there waiting too. Punch that little bastard when you see him for stealing my kill or better yet get your shit together and kill him so all this shit can be done." I watched his projected form run a frustrated hand down his face and shake his head.

"We can't do that until the Reaping, and you know it. What did he do now?"

I went back to working on my hair. "Too much for the little time we have. So what have you heard out there?"

Blake scoffed. "Silence, my brother is on to his next sinister plan. James has taken members of the Magical Council, and now you said he took Pearl. He has Walter keeping me busy, so I haven't been able to find out much, but that's because no one is talking. I went to the Nephilim bar and have been trailing Lilith in Vegas, but so far nothing. Radio silence, man. And if I had to guess, that's because people are preparing for the Reaping. If the Magical council is gone, who is going to play mediator? Little fucker is up to something bad this time. I would start down here in Hell for the answers about her blood. You know you could always ask the twins to help."

"Fuck. Yeah, and I trust them as much as you do." I cussed, finishing my hair and turned to face him. "Thanks anyway, man. I appreciate you trying."

Blake nodded once and then disappeared.

I took a deep breath to calm my nerves, and they weren't even from the wedding. It was all this other shit. The apocalypse was getting closer and closer, and the entire supernatural world could feel it. It was dumb for any of us to think that things would always stay the way they were. I reached over, grabbing my whiskey while concentrating on hearing Akira again. Stupid shits blocked me. Her inner thoughts, no matter how chaotic they were, calmed me. It calmed me to be able to check in on her and know she was okay. Know the baby was okay. My guess was Akira was a critical piece to the Fated, and that scared the shit out of me. Why else would her mother be so important she'd have a guardian angel? And why else would

Lilith need her blood? Something weird was going on, I could feel it, and it grated my nerves.

This would all end one way or another, and soon. I just hoped we made it out alive.

I turned to the door right as Chort busted in, half-drunk already. "Time to get married, fuck boy." He sang before stumbling into the door.

I scoffed at his idiocy, and I stopped thinking about the blood matters. I was getting ready to watch the most beautiful woman I'd ever seen walk down the aisle, and we still had plenty of time to think about all that other stuff. Tonight was about her and me. As we walked through the living room, I tried to glance through to her adjoining space, but Chort steered me to the steps.

The last time I was married, there was no wedding, ceremony, or vows. Just an exchange of rings. I mean holy matrimony wasn't a thing here. Technically in Hell, there wasn't a cause for weddings. Demons didn't get married, and that's what pissed me off so bad about Ariel's betrayal. She said she would only be with me if I married her to prove my faithfulness, and then that bitch was fucking Jax the whole time. I shook my head clear of the thought as I stepped out into the garden, lit with hanging lights from the trees and fireflies. Akira was going to eat this shit up, and my fucking dick was hard just imagining the look on her face when she walked down the aisle.

I was the luckiest son of a bitch alive.

THE WEDDING

I thought Elijah and Cain would be walking me down the aisle, but I was told this wasn't like a human wedding. The entourage that helped get me ready, all waited with me in the most gorgeous library I'd ever seen. It matched the expensive taste of the rest of the mansion but was a lot more inviting. A gigantic fireplace sat in the middle of the room, and reading nooks with windows leading out into the garden were evenly spaced throughout. It screamed book worm paradise. I was a little shocked when Elijah told me that Anock had had this made just for Mikayla. That girl must be something special.

I walked over to one of the reading nooks and peered out the window to get a peek at the decor, while the twins fought with Envy and Strife about what color theme the wedding should have been. They apparently said blue was more practical. I was not even getting in that conversation. Those girls came from the realm of colors, and I was definitely outmatched in my knowledge compared to them. I rolled my eyes, hearing Elijah gasp and looked out to the string lanterns hanging beautifully from the trees. They had been strategically placed so that there wasn't too much light, but just enough. I could hear some type of fancy orchestra music, but couldn't tell where it was coming from. I also couldn't see the aisle I would be walking down either. My heart thumped in my chest as my nerves started to pick up. As I looked all around the space, it was a dream come true. Cain and Elijah had set up the most beautiful wedding I'd ever seen, and I couldn't believe I was actually the bride.

Tables were set with an array of red, gold, and pink décor along with flowers. They were placed around the luscious garden flowers, trees, and bushes that matched perfectly. It looked like fall colors, but the way they pulled it off in this summer garden was outstanding.

The sound of someone clearing their throat had me turning around to see Crow. His eyes bulged for a second before he froze and stared at me in shock.

I laughed, feeling a blush heat my cheeks. "Come on now. I don't look *that bad*."

Crow opened his mouth and shut it before answering. "No. *Never*." He swallowed hard, and I looked down, picking at my dress, feeling awkward all of a sudden. "*You look beautiful!*" He exclaimed, and it brought my attention back to him. He grabbed the back of his neck like he was nervous, and I tried not to think of how he pretty much said he wanted me back in the trials. Or the fact I'd been having visions of us hooking up. I wondered if this was hard for him to see me marry Cander.

"Thank you." I smiled, gesturing to his soft gray suit and tie. "You look pretty good yourself."

"First time in a suit. Cain and Elijah dressed *all of us*." Crow shook his head in annoyance. "They made it a requirement on the invitations."

A laugh burst from me before I could stop it. "That sounds like them, and I didn't even know we *had* invitations." I looked over to Cain in disbelief, and he saluted his drink to me in the air. "I don't know how they put this together so fast. Well, I mean, I guess with their magic." I pursed my lips, feeling stupid for forgetting that.

Crow laughed. "Exactly." He reached over, grabbed two champagne glasses from a side table that also held chocolate-covered strawberries, and passed me one. "There I was, making drinks in my bar and this thing just, *poofed* in my face raining glitter all over me and the bar. When it finally cleared, something was floating in the air. *Literally*, it made a poof sound and everything. And that damn glitter... I'm still finding it everywhere! I almost rushed here just to kill one of them for making me look like a male stripper behind my bar the rest of the night." I laughed, imaging the whole thing. "I grabbed it, already knowing it looked like the twins' work, and sure enough, there was yours and Cander's wedding invite. And right at the bottom was their dress requirement code. It said: We will dress you, and that's a requirement."

I almost spit my champagne out laughing so hard. Those two were something else, but they *were* amazing at this stuff. I looked around the room to see all the girls wearing beautiful flowy, Greek looking gowns in colors that match the décor outside. Each one of them was given delicate gold jewelry that matched the gold dusting they coated me with. Both Cain and Elijah wore a dark brown suit. Not ugly brown, but sexy brown. I don't know how they pulled it off, but they made brown look good.

I focused back on the conversation. "Well...that sounds exactly like them."

Elijah clapped a couple times, addressing the room, and everyone went quiet. "It's time for our beautiful masterpiece to come to life." He said, gesturing to me. An array of excited squeals and claps sounded around the room, along with jumping and hugging. I smiled back nervously, but it probably looked like a grimace since my cheeks suddenly felt shaky. This was really happening.

It was weird. I was so nervous all of a sudden. Growing up in the Hollywood spotlight, I was used to attention, but this felt different for some reason, like a nervous excitement. What would Cander think of my hair? We ended up putting it up. Would he think my neck looked too long? I glanced down at the bottom of my puffy dress. Hopefully, he wouldn't think I looked fat in this.

I blew out a couple nervous breaths trying to calm my suddenly rapid heartbeat.

"Oh, hush those thoughts." Cain griped, coming over and grabbing my hand to guide me towards the double doors. I couldn't see much through the glass but the twinkling of fireflies, so I focused on them trying to take his advice. "Remember, I am lifting this little blocker the moment you step outside." I looked at him, feeling a moment of panic towards that. So Cander was probably going to hear me freaking out the whole way down the aisle. *Great!*

Cain laughed, spying on my thoughts. "So, all you need to do is focus your pretty little thoughts on your man."

"Plus," Elijah said, coming over. "It's not good for the baby. No stress."

I laughed, handing my champagne flute to him, and he exchanged it with a bouquet of flowers. "But alcohol is fine," I said sarcastically, rolling my eyes.

The music outside suddenly played around us inside the library. The twins stepped away, waving their hands towards the doors. I watched with bated breath as they opened slowly outward, giving me my first look at the aisle and the man waiting for me. I barely felt the tickle running through my mind signaling the twins had lifted the block because of my shock and awe.

Butterflies erupted throughout me.

Goosebumps covered my arms.

Nerves electrified my veins and *holy fuck*, Cander was about to be my husband. Mine.

Everyone and everything faded away from us. I couldn't look away from him. His beautiful eyes cast a golden glow to his tall, muscular body filling out every inch of his sexy black on black tux. *I was mesmerized*. I wanted to simultaneously orgasm and have a stroke at the same time, but instead, I took my first step forward, clutching tight to my bouquet of flowers. I looked down and bit my lower lip hiding my blush when he flashed me a sexy smirk. His hair was perfectly gelled back, captivating more of his high cheekbones, kissable lips, and hard jawline. That sight alone was enough to kill me, but *fuck*, when he smiled, I was blown away. I watched as my dress swished gently around me as I continued down the aisle. I was only able to glance up at him every once in a while, because the closer I got to him, the stronger my emotions stirred within me. It made it impossible to hold his intense stare for too long.

I reached him and slowly turned to face him as I took a slow breath in and let it out.

Baby?

At his sexy voice in my head, all my fears dropped instantly. My gaze lifted and met his, and I smiled gently at his enamored face. He looked at me like I was the most beautiful thing he'd ever seen.

"You're fucking breathtaking, Akira." He said in a deep voice, low enough only for me to hear.

I chuckled lightly and bit my lip to hold back another smile as my blush was back in full force. When he chuckled too, I reached for his hand, unable to keep from touching him any longer.

He took it and gave me a devilish grin. "Ready, baby?"

I smiled back. "Fuck yeah!"

378 | THE IVY TRIBE

*A*nock was the one that performed the ceremony. At first, I was shocked, but Cander kept me distracted with his promises to make our wedding night one to remember. I honestly had no idea what Anock even said because of our inner dialog. Cander was teasing me relentlessly, and by the time we walked back down the aisle, he had me soaked and aching. And he was now taking great pleasure in watching me squirm.

"A toast!" Crow said, standing up from one of the round tables positioned in front of our long one. Everyone quieted, and Cander took my hand, rubbing his thumb lazily over it as we listened. "To Cander and Akira! May your marriage be full of hot demon blood, sex, and gore!" A roar of demons agreeing along with table slapping sounded throughout the garden, making me laugh.

"To Cander-"Crow continued after they'd quieted down. "He was ordered from our Queen to kill me *at least* thirty times, and yet somehow, I have always changed his mind." I laughed along with the guests and looked over to see Lilith frowning.

"Oops. You know you love me, Queen Lilith." He said, and more chuckles went out. I was guessing he was a bit drunk by his lapse of speech with his Queen. He was acting completely different towards her now compared to before our trials.

"And to Akira. For what started out as you saying I wasn't your type."

I laughed, putting my head into my hands to hide the embarrassment. I was an idiot. I looked to Cander, and he chuckled, rubbing my back. "You've ended up being a close friend who I have sacrificed myself not only once for, but twice now, and I wouldn't have it any other way. We've been through a lot together." Crow let a pregnant pause fill the air.

I didn't think it was lost on Cander how Crow's tone was starting to seem a little too friendly when mentioning our closeness. I took a drink, wishing Crow would wrap it up before he said something that got himself killed.

"So to my two closest friends, may your marriage be successful and happy. Cheers!" He held up his glass, and I glanced to Cander as we held ours up, but couldn't read anything from his face.

"Now...it's time for the real party to begin!" Elijah said into the microphone he stole from Crow, and the growls and table slapping with excitement was back.

"Come with me," Cander whispered against my neck, and chills ran through me at his hot breath. He moved my chin and gave me a slow kiss. *Fuck* I was hoping he was taking me somewhere for a quickie.

"Didn't this thing just start?" I asked as he gently pulled me through the crowd. Apparently, the dress code was only for the demons who attended the wedding. The reception was full of demons, *not* in human form. A lot of them stopped us along our way to give congratulations and also give Cander a hard slap on the back. Each time he got one, I couldn't help but giggle at his angry face.

"Yes, but I want to give you my present."

I froze. "Ugh." Oh my God. I didn't get him anything!

He laughed, hearing my thoughts as we passed by a massive fountain with flowing red blood. I moved my glance away, suddenly feeling sick. "Your gift is going to be me seeing that sexy lingerie you have under that dress you're wearing."

"Oh," I said as he opened up one of the library doors and rushed me in before shutting and locking it. I laughed at his sneaky behavior.

"Cander, there are like a million windows in here. Why lock the door if they are just going to see us anyways."

He chuckled, pulling me through the room and into the hallway. "We aren't staying in there." He paused, opening up a door that led to another corridor. This place was so freaking confusing. "And we aren't having sex...*yet*."

"*Okkkaaayy*? So what *are* we doing?"

He stopped us at a random spot in the hallway before looking around again.

I laughed, unable to help it. "Oh, my God. Would you just tell me already?"

He smiled and pulled out his phone.

"Ugh."

He shushed me, going to work doing something on his phone that I couldn't see. "Just a second."

I giggled at the concentration on his face. Whatever he was trying to do on his phone was clearly taking a lot of thought. It was sexy watching him do stuff.

Before I could ask what it was again, he turned the phone towards me and shoved it into my hands. I couldn't believe what I was seeing.

I gasped.

"You little bitch! You went off and got married without inviting us!" Immediately tears sprang to my eyes. Alex, Kay, and Liz were all sitting in my living room on a video call.

I looked to Cander in shock as my hands started to shake. "How?"

He sighed. "It doesn't matter how." He leaned over and kissed me. "It's my wedding present to you."

I ugly bawled right then and there while Cander and the others on the call laughed at me.

"I thought I'd never see you guys again!" I gushed.

"Oh please. We are a lot harder to get rid of than that! We are like herpes!" Kay said. She looked even more beautiful than the last time I'd seen her. Her long red hair had more of a shine to it, and her green eyes seemed to sparkle.

"Ugh, no bitch we aren't," Alex said, glaring at her. God, I missed these guys.

"But I thought they erased your memory?" I asked, confused.

Liz scoffed, sitting up straighter. "I can do anything those little boys can do and more. Cander told me to reinstate their memory after you left, so I did."

I glanced at Cander then back to the screen, unsure of what to think about it all.

"I don't even know what to say." Tears clogged my throat again, and I sounded so stupid. "I've missed you guys so much."

Cander leaned over, squeezing my shoulders in support and giving me a gentle kiss on the head.

"I still can't believe you married the waiter," Kay said, looking at her nails.

I laughed and rolled my eyes. "We caught you up before your mind was erased, Kay. You know he's not actually a waiter, right?"

Alex rolled his eyes. "She said that's probably his job in Hell too."

"What is wrong with a waiter?" Liz asked.

I laughed again and looked to Cander, who just shook his head and rolled his eyes. "There aren't any restaurants in Hell." He said, chiming in.

"Oh my God, that's the first time you've spoken to us," Alex said in shocked excitement.

Cander chuckled and went back to surveying the hallway, clearly not planning to respond to that.

"Well, I mean honestly, Akira. You've got like a real-life brooding alpha male who literally growls, at people who get too close to you, and specializes in silent death glares."

Kay perked up from where she sat. "Oh! And he's supernatural!"

I rolled my eyes. "I'm *supernatural*."

She looked to Alex and Liz, completely ignoring me now. "This bitch is living every book nerd's dream!"

"Language!" Liz corrected her, making me snicker.

"Hey! You don't yell at Alex for doing it!" She argued, and I watched as Liz reached for a magazine. She started to roll it up to smack them both with, and I was now laughing so hard I could barely breathe.

"Just a couple more minutes, babe. Crow said Cain and Elijah are looking for you." Cander said.

The reality that this call probably was something special and was not going to happen all the time hit me hard. A somber feeling fell over me, and I sighed.

"We will talk again," Liz reassured. I'm guessing she could tell from the look on my face I wasn't ready to say goodbye.

"Yes, we will! And by the way, you look gorgeous!" Alex said, and Cander growled.

"See!" He jumped up, pointing to the phone, and I laughed. "Did you hear him?" Alex picked up the phone from wherever it had been sitting and was actively trying to find Cander. "He growled!"

I glared at Cander, and he just winked at me. *Ugh. Men.*

"Before you go-"Kay wrestled the phone away from Alex and set it where it had been before. "I just thought you should know that your dad is awake." She said, and my heart stopped. My dad was awake. Would he come and find me and act like the father he pretended to be? Or would he be his true self? I got a glimpse of him in Cander's memory and he had acted like I didn't matter.

Before I could think any more about it, Kay continued. "So, we've decided to go with Liz."

"What?! What do you mean to go with Liz? Where's she going?!" I looked at Liz. "Abuela?"

Liz leaned forward, still holding the rolled up magazine in her hand. "I am no longer needed here. Lilith knows about your friends. I will take them and keep them safe. I will not allow us to become captured again."

"Shit, they're coming." Cander cussed. "Time to go now. If Cain and Elijah find out they still have their memories, I can't guarantee they will let them keep them or that Liz won't be punished."

He reached for the phone. "Wait, there's something I need to tell you guys!" I said as they all spoke their I love you's and goodbyes all at once.

"I'm pregnant!" I shouted right as Cander took the phone.

Alex's shriek of "WHHAATTT?!" Was the last thing I heard before he shoved it into his pocket.

I sighed, leaning against the wall feeling both happy and sad.

Right as I was about to thank Cander for my gift, he shoved me against the wall, slamming his mouth on mine, right as the sound of a distant door banging open sounded to my right. I moaned when Cander's tongue shot deeper into my mouth, sucking on it, and making him growl. I realized this was a ploy, but he was one hell of an actor, so I couldn't help immediately diving into character.

"There you two are!" Cain said, clearly angry. "We have an agenda!" He yelled, and Cander stepped back, winking at me while trying not to growl at his unfinished sexual attack.

Cain clapped his hands together impatiently. "Come on, you two, there is lots to do!! Plus." He said, waving us to follow. "It's time for presents!"

"Thank you," I whispered to Cander, and he leaned down, giving me a quick kiss as we walked.

"Always, baby."

---

*C*ander was deep in the whiskey with another Watcher named Chort, who he had introduced me to. They were busy locked deep in a conversation at the end of the table, talking about something called soul sharing. Whatever that was. The girls and I were talking about the do's and don'ts of Hell. It was kind of cool getting a rundown of things not to do.

"Oh shit." Envy said, standing up.

I followed her gaze, and my heart dropped. Queen Asgret.

I could hear her cane hitting the cobblestone path through the garden as she made her way towards me.

Before I could freak the fuck out, Anock flew down in front of the table in a woosh of black feathers and force, blocking her path. I watched as Cander walked over, standing next to Anock.

"I wondered why I hadn't got an invite to a Watcher wedding, but now seeing that pregnant son killer, I understand why I wasn't." I tried to stand to see what was going on but Envy and Strife, who sat on either side of me, held my shoulders down.

Strife shook her head. "Stay down." She said under her breath.

Before I could argue, a hiss had me looking back to see Andy and Rose at my back. If I needed to be surrounded by the most powerful immortals in Hell, this must be serious.

"And what brings you out of your bubble, Asgret?" Anock asked calmly.

"Oh, I thought I'd come to give the couple a little present." I heard her say with a wicked laugh. I looked to Envy and then to Strife, who both looked equally terrified. My heart dropped in fear. These girls were hard as fuck battle-ready warriors. If they looked scared, I was probably in trouble.

I also didn't miss the shared look between Cander and Anock, either. "That won't be necessary, Queen Asgret," Cander said, crossing his arms.

She cackled. "Oh, but it is!"

"NO!" Anock shouted, making me jump in surprise.

"But you see, Anock Prince of Purgatory, and Cander Keeper to Lilith…It is already done."

A black cloud of smoke appeared suddenly. Anock roared in anger, searching the smoke for where she had been, as Cander headed my way.

"What?" I asked no one in particular. "What does that mean, it's already done?"

Cander walked over and kissed my head, and I noticed his hands had a slight shake to them. What the hell was going on?!

Anock walked over to our table, and I turned to face him, still in Cander's arms. "Asgret has the power to curse." He said, and I looked around to try and read everyone's faces.

"And?" I asked when I saw nothing but fear. "So, like, she cursed me?"

Cander cussed, letting me go to grab at his head.

"Or your baby." Strife said with a sigh.

I gulped in fear, putting a shaky hand over my stomach. *What have I done?* The silence was deafening, and I couldn't stand everyone staring at me, so I turned to Anock. "It's safe to say this reception is over."

I turned to grab Cander's hand and walked back to the library in silence until I slammed the door shut behind us. Nausea swirled through me, and it took me a couple tries to get the words out.

I looked into Cander's wild eyes. "Did I just curse our child?"

FUTURE CONSEQUENCES

*O*ur wedding night didn't turn out like I'd thought it would. Instead of an all-night sex marathon, Cander and I spent the night in an all-metal medical room, being checked for a curse. While the twins used all sorts of magic checking my body's health, Anock worked hard checking my head. Every test came back fine, and they couldn't find anything wrong with me, but that only led to the baby.

So then they moved to the baby. When I asked how in the world they would be able to tell anything from a three-day-old pregnancy, they said I was equivalent to three weeks along. After I pestered them enough for an explanation, they finally explained that every day pregnant equaled one week pregnant in demon terms. Which meant I would be having a baby in forty days. I found it a little hard to believe but said no more about it.

Anock stepped back and leaned against the counter, crossing his arms. "The only other thing I can think to do is to get a Worm demon."

I sat up on my elbows. "What!?"

Cain and Elijah sighed. They looked exhausted, and so did

Anock. Even if they had tried everything at this point, that sounded a little extreme. I sat up fully and grabbed Cander's arm for support. He looked defeated and stressed. I'd never seen him like this before, but ever since that stupid bitch did this, he was like a whole other person. He seemed checked out most of the night and just stared at the wall. I didn't say a lot about it because I could tell whatever Asgret did to me was serious, but I didn't know how to make it better. And I couldn't assure him that the baby and I would be okay because I didn't know that.

"It may be the only way," Anock said, looking to Cander, who sat in a metal folding chair by my bed. "Cander?"

Cander took a deep breath and rubbed a hand down his face. "And what if we can't get it out? Or what if it goes to the baby instead?"

"Wait!" I said, holding up my hand. "You're talking about the Worm demons that come from Asgret's realm? The same bitch who did this! I just had a damn demon on my soul from that realm, and it was torture, and now you want to put something else in me?! Are you shitting me right now?!" I looked accusingly around the room to the group of men. "I already have a baby in me! I don't want anything else!" I growled, crossing my arms.

Elijah leaned over to Cain. "Unless it's Cander's cock." He mumbled under his breath, and they both snickered.

"THAT'S IT!" I jumped off the medical table, unleashing my arm blades, and headed to beat those little shits who shrieked in fear and ran to Anock. Before I could get too far though, I felt Cander's arms wrap around my torso before picking me up from behind.

"Calm down, babe." He said, squeezing me tight around the middle while I raged like a bull. I tried to fight off my anger, but I was just too stressed and too tired.

Anock sighed. "Alright, I say that's enough for tonight. Get her calmed down and rested, and we will come up with a plan." He glared at the twins as he walked out of the room, who scrambled quickly out after him.

Cander released me once the door was shut. I immediately turned and rushed into his arms, hugging him tightly. There was so much that kept getting thrown at me, and I just wanted to catch a break. I was never good with constant drama, even with the lifestyle I'd had. I thought the Ivy Tribe was going to be my only issue. Ever since then, my problems have only escalated into a giant snowball raging out of control down a hill. We have no idea why Lilith needed my blood. I didn't know what was going to happen with my father. And now, my child and I could be cursed, and no one knew what kind of curse it was. Was this like the sleeping beauty fairy tale curse? Or was I just cursed with bad luck for the rest of my life?

"I know we have a lot of unanswered questions, but we will figure it out," Cander said into my hair. I was sure it looked like a mess, they had come and gotten us as soon as I took off my wedding dress. So I just let down my hair from the millions of bobby pins and threw on a pair of Cander's sweats and a tank top. Which irked me, I still hadn't got to see him wear these.

Holy fuck, my hubby in grey sweatpants would for sure give me a heart attack.

"Why are you thinking about my junk right now and not answering me."

I laughed into his muscular chest before stepping back. He still looked beyond stressed, but his eyes held a bit of humor, telling me maybe this might all turn out okay. I didn't want him falling into himself or backing away from me like he had before.

I put a hand on my stomach and shrugged. "Maybe I'm hungry?" I asked with a sly smile.

He laughed and grabbed the back of my neck before kissing me. "Then let's get you taken care of."

his was my first official Watcher's meeting, and I was kind of nervous. I wasn't really sure why, I knew a lot of them already, but I chalked it up as first day jitters. It had been two days since the wedding and Cander and I had done nothing but lay in bed naked. Apparently, the time for play was over, though. I was okay with that as long as I had Cander with me. These past couple of days, we'd grown inseparable. I mean, the man didn't even let me pee in peace, acting like some random villain was going to come out of the toilet. But I guess he *was* my husband now. I could tell to an extent it was the curse that had him on edge and acting like a bodyguard.

"We have a lot to address tonight, so get comfortable," Anock said to the table. I was sandwiched between Cander on one side and Strife on the other. I had met Chort already from the Ninth Realm, but I had no idea who his partner was. I continued to look around at all the new faces until Anock brought my attention back to him.

"Akira." I looked at him, and he chuckled. "I'm going to get this quick intro out of the way so we can begin. All of them know who you are thanks to the attention of your trials and wedding, but I'm sure you have no idea who they are. So-" He paused, gesturing to the end of the table where two red-skinned demons sat. They had horns and were freaking huge. They literally looked like what humans called the devil. I gulped when they stood.

"This is Remy and Lanthrian from Queen Mandra's Lava Realm." They sat back down when Anock gestured to the next introduction. As the next two stood for their intro, I was a little more than confused. They threw me for a loop, and I had no idea what to make of them. There was a little girl that looked to be about ten years old, and I swear, looked like the girl in Stephen King's movie, *The Shining*. Like, literally, the *same* exact girl. Her partner was a decrepit old man. Old as in had a walking cane, and it made no sense.

"Ancitif and Amon. They are from Queen Irrithal's Greed Realm." Anock said, and they sat, and the next stood.

"Focalor and Chort. From Queen Sitri's Sorrow Realm." Anock paused to laugh. "It's probably a good thing you got a pass on going into their realm." I looked at Chort's partner and had to hold back my drool. I had no idea how to repeat his name but, *holy baby mermaids, he was hot*! Focalor looked like an Egyptian King and even dressed like one. I got a good look at his attire below his waist before he sat back down. Right up until Cander's growl broke my attention, and my face heated. *Whoops.*

Focalor gave me a wink, and I immediately looked down, feeling super embarrassed. I was a married woman now. I couldn't be doing that shit.

You do that shit again, and I'm tying you up and leaving you aching for my cock for a whole week.

I looked over to Cander and lifted an eyebrow in defiance before silently answering back. *You wouldn't dare, I need to eat.*

Don't test me. He growled back into my mind before reaching under the table and squeezing my thigh hard. I suppressed a grunt of pain, watching the next pair stand. They looked oddly normal. Looking around the table, well, other than the old dude and little girl, everyone seemed to have some supernatural beauty to them. But these two men just looked like ordinary average Joes.

"Emil and Manic from Asgret's Realm," Anock said, trying to hurry and move past them. I caught the clench of his jaw, and it was clear he wasn't happy that someone from her realm was here but couldn't do anything about it. Right before he opened his mouth to introduce the next pair, one of the guys spoke up.

"I'm Emil." The short, chubby looking one said. "We're sorry about what happened with our Queen." I just looked to Cander and then back at them, unsure if I should say anything. "What she did wasn't fair, but you have to understand, in Hell, revenge is something you should always expect when you cross someone. Cander, you had to have some idea that you were putting her in danger when you had Jax killed." He explained.

Cander stood from the table as his eyes turned red. "And who said I had him killed?"

Emil's partner Manic, who was a tall, scrawny looking demon, spoke up now. "Like we all haven't heard the rumors of how Jax died. You got the help of the lesbians over there, and even one of the Fated to help. Then took him out because he killed your brother and slept with your wife!"

I stood to put a hand on Cander's back to hopefully calm him.

"He got what he deserved, either way, Jax had to die for what he did." Cander grounded out through his clenched teeth.

Emil scoffed. "Exactly. He fucked you, and you needed revenge." He paused, pointing his finger at me. "Now she killed Jax, and his mother wants revenge, and round and round it goes."

Anock slammed his closed fist down on the table so hard I jumped. "ENOUGH!"

"All I'm saying is they should have known not to fuck with our Queen," Emil said to Anock in explanation.

Anock growled as his wings opened wide. "And your Queen should have known better than to curse someone who could supply my army! For that, she will pay!"

Cander grabbed my hand as we both sat back down. It felt weird to me how nice Anock had been, but with everything going on, I hadn't had time to even think about it. Now it was all too clear. He was nice because he needed me. He was trying to cure the baby and me of this curse because we were important.

"Enough introductions for the day," Anock said. Cander

reached to the middle of the table and grabbed a pitcher of blood, filling up my wine glass before kissing me and shoving it into my hand. I was just about to set it back down, not interested when the scent of metallic salt hit me, making my stomach growl. Apparently, the baby was hungry, *Little demon.* Cander placed a hand on my lower belly and rubbed softly in affection as I took a sip. The delicious taste made my mouth water, and I immediately wanted more. I tried to drink it slowly and not chug it like a beast. Cander caught my hunger and laughed under his breath at me.

"Thanks to our newest little Siren, we now have close to a hundred Pit demons to capture and kill roaming the realms." Anock gave me an exasperated look, and I shrunk back in my seat. Amon growled at me from across the table, causing Strife to lean over, and hiss at him in my defense.

Anock ignored the angry growls coming my way and continued. "So that is our first task. I still require you to collect the souls for your realms and do your normal duties, but I think it would be best to work in teams to eradicate these demons. It will be quicker and more efficient."

He paused to drink from his cup. "Next is the little issue of pissing the King off. Now that his favorite lover is dead, it's safe to say that he will want more revenge than just sending some of his Pit demons to cause chaos."

Emil scoffed. "So, just let him kill her."

Cander's eyes flashed red, and his demon claws started to grow.

Babe, I warned via mind speak. Cander huffed out loud but put the claws away.

"I need her, and so does the realm. If we don't get Mikayla captured before James and Blake face off in the Reaping, the Apocalypse *will* happen. We need an army, and we need one fast, so no harm is to come to her." Anock glanced at me and then Cander.

I looked to my husband, wishing there was something I could do. I hated being dangled in front of Anock on a string because of my magical vagina.

"The only thing I can think to do at this point is to allow a run…and gather a massive amount of souls to appease him." Anock said, pinching the bridge of his nose.

The whole table erupted into excited chatter all at once. I was confused about what was going on.

"What's a run? What does he mean?" I asked Strife.

"It's when we are allowed on Earth for a certain number of hours to collect as many souls as possible. It's something fun for us. As you can see." She gestured to the table, showing everyone asking Anock who would get to go. "It's a big deal."

Right, when I opened my mouth to ask how we collected souls, Anock yelled. "SILENCE!" And the room quieted.

"Now, because we still have the Pit demons to take care of and the realms to guard, I decided to split you into two teams. While team one is running on Earth, team two will be ridding the realms of demons. After the twenty-four-hour mark, the teams will switch."

"I SAY THAT BITCH CLEANS UP HER OWN MESS AND WE ALL DO THE RUN!" Remy from the lava realm shouted, pointing at me.

I stood fast to defend myself, but my knees buckled. The last thing I saw was Cander reaching out to catch me.

○

$\mathcal{I}$ was no longer sitting around the table with the Watchers.

Now I was standing on a mountain in the greyed daylight during a blizzard. I shivered, looking down at my new black Watcher's uniform. This thing did shit to stop the cold. I turned around in a circle, trying to see anything or anyone but couldn't. *Was this a vision?*

"Hello?"

I turned towards the female's voice and saw an angel calling to the wind.

Her skin had a slight white glow that also surrounded her fluffy white wings. She had long brunette hair and emerald green eyes, and she was simply beautiful. I took a step closer.

"Who are you?" I asked, but it seemed like she couldn't see or hear me because she didn't respond. I walked closer to her, watching as she looked around in confusion.

"Can you se-" Before I could get my question out, Anock fell from the sky.

I stumbled back in shock at first but then realized he might have come to save me. Maybe this wasn't a vision. I walked up to him, calling his name, but he was acting like the girl. Okay, this *was* a vision. Which was strange because it wasn't like my other ones. This one I was just a spectator, whereas the other ones, I was involved. I didn't think Anock or demons could leave Hell, but here he was in a red leather gladiator outfit. But he was just talking about going on a run so I guess we could leave Hell. His chestnut-colored hair was longer than it was at the table just now, and instead of tied back behind him, it was hanging down over his shoulders.

I watched as he walked to the angel with love and adoration clear on his face. "You've become your true self." He said to her. A thought struck me, and I wondered if this was the Mikayla everyone had been talking about. I wasn't sure though, because I didn't think she was an angel and this girl clearly was.

She looked back to Anock with a blank face. "How did you get in my dream?" She asked. Holy shit! Her voice gave me chills and unlike James who had the white wings, this girl was the real deal. I immediately wanted to drop to my knees and weep in awe. When she spoke, her voice tingled across and through me like a million beautiful notes to an enchanting song. All I could do was stare in shock.

Anock stepped towards her also in awe. "Why are you sleeping, angel?"

A gush of wind howled past me, and I lifted my hand up, blocking my eyes temporarily to keep the harsh snow out.

"Anock, you've never had the power to enter dreams before." She said to him.

I struggled now to keep upright by the sudden strong wind of the storm. They both seemed unaffected by it, though. I missed what they were saying now as I was being pushed back by the wind. I bent down and put my hand through the freezing snow to hold the ground. I gained a little traction and looked up to see Anock slap his hand onto her arm. I didn't miss her confused face as she looked down at the round black tattoo that was now there from where he touched her.

Before I could stand or see anymore, the vision faded.

I sat up fast, gasping, and coughing up blood. Cander sighed in relief before hugging me tight and cradling my head to his chest. It was clear I'd scared the crap out of him. I looked up to see the other Watchers looking at me as well. Apparently, I'd scared them too.

I swallowed the blood that had come up feeling confused by it. *I'd never done that before when I had a vision?* But, this time it *did* feel different.

Anock walked over with an evil grin on his face.

I looked to Cander, confused, and then back to Anock. Why was he looking at me like that?

"It will work!" Anock shouted in excitement. "And it's all thanks to you!! We will finally get Mikayla!"

Huh?

Cander released me so suddenly that if Cain hadn't been at my back, I would have hit the ground. He looked at me suddenly frightened and enraged like I'd never seen before.

"*Cander*?"

I barely noticed the cheers of excitement from the Watchers around me or Anock's laughter…just Cander.

And he acted like I had the plague.

Cander stood and shook his head, backing away from me when I went to touch his face.

His actions made my lips tremble, and tears fill my eyes. *Why was he looking at me like that?* His face was filled with hate. *Why was he acting like this all of a sudden?*

I didn't understand.

When he opened his mouth, I was hyper-focused on him, trying to hear through the victorious yelling going on around me. And even though he was back by the door, I heard him loud and clear.

"What have you done, Akira?"

The End. For now.

EPILOGUE

*M*y vision changed everything. From extreme wedded bliss of newlyweds to a heartless marriage. From badass newly made Siren to a super pregnant lonely demon. I went through many stages of grief after what had happened, to the point where I wasn't sad about it anymore. This was my reality, my new life, and it really was Hell.

After Cander walked out of the ballroom that day, that was the end of us.

Now I only saw him in passing, and even then, he avoided eye contact and acted like I didn't exist. He had moved me to another part of the mansion and had his door spelled to keep me out. At first, it pissed me off and I did everything I could to get in his face and make him listen. I pleaded and begged for him to understand that I had no idea what I did wrong. Eventually, he snapped, and the last time I tried was when he slammed me against the wall and choked me out. He said I was better off dead, and if I came around him again, he would make sure I'd end up that way.

Since Anock's plan went into action, he was hardly here now, which was a good thing. Cander had gone from ignoring me to lashing out at me in every way possible. After he had me moved, I wasn't sure how to feed, and stubbornness kept me in my room crying and angry for a long time. When I could no longer stand the stomach pains and the baby's persistent kicks for food, I ended up portalling to Crow's bar. I didn't give a shit who I fucked or drank from, I was starving. I'm not sure how Cander found out because Crow swears it wasn't him, but somehow he did. I had no sooner started to straddle a guy before Cander threw me off him and tore the guy's head off.

From there, it got worse. I was restricted from leaving the mansion, and after Cander sought permission from Anock on the matter, Anock agreed for his own reasons, and now I was stuck here. Now they sent Cain and Elijah to push power into me and keep myself and the baby alive, but it was never enough. I was also put on clean up duty to keep me busy while the other Watcher teams did their runs or killed Pit demons. It entailed me escorting some demon who disposed of Anock's dead mates to either Rose or Andy's rooms through a door in the basement. I wasn't even sure why I had to escort this guy. He seemed to be doing fine on his own but if I had to guess, it was another one of Cander's demands to keep me busy so I wouldn't see the women he brought in and out of his room. Not that he cared if I saw. That much was evident at the Watchers' meetings where he'd had a Succubus on his lap for most of them. I remember the first time I walked in and saw a woman straddling his lap wearing nothing but lingerie. My heart broke so bad I thought my chest was caving in. I just remember I couldn't get enough air into my chest and had to turn and run before he got the satisfaction of seeing me cry. I just couldn't believe he'd moved on so fast.

How can you go from wanting someone, liking, or maybe even loving someone so much to just doing everything you can to make their life Hell? And he just didn't care that my visions weren't my fault. When I broke down to Anock about all this, he had Cander, and one of his sluts brought in, and the truth was revealed.

It *had* been my fault.

That tattoo I saw placed on Mikayla's arm, which was the angel in my vision, was a demon's deal mark. Apparently, Anock had tried to seal a demon mark on her before, and it hadn't worked. So they decided to experiment, and that's where my blood came in. They figured if they could get my blood mixed in with Apollo's serum, bad batch or not, it would contain enough light to stick to her. They figured my mother had to have more light than the average human to have a guardian angel. Lilith was in on it to save her sons from the Reaping. She didn't want them to fight to the death. If Anock got Mikayla to prevent that from happening, one of two things would happen. Either things would stay the same if Hell decided not to attack, or Hell would attack with its army and take over Earth. Either way, she wouldn't lose a son. And well, Anock's reason for it was simply to experiment until he could find a way to get Mikayla.

So my blood caused the demon seal to work on Mikayla. When I had asked what deal Anock stuck to her, he told me that was on a need to know basis and then dismissed me after I was told to leave Cander alone. I shouted and screamed at Anock, this whole thing was bullshit. Leave my husband alone? Why? Because he was mad at me because I gave his friend's girl to Anock? I tried everything to get Anock to see reason. He was siding with Cander saying to leave him alone when Cander was literally mad because Anock was going to get Mikayla. It was clear to literally everyone Cander was rooting against Anock. But Anock didn't care, none of this shit made sense.

I was being ignored, starved, and overall treated like shit, and no one cared. Well, Crow, the twins, Envy, and Strife did, but they were hardly around. Rose and Andy were ordered not to have contact with me from my oh mighty piece of shit husband, and well, I guess those bitches decided to side with him, because I hadn't seen them since my wedding day. The twins were busy protecting and acting as gatekeepers to all the realms, while the other Watchers had been split into teams. Envy and Strife stopped by, only for a few moments to check on me when they got back from a run or back from killing Pit demons, but it was never long enough. Cander had tried to pull the same, keep away from her and let her think about what she did, shit on them too, but they told him to get fucked. That left Crow, and well, he was struggling to keep his bar safe. He visited me every chance he got, but he always kept his distance. He gave me a power boost when he could but only by using his hand, so there was that. His visits were getting less frequent as the days went on. He said Cander was having me watched, and I guess that was why.

Crow didn't agree with what Cander was doing but said there was nothing he could do to make him quit acting like a piece of shit. I guess he had tried, and they fought, and since then, he stopped working to change Cander's mind and instead started visiting me. I could tell Crow was genuinely torn about losing Cander as a friend. Both him and I didn't understand why he would act in such an extreme way. Was our wedding just a joke to him? Had he ever really felt anything for me? All the words he told me were obviously lies. He said he would never pull away from me again, and yet he did.

The hunched over grey goblin hobbling in front of me pushed a wheelbarrow full of dead women down the dripping concrete basement hallway. He whistled *It's a Small World After All*. Over and over again. And it was the same thing every day. I walk into the birthing room, where they spent their pregnancy chained to a wall. After they pop out Anock's baby, I snap their necks and put them in the wheelbarrow. Then I follow him through the usual halls, through the basement halls, and then to the dumping room. At first, I couldn't stop throwing up. These mortals had been captured, raped, and tormented, and the moment Anock gets his wanted result, they are killed and trashed for food. Now, I was so numb to the mind fuck of my life, I had nothing left in me at this point. So I just went along with it. What choice did I have?

I sighed and looked up at the swinging lights that hung from the ceiling as we walked. Well, he *hobbled* from a hunched back, and I *wobbled* from a huge pregnant belly, so I guess it wasn't really walking. Just a pathetic parade of demons that no one liked, doing a job no one wanted to do. The door where we dumped the bodies came into sight, and I perked up ready to be done for the day. My feet were swollen and killing me. I was ten days away from having this baby if what the twins estimated was right. So I was majorly ready to go to my room and sleep until I had to start this miserable shit all over again.

And that sucked worse.

I ended up night after night lost in my thoughts, worrying about my baby. Cain and Elijah came last week and had given me some type of test to see the baby. It was like a human ultrasound except they used magic, and the live video was in 3D displayed above me.

The baby so far had displayed signs of both mine and Cander's demon form. Cander had two long thick vampire fangs that dropped from his jaw whereas I had millions of sharp serrated teeth. The baby had two tiny little fangs on top and a row of small serrated teeth on the bottom. We would have never known that, but he yawned while the twins had the ultrasound going. I was shocked, scared, and weirded out all at the same time. I remembered whispering so the baby couldn't hear and asking Elijah if he would eat me from the inside out but didn't really get an answer. Only a laugh and don't be silly, followed with an I hope not, from Cain. So far, that hasn't happened, but every sharp pain has me worried because the baby also had tiny claws. Which had only come out along with his arm blades when he started to cry during the ultrasound. Thank God there were no claws on his tiny feet because that would suck ass.

All in all, the baby's demon features hadn't hurt me *yet*, and they chalked it up to me having a supernatural pregnancy, but the birth we really had no answers to. They said I couldn't die because of the whole needing a knife and someone eating my heart thing, but I was worried about the baby. No one knew the status of the baby. Based on Anock's babies, they were all considered dark Nephilim and were shapeshifters. Since we didn't know the status of my mother, or me really, what would Cander's and *my* baby be?

"Help me with the door yah, wench! Why yah standing there lookin' at the lights? Ye lame?!"

I looked at the goblin scowling at me, and I growled back, feeling the muscles in my belly tighten in frustration. "You'd do well not to call me that again, or you won't be alive to wheel your next wheelbarrow of bodies, goblin."

He sputtered out a laugh that ended in a nasty cough before stepping out of my way as I came over to open the door. "*Yeah, yeah.* So then why are ye here if yah so important?"

I ignored him and let out a sigh as he wheeled past me with the bodies. If I had the nerve, I would lock that little shit in the room with the dead bodies and let Rose and Andy eat him. Instead, I ignored him as he walked back out, and I slammed the door behind him.

"Are you satisfied with your escort today, *princess*?" I asked him in spite, causing him to turn and frown at me before hobbling on *stupid little goblin shit*. It was clear I hated him, just as much as he hated me.

I huffed and made my way to my room. The same day, the

same pile of shit as always, and I was *sooo* done. As soon as this baby came out, I was taking off. I was a Watcher now, and they fucked up when they taught me how to portal. Granted, the assholes blocked that power from me, but still, I would find a way. Then I was leaving *with* my son, I'd already mapped the whole thing out. I needed to find Liz, Alex, and Kay. If Liz was as powerful as she let on to be, she could hide us, or at least my son. I didn't want this life for him. The life of a captive demon treated like a slave because that's exactly how I was treated.

I pushed open the door from the basement hallway and into the regular hallway. I paused when I saw a group of giggling Emotion demons stumble out of Cander's room.

Instead of feeling my heartache, I bit my lip, held my breath, and looked away. I just loved how he kept a parade of girls coming in and out of his room like I didn't exist. I scoffed out loud holding in a laugh because all this was so stupid, it was funny. Literally, my own husband threw my ass out, not even after a full week of marriage, because of something I had no control over? He was there when the snake bit my neck. It wasn't like I willingly gave my blood, yet he acted like I crafted that demon deal into a perfect little handmade box with a bow and sent it to Anock. *It was crazy.*

"What's funny?"

The shock of his voice gave me a sudden stomach cramps. "Ahhh!" I gasped, leaning over and clenching my lower stomach to ease the pain. I slammed my eyes shut and willed him to go away.

"Did you not hear me? Or did pregnancy make you deaf?" His voice still played havoc on me even after everything he'd done to me.

I took a deep breath to ease the pain as my son kicked hard in my belly. He always did when he heard his father's voice. It was the one reason why I hated being a partner to Lilith's

Realm with him. I turned and glared. "What do you want, Cander?"

God he looked terrific in his black Watcher's uniform, and I fucking hated him for it. Why couldn't he be ugly? I hated his perfect gold eyes and his stupid kissable lips. I suppressed my hunger and started to walk on to my room.

I heard him scoff and then follow behind me. "Well, I was on an assignment in the Ninth Realm clearing demons, until dumb and dumber summoned me here for you."

It was my turn to scoff. I rubbed my belly as we walked to calm the baby's kicks. Ever since I blew up like a balloon, I was in sundresses or anything conformable to put on. In reality, I probably looked like a tent. That's probably what that asshole thought anyways. So I was waddling in a yellow sundress trying to get away from my current asshole husband and not getting very far. This was not how I saw my next meeting with him going.

Another contraction hit me, shooting piercing pain straight up my vagina into my body while it went down both my legs.

Fuck, that hurt!

I stopped walking and held on to the wall, refusing to look at the piece of shit to my left. Why did these things have to stir up now? I wanted to get *away* from him.

When the contraction ended, I slowly waddled on and tried to talk through the pain. "Why the hell would you come if they summoned you for *me*? You hate *us*." I paused at the start of another contraction. "Or did you forget?"

"You're in labor, Akira." He said in annoyance.

I turned faster than I thought humanly possible and put both hands protectively over my baby bump. My fangs, claws, and blades came out quickly, and I took a step towards him, letting red fill my vision. He hadn't cared about our baby boy this whole time, so why was he here now?

"After everything you've done to me, if you think you're

getting this baby." I paused as my demon struggled to take form on dry land.

I watched in return as his eyes turned red while his demon formed.

"*You have another thing coming*!" I growled, ready for a fight.

"I'm not going to take the baby, Akira!" Cander said, rolling his eyes.

"Yeah?! You're right, you won't!! This is my son! Mine! As soon as you found out I was pregnant, you all but bolted. I bet this whole, you're pissed at me because of my blood, thing is just an excuse to bail on your son. *You're such a piece of shit*!" I yelled.

Right as I aimed for an attack, a deep voice broke my attention from behind me.

"*Akira*?"

It couldn't be…

I turned around to see my father standing there. At the end of the hallway, by my door with his band.

What in the holy fuck!?

My heart stopped, and another twinge swept across my stomach, making me cry out in pain.

The sudden hand on my back made it both better and worse at the same time because of how much I hated yet craved his touch.

"Step away from my daughter and grandson, or you die."

The hand left, and I straightened to see my father and his band now making their way towards Cander and me. Seeing my father turn into his demon scared me.

It was too much, the pain, the confusion, the hurt.

And it was obviously clear on my face.

"Don't worry, Bear. I won't let this piece of shit near you again."

Thank you for Reading!

STAY CONNECTED

Want to read samples from the Beloved Series? Go Here-

https://www.authorchelsiiklein.com/

Connect with me!!
https://www.facebook.com/chelsiiKlen
https://www.facebook.com/groups/2635684956688972
https://www.instagram.com/authorchelsiiklein/
https://twitter.com/chelsi_fountain

Made in the USA
Columbia, SC
22 October 2024

44502599R00233